DEDICATION

This book is dedicated to my husband who read and reread (including the mushy parts), answered silly questions, ate out a lot, sometimes handled the kids by himself so that I could write, and who told me he was tired and begged me not to make him do English. Thanks for all your support.

CHAPTER 1

"**P**OTENTIAL HOSTILE INCOMING AT THREE o'clock," Miranda trumpeted through my earpiece.

Her sudden voice invading the silence succeeded in startling me into dropping my two day old bagel. There went breakfast, if I dared to label it that. I kicked the half eaten bagel aside in disgust and picked up my modified tranquillizer gun.

Turning in the direction she'd indicated, I looked through the scope. It took me a minute, but I found him. The "potential hostile" was my target, Kenny. He was carefully picking a path through the woods that was bringing him slowly closer to me.

Relief mingled with excitement surged through me at the thought of ending my exile in these mosquito infested woods. I'd already been here three days just waiting for him to make an appearance. Hopefully, my patience was now going to pay off.

"Finally, show time," I said, quietly echoing Miranda's enthusiasm.

Through a bit of research, I'd determined he came to this particular little patch of woods at least once a week. The reason for his visits was still officially unknown. Actually, all of his unauthorized escapades out of the Colony boundaries were unknown by anyone official, except for me and Miranda, and we weren't telling. Yeah, we were rebels at heart.

"Got 'em," I verified as I watched Kenny continue to move toward me. "Additionally, I'd like to congratulate you on the nice piece of grammatical lingo work."

"I know, right?" she said, her voice bubbling with enthusiasm. "Military talk is so cool."

She'd been at the military movies again. I'd roll my eyes if I wasn't trying to focus.

"What are you aiming for?" she asked.

Considering the possibilities for a moment, I smiled at my decided point of entry. "As big a pain in the butt as he's been, I'm hoping to return the favor."

"Ah, a kiester shot," she snickered in understanding. "Serves him right."

I didn't know if it served him right, but it was what I'd been tasked with. Getting the DNA sample, not shooting him in the rear. I wasn't happy that I had to be the one going after him like this. But if it wasn't me, it'd be someone else collecting the sample. Probably a lot less nice someone else. I wasn't trying to justify my actions, much.

"Yep, right in the kiester," I whispered. As long as my aim was true. Until the last few weeks, I hadn't had a lot of practice. I was from Texas, but I hadn't shot a gun since I was a kid.

"That's one heck of a gotcha. A big needle in the butt," she snorted.

Her continued chatter was more evidence of her excitement. I tried to tune her out, but it was difficult. I didn't fault her for the sudden onset of merriment. Over the last three days, there hadn't been a lot of conversation or creature comforts, like bathing for instance. Not many gal pals would stick with you through that. But that was Miranda for you. Research partner extraordinaire and the other half of our self-titled duo, M&M, short for Macy and Miranda.

When we met roughly ten years ago while working on another project, I didn't think we had much in common. I was from the South, and she wasn't. I was seventeen, and she was twenty-two. I wasn't even of legal drinking age yet, but she more than made up for my lack of participation. I was so focused on school and research that I had no time for boys, and she spent every free minute she had chasing them. She thought I was a stick in the mud, and I thought she was the mud gumming up my life.

That started changing the day the cafeteria began serving Tex Mex.

When she happened to be the only other person in the room who knew what to do with the grilled chicken, tortillas and fixings, it was the start of a beautiful friendship.

She took one look at the confused scientists milling around the lunch line and very dramatically and loudly drug a chair to the middle of the room. She then stood in the chair and yelled, "It's called fajitas, People!"

After that pronouncement, she began to methodically instruct them in the art of fajita construction. It was so beautiful that it brought tears to my eyes. Well, that was probably due to the jalapenos, but it was still a beautiful thing to behold.

Our friendship grew from there, and we'd essentially been best buds ever since. We were still very different from one another personality wise, but we found that we had more in common than not.

Sometimes, I was certain she put the mental in the second M of our title. Obviously, I was the moxie. My M also currently stood for mosquito bitten.

I winced as I brushed away another grape sized mosquito intent on making a meal out of the only exposed skin on my body, my face. I should have gotten one of those hats with the mosquito netting, but I hadn't considered their tenaciousness or the impossibility of warding them off while I slept. Maybe next time.

God I hoped there wasn't a next time. My body itched in all sorts of places from bites where there ought not be bites. I still hadn't figured out how they kept getting inside my underwear.

Yep, mosquito bite and mental. The meaning of M was a fluid thing.

Miranda was currently positioned in my truck at the edge of the woods where she was working the infrared. Nothing but the best for this operation. That was a slight overstatement of the truth, but I'd learned to work with what I had. Plus, I'd promised Miranda to start trying to look on the "bright side of things."

Those were her words, not mine.

But, I had managed to gather a certain joy from this on a number of occasions, like after I've had to open her blinds in the morning to get her moving. Then, with much gusto, remind her to look on the bright side. I'd also learned to do the reminding while hiding behind the bedroom door. Her aim with paperbacks was painfully accurate.

I was still waiting for the best time to use the new nickname I'd given her, Little Miss Sunshine. Oh, she would rue the day she foisted sunniness upon me.

Realizing my mind had drifted during her monologue, I hissed, "Miranda, be quiet so I can focus on shooting him."

She didn't even pause to take a breath, just changed the subject of her rambling. "Yes, Ma'am. General, Sir. Head Honcho. El Capitan…"

"Your respect is touching," I grumbled.

"Fearless Leader. Big Kahuna…"

There it was, mental. Not sure what it said about me that she was my best friend. But it took all kinds to make the world go round. At least, that was what I'd heard from her. Repeatedly.

"I'm shutting you off now," I told her as I reached up and muted the earpiece. So glad I sprung for the more expensive model that had this feature. I had a feeling I would need it sooner or later.

Without her distraction, I was able to focus on Kenny again. He was still moving cautiously and constantly scanned the area, like he was afraid of being followed. I didn't know who would be following him, besides me of course, but we could all leave these woods if he would just come a little bit closer.

I had my suspicions of why he was here, and if I was right, it would open up a big old can of trouble. So, I wasn't investigating it, officially or otherwise. To report conjecture and suspicion would be unprofessional of me. And that was my unofficial official opinion on the matter.

But, if I let myself study the matter, I would think Kenny was being careless, which was out of character for him. It was almost as if he wanted me to know he was in these woods, perhaps even why. I was really hoping that I didn't have to delve too deeply into the situation. At least not yet, but I was really in favor of not at all. That might be possible if Kenny would just work with me a little.

Unfortunately, I hadn't observed teamwork as one of his many skills. On the contrary, he was more the leader type. I knew he was the undeniable leader of the pack of teenage hybrids. For whatever reason, they all deferred to him.

I had to admit that there was something different about him. Like his DNA had made a leap that had bypassed the other hybrids. I was still trying to figure that out, which was why I needed his DNA.

Kenny may not have been the run of the mill hybrid, but he was in possession of the normal teenage boy attributes, which equaled tons of bravado, raging hormones, and not much sense. He wasn't dumb by any measure, quite the opposite. He was just subject to the lapses in judgment that plagued all teenage boys.

I suspected that he was beginning to figure out things that the government wouldn't approve of him knowing. Combining that knowledge with not much sense could be a dangerous mix for everyone.

I was purposely ignoring that truckload of dynamite as well. I hoped that didn't blow up in my face at some point in the future.

I wiped my sweaty palm across my jeans. Wouldn't do to miss because of a slippery trigger finger. That would give up my location for sure. As it was, it'd be a miracle if he didn't already know I was here simply by the smell wafting from me.

But, then again, maybe I blended right in with my new woodsy smell, Cologne eau de earth. It definitely wasn't a scent I'd recommend. I'd stand up wind of myself if it were possible.

My concern didn't extend to him seeing me. Too much woods gunk was now part of my outfit. I liked to think of it as natural camouflage and not dirt, stuck to sweat, on top of bug bites, and only God knew what else. Choosing to view it that way kept me from running out of these woods like a crazed woman.

I watched Kenny take a few more steps and then freeze.

Through the scope, I could see his nostrils flare as he turned in small circles. Crud, maybe he could smell me. This range would have to do. Zeroing in on the target, the back pocket of a worn out pair of jeans, I pulled the trigger.

Seconds later, a chorus of cursing erupted from Kenny. I knew by his particular phrasing that my dart had been right on the mark.

Was it wrong to be so happy about shooting someone in the rear? I couldn't decide with the thoughts of my impending shower so prevalent in my mind.

"That was uncalled for, Doc!" he shrieked, his voice fading quickly as he increased the distance between us.

I couldn't blame him for retreating. I had just shot him in his derriere. "Sorry, Kenny," I yelled. "You could have given it to me willingly!"

I let the gun rest on my hip as I savored my victory. "I didn't have to shoot you in the butt," I muttered to myself, and sadly, I realized that I wasn't very sorry either. I could have been home two months ago if not for his evasive maneuvering.

I understood his unwillingness to participate, even secretly approved of it. But that didn't change the fact that the government was going to get its sample one way or the other. My boss was already chaffing over the delay in my report and had hinted at a dead or alive scenario if warranted.

Remembering that conversation stirred my anger and made my victory kind of hollow. I knew I was on Kenny's side. Deciding how to translate that into my job was hard and becoming more difficult all the time.

At least, I had avoided the death part of the scenario. Still alive equaled good. Alive meant there was still a chance of escape.

Escape? I stilled at my own thoughts. Where did that come from?

Still deep in thought, I slipped the gun's strap over my head. Placing the butt of the gun against my hip, I mirrored the stance I would use if I was holding a heavy fishing pole. Since I'd welded a heavy duty reel to the end of it, I sort of was.

I had tried to make do with the standard model tranquilizer gun, but it was made to fire a dart that dispensed a substance, not collected one. It also had no way to prevent the sample from being contaminated.

The dart I designed did both, and as a bonus, it was attached to a fishing line that could be reeled in quickly. It was red neck engineering at its finest, getting the job done and costing next to nothing. Just like my budget, oddly enough.

It wasn't that I wanted to gain my samples this way. Stalking through the woods and swamps was not my idea of fun, but Kenny had left me no choice. I had tried to just tranq him and then draw the sample. Actually, I had tried multiple times with multiple drugs. I had even combined them and went way beyond maximum dosages, but still, I couldn't bring him down. That left me seeking alternative methods of collection.

It was almost like a game now with the goal being to capture the elusive sample. Annoyingly, up till now, Kenny was just as good at the game as I was.

I began reeling in the sample, shifting my stance to gain more leverage as the dart snagged on something. Seconds after I moved, the tree behind me exploded.

"What the..." I shrieked, dropping to one knee.

Covered in bark and wood bits, I turned and viewed the now scarred trunk. I traced my fingers over the area of impact, allowing them to fill the deepest groove in the center of the wound. My fingertips scraped against warm metal. A bullet?

I twisted back to the front and scanned the woods in front of me. Another shot splintered the tree on level with where my head had been just moments before. Had I not swiveled, it would have been a head shot...a kill shot.

Dropping the gun, I scrambled to the other side of the tree. With my back pressed firmly against the trunk, I quickly skimmed the woods in front of me. I knew full well that I didn't stand much of a chance if I was surrounded.

Re-engaging my earpiece, I filled Miranda in. "I've got someone out here shooting at me. Can you see anything?"

"Shooting? Like bullet shooting?"

I tapped my ear piece as her voice came across sounding garbled. "Way like. And a good shot." Too good. He almost had me twice. Only coincidence or providence had spared my life.

"The only thing I've seen is what I assume to be Kenny hauling butt off my screen. I think he's getting faster."

She was talking like she had a mouthful of marbles. "What's wrong with your mouth?" I asked her. Bearing in mind that I was being shot at, I was becoming worried she was in some similar predicament.

"Eating," came her muffled reply.

Eating? I was brushing off tree, and she was eating? How was that fair? And had she stuffed it all in her mouth at one time?

"Eating what?" I asked bewildered.

"Moon pie."

Ah, that explained it. The marshmallow got you every time.

"Do you think it's that extremist bunch we've had so much trouble with lately?" she asked.

"Don't know. They didn't identify themselves."

I reached up to brush my bangs aside and realized my hair was still covered in wood splinters. I leaned slightly forward and gave my head a gentle shake, dislodging most of the debris. One particularly large shard refused to let go, and I had to pull it free of my scalp.

I held it up for inspection. It was about six inches long and tipped in blood. "I've been staked," I informed her.

"Good thing you're not a vampire," she replied sarcastically.

I frowned as I continued to brush the remaining splinters from my clothes. Being out of infrared range meant he was shooting from almost two miles away. Wasn't that close to world record distance?

When I didn't respond to her jibe, Miranda's tone turned serious. "Macy, are you okay?"

I thought I heard honest to goodness concern in her voice. "So good of you to quit eating long enough to take notice of my predicament. And yeah, I'm fine. For the moment, anyway."

"Hey! I'd be no good to you if my nutritional needs were not met."

Oh Lord, here we go. I was already being shot at, wasn't that bad enough?

"I'm not sure moon pies qualify as meeting nutritional needs," I argued, but she marched on, undeterred by the truth of my statement.

"I could suffer debilitating side effects that, eventually, would lead to my death of starvation."

There really was no stopping her when she was tirading. You just had to ride it out. "Side effects?" I queried, not trying to hide the skepticism coloring my voice.

"Yes," she stated firmly. "Like energy depravation, and foggy brain syndrome, and...and,"

She was reaching this time.

"Biteyourheadoffitis," she finished.

That was new, but not very original. Still, I couldn't help but grin. "The last one being purely to alleviate the prior two symptoms, I'm sure."

"Precisely. Anyway, the taste benefits in my scorebook, as you well know, way exceed any nutritional benefits, which are considered merely an added benefit of marginal importance."

What? I shook my head in amusement. "There were a lot of words in there, Mir. Just save me a moon pie, okay?"

"Already done. Where are you now?"

"Same place. I'm pinned behind a tree. No one's shooting at me from this side, so I think there's only the one shooter."

I heard rustling in the trees to my right and inched my way closer toward the sound. Another shot rang out, confirming the shooter's continued presence.

"Dad gum it!" I swore, quickly jerking my foot back. That was three shots now.

"Still with me, Greer?" Miranda suddenly belted in my ear.

I jumped again at the sound of her voice. Pressing my hand to my chest, I took long deep breaths, trying to calm my heart. I wasn't afraid. Startled, tired, hot, hungry and really annoyed, but not scared of the person with the gun. Maybe I was getting used to being shot at. It had been a rough couple of years.

I angled my boot to look at the bottom outside edge. It had a rivet running the length of it. Once again, that was too close. Thank goodness for thick soled boots. My shooter obviously wasn't the shoot and run type, which meant he was probably a professional. As if the impossible distance and near misses weren't indication enough.

"Macy!"

"Yeah, I'm here," I confirmed. "And, stop yelling."

"Sorry, Big Chief. It's a little stressful."

"It ain't all that and a bag of chips here either."

I wiped the sweat from my eyes with the back of my hand. I could do with some chips. Barbeque flavor maybe. Yeah, barbeque potato chips with a homemade hamburger right off the grill sounded great. And a big slice of apple pie. Or peach. Any fruit pie would do.

My food reverie was interrupted when I spotted Kenny through the undergrowth. He was bent down working at something on the ground. With a knife?

Making sure to stay firmly hidden behind the tree, I angled myself to get a better look at him. He was cutting the fishing line! Great. Just freaking great.

"Kenny is making off with the sample," I relayed to Miranda.

"Oh, no," she groaned. "This is unbelievable."

I completely sympathized with her groan.

"That makes this what, five failed attempts? And now, we have to do this all over again?" she whined.

Yep. Assuming I lived and that he'd be dumb enough to fall for this again. "Way to boost my confidence, Mir. I was feeling a little down in light of my still smoking failure."

"You know I live to be the wind beneath your wings," she retorted.

"Oh, I'm soaring. Where eagles fly."

"And mountain's high?"

"Something like that," I sighed.

Kenny grinned and waved the dart at me.

Yeah, I see you. I smirked at him and waved back. Didn't he know I was being shot at? He probably thought I deserved it. Maybe he was right. Then he was gone. He was getting faster.

Miranda's voice was sullen when she asked, "What do you want me to do?"

I sighed again. Not much we could do. We weren't supposed to be here, and what we were doing here wasn't supposed to exist anymore. Leaning my head back against the tree, I thought about my options.

"I guess I'll have to wait him out. It'll be dark in a couple of hours. Maybe I can shake him then." Unless he had night vision equipment or infrared or buddies helping him pinpoint my location. Crap. Where was that bright side?

"How do you know it's a him?" Miranda asked.

"I don't. But aren't two crazy women in this movie enough?"

Resigned to wait, I dropped to my bottom, immediately alleviating the burning in my thighs. One problem solved. Now all I had to do was hope that he was working alone, didn't move positions, didn't have infrared or night vision goggles and wait till dark, at which time, I was going to somehow escape from my attacker by maneuvering silently through the woods in the dark. How could it possibly fail?

"I could place an anonymous call for a local police unit," she offered.

"Because that wouldn't draw attention to us at all," I muttered. She probably didn't deserve my sour tone. It wasn't a good idea, but not a terrible one either. I'd save it as a last resort kind of thing.

"It wouldn't draw any more attention than all those crazy protestors are," she said defensively.

We did have some crazy protestors, complete with unwashed looks and wacko signs. But they weren't all crazy or wrong.

"You do realize some of them are right, don't you?" I asked her.

"We're going to hell like Satan because we're playing God?"

"No! Not those crazies, the ones that are accusing the government of continuing the hybrid program."

"Are you sure?" she asked bluntly.

What was I supposed to say to that? In truth, no, I was not absolutely sure. Maybe being shot at was a sign, but then, me surviving could also be a sign. Either way it didn't matter. It wasn't like I lived my life by following supposed signs. But being in these kinds of situations, which seemed to be happening more frequently, did make one stop and think.

I took a deep breath and rolled my shoulders. It wasn't this difficult when I first started this project. It had been research pure and simple. Now, it had become something more. Enough to warrant a trip to hell? I didn't know. But I hadn't been consumed by fire from on high nor had the ground opened up and swallowed me. That had to mean something, right?

Maybe the Big Guy didn't care. After all, other species evolved without divine intervention. Except for those pesky major earth extinction events. But those had to be purely due to chance. I mean, what could the dinosaurs have done to tick him off that much?

Besides, I couldn't find it written down anywhere that we weren't supposed to alter the genetic code. Evolution itself was a slow alteration of the genetic code, and He put that in motion. For that matter, all sorts of things, like epidemics and natural catastrophes, impacted the human genome. Heck, even a person's choice of mate could potentially alter the genetic code.

I didn't understand why people were so upset about something that happened all the time. Maybe the creation of human animal hybrids was a little more conspicuous than what nature produced. But it was still just science, the manipulation of a formula.

Most cutting edge medical research was heading in that direction, too. Why would it be okay for one and not the other?

Anyway, I rather thought God and I had a lot in common. I was a scientist...He was a scientist. That was another thing I didn't understand, all the hoopla about God and science. To me, science was just figuring out how He did what He did. He created the puzzles, we solved them. It was a good setup. Unlike my current dilemma.

"Did you go to sleep on me?" Miranda asked.

I smiled at her poke. She was not one for silence. "No, just thinking about the morality of the human evolution of humankind."

"It is a conundrum."

I nodded then remembered she couldn't see that. "Right you are. I think I have to choose to believe that He and I are on the same team until I know otherwise."

"Otherwise being?" she prompted.

"Giant meteors hurtling toward earth?"

"Yep," she concurred, "extinction events might qualify as otherwise."

This wasn't the first or even second time we'd had this sort of conversation. Only the accompanying circumstances seemed to vary.

"But, then again," she lectured on, "many world cultures, even the Good Book, predict the end of the world."

Wow, this was such an emotionally uplifting discussion we were having. I took a breath prepared to rebut her, when I suddenly had a new brainstorm about the hunt for Kenny's DNA. It was so obvious. I couldn't believe I hadn't thought of it before.

"Hey Miranda, assuming I live through this, I think I have another idea about how to get Kenny's DNA."

There was a long pause before she answered. "Does it involve me being stuck in this truck for three days again?"

"I don't think so, but I haven't worked out the details yet. I could arrange it, if you like."

"I don't," she hissed.

Her response was so filled with hostility that it made me laugh out loud. I quickly stifled the laugh behind my hands, but I was sure the damage was done. Letting the shooter know that I was still here probably wasn't the smartest move.

I dropped my hands and grimaced as I spit out the errant pieces of stuff that had transferred from my hands to my mouth. "Do believe me when I say you got the better deal."

"Just so we're clear. I am not agreeing to the plan itself, only to listen to the plan."

I maintained my silence, knowing she wouldn't be able to hold out for long. I could have heard her sigh even without the earpiece.

"What's the plan?" she said dejectedly.

I opened my mouth to respond and then snapped it shut again when a sudden eruption of noise drew my attention. Listening intently, I determined it was coming from a good distance away on the other side of the tree.

"Just a minute," I told her.

Tilting my head to the side, I strained to capture the sounds. There were several thuds followed by someone or something crashing through the woods. Whatever the origin of the sounds, there was no effort at concealment. The noises gradually faded until it was silent again. If I had to interpret what just happened, I'd say it sounded like a struggle of some kind.

I resumed my crouch and ventured a quick look around the tree. No corresponding shot was fired. More slowly, I peered around the tree again. My head remained attached, always a good sign.

Staring in the direction of the shooter, I didn't see anyone. But I didn't really know what I was looking for, and it was hard to see through all the foliage. There was no sun glinting off metal—learned that tidbit from one of my rare nights of watching television.

I pulled back behind the tree as I mulled it over. If the shooter had still been there, he would have taken the shot. There was no hesitation in any of his previous attempts. Then there was the fact that I really detested waiting. Actually, it was the wasted time associated with waiting that I hated. Every now and then, there was a purpose in waiting. A really good one, like remaining alive.

"Miranda, I'm going to start heading your way."

"You sure the coast is clear?"

"I live in the gray, remember? I'm not absolutely positive,

but I think so. I think I heard a fight. Maybe I have a guardian angel that beat up my assailant. I'm going to check it out. Keep your eyes open."

"The infrared doesn't indicate the presence of wings," she replied flatly.

Ha, ha. "I meant watch for movement of any kind that would indicate I am not alone."

"When did you become the detective slash investigator person?"

"Apparently, when I took this job," I said, standing up. "It must have been in the fine print."

"Didn't read it, did you?" she said accusingly.

"Does anybody?" I said exasperated. "I just pressed accept."

With her voice still dripping with sarcasm, she asked, "Wonder what else you'll become before this is done?"

Taking a deep breath, I let it slowly blow out through my lips. Me, too, I thought. Me, too.

I scanned the area one last time then told Miranda, "Ok, I'm signing off now, catch you in a few."

"Copy that, Tango. Meet you on the flip side."

Roger that, GI Wannabe. Now it was my turn to play the soldier.

With my attention still fixed on the woods in front of me, I pulled the ear piece loose. I didn't trust Miranda not to startle me when I was trying to be all stealthy like. Having tucked the ear piece into one of my pockets, I carefully eased around the tree.

Kenny's voice boomed into the silence. "Coast is clear."

I nearly jumped out of my skin.

"Dang it, Kenny!" I yelled. "Do not sneak up on a girl when she is being shot at." I crouched back down, elbows on my knees and my head resting in my hands. I knew my legs were going to pay for all this squatting at some point in the near future.

"What are you gonna do?" he asked snidely. "Shoot me with your little gun again?"

Out of the corner of my eye, I could see him mime a gun shot with his hand. I rolled my head to face him. "You gonna make me?"

We regarded each other silently for a few moments. He the rebellious teen and me the what? I didn't like any of the words that I could fill the blank with.

"You could just give me the sample," I finally said.

"Where is the fun in that?" he snorted.

I placed my hands on my knees and pushed to a stand. "Yeah, because crawling around the woods and being shot at is so much more fun."

"Works for me," he affirmed.

Well, I didn't like how it was working for me. I knelt and began gathering my supplies when it occurred to me to question just how he knew the coast was clear. Pausing, I turned back to him. "Kenny, how do you know the coast is clear?"

As I waited for his response, I noted the absence of his usual cocky smile. He looked dangerous and scary. I'd never seen him look scary before. Kenny was growing up.

He held my eyes as he said, "I know because I cleared it."

Alarm bells began ringing in my head. How serious was he? Deadly serious? My alarm grew with the thought that, one, he might have hurt someone. And two, because he did it to protect me? Or maybe he was protecting something else in these woods. If he was after my full attention, he had it now.

Supplies forgotten, I slowly stood up and faced him. "Kenny, what did you do?"

He cocked his head sideways at me. It was an oddly reptilian move. He was studying me now, and I didn't like it. It felt like I was in the presence of a predator, and I am not prey.

"Let's just say he won't be bothering you anymore."

What did that mean? Was he admitting that he killed someone?

Stunned by his answer, I was unsure what to say next. If I asked him outright, I wouldn't have plausible deniability, should I need it. I also didn't want to wrongfully accuse him of something. Not to mention, the unease I currently felt with his behavior. I truly hoped I hadn't just witnessed the birth of a killer.

One thing was certain, if Kenny now possessed the wherewithal to pair action with his teenage bravado, then I needed to know. For all our sakes.

I swallowed and asked softly, "Could you define not bothering me anymore?"

He must have seen the worry etched on my face. The cocky smile reappeared, and he looked like the Kenny that I knew.

"Don't worry, Doc," he said. "He's still alive. We just came to a...understanding."

Understanding, right. Whatever that meant.

I didn't know who was behind this most recent attack, but I did know that I didn't want Kenny caught in the middle of it.

"Kenny, you don't want to do something that the HCF could use against you to deem you as a liability to them." I put my hands on my hips, thinking about the best way to phrase what I wanted to say next. "If that happens, I don't know if I could protect you, or they may decide to get rid of me and get someone in here that's not as nice as me."

His response was immediate, and he made no attempt to hide the threat in his voice. "Maybe, I wouldn't be nice either."

I nodded. I wasn't going to condemn someone for protecting themselves. But if he was entertaining the thought of violence, then I knew Kenny well enough to know that he was definitely hiding something out here. My hope of staying out of it seemed to be vanishing right before my eyes.

"I don't know what you are currently up to or what you're protecting." I put my hand up to forestall his answer. "I'm not sure that I should know...that it's safe for me to know." I waited until understanding dawned in his eyes. "Just be careful. If it reaches a point where you feel I need to know or you need my help, then you fill me in. Okay?"

"Sure thing, Doc," he nodded.

What had I just gotten myself into? I just kept digging the whole deeper and deeper. Would someone please take the shovel away from me now!

Regardless of my implied pledge of help, I was relieved at Kenny's assurance. Maybe he wasn't in over his head, and maybe he wouldn't drag me down with him. Not that I would have minded the death of my assailant. He had tried to kill me. But I wouldn't want it at Kenny's expense.

Having retrieved a sterile cup from my duffle, I held it out to Kenny. "Would you mind peeing in this cup for me?" I knew it wasn't the best DNA sample to have, but it would at least be something for all my trouble.

A sharp laugh escaped him as he looked with contempt at my extended hand. "You're funny, Doc." Then he took off again.

Yeah, didn't think so. That would be too easy.

I belatedly realized that I had forgotten to thank him for rescuing me. "Thanks for saving me, Kenny!" I shouted at his retreating form. I hoped he heard me. And I hoped he stayed on my side, especially when I finally won this game.

I finished packing my supplies and made my way over to where I thought the fighting sounds had originated. I knew I was there when I spotted the shell casings on the ground.

I retrieved a pair of tweezers from my duffle and picked one up. The letters DTP followed by a space and then a smudged GM were stamped along the top. Unless the Department of Transportation and General Motors did a whole lot more than transportation related goods and services, I had no idea what the letters stood for.

Using the tweezers, I collected the other casings and put them in a baggie. I didn't know what good it would do me, but evidence was evidence.

Turning in a circle, I surveyed the rest of the area. There were definite signs of a struggle, but no blood. Perhaps Kenny had been telling the truth about not killing anyone, though there were plenty of ways to kill someone without shedding blood.

"Bright side, Macy, remember?" I scolded myself.

There were animal tracks on the ground where the dirt was softer. Kneeling down, I placed my hand in one of the imprints left behind. It was much larger than my hand.

Looking up from the paw print, I saw fur stuck to the bark of a nearby tree. Using the tweezers again, I worked the fur free and studied it a moment. It might not be related to this at all, but I put it in a baggie, just in case.

Further up the tree, there were fresh claw marks. By the spread, I thought they probably belonged with the prints on the ground. The prints on the ground, however, did not have claws attached.

Kenny didn't have paws, claws or fur. That left only the sharpshooter. A sharpshooter with those features implied another hybrid. Was someone from the Colony protecting Kenny? But if that was the case, then why would Kenny have fought them? And how would a hybrid have become an expert sniper under the noses of the guards?

I frowned at the conflicting evidence as I took one last pass through the scene. I almost missed the dull gray object barely sticking out of the ground. By the footprints crisscrossing it, I'd apparently stepped on it several times already.

I nudged it with the toe of my boot, but it didn't move very much. I knelt down and used my hands to clear away some of the dirt. I didn't see any pins or rings like what I thought I would find on a grenade. Because I'd already stepped on it, I knew it wasn't a land mine.

I carefully worked it loose and then used my shirt to wipe away the dirt. It looked like some kind of weird tongue depressor. I turned it over in my hands and recognized the lens right away. It was some kind of camera. Cameras usually had serial numbers. I put it in baggie number three.

Seeing no more clues, I tucked the little bags of evidence away in my duffle and began the long trek back to my truck.

I saw Miranda before she saw me. She had the radio going full blast and was dancing wildly—as much as she could within the confines of the truck—to the local country station.

I really should remember to never let her stand guard again.

She turned the music down and called a greeting through the open window when she saw me. "Welcome back."

"Good to be back," I answered her.

"I see you managed to stay in one piece," she said, her eyes lingering on the spot where the tree had staked me. I knew there was blood. Head wounds always bled a lot.

"One piece is always good," I said. "Except when it comes to dessert."

"Two pieces of dulce de leche caramel cheesecake are divine," she sighed.

"Definitely a match made in heaven," I agreed.

We both envisioned that little piece of heaven while I closed the distance between us.

As I reached for the door handle, Miranda shook herself out of her sugar and cream cheese induced daydream. "I saw Kenny," she said. "He waved as he leapt across the road."

"Leapt, you say?" Huh? "Did he happen to be covered in fur?"

"No, just regular Kenny in all his leaping glory."

I opened the back door and chunked my bag in. "Now his leaping is glorious?" I asked, looking at her sideways as I set my gun down on top of the duffle.

"I saw the leap," she said while hanging over the seat as she stowed the equipment in the back. "Definitely glorious."

"Recorded?" I asked hopefully.

"Not a chance," she laughed.

I slung the back door shut. Dad gum it again. Nothing to show for this outing but bug bites and a heart spike. Actually, three heart spikes. That ought to count for at least one work out.

I opened the front door and pulled myself into the truck. I turned to find Miranda holding her nose.

"Seriously?" I said, narrowing my eyes at her.

"As a heart attack. Dang girl, you stink. With a capital P," she said while furiously waving her free hand in front of her face.

Ignoring her theatrics, I started the truck and rolled the windows up. Air conditioning, now that was something glorious.

"You are not a bouquet of roses either," I informed her as she continued her histrionics.

"At least I didn't sleep in raccoon poop or possibly with skunks," she managed to choke out between ragged breaths.

And the Oscar goes to...

"I think I would have noticed if I'd slept with skunks," I said indignantly. "And stink doesn't even start with a P," I argued while swinging the truck in a wide U-turn. Just to check, I sniffed my shirt. I had to admit the scent wasn't pleasant. "Maybe on the sleeping in poop," I conceded.

"Oh, I think it's a definite on the poop, and the P belongs to Peeyew."

I sniffed my shirt again. It didn't smell that bad. Maybe I'd gotten used to the smell. That did happen.

"Do you have a tissue?" she asked. "My eyes are watering so bad."

I rolled my eyes and kept driving. She'd get over it when she got over it. Anyway, I needed to figure out how to tell her about Kenny. I wasn't exactly sure what to say that wouldn't freak her out. I practiced the conversation in my head.

Hey Mir, Kenny could be a hybrid pyscho killer. Too frank. I needed to soften it a little. Then there was the other important part. *Also, I may have inadvertently agreed to aid in a teenage hybrid rebellion against the government.* Nah, best to leave the last part out.

"I think Kenny just crossed over from being annoying teenager to potential threat," I told her.

"What, did he stay in the woods as long as you? And what the heck happened to your face?"

I glanced over at her. She was dabbing her eyes with leftover fast food napkins. Drama queen.

"Yeah, ok, enough. I'm serious. He took out whoever was shooting at me." I should have said whatever, but I thought that might be too much information for her to process, especially given her current state.

I snuck a glance at my face in the rear view mirror. Good grief! I looked like I had the measles. I must never ever camp again without mosquito protection. I was really surprised Kenny had refrained from commenting on it. He usually took every opportunity he could to zing me.

Miranda coughed suddenly and loudly, drawing my attention

once more. My eyes widened as she smothered a gag in her wadded up napkins. There was no puking allowed in my truck. To be safe, I rolled her window down. She put her head so far out the window that if she'd had a long tongue, it would have been flapping in the breeze.

We rode in silence for a while until she pulled her head back in long enough to ask a question. "Where'd he take him?"

I gathered she was referring back to my previous comment about Kenny taking out the assailant. "I have no idea," I said, shaking my head. I really didn't.

CHAPTER 2

"**S**oup's on!" Miranda yelled from the kitchen of our rented house.

Having tired of the repeated hotel stays pretty quickly, we had rented a little wood frame house in a definitely old but decent neighborhood on the outskirts of New Orleans. It kept us within easy driving distance to work, and boudain was even closer. It was a win win all around.

I walked into the kitchen still towel drying my hair. I smiled as I recognized the scent. Soup today was gumbo. Yum, and again, yum. For a northwesterner, she could make a pretty good gumbo. That was good because I was a pretty good eater.

As usual, she had the television blaring. Most people opted for the small television in their kitchen. Since we spent most of our time there, we had installed a fifty inch right behind the table. Sometimes, it was like they were seated there with us. We thought about getting one of the new 3D versions, but decided it would add too much trauma if it seemed like they were reaching for our food all the time.

I laid my towel across the back of the nearest chair and picked up the bowl and spoon Miranda had placed there. She was better than she knew at the homemaker thing. Someday, some man was really going to appreciate that about her. But for now, that was joyfully my job.

"Thanks for cooking," I said as I walked over to the stove.

She'd even made rice. I ate just about everything with rice. It was cheap and filling and how I grew up. I didn't know if it was because my Mom was originally from Louisiana or because we were poor. As long as it tasted good, I didn't care one way or the other.

"Wait until you taste it to thank me," she said through a mouthful.

We weren't big on formality here at M&M's. Good taste was required, but manners were strictly optional.

I spooned in rice and ladled the gumbo over it. It was chicken and sausage this time, my favorite gumbo combo.

When I heard the special alert signal interrupt the current program, I turned to watch the screen. The on air reporter was a woman I didn't recognize, but that wasn't surprising given how little television I watched.

"We interrupt this program to bring you the latest from Capitol Hill," she said. "As a result of the report issued by the extremist group, God's Light, Congress has decided to call for hearings on a possible investigation into the purported actions of the HCF."

Translation, they were going to have hearings to see whether they were going to have hearings. I wondered how long they'd chase their tails this time.

Recent events included an extremist report giving detailed descriptions of alleged propagation of hybrids. The report included photographic documentation, some of which they were showing on the screen right now. I would have been more nervous, but I didn't recognize anyone in the photos, and the report was centered on some place in Tennessee, a far cry from Louisiana. As it was, I just thought it was curious.

"As you may recall," the reporter continued, "HCF is the acronym for Hybrid Containment Force, the governmental agency responsible for the cessation of all hybrid related activities within the United States."

Miranda, who seemed completely absorbed with the update, had already taken her seat at the table. "She should do something about that hair," she said while making little jabbing motions at the screen with her spoon.

Glancing back up at the screen, I thought her hair was okay.

The television lights just made the red look a bit harsh. "I think they just need to soften the lighting," I commented.

Miranda grunted in response.

Crossing to the table, I hooked the chair opposite her with my foot and slid it out to sit down.

How she could think that the most important aspect of the report was the state of the reporter's hair was beyond me. The possible worldwide exposure of hybrid research, which could have serious, devastating repercussions for us, was right in front of her, and she had isolated that for discussion.

I never would have noticed that detail without her pointing it out. She often pointed out details that I didn't think important. Like a character from a child's book, everyone should have a Mirandawumpagump for missed details.

I snickered at my own joke. We were so different.

She briefly cut her eyes in my direction, but when I offered no explanation, she let it go. Some things were just for personal enjoyment. Besides, if I explained, she'd only tell me I had reached the state of silly tired. She would of course be right, and I couldn't let that happen too many times a day.

Slowly, I began to mix the contents of my bowl while I watched the update. The news station was now airing a video of an extremist rally. The poor quality of the footage led me to believe it was recorded by the extremists themselves. They did manage to hold the camera still long enough to capture one guy's rant. He very passionately listed "facts" supporting his claim of the government establishing a hybrid zone. All that was missing was the foaming mouth. The video ended with the camera taking a nose dive.

The reporter came back on the air. "We apologize to our viewers for the poor quality of the previous video footage. In an effort to bring you the latest breaking news, the footage was aired without prior review."

The camera angle switched, and she began again. "The central charge of the report issued by God's Light is the establishment of a hybrid zone within the continental United States. To clarify, the definition of a hybrid zone is an area where two species meet and interbreed with the resulting hybrid offspring maintaining distinct characteristics from either parent species and thus forming its own unique species."

When she said it, it sounded reasonable. It lacked the flavor of fanaticism that came with the extremist report. She made it seem totally believable. That was probably due to the fact that I already knew the government was doing exactly that. But the purely scientific definition made it sound too clinical. I had firsthand knowledge that it was everything but clinical.

In my somewhat longer and much more convoluted definition, the two species that met and interbred were not a result of nature. They were created by humans. Also not included in the clinical definition were the two years of me sweating my butt off, constant travel, and the forever whacked out hair—thank you ninety degree weather and the humidity to match.

"You going to taste it or just move it around the bowl," Miranda said, cutting through my thoughts.

I transferred my gaze to her and smiled at her sour expression. Miranda had a way of saying even the simplest of things in a tone of voice that made it seem like an insult or accusation. If you were not careful, you could feel immediately guilty, even when you were completely innocent. I, having known her this long, was highly aware of this, and thus, not moved by her manipulations.

Ever so slowly, I lifted the spoon to my mouth. Her eyes narrowed to slits as she watched me. What were friends for, if not to rib each other every now and then? I closed my mouth around the spoon and sighed inwardly. It was good. Really good, but I buried that reaction.

"It's not half bad," I teased. "You could probably get someone to buy it in one of the fine eating establishments they have around here."

She knew, as well as I did, that the only eating establishments close to us were a couple of mom and pop diners. Little more than holes in the wall really. But their food was good, to die for even. That was not a cliché. It was, after all, like eating really tasty grease on a spoon. Over time, I was quite certain that eating a regular diet of their offerings would most likely lead to an early grave. But you would be buried with a smile on your face.

I brought another spoonful to my mouth, mindful of her persistent glare. I couldn't keep the straight face any longer. "It's good," I laughed. "Really."

"You're a real comedian," she sneered with her upper lip curled.

All I could do was laugh some more.

"Just shut up and eat your dinner," she said in disgust.

She acted upset, but I saw the small smile she tried to suppress. Having firmly established her master chef skill level, we both turned our attention back to the television. I didn't have the heart to remind her that I was the one who taught her how to make gumbo.

The female reporter was back again, and now she was interviewing the president of God's Light, a Mr. Kevin Randall.

Mr. Randall looked so normal on television, but I knew he was crazy firsthand. He'd been in New Orleans a time or two, and I'd witnessed his vitriol close up. I didn't think he had seen me either time. That was something else I owed Kenny for.

But even if he could identify me, it would just be part of the good stuff that was now my everyday life as the number one HCF field agent. Yeah, good stuff, like death threats from extremists and harassment by the locals, who were clueless as to my real position. Dealing with the unbelievable bureaucracy that was the HCF was its own particular delicacy.

I forgot to include the growing list of actual attempts on my life. Somebody out there knew what I was up to, even if it wasn't the wacko extremists.

I looked back at the television as Mr. Randall started picking up steam. His face was flushed, and his voice had taken on a preacher like cadence. "If God had intended for us to be able to smell like a bloodhound, He would have given us that kind of nose..."

"That's an ugly picture," Miranda commented, doing her best imitation of snarling like a dog and snapping make believe jaws.

I grimaced as I watched her. It sure was. I didn't know what it would really look like on a human, but the picture she was presenting wasn't pretty.

"…if we were supposed to swim like fish, He would have given us flippers not fingers—"

The reporter interrupted her guest and said, "Then you must believe that if human beings were meant to fly, then God would have given us wings and not airplanes."

Score one for her. She'd just gone up a notch in my book.

Her comment had the desired effect of stalling his rant. He looked completely flustered before he took a moment to gather himself.

"The technology for flying and the alteration of human DNA are two very different things," he said confidently. "As humans, we should protect our DNA, not destroy it by creating monsters."

I took objection to that. Hybrids were not monsters. Altered humans, yes, but not monsters. Incorporating animal abilities into the human genome made them humans with extra capabilities. But it didn't change their personality or how they related to others. Granted they looked different than humans, depending on what had been altered. But they still thought and acted like humans.

"Is it so different, Mr. Randall?" the reporter argued. "All technology is the advancement of knowledge of one kind or another. Each successive generation more advanced than the last. Your attempts to squash technology in this area may very well be dooming us in the future."

She'd interrupted him again. How very unhostess like, and good for her. She was right on the money.

The next generation hybrids were more advanced than their predecessors. From the new gene combinations created, the children had abilities not seen in either hybrid parent. And, where the originals had only one or two traits, their children had any number of traits. Beyond that, the individual traits themselves had been magnified so that the abilities of the offspring far exceeded that of their parents.

The second generation hybrids had also avoided the problems that plagued their parents. Unlike the original man-made hybrids, their creation produced a stable DNA structure that perfectly blended the human and animal genes. In general, the next generation of hybrids possessed heightened senses and were stronger and faster than anyone had thought possible. Vampires and werewolves they were not, but they were dang close to Hollywood's version of shape shifters and mutants.

I tuned back in just in time to watch Mr. Randall dial up the crazy.

"All of this genetic manipulation will be our doom," Randall cried vehemently.

Both I and Miranda involuntarily pulled back in disgust as a drop of his spittle splatted against the lens of the television camera. The reporter wasn't fazed in the least. She soldiered on in that professional demeanor she possessed.

"You are not concerned then, that the potential benefits to human kind, through our increased knowledge of human DNA and its operation, will be lost through your efforts?"

He looked dumbfounded. I didn't think he understood her question. I knew what she was saying. The better you knew how something functioned, the easier it was to fix when things went wrong.

"We should not be altering human DNA," he tried again. "God does not approve—"

"You have proof then?" she said, cutting him off.

Again, with the deer in the headlights look.

"Mr. Randall? You just stated that God did not approve of genetic alteration. Do you have proof of your claim?"

I high fived Miranda across the table. The reporter lady was nailing his butt to the wall. Randall was fuming. It was great.

Mr. Randall yanked off his mike and stormed off the set.

What a loser.

Miranda mirrored my thoughts when she held up her left hand with her thumb and forefinger creating an L. Then she flipped it and shot at the screen where he had been. If only it was that easy.

The reporter lady did not seem surprised by his swift departure. I was pretty sure it was what she'd been going for, all the better to emphasize his insaneness. But it was risky for her and the news organization she worked for. I didn't recall the press being a big fan of hybridization. One might wonder why she was taking such a hard line with this story.

"As with any other news organization, reported facts must be supported by evidence. As Mr. Randall cannot produce evidence of his claim that God is against genetic manipulation of the human genome, we must believe it to be merely his opinion and not a fact."

I couldn't have said it better myself.

"Any new developments regarding these events will be reported as speedily and accurately as possible. In the meantime, please join us tonight at eight for an in depth look at the history of the HCF and genetic manipulation."

Miranda picked up the remote and turned the TV off. "Think that will be worth watching?" she asked.

I shrugged. Didn't we already know the history?

It all started about forty years ago when a company called Biometrics announced to the world that it had successfully implemented the integration of animal DNA into the human genome. For proprietary reasons, they refused to release their research, but they did parade their results, a series of human animal hybrids, in front of the cameras for all to see. As might be expected, by the time the news conference was over, the proverbial scat had hit the fan.

Three primary schools of thought regarding genetic engineering developed fairly quickly after that. There were those that hated it, those that didn't care one way or the other, and those that did everything they could to sign up. It was astounding the number of people that thought having a tail would be "groovy."

Protests pretty much became an everyday occurrence. Some were in support of the hybrids, but most were against. People didn't understand the process and fear of a mutant epidemic began to spread. As the fear grew, the protests turned violent.

Federal troops had to be called in to maintain the peace in a lot of large cities throughout America.

The Federal crackdown on protests caused more unrest in the populace. Americans needed somewhere to channel their fear and anxiety. That translated into the majority of the people in the nation becoming survivalists. As the people learned to do things for themselves again, grow their own food, make their own clothes, etc., there was almost an undercurrent of revolution in the country. It was a strange time in American history.

All the uncertainty and fear circulating around also spurred the growth of local militias. Gun sales skyrocketed. By the 1980s, statistics showed that almost every household in America owned at least one gun.

Then there were the foreign governments insistent on getting access to the technology while simultaneously accusing the US of both heinous crimes against humanity and seeking total world domination. They didn't accept that this was the work of a few scientists not under government control. Even allies of the US began to question the government's motives.

With Americans armed to the hilt and on the verge of civil war, and the rest of the world in an uproar, the president decided to step in. In an unprecedented move, under the heading of "Homeland Security," the president ordered the seizure of Biometrics. He established the HCF to dissemble Biometrics, and the world was told that both the research and the hybrids had been terminated. Congress then followed suit by passing laws that banned genetic manipulation for anything other than medical research.

Until recently, the HCF had faded from public consciousness to largely exist in internet searches for the latest conspiracy theories. Given the public's fascination with the supernatural, there were some doozies out there.

"You know," Miranda drawled, "the history that we think we know, came from the same government that told the rest of the world that hybrids didn't exist anymore." She paused, letting the thought hang in the air.

"Your point?" I asked.

"It might be interesting to watch. Maybe she knows something that we don't."

I hoped not. I kind of liked her in your face style and her level headedness. I didn't want her to disappear like the scientists originally involved in the creation of hybrids. Who knew where the government had sequestered them away. As we sat here, their existence was slowly being scrubbed from the history books.

"Well, if she knows something, I hope she doesn't report it," I said.

"Too dangerous?"

I thought about the recent escalation of extremist activity and the spotlight that was now trained on the HCF. Whatever part of the government that had worked at pushing the HCF into history wasn't going to be happy about the latest developments. "Little bit," I nodded.

"Still, I think I'll watch," Miranda said thoughtfully. "Maybe they'll mention the Colony."

"God, I hope not," I breathed. That was the last thing any of us needed.

The Colony, as we referred to it, was where the supposedly terminated hybrids were housed. But that only happened recently. I didn't know where they'd been before. I also had no explanation for the rationale behind choosing to place the Colony in New Orleans. Other than it must have been decided by a paper pusher or someone with a soft spot for New Orleans.

The exact location they had chosen to establish the Colony was on land that had been decimated by Hurricane Katrina. The city didn't have the funds to fight the encroaching wildlife or fix the damaged infrastructure and was happy to sell the land to the government.

At least they'd had the good sense to let someone who knew what they were doing design the facility. Excluding Kenny, it did a good job of keeping the hybrids in and everyone else out. It helped that the facility was rumored to be a Centers for Disease Control outpost for quarantine of individuals with horrific, highly contagious diseases. The flesh eating bacteria was a particular favorite of the bloggers.

I thought this explained why the crowds Randall managed to gather for the protests in New Orleans weren't all that big. Nowadays, normal humans wouldn't go near the place. The extremists, however, had no such qualms. They were becoming a constant source of irritation. But extremists were never normal, were they?

Being that it was New Orleans, it could have been that the government wanted an easy way to explain away any lapses in security. It wouldn't be that hard to blame the overconsumption of alcohol or voodoo practices for any strange sightings. Strange sightings were something New Orleans was never short of.

One time, I actually saw a picture of Kenny on the cover of one of the local rags. I framed it and gave it to him for his birthday. I couldn't tell by his response if he liked it or not.

"You think Randall will ever turn his attention back to exposing the Colony?" Miranda asked.

I walked my dishes over to the sink and started to wash them. She set hers in the sink next to mine. That was the deal. Whoever didn't cook had to clean. Consequently, we ate out a lot.

"He might. He was really intent on it before." It would not be good if he succeeded. There was no telling what fiction he might report as truth.

She nodded, recalling last year's incidences. "Last year we got lucky. If that hurricane hadn't been in the vicinity, who knows what might have happened," she said and absentmindedly picked up a drying towel.

I noticed that she was about to participate in the cleaning, but I wasn't going to call her attention to the fact. Hey, the gumbo was good, but she was a messy cook.

She frowned as she dried the first dish and put it away. "If he does come back, he's going to be madder than a hornet after that interview."

I eyed her over the skillet I was scrubbing. Madder than a hornet? When had she ever even seen a hornet?

"They'll just increase security," I assured her. "No way would they let him get in. There's too much at stake."

I might have sounded confident, but I wasn't sure the officials in charge of the HCF were ready for all this. I didn't even have confidence that they were aware of the potential powder keg that existed. Which was why I was glad that, all in all, it wasn't that hard to contain the inhabitants of the Colony. Certain determined teenage hybrids notwithstanding.

The hybrid population as a whole was small, and they knew more than anyone what the stakes were. They also knew why the population was now down to less than five hundred. It hadn't started out that small. Humans could do really bad things when they were scared.

"Even so," she said. "It'd probably be best if we wrapped up our work here sooner rather than later."

I was thinking the same thing. Securing our exit before any more trouble had a chance to brew via the extremists or the government. I did not want to be caught in a government cover up or the government deciding to cut its losses and start over by torching the whole place, inhabitants and related scientists included. Would our government do that? Certain factions would.

Regardless of the rhetoric fed to the public, I knew the government had no intention of ridding the world of hybrids. What would the public do if they found out their government had been lying to them all this time?

"Agreed," I said as I watched her put away more dishes. "I do not want to be the target of America's wrath."

"You'd be the bigger target."

She was right. If what I did for the HCF became known to the public, it would definitely make me a target. I was the one conducting all the research for the HCF. And, it was my name stamped on the reports. Which was why I was using the HCF's directive's regarding my work as more like guidelines than hard and fast rules.

The heads of the HCF had no interest in studying the first generation of hybrids that were rapidly dying off. They insisted on limiting the scope of my work to the second generation hybrids. Idiot bureaucrats. Since the second generation was directly descended from the first, it was important to know why the first generation was dying prematurely. Seemed like common sense to me, but whatever.

Despite the HCF, I had discovered that the first generation's transformations had begun to affect more than the targeted areas, unleashing a massive rejection backlash in their bodies. It had even affected gametes, which was not normally the case with mutations to adult DNA.

It was the successful mutation of gametes, if you wanted to phrase it that way, that allowed the second generation to exist at all. But they were more than existing, by every indicator, they were thriving. Most had reached their teen years, and I was warily anticipating the arrival of the third generation any time now. What with teenagers being teenagers, plus the added bonus of insufficient parental supervision.

Oh, there was government security in the form of guards and rules and such. But teenagers had been thwarting lockdown since the dawn of time. I didn't think they were going to stop now. If anything, their special skills aided them in their great escapes. Kenny was a prime example of that.

I was quite certain he shouldn't have been able to leave the compound, but he did. Regularly. From what I had observed recently, he wasn't the only one. It was clear they were becoming restless. Nobody liked a cage, no matter how gilded.

And if they escaped and this whole thing went south...with my job description? I'd be right in the crosshairs. I already was for someone.

"One last sample to get and then we are out of here," I said.

"You said it, sister," she replied emphatically and hung up the drying towel. Then she realized what she'd done. "Hey! You let me dry and put away the dishes without saying a word!"

"I said words," I replied sheepishly. In conversation, but still words.

She huffed out of the kitchen, leaving me to finish alone.

Unfortunately, this meant I would be cleaning the pots alone. It would help if she would pick the right size pot to begin with and quit having to transfer to bigger pots. It was like the three bears of cooking in here.

I began scooping the gumbo into the storage container. It was true that I hated cleaning, but the gumbo had been worth it, and it would taste even better tomorrow.

She returned a few minutes later intent on ignoring me and carrying her laptop, which she plunked down on the table. She sat down with her back to me. Maybe she really was upset.

"Did you upload the newest list yet?" she asked coolly.

"Check your email."

I needed a penance offering. Good thing I'd picked up a carrot cake on the way home. It was still on the entrance table in the foyer with everything else I'd dropped when I came in. Yeah, I wasn't so good at the homemaker thing.

"Be back in a sec," I told her. I didn't take offense to her cold silence. It'd only make what was coming all the sweeter.

Returning with the distinctive box in hand, I detected her eyes following my prize. Just like I knew they would. This cake was no ordinary cake. It was from the bakery Cake Queens, which, in my expert opinion, was just this side of heaven.

I made a production of rummaging around for plates and forks. Then took longer looking for the cake knife. I heard her sigh and smiled at her disparaging of my acting skills.

"Just cut the cake already and give me your I'm sorry gift," she grumbled.

I set the piece of cake beside her. "I offer cake for my transgression," I said solemnly. "Though, I'm not sure of its validity, seeing as how I'm not really sorry. Maybe I should just eat your piece too."

She quickly confiscated the plate before I could reach it.

Apology made, or at least a close approximation of one, I picked up my plate and began to eat.

"Your apologies stink," she said, picking up the fork I'd provided. "Good thing you know how to pick a bakery."

"Oh my god, it's so good, isn't it?" I moaned.

She couldn't respond. Her eyes were closed in carroty cream cheese bliss. If you needed an explanation for such a display, it would be fair to assume there was no help for you. After a few seconds, she opened her eyes and resumed eating.

"Did you find the file?" I asked her.

She nodded.

As my research partner, she did most of the leg work of typing my notes into a format the HCF would accept. What we were currently working on was our second objective on this project, cataloging potential hybrid traits. That included which traits were dominant, how they influenced one another, what combinations of genes produced the most viable hybrids, etc.

From the work I had already done, it was apparent that some species DNA seemed to coexist or merge with human DNA better than others. The government wanted to know why, how and which ones. That was also my job. Basically, I was your modern day Dr. Frankenstein but with updated technology. And the fact that I didn't actually create anything.

"Did you receive their latest memo?" she asked.

"You mean the breeding program?" I said skeptically.

"That would be the one. I take it you don't approve."

"Do you?" I asked with raised eyebrows.

"Not even a little. In fact, I'm seriously beginning to question the validity of our being here at all."

She wasn't the only one, I thought, nodding my agreement.

Did they really not see anything wrong with forced breeding? It was almost as if they had relegated the hybrids to the status of lab animal. I knew the bureaucrats at the HCF had hopes that the third generation would produce an even greater variety of traits that were viable. And, apparently, if left to them, in largely predictable combinations.

So what was the purpose behind a bunch of politicians wanting made to order hybrids? The military I could understand, but politicians? The possible answers to that question made me very uneasy.

With this new breeding program dictate they had issued, the HCF had crossed another line. It was one of many they had crossed in recent days. The sudden change in direction at the HCF left me wanting to know exactly who was in charge. I also wondered if the rest of the government knew what the HCF was up to.

"Who do you think is behind the changes at the Colony?" I asked Miranda.

She stopped typing and looked up at the ceiling. After a moment, she said, "Someone who's after something."

I pursed my lips in concentration. "They are definitely after something," I agreed.

"Who do you think it is?" Miranda asked.

I thought about my boss. It certainly wasn't him. But there was someone or somebodies up there calling the shots. Someone who was intent on seeing their plans carried out. I could see things going really bad really fast if they felt like they were losing control of the situation. And if they got wind of Kenny's covert ops...

"I know it's not Mr. Cain. It's got to be someone higher up. Who? I don't know. But I don't like the changes being implemented. It feels like a setup for something bigger. And, I don't like where they seem to be aiming toward in relation to the hybrids yet to come."

We grew silent as our thoughts consumed us. It seemed the world was right on the edge of disaster and didn't even know it. What happened if we didn't stop it in time or couldn't stop it at all?

"We're too young to be deciding the fate of the world, you know," Miranda sighed heavily.

"Probably," I agreed, smiling at how our thoughts had mirrored one another's.

"You haven't even gotten your wisdom teeth in yet."

My smile quickly faded. "I don't have any wisdom teeth," I sternly reminded her, even though she knew full well that I didn't.

"Even worse," she said dismissively. She picked up her fork and began tapping it gently against her plate. "It could be that we might need to make some decisions soon."

I looked steadily at her. "It could be," I nodded.

"Might be dangerous," she warned.

"When has it not been?"

"We might have to go on the lam."

As she was completely serious, I swallowed the laugh that suddenly threatened to escape. "I'm a pretty good runner."

"Let's hope so," she whispered and set her fork neatly on her plate.

If I was being honest with myself, I had already decided some things. Like research no longer being my number one reason for staying. Now, it was to act as a barrier between the hybrids and the government. I readily admitted one hundred and fifteen pounds wasn't much of a barrier, but what I lacked in mass, I made up for with my brain.

Originally, I thought that if I could give the government the answers they were looking for, then maybe I could avoid a hybrid rebellion and all the subsequent trouble that would cause. Problem now was, I didn't know if I wanted to hand over my work to them.

I was still considering going directly to the military. I still had some contacts there from previous projects. I wasn't sure how they would react to this bombshell, but if it got much worse, I'd have no choice but to approach them.

I thought the whole project would have been better off in their hands, anyway. At least with the military, there would have been a secure command structure and no lack of willing participants. I just had to work out how to bring them in without starting a civil war and without leaving the hybrids to fend for themselves against the government.

I sighed at the responsibilities weighing on me. "The negatives associated with this job sure are starting to pile up. It's a good thing they pay me so well."

"They don't pay you at all," she answered without looking up from her computer screen.

She never let me pretend for one second that I was the highly paid scientist. "Thanks for shattering the dream."

"Just keeping it real."

Her eyes were starting to take on that glazed look she got while working on the computer. Pretty soon, I'd be able to perform a complete tap routine right in front of her, and she wouldn't even notice. Assuming, of course, that I could tap dance.

Scooping up our plates, I headed back to the sink and left her in her spreadsheet world.

Why was everything in life so messy? Cooking was messy. Managing relationships was messy. My job was definitely messy. Playing backup parent to basically a whole generation of kids who were losing their parents was beyond messy.

To be fair, most of the kids were really great, and I didn't mind helping where I could. But they had real issues, and I was no teenage expert. I barely made it through myself, and I didn't have super speed, or vision, or anything. Except maybe my curiosity. And everyone knew what happened to that cat.

No, I didn't have a good feeling about where all this was headed or the part I was playing in it. I couldn't shake the nagging feeling that I was going to be right in the middle of it when all hell broke loose. I didn't count myself as a psychic, but I could read the warning signs. Seeing as how they were seemingly waving at me like some big red glowing beacon, they were hard to miss.

CHAPTER 3

'D FINALLY MANAGED TO CONVINCE Miranda that my latest plan to get Kenny's DNA was great, fool proof even. She'd said that sounded about right considering who was in charge. At which point, I enlightened her as to who was the greater fool, the leader or the follower. We concluded that we were both fools for science and left it at that.

My plan had us stalking Kenny around the Colony campus. He knew what we were doing, but we had a serious weapon on our side this time, teenage male hormones. I knew if we waited long enough, his attention would be wholly focused elsewhere. Then, I could nab his DNA. It was just a matter of time.

Weeks, as it turned out. He had more self-control than I had given him credit for, or he had hiding spots we didn't know about. He had managed to slip by us a time or two. I blamed this entirely on lack of proper nutritional support from Miranda.

She had me so hopped up on junk food that I was beginning to live in a hazy sort of fog. I had no idea where she was stashing the stuff. She pulled it out of every conceivable pocket or pouch. I had just about determined that if she shoved another cellophane wrapped, gooey, cream filled, imitation chocolate something or another at me again when I said I was hungry, I was going to shoot her instead of Kenny.

After more than one empty goose chase, I gave up trailing him and decided that a zone offense might be more productive. Early one morning before anyone was up, I stationed us on the roof of a maintenance building that overlooked some fairly secluded spots. For cover, I used the exhaust fans that dotted the roof here and there.

Our moment arrived when Kenny led his lady love, Crystal, to a spot directly down and across from us. I waited until he gave his full attention to Crystal, and then I grabbed my gun and carefully stepped out from behind the exhaust column.

It was the perfect setup. I had Kenny in my sights, and I'd modified the gun to have a spring action return. No more cutting the fishing line. Then Miranda decided to liven things up.

She peeked over the edge of the roof and yelled, "Smile!" at Kenny—something that was not part of the plan—and then ducked back into hiding. When Kenny spun around, understandably startled, all he saw was me standing there with my gun pointed at him.

In one motion, he stepped in front of Crystal, abruptly lifted his head, and fired thick mucousy goo from these frilly gill things that popped out of the sides of his neck.

Why was it always me? Who knew he could spit goo? And with such accuracy and speed. I was so shocked that I didn't even attempt to use my gun. I'll admit it, when the goo hit, I freaked a little.

Miranda silently regarded my goo splattered face for exactly two seconds before dissolving into hysterical laughter. It was always nice to have friends you could count on.

"Nice one, Kenny," she choked out as she lay back on the roof with both hands pressed to her stomach.

Congratulating Kenny? Oh, that was lovely. I couldn't believe she had forsaken me in my time of need. The goo could have been acidic and burnt my face off or some sort of neurotoxin that could have induced paralysis causing me to fall off the roof. I had to give her the benefit of the doubt that, in her two second delay, she had considered and discarded those possibilities. But even so, not cool.

"Little help here, please," I demanded while watching her roll from side to side.

She didn't stop laughing, but she did sit up and start fishing around in my duffle.

The goo smelt terrible, like burnt beans. I was working hard to overcome my gag reflex. I kept repeating to myself that it was only molecules arranged in specific configurations. That it might have been, but I just wanted to do one of those really girly screams accompanied repeatedly by, "Get it off!" The fact that I could feel it sliding down my face didn't help.

I bent forward at the waist, hoping it would fall off me entirely. "Remind me again why I signed up for this," I said.

"You won the lottery," Miranda replied and handed me a plastic storage tube.

"Not the help I was looking for, but thanks." I had almost forgotten about securing the sample, but, as gross as this was, I still had a job to do. "Eww! I think some got in my mouth," I squealed.

Miranda handed me an open water bottle, and I very vigorously swished and spit while she snickered. I was tempted to aim at her as I repeated the process but refrained from doing so. Only because I still needed her sane for my personal cleanup efforts. That would never happen if she was suddenly wearing the slime. She'd probably run off the roof or strip naked in an effort to rid herself of the putrid stuff. I didn't want to witness either of those options.

"I am never playing the lottery again," I vowed, taking the swab from her outstretched hand. Carefully, I stroked some of the goo into the tube. "They couldn't pay me enough."

"They aren't paying you anything," she reminded me.

I sealed the tube and my ire at her comment. There had yet to exist the time when she did not take the opportunity to remind me of my current undercompensated status.

"Then definitely never again," I stated with conviction, and I meant it too. I never wanted to find myself in this situation again. "This is disgusting," I moaned and spit again.

"Are you referring to wearing the goop or tasting it?" Miranda asked, eyeing me warily as another chunk broke away and splattered against the pebbled roof.

"I've got to go with both A and B."

"Good call," she agreed.

Straightening, I brushed away another large clump headed straight for my right eye. The sheer volume Kenny had been able to dish out was impressive and quite effective for startling his opponent. It was too bad that, on this occasion, his opponent was me.

I slung the dripping goo from my hand and held the tube up to the security light on the roof. Finally, I had in my hand, the somewhat revolting, but coveted sample.

"What species could this gunk possibly be from?" I wondered aloud.

"I'm thinking dinosaur. Remember the one from that dinosaur movie that shot the gunk into that guy's face before it ate him."

Miranda loved movies. All kinds of movies. Me, not so much. I tended to sit and think about all the things I could or should be doing while the movie was playing. By definition, that didn't create a very relaxing pastime for me. But, if food was included as part of the package, I could be persuaded. Everyone had to eat.

"That's real scientific, Mir," I said and handed her the tube.

"You do employ me for my skills."

"And your baby wipes." I wiggled the fingers of my extended hand for emphasis.

She grunted in agreement as she tossed the box to me. "They are one of life's essentials."

No argument from me there. It was amazing all the things one could use baby wipes for that didn't involve a baby.

Miranda labeled the tube and tucked it away while I scrubbed furiously at my face. I went through ten wipes before I was satisfied there was nothing but face on my face. Thank goodness my cap had protected my hair.

I tossed the last wipe and my cap into the trash bag she produced and surveyed the scene below us. The Colony was very quiet tonight.

"You ready to head out?" she asked.

We'd been here six weeks this time. The goo was the last sample I needed. It was bagged, tagged and ready to go. Consequently, so was I.

"Yep. Let's hit it."

"What, no victory dance?"

"Nah, I left my dancing shoes back in Houston. And, I don't trust Kenny. I want to make this my sixth and final attempt to get his DNA." I left unspoken the angst I was feeling about the conclusion of our work here and what that meant, but she read my mood anyway.

"Gottcha. I always preferred victory dinners to dances anyway."

Now she was speaking my language.

We packed the rest of our gear and headed to the ground below. Halfway down the stairs, I realized that I'd left my phone on the roof.

"Hey Miranda, I left my phone."

"You want me to wait," she called from below.

"No, I'll meet you at the truck."

I started up again, taking the steps two at a time. When I reached the door, I pushed it open slowly. Walking to the edge of the roof, I stood and looked over the Colony grounds. I couldn't help but feel bittersweet. I had gotten what I came for, but at what price?

My phone rang, and I walked over and scooped it up. It was Miranda. "Yeah?"

"Just wanted to make sure you found your phone. The protesters are getting a little crazy. You might want to hurry up."

"I thought they were already crazy."

"Just get your butt down here," she said and hung up.

I put the phone in my pocket. Two more teens filled the spot that Kenny and Crystal had recently vacated. Yep, third generation coming soon.

With a heavy heart, I left the roof and aimed toward the truck. Choices and consequences was the name of the tune that repeatedly played through my mind. I feared that I wouldn't be able to change the channel any time soon. It was going to make for a long six hours back to Houston.

Houston, Texas was the location the government had chosen for my lab. Miranda hadn't been kidding when she said I wasn't paid. Officially, the government didn't pay me. I was paid a salary by the University of Houston where I was required to speak as part of a guest lecturer series sponsored by a special grant from the government. See how that worked?

The government did arrange for the lab itself and all the supplies I needed. The hoops I had to jump through just to open the door were a bit overdone I thought. But it kept the HCF from having a molecular geneticist on their payroll and me out of prison for conducting illegal research. So, I guess it worked out alright.

The trip back to Houston was usually uneventful. The highlights being our pit stops and our joy if we missed any traffic on the freeway. Once you've been detoured to some podunk town where your vehicle's GPS did not work, and the workers forgot to post the rest of the detour signs, a straight shot to Houston was something to celebrate.

So far, tonight's trip seemed to be taking the uneventful route which, as feared, left lots of time for thinking. As a consequence, it took me a while to figure out that we were being followed.

"Hey Miranda, don't turn around, but do you see the black SUV about a hundred yards behind us?"

She shifted in her seat and pulled her visor down like she was adjusting her makeup in the mirror. As if. She was one of those natural beauties. Perfect skin, perfect hair, blah, blah, blah. Everywhere she was dark, I was light. I wasn't bad to look at. But she looked exotic, and I looked like blonde haired, blue eyed, American apple pie.

"How far is a hundred yards?" she said, still peering at the mirror and totally missing the look of incredulity on my face.

"Are you serious? Think football field," I told her.

"Not helping, but do you mean the only vehicle on the road besides us for like for-ev-er?"

She'd punctuated each syllable of forever clearly in an attempt to cover her yardage incompetency. I knew she'd grown up in the Northwest, but how could she not know how long a football field was? They had football up there. Being that we had more pressing issues to pursue, I chose to let her poor sports education slide for the moment.

"That would be the one. It's been following us since at least Baton Rouge."

"Are you sure?" she asked doubtfully.

She was doubting me? After she'd tortured me by making me watch every episode of that ridiculous detective show, with her only lure being her attempts to learn Chinese cooking? That was one mistake I'd never make again.

"Are you doubting me? Who else could they be following? As you so astutely pointed out, we are the only ones on the road, and it's two in the morning."

"This sounds like one of those spy novels."

I honestly didn't know where she found the time for all her extracurricular activities.

She lowered her voice and in true movie trailer fashion began her intro. "There were two of them. At night, travelling through the wilds of Louisiana. When the darkened SUV—"

"The wilds of Louisiana?" I interrupted. "Don't you mean swamps or uninhabited lands? How about mosquito infested woods? And thanks for comforting me in my distress."

She flipped her visor back up and nonchalantly said, "It's the only major freeway from Baton Rouge to Houston. I'm sure they have a legitimate reason for being here at this time of night, other than following us."

"Yeah, it's not like we're carrying cargo filled with mutant DNA that the general public thinks doesn't exist anymore." I looked over at her as I said it.

"There is that," she said, pursing her lips. It was the look she always got when she was thinking.

"You've got that look again."

"What look?"

"Your thinking look. That's gonna make wrinkles when you're older." I snuck a quick look in the rear view mirror. "I think that we should pull over somewhere and see if they follow."

"We could do that," she said slowly. "But I think it's too late."

I snapped my eyes back to the rear view mirror. The SUV was speeding up. Crud. What should I do? Speed up, slam on the brakes...remain calm as they passed us. Oh, well, that was anticlimactic. I checked my speed. The dial said eighty. They sure were in a hurry all of a sudden.

"I guess they had somewhere to be," I said quietly.

"Maybe they got a call?" Miranda guessed.

We watched silently as the SUV pulled further away from us. I was just about to chalk it up to coincidence when their brake lights came on. I let off the gas pedal.

"Macy," Miranda said.

"I see'em." They were stopping fast.

"Macy!"

"I know!" I shouted back at her.

My tires squealed across the asphalt as I slammed on the brakes. The truck came to a stop about thirty feet away from the SUV.

"Do we have any weapons?" Miranda asked.

Once again, she had completely stunned me. "Weapons?" I asked, turning to look at her. "Are you kidding me? You won't even step on a cock roach."

"They're disgusting," she groaned. "And stuff always squishes out when you smash'em."

We both shuddered. She was right.

"Do Yoohoos and Mr. Goodbars count?" she asked, holding them up.

"Unless Mr. Goodbar is the tire jack, I'm thinking no, but if they need a sugar fix, we got'em covered."

Idiot. She was a whiz at molecular biology, but the common things seemed to escape her sometimes. Perhaps we could hit them over the head with a Yoohoo and shove the candy bar in their mouth if they tried to scream. The ridiculousness of that thought caused me to smile in spite of the seriousness of the situation. But it quickly faded as I stared at the very real SUV in front of us.

It had done one of those sideways turning stops that blocked the whole road. I'd only ever seen that in the movies. Staring at its black length stretched across the road, I knew there was no getting around it. I was also pretty sure driving really fast in reverse was a bad idea.

"Why haven't they got out yet?" Miranda asked.

I glanced at her. Her face revealed the various scenarios she was playing out. It didn't look like they were pleasant ones. That was probably why they hadn't gotten out yet.

"Intimidation," I said confidently, turning my gaze back to the SUV.

"Intimidation?"

"Yeah, they think we're scared poopless right now."

"They got that right," she said, nodding vigorously.

"Yep, I'd say they nailed it." She wasn't the only one with an imagination.

I drummed my fingernails on the steering wheel. This was a situation I never thought I would find myself in. I didn't know why, especially considering what I had been through lately. Sure, it was always a possibility, in some obscure, remote, most likely never way. One I'd never really entertained. All of my attackers had been unidentifiable somebodies somewhere off in the distance, but now, they were right here in front of me.

"Here they come," Miranda singsonged.

For goodness sakes, I was a researcher. Now I was being cornered by tall, dark and packing? In the beam of my headlights, I was able to see a shoulder holster peeking out of his unbuttoned jacket that swung as he walked. Great. He was probably trained in all sorts of ways to kill me.

My weapons training consisted of hit the beer bottle on the fence when I was ten. I didn't have any training in survival or what to do if hemmed in by a SUV sporting baddies. All that stuff that, right now, seemed like a really good idea. Where were all my spy gadgets? They were new line items in my budget that was where they were.

As focused as I was on my internal debate, I hadn't realized he had reached the truck. The tap on the window clued me in.

With my first close up look at him, I could not keep the smile off my face. As my eyes swept his form, I came to the conclusion that I was being stalked by Men in Black. He had the suit, the glasses, the chiseled jaw...

I rolled my window down and, with what I hoped was a totally used to dealing with this kind of thing voice, asked, "Do you need directions?"

He didn't even crack a smile. But he did look me in the eye...maybe. Hard to tell with the sunglasses on...at two in the morning.

"We need you to come with us, Dr. Greer," he spoke in a rich, even voice.

That was me. For better or worse, they knew who I was. Leaning across the open window, I propped my chin in my hand, partially concealing my smile. I didn't expect him to fill in the blank, but I asked anyway. "Why would I come with you, Mr. ...?"

"Please get out of the vehicle, Ma'am."

Just as I suspected, we weren't exchanging names.

I took a breath and righted myself. Putting both hands back on the wheel, I stared out the front window. "Well, Mir, it looks like I'm getting out of the vehicle."

When she didn't respond in her usual rapid fire mode, I turned to look at her. She was sort of sunk down in her seat as far away from my side as she could get. Her eyes were darting back and forth between the Goon at my window and the black SUV. Maybe she was in shock.

"Miranda, you ok?" My query was met with silence. "Miranda," I said sharply.

It seemed like her eyes were in slow motion as they slid to me. "Where is my tall, dark, and delicious?"

Really? She was thinking about possible mates at a time like this? Unbelievable. My concern was replaced by anger at the accusation in her voice.

"Are you accusing me of hogging the Goons?" I asked coldly.

She straightened in her chair, seeming to puff up at the same time—like a chicken or something.

"I know how this goes. The leading lady is always the one who ends up with the hot guy."

Yep, she was thinking about it.

"Miranda, need I remind you of all the times I have made this trip alone because you made other plans involving Goon like beings. I think you are quite capable of getting your own Goon!"

As if on cue, a door to the SUV opened and out stepped Goon Number Two. We watched in silence as he walked to the back of the SUV. At least the momentary interruption served to quell our anger, which I suspected was born out of the stress we were currently enduring.

"He's back," Miranda whispered, pointing at the window.

I turned back to the window. Goon Number One was still at eye level with me and had one hand gripping the door handle and the other resting on top of the truck. How tall was this guy? Of course, I was only five foot three so almost everyone was tall to me.

"I'm going to have to insist that you get out of the vehicle, Ma'am," he said a little more forcibly.

"Sticking to the script, I see," I told him.

Facing Miranda once again, I started to speak when she beat me to it.

"No goodbyes, MG," she spit out rapidly and held up her closed fist.

I raised my eyebrow at her. "We do fist bumps now?"

"It's a new thing. I thought it'd make us look more tough in front of tall, dark and PUSHY!" she yelled as he opened the door.

He ignored her outrage and responded with the requisite phrase. "Out of the vehicle now, please."

He was polite, if not original, for a kidnapper.

"I'll see you later," I said quietly to Miranda while returning her fist bump. Most definitely I would. Probably.

I climbed down from the truck, jumping the last foot or so to the ground. My truck was a jacked up 4x4 with oversized tires. Miranda has repeatedly told me that it was too big for me and that I needed to downsize. But I worked hard for this truck. I loved my truck.

He obviously didn't know this. He had already started walking away while ordering, "This way, Ma'am."

I crossed my arms and stared at his retreating form. Did he think I was an idiot? There was clearly only one way to the SUV. Obviously, it was that way.

When he realized I wasn't following, he pivoted and raised an eyebrow at me. Apparently, I didn't have the market cornered on eyebrow raises. "What about my truck?" I could tell by his hesitation that he was not expecting that question.

"The truck?" he asked in confusion.

"Yeah, the truck," I repeated mockingly. "What is going to happen to my truck?"

"My partner," he said, motioning toward Goon Number Two, "will see to the return of your truck and associate."

"How convenient," I said dryly.

"We plan it that way," he said and resumed his march to the SUV.

Goon Number Two and I started walking to our respective destinations, trading places as we went. I noticed he had latte colored skin as he crossed through the headlight beams. I wondered if that meant he had the light brown eyes that were so often paired with that color skin. But even if he did, being pretty did not earn him a pass to drive my truck.

My glare followed him as I paused and watched him climb behind the wheel. Shifting my gaze sideways to Miranda, I gasped in disbelief. She was grinning from ear to ear.

That girl was a hopeless romantic. She'd probably already cooked up any number of romantic scenarios to enact. Goon Number Two didn't know what he was in for. They'd probably be engaged before they hit Houston.

I looked back at the SUV and the Goon waiting by the open door. What else could I do? By my calculations, running in Louisiana at night would be just as dangerous as getting in the SUV. I figured they wanted me alive, didn't know about unharmed.

He must have sensed my hesitation. Stepping away from the door, he looked prepared to take off.

"I'm not running," I said. I could at least spare myself the humiliation of being chased down.

Sighing more loudly than I intended, I let my shoulders slump forward and walked over to the SUV. He held the door open for me, but I shunned his reach for my elbow. This vehicle wasn't any taller than my truck, and I climbed into it unassisted all the time.

Once inside, he made me move over to the middle seat next to another Goon already in position. Then he climbed in beside me, taking up all the free space.

In the front of the SUV, there were two more Goons dressed exactly the same as the others. "Do they clone you guys?" I asked jokingly. Nobody laughed. Given what I did for a living, it probably wasn't that funny. They could be clones or more.

After a few minutes of driving in silence, it became clear to me that no one was going to volunteer any information. We were going to have to do this the old fashioned way.

I angled myself to face my Goon. Since he'd been the one to fetch me, I'd designated him as mine. "Who's we?" I asked.

I got the eyebrow raise again. It was kind of funny watching the one eyebrow ascend above the sunglasses. I couldn't help smiling as I explained my question further. "You said we plan it that way. Who's we?"

"All of your questions will be addressed by the Director."

At least, he'd dropped the Ma'am. "We is the Director?" I teased. He didn't find my comment amusing. Tough Crowd.

"And that would be Director of...?" I drew out the of for emphasis, but he didn't answer. "When do I get to meet the Director?"

Still no response. I guess I had gotten all I was going to get on that, so I changed the subject of my questions. "Can you tell me where we're going?"

The only sound was the whistling of the wind against the SUV. The old fashioned way was annoying.

"How about, when will we get there?" I tried again.

Nada. Were these guys breathing? I looked at Goon Number

One's abdomen. His jacket was still unbuttoned and underneath was a nicely fitted white t-shirt. Yep, breathing.

He caught me looking, and I innocently batted my eyelashes at him, but I couldn't wipe the stupid grin off my face. I was trying to stop smiling, but the harder I tried not to, the stronger the urge became.

I sat back between the Goons again, laying my head against the back of the seat until I could stop grinning like an idiot. There really wasn't anything funny about the situation.

"Sure would be nice to know why you've kidnapped me," I said to the quiet interior of the SUV.

They didn't even bother to acknowledge the fact that I was speaking. They were going to sit here and ignore me. They really were.

I could make it difficult for them, but they could probably make it difficult for me too. I was betting there difficult would be a lot worse than mine.

Using my hands to cover a huge yawn, I squeezed my eyes shut. The driving combined with the ebbing adrenaline was starting to make it hard for me to keep them open. I hadn't slept since five this morning. Counting backwards, I calculated I'd been awake for twenty one hours. It was definitely time for a nap. Lucky for me, I had my own personal Goon snuggly, and I was going to use it.

I laid my head against my Goon's shoulder. He smelled like a bonfire and fruit, an odd combination on a man. Turning my head slightly, I pressed my nose into his bicep and took a deep whiff. Maybe it was his fabric softener. I'd never seen one labeled backyard bbq with grilled fruit, but that didn't mean it didn't exist.

I could feel him looking down at me. He probably even had that eyebrow raised. That made me grin again, and I pressed my face tighter against his arm to hide it. If he objected, he never said a word.

As I waited for sleep to overtake me, I revisited the events of my day. Assuming that Miranda didn't become too distracted to store it properly, I had obtained the last sample I needed. The one official reason I was still on the job. It would take me a little while to complete the analysis, but then what?

Did I trust the HCF enough to hand over my report? Not currently. There would be trouble either way. Turning it in was probably the safest choice for me. But, if I did turn it in, would I just leave? How would I explain that to Kenny and the rest of the group? Or to myself? That would leave no one standing between the hybrids and the government. What would happen to them then?

There had to be a way out of this mess that didn't involve manipulation or annihilation of the hybrids or rebellion against the government. I just couldn't see it yet. Depending on what these people wanted from me, I might not have to worry about it at all.

My pillow shifted further away, and I leaned in closer, claiming the space he'd given up. He'd just failed if he was trying to get away. That was ironic. Shouldn't I be the one trying to get away?

I covered another yawn and curled my legs beside me on the seat. Leaning more heavily against my Goon, I wrapped my arms around his arm and pulled it toward me. He resisted briefly before he let me adjust him. That was better. Now maybe I wouldn't wake up with a knot in my neck.

Well, here was hoping I didn't drool.

CHAPTER 4

I T WAS DAYLIGHT WHEN I woke up, and I felt more tired than I had before I'd slept. I hated when that happened. But not as much as I hated my body informing me that I hadn't moved while I'd slept. I couldn't feel my legs at all.

Gingerly, I moved them back to the floor and waited for the pins and needles to start. Unwrapping my arms from my bicep pillow, I sat up and began to roll my head from side to side. Neither of my captors seated on either side of me paid me much notice.

Peering out the front window, I observed we were no longer on the interstate. I probably could have deduced that without seeing the road simply by all the bumping the SUV was doing.

The smooth interstate had been replaced by a dirt road lined by very tall weeds on either side. I was summarily being tossed around, constantly rebounding off the nearest Clone—I'd updated their designations this morning, more scientific. All this movement was probably what woke me up.

I didn't often ride in the middle seat, but it didn't take long to form my opinion. Riding in the middle was the worst. There were no places to hold on. I had to grip my Clone just to stay in the seat. If I didn't think he was emotionless, I would have sworn he was enjoying the steady jostling I was enduring. I certainly wasn't, particularly not with the needle sensations throbbing every time my legs bounced into something.

We fielded one long string of incredibly large ruts that slung me everywhere, including into his lap. He seemed truly startled that I was there.

"Don't look at me," I said accusingly. "I'm not driving."

He didn't say a word, just deposited me back in my seat, which was fine with me. It was where I was headed anyway.

The ride smoothed out after that. The vehicle climbed onto a blacktop road right before we entered an airstrip, a private one by the looks of it. A sleek jet was parked at one end, and there didn't seem to be any other vehicles around.

I wondered if the current Clones were going with me or dumping me here to be ferried somewhere else. I found myself surprisingly not wanting to give up the little bit of familiarity I had gained with my Clone. Not like we had connected or anything. He hadn't spoken to me since the night before, and even then it was the bare minimum.

Come to think of it, I hadn't heard them make a sound all night either. Maybe I had slept really soundly or maybe these guys didn't talk the whole way there. That would require more discipline than I possessed. Maybe they weren't communicating verbally, yet another interesting and frightening thought. I'd have to experiment with that later.

The SUV pulled to a stop alongside the jet, and my Clone didn't waste any time escorting me to the gangway. It appeared my Clone was the only one accompanying us because the SUV carrying the rest of them drove away as soon as we stepped onto the ramp.

I found it strangely comforting that he was going, and odd that they thought it took an SUV full of Clones to accompany me to the airport. They either held the belief that I was tougher than I actually was, or they were expecting trouble. I kind of thought it had to be the latter.

As I reached the top of the ramp, I paused and looked around. The swamps were gone, but that didn't tell me much. In my estimation, we had driven about six hours. Six hours in any direction and still managed to end up in the middle of nowhere. For all I knew, they could have gone in circles the entire time. It didn't look like Houston, but it could have been. Houston zoning was weird.

Not recognizing a single thing settled it. I had no idea where we were. I didn't really think I would pursue an escape plan, but it would help to know where I was, if the need arose.

My shadow suddenly grew much larger, and I knew without turning that my Clone was behind me. In response to the ever so strategic clearing of his throat, I muttered, "I'm going," and stepped onto the plane.

"Swanky," I said, clasping my hands together in front of me. To no one in particular, I said, "So, what's on the breakfast menu, and please point me in the direction of the bathroom."

"Last door on the right," said a pleasant voice from what I did not think was a flight attendant. She wore no uniform to speak of, no sun glasses, and her suit wasn't even black. Like me, she had blond hair, which she had pulled up in a bun, and her eyes were blue. She even looked a lot like me. I found that to be the slightest bit creepy.

In response to my staring, she lifted both her eyebrows, the universal equivalent of asking "what?"

I smiled and walked past her to the bathroom. My Clone, who had brushed past me already, had taken a position just over the wing. Someone had read the safety reports.

I finished my necessities and was happy to see a tray filled with breakfast goodies at a table directly across the plane from my Clone. The look alike, non flight attendant woman was nowhere in sight, which left only me and my Clone in the immediate vicinity of the food. Since he hadn't bothered to claim it, I assumed it was for me. If I was wrong, I'd still rather eat now and make apologies later.

There was the possibility that the food could be drugged, but it seemed unlikely. If they were going to pursue that route, they would have done it in the beginning, when escaping had the greatest likelihood of success. There wasn't much escape to be had at thirty thousand feet up, if you excluded parachutes, which I did. If it came down to that, they could just shoot me. There was absolutely no possibility of me willingly jumping out of this plane.

Without further delay, I sat down and commenced eating. In the five minutes it took to clear the tray, we were wheels up. There was no greeting from the pilot, and I didn't even get a safety lecture.

But I wasn't left completely on my own. There was my Clone, of course, and my unexpected twin had returned and taken a seat across from me at the table. She was perusing a report of some kind, waiting for me to finish.

Although I had eaten everything on the tray, including the token grapes, I was still hungry and began to scope around for more.

"I can get you another tray," my look alike offered.

I liked to give people labels, especially when they didn't offer an alternative. Maybe it was a scientist thing. Miranda said it was just me being neurotic. Being that she herself was neurotic, she should know.

"You could be my new best friend," I said, secretly hoping I wouldn't need one.

When she left to get my seconds, I crossed the isle and scooted in next to Clone Number One. "Did Miranda and my truck make it back to Houston okay?" I asked him.

My question didn't even rate a head turn. His delay in responding allowed me to study him closely. Now that I could see him in the daylight, I made a very astute scientific observation. He was quite handsome.

Yes, handsome was a scientific designation. There had been studies done that showed men who were considered handsome by potential female mates had the greatest chance of mating and thus propagating the species. Not that I was looking for a mate or interested in propagating. Okay, maybe his hotness was not entirely scientific, but it was definitely worth noticing.

"They have arrived and everything including the cargo is secured," he finally answered.

Secured? What did that mean? Being the practical person that I was, I asked him. "What do you mean by secured?"

His tone of voice clearly indicated he was irritated with

being disturbed. "Your associate and the cargo are where they should be."

I placed my elbow on the table and rested my chin in my hand. Could he be any more evasive? Miranda could be tied to a chair and be where she was supposed to be. By cargo, I assumed he meant they knew what we were researching and hadn't exposed us. That was good. But I was starting to get irritated with his irritation. I just wanted a straight answer.

"Is your should be the same as mine? Because my should be is at my lab," I stated definitively, then added, "Unharmed," for good measure.

I thought I detected a sigh. It was such a minute movement it was hard to tell. I didn't think he could be more condescending. I was surprised. Not pleasantly.

"The cargo and your associate are unharmed and currently doing whatever it is they do when they are not graced by your presence."

It was my turn to arch my eyebrow at him. Feathers were a little ruffled, weren't they? I had to admit it, I was beginning to enjoy this interplay. That was the biggest reaction I'd gotten from him yet.

I wondered what branch of government he was. I assumed these guys were government. They just had that feel. You learned to recognize it once you've dealt with the government long enough.

Squinting my eyes at him, I asked, "Are you with the DOD?"

He declined to respond.

"Homeland Security?" I paused, but at this point, it was only in pretense of waiting for a response. "CIA, CDC, Super-Secret Agency I've never heard of?"

Still nothing. How did I get this guy to play ball? I didn't know what it was about him, but to me, it felt like he was the leader.

I straightened in my chair and considered him a moment. His hair, which was a very dark brown, was longer on top and slowly tapered to right above his suit collar. It would probably have been soft curls or at least wavy if he were to let it grow. I wondered what color his eyes were.

Bingo. He still had his shades on.

At the risk of being subjected to his brand of irritation once again, I said, "You know, we are not in the sun. You can take off your shades."

He turned his head to face me. It was kind of creepy. Now that I had his attention, I wasn't so sure I wanted it. With one finger, he raised his glasses above his eyes.

To say his eyes were peculiar did not do them justice. They were not strictly human eyes. I would know. Anyone who got a peek at them would know. They were a brilliant green color, and the pupil was elongated. Some sort of cat DNA maybe?

"The Director will answer all your questions," he stated sharply, then he let the glasses slide back in place and resumed his non-interested pose.

He was a hybrid not at the Colony and clearly in a position of authority with some other government agency. That was disturbing on so many levels, but mostly because I was ignorant of his existence.

"You're a hybrid," I said, slightly confused.

He didn't acknowledge my comment. Big shock.

"Are all of the Clones hybrids?" I asked.

His non response signaled that he was back to ignoring me. This could get old fast. I needed to rattle him. I knew I really shouldn't poke the tiger, but if he thought this was over, he obviously hadn't studied the dossier on me enough. Did he think I'd be afraid of his kitty cat eyes? Scared into silence? Please.

"Oh, my God! You're a werewolf!" I exclaimed.

His head slowly swiveled back to me. I opened my eyes real wide and put on my most innocent face.

"I am not a wolf," he growled softly.

I changed my mind. I could keep poking the tiger all day. Except that the twinish, non flight attendant, food lady was back, and I was distracted by the bacon and eggs she set in front of me.

Thus, I officially ended our staring contest. It wasn't really fair anyway. I couldn't tell if he was blinking with the sun glasses on.

While I tucked into my second tray, I wasn't positive, but I think I saw a small lifting of the right corner of his mouth. Maybe a smile, a tiny one.

After my stomach was satisfied, I decided I needed a new dancing partner. I'd just taken my original seat back when the food lady sat down and introduced herself—I'd shortened her label to what was most currently relevant to me.

"I'm Olivia Needham," she said smartly and a little too perky. But I thought her name fit. She was well put together, sophisticated, elegant even, except for the perky. Perky made me nervous. Made me want to find out what you were hiding with your perkiness.

Perky or not, she definitely didn't seem like someone who should be serving food. "And what is Olivia Needham's part in all this?" I asked.

"Besides being your new BFF?"

Clever. I smiled, acknowledging her wordplay.

"I'm a liaison of sorts. I'll be showing you the ropes. Helping you with whatever you need. But until then, the Director—"

"The Director will answer all my questions," I finished with her. "Yeah, I've heard that a time or two." I smiled real big and waved at Catboy.

Nothing. That boy was a statue.

"You learn quickly," she quipped.

I think she was amused. Glad I could entertain. I also wondered if she was talking about the situation or Catboy.

"Will we be landing soon?" I asked. All this travelling and non talking, talking was annoying.

"In about an hour," she said. "You then have another short drive. You'll see the Director first thing in the morning."

She was a lot more informative than my last interview. Considering he told me basically nothing, that wasn't saying much.

"And he is Director of what exactly?" I asked.

She regarded me with a half-smile on her face, but didn't offer an answer.

Statues, the whole lot of them.

She then pulled out a brief case and began sifting through some paperwork, completely ignoring me. Question and answer time was apparently over.

I sighed and looked out my window. Not that I would recognize where we were, yet again. But there was nothing else to do but wait and mull over my future.

They obviously wanted me for something. If Catboy's eyes were any indication, it was related to my work with hybrids. I thought if they wanted to harm me, they would have done it by now. I figured the hurting part wouldn't come until and if I refused their offer.

Once we landed, Ms. Needham took a different vehicle, and I was back to the Catboy and Clone snuggly. So there was no talking, no iPod or Wi-Fi, not even a magazine. I had napped on the plane and wasn't tired, but I was hungry.

"Are we going to eat anytime soon?" I asked.

In what was a shockingly immediate response to me, both Catboy and the Clone looked at me.

"What? Am I not allowed to eat?" I said defensively. Was this the way they were going to be feeding me? I'd be keeping this in mind when the negotiations started. Hopefully there would be negotiations instead of do this or die.

"Did you not eat on the plane?" said the Clone, who obviously had no appreciation for my appetite.

I turned to face him, as much as I could while stuffed between the two of them. "Yes, in fact, I did eat on the plane. However, I am no longer on the plane, and I'm hungry. Hence, the question." A little snarky, I knew, but I was hungry, and he should have been able to figure that out because I wouldn't have asked otherwise.

As if by magic, a goodie bag materialized in front of my face. It dangled from Catboy's long fingers. Look who else had figured out that food was important to me. I threw a glare at the Clone and greedily reached for the bag.

Opening it, I peered inside hopefully and found that he had far surpassed my expectations. I thought perhaps some cheese and crackers, but that was not what I was looking at. He had covered all the forms of chocolate, liquid, solid and gooey.

He was no longer Catboy. He was now Catman. I could show respect when it was due. Anticipating my needs, particularly my food needs, and meeting them definitely qualified for respect in my book.

You might think with my love of eating I'd be huge. Or, as we say in Texas, as big as the side of a house, but I wasn't. I kept up with my eating by running and weight lifting. I knew exactly how far and how fast I had to run to outpace the Oreos. And if I do say so myself, I looked good. Curves in all the right places. I was a lot more solid than I looked thanks to the weights. No waify model here.

I busied myself rifling through the little bag of heaven. I froze when my eyes locked on a familiar wrapper. Was that…a fried chocolate pie? I hadn't had one of those in at least a month. I ripped the package open and took a bite, sighing as the chocolate pudding filled my mouth.

It was official, Catman loved me.

My chewing slowed as I eyed Catman who was suddenly making a strangled coughing sound. Was he trying to smother a laugh? Was Catman telepathic? Cats weren't telepathic. No animal was telepathic. However, the only time that I had heard him speak was when he had addressed me. How was he communicating with the other Clones?

I wanted to ask what was going on, but I knew what I would get in response. It seemed I had no choice but to wait for the Director to answer my questions. Knowing I wasn't going to figure it out right then, I settled in to finish my assorted chocolates.

It occurred to me that though I might not be able to figure out everything, I could conduct a little experiment. Focusing solely on Catman, I told him, *Thank you.*

He had no verbal response, but he did slightly nod his head.

Oh. My. God! He could hear me. This could be really great

or really embarrassing. I cringed as I tried to recall all the things I'd thought since being with him. Only about thirty or forty embarrassing things. No big deal, right?

I wanted to run and hide, but there was nowhere to go in here. And how could you hide from a telepath anyway?

My mind began spinning with all the possibilities associated with telepathy. I had a whole new set of questions now. Did he hear everything or only things I directed at him? Could everyone hear me or just him? Was I broadcasting everything I thought?

Good Lord, these people would get tired of me real quick. I never really shut up mentally. I thought a lot. Even if I wasn't verbalizing, the brain was still going.

Did that mean I needed to erect some kind of telepathy barrier? And how the heck would I do that? Really, I needed the telepathy handbook and a note pad to write down my questions.

But no one handed me pen and paper, so maybe I wasn't broadcasting, or they were ignoring me, as usual. Or maybe they had erected their own barriers against me. Not sure how I felt about that possibility, but I could understand it.

I crushed the bag with the leftover trash in my hands. I couldn't wait to get my hands on the Director. And God help him if I came across pen and paper.

CHAPTER 5

I T WAS RIGHT AROUND DARK when we finally arrived at what I called an estate. Given that it was late summer, that put it around eight o'clock in the evening. I'd been traveling all day on two breakfast trays and a bagful of chocolate. I needed a shower, a change of clothes, and something to eat. As I had nothing with me, I hoped they'd thought of everything.

Catman held the door open for me while I exited the SUV. My muscles severely protested their engagement after so long a rest. Yikes, I was stiff.

He raised his eyebrows at me questioningly.

I assumed it was in response to the grimace on my face, but I was not going to tell him that my butt hurt. Or think it. Dang it. I'd already thought it. Shaking my head in disgust, I motioned for him to lead the way.

He shut the door to the SUV and started up what was a very long stone patio area. "You will find the showers refreshing," he tossed over his shoulder.

Was he amused? He sounded amused. I was not amused. Some things just didn't need to be shared on a first date.

My view of the grounds was somewhat limited by the descending darkness, but I could determine there were rolling hills off in one direction and woods in the other. The house itself appeared to be your standard stone mansion or palace. Not like I'd know the appropriate term. What I did know was that it was beautiful, especially all lit up.

Stepping through the door into the foyer left my mouth hanging open. "Wow," I breathed.

From floor to ceiling it was opulence. A black and white diamond patterned floor stretched as far as I could see. Dark wood paneling and woodwork were everywhere, including the twin gigantic curved staircases we now faced.

Walking across the foyer, I suddenly felt small. This place was a lot bigger on the inside than it looked on the outside. It reminded me of something you would find in the English countryside. Well, I guessed you would. Again, not an expert in this sort of thing.

"It's a mix of European architecture," Catman supplied.

I'd forgotten he was standing there. Looking up at him, I got my second look at his eyes without the glasses. They were still green, but they no longer had the elongated pupil, which meant he had the ability to reverse his trait. Very interesting. And, he'd just answered my unspoken thoughts. Were we acknowledging the telepathy thing?

He maintained eye contact with me for just a moment longer than necessary before turning his back to me. "I'll show you to your room," he said.

Guess not.

Taking the lead again, he preceded me up the stairs. Gotta love the view. The sculpting in this place was amazing. He harrumphed at my assessment, and I smiled at his backside as we continued to climb.

At the top of the stairs, we turned right, and that was about the only turn direction that I would remember. We wove right and left so many times that I thought we should have ended up where we started. Finally, we stood before a door that I presumed led to my room.

He knocked and opened the door to reveal Ms. Needham seated in a receiving area. She looked up as the door opened and nodded once to Catman.

"Welcome, Dr. Greer. Please come in and forgive the intrusion, but I have some details to go over with you before you turn in for the evening. I have also been apprised of your nutritional needs," she said, motioning toward the table between her and an unoccupied chair.

On the table were a couple of platters with meats, cheeses, breads, fruit and a lonely can of soda.

"Was the apprising your doing?" I asked, looking back at Catman as I stepped into the room.

He was leaning against the doorframe with his arms crossed over his chest and one foot braced against the trim, watching me intently. What did he expect me to do? Fall on the trays and devour them? I wasn't a food vampire. I just liked to eat. It might have had something to do with a shortage of food growing up, but I wasn't going to psychoanalyze it.

"What?" I asked in irritation when he continued to stare.

He lowered his foot and uncrossed his arms. "Enjoy your shower," was all he said as he turned to leave.

Why did he have that look on his face?

I frowned and walked back to the door. Peering down the hallway, I watched until he turned a corner, putting him out of sight. I didn't know what the look meant, but I didn't think it was good. Catman was mysterious.

I supposed I'd have to learn his name eventually. I'd make it my mission. Something to look forward to tomorrow.

"Everything alright?" Ms. Needham called softly.

I closed the door and turned my attention back to the room and its contents. "Hunky Dory," I said without emotion.

This was one weird kidnapping. Totally not what I would have expected. Not that I had dreams about being kidnapped. But I was pretty sure that if I did, private jets and mansions wouldn't have been a part of them.

I slid into the chair opposite her and started making myself a sandwich. "So, what are these details I need to know?"

She picked up a notepad and flipped the page. "For starters, once I leave this room, you will not be allowed to leave until I come to retrieve you in the morning."

I had a new mission, to make that notepad mine.

I rearranged my sandwich, adding a good deal more cheese to one side and then carefully cut the sandwich in half.

"No nighttime escapades. Got it," I said.

She checked off the first item on her list, and then she noticed me eyeing the notepad. "I like to make actual physical lists that I can have with me. That way I don't forget anything. I know I could do it on a tablet device," she shrugged, "but I just haven't made the transition yet."

Whatever. I was only interested in divesting her of the notepad, not her reasoning behind it. I was counting on the hope that she, like me, hadn't eaten yet.

"What's next?" I said through a mouthful of pastrami and Colby Jack.

"This will be your suite for the duration of your stay here. You are free to go into any of the rooms in this suite. If you need anything, you can ring the—"

"How many rooms does it have?" I was curious. I'd never stayed in a suite in a mansion before.

"There are six rooms in this suite. This one, the bedroom, bathroom, exercise, office and a casual living area that has a small kitchen."

Just like an apartment, and had she rattled that off rather quickly?

"As I was saying, if you need anything, there is a list of phone numbers by the house phone that tells you who to call for whatever you need."

"Where is the house phone?"

"In the office."

"Which is where?"

She looked up from her list, irritation clearly written on her face. I suppressed the urge to smile at her. She was getting grouchy, and her words had lost that professional detachment. Also, just as hoped, her eyes were greedily following my sandwich as I took another bite. Can't say I was too impressed with the lack of priority they attached to eating around here.

I waved the other half of my sandwich in front of her, drawing her angered attention back to my face. "I'll trade you this half of sandwich for your notepad."

She didn't hesitate. She ripped off the front page and pushed the notepad over while simultaneously grabbing the proffered sandwich. "Thank God," she mewed. "I'm starving."

"I noticed that the Clones never seemed to eat. Don't they feed ya'll?"

She barked out a laugh, sending a piece of pastrami flying. "Clones. Too true." She swallowed and took another bite. "Oh, they eat," she garbled. "A lot. Just maybe not at regular intervals. You'll see."

"Will I?" I studied her face, searching for any clue as to the reason I was here.

"Yes, I think you will," she said as she continued to eat her sandwich, albeit not as fast as she had in the beginning. Little gummy was it?

Back on task, she returned to her list. "There are clothes in the closet. Everything you need should be there and in your size." She was visibly struggling now. "But if you don't find something you need…"

I couldn't make out that last part. "What?" I asked innocently. I had to work to keep the smile off my face as I popped the top on my soda.

She quirked her eyebrow at me. Could everyone do that here?

"Trade you the soda for your pen."

She put her hand over her mouth as she put effort into plying her jaws apart. The cheese worked better than I had anticipated. Granted, the ratio of pastrami to cheese on her sandwich was probably ten to one, but I hadn't realized the difficulty it presented. I was just after her pen and paper, not her death.

She coughed raggedly before swallowing, and then while smiling behind her hand, she managed to get out, "You're a real tough negotiator."

I could tell she meant the exact opposite, but she handed me the pen, and I handed her the soda. Maybe I wasn't the best negotiator. But I knew enough to pile the cheese on her half of the sandwich so that she would most definitely need a source of liquid, and I got what I was after. I'd call that a success.

"So what else is on the list?" I asked when I thought she'd recovered enough to continue.

She was currently swishing the soda around her mouth in an effort to thin the layers of cheese glued to her teeth. She flipped the list around and pushed it toward me.

I was going to have to rethink the elegance I had attributed to her when we'd first met. She was appearing less and less elegant with every second that passed. Since I myself made no claim to elegance, I much preferred her this way.

I scanned down her list and checked off her number four and five. Reading further, I went through the next items. Wake up call at six a.m. She would be escorting me to the Director at seven a.m. sharp. Wear a suit.

I lifted my eyes from the list to find her disassembling her sandwich. She had given up eating the sandwich as a whole and was peeling the layers off and eating them separately. Now this was the portrayal of a woman I could respect, letting nothing come between her and her food.

I tapped the offending note with the pen. "You do not trust me to dress appropriately?"

She paused with a wad of pastrami between her fingers. "At this point, your actions still reflect on me. I thought I'd cover my bases." Then unashamedly, she popped the chunk into her mouth.

Looking into her eyes, I could discern her unspoken comment that she knew what my preferred attire was, and it wasn't a suit.

"And, there's the fact that you have a tendency to be a little...unpredictable?"

Was she commenting or asking? I couldn't tell as I glared at her. I wouldn't characterize myself as unpredictable. I just liked to do things the way I wanted to.

"Is stubborn a better word?" she asked as if she already knew the answer.

I'd been called that a time or two, or more. But who, when given the choice, would choose to wear a suit over jeans?

I shifted my eyes to the page for one last look. "Alrighty then, I think we're done with the official welcome." And insult, I added silently.

"Actually, that won't come until after we know your status here."

That was an interesting choice of words. "Do I have a choice in my status?"

"There are always choices. Do you have any questions related to what we have gone over?"

"Let me guess, if I say no, then we are done for the evening."

She swiped one of the provided napkins and wiped her face and hands. Scooting her chair back, she started gathering her stuff. "As I've said, you do learn quickly, Dr. Greer."

Just for that, I wasn't telling her she missed a good size piece of Colby Jack stuck to the side of her face. Instead, I smiled and said, "I do my best." Doing my best not to stare at the Colby Jack, I clarified my previous statement. "When I want to."

She scooped up her brief case and walked toward the door. As she reached for the handle, she turned and looked me in the eye. "Let's hope your best is good enough."

That sounded ominous.

"Good night, Dr. Greer."

"Good night, Ms. Needham."

She pulled the door closed behind her, and I pressed my ear against it. Her heels clicked loudly on the tile floor and then faded to a stop. I heard a soft male voice, then her irritated growl. The guard must have pointed it out to her.

Her raised voice quickly followed her growl. "Two can play that game, Dr. Greer. Sleep tight."

Uh oh. I hoped I hadn't bitten off more than I could chew. The irony of that thought, more than I could chew, caused me to shake with laughter. I never would have bet being kidnapped could be so much fun.

Wiping tears from my eyes, I walked over and picked up the pen and notepad. It was time to get to work and, more importantly, to take a shower. With essential writing instruments in hand, I opened the pocket doors leading to the rest of the suite.

Immediately after the receiving room was the casual living area Ms. Needham had described. There were three doors leading out of this room, two to the left and one to the right. I chose the first door on the left. It contained a nicely equipped exercise room. The second door opened to reveal quite a large bedroom that included lots of soft yellows and bright reds.

I tossed the notepad and pen on the bed and walked toward the bathroom that I could see through a large archway on the other side of the room. Feeling for the light switch, I found it and flipped it on.

"Goodness," I breathed.

It looked like some sort of Roman era bath. It was huge with marble everywhere. The tub by itself took up one entire wall, and there were stairs I would have to climb to get into it. And, I guess that was the shower?

Entering the bathroom, I came to a stop in front of a glass contraption. It did not fit the old world theme at all. The back wall had a large control panel with the word NOLA engraved in its center. Surrounding it were all kinds of nozzles and gadgets with even more spaced irregularly throughout the shower. Some of them looked like they had moving parts.

I stood there baffled, wondering whether I should put me or my dishes in. Stepping inside, I studied the controls, but I didn't know what the various terminologies meant. I'd never encountered a shower like this before.

"This should come with a warning label. Must have license to operate."

I reached my hand toward the controls and heard a whoosh behind me. Turning swiftly, I found that I was sealed in. Oops, it also came equipped with an overly sensitive touchpad. I pressed against the glass door that had appeared out of nowhere, but nothing happened.

"NOLA activated," said a creepy female computer voice from the control panel.

"What the..." I spun back around to face the control panel. I hurriedly searched for a button controlling the door, but I found none. There were just numbers and unfamiliar symbols.

"Open the door, NOLA," I demanded. Nothing happened.

"NOLA, open the door," I tried again. Why wasn't there an exit button or an off switch? "Don't make me count to ten," I threatened under my breath.

"Cycle ten engaged."

Oh, *that* she could hear.

My eyes widened as various attachments began whirring and spinning. I backed up giving them plenty of room as they gained speed. When they started moving toward me, I whipped around and began to pound on the glass while yelling, "Let me out!"

Water began shooting at me from every direction. Who puts shower jets in the floor! And it was HOT! "Hot, Hot!" I sputtered through the water hitting my face.

"Temperature increased."

No, no, no. "Temperature decrease, temperature decrease!" I yelled.

"Temperature returned to normal level."

I turned around to face her. Maybe if I could grab one of the attachments moving toward me, I could use it to break the glass. I lunged for the nearest nozzle and pulled. It slid free of the wall, and I turned to slam it against the door.

Before I could, my head suddenly yanked to one side, almost pulling me off my feet. In the effort to stay upright, I dropped the captured nozzle.

Did she just grab my hair? My head snapped back in the opposite direction. Oh, no she didn't!

"Let go of my hair!" I shouted while trying to wrestle my hair out of her little metal hand thingies. "Bad NOLA!"

I strained with the effort against her, but she was too strong and too quick. I had managed to free only a single clump of hair when white foam began to cascade down my body.

Oh goodie, soap. I'd been worrying this was a rinse only cycle. I hoped I could get out before the hot wax started.

Along with my head being jerked from side to side by NOLA, I now had the added pleasure of being covered entirely in bubbles. I gasped and spit as the cascade of soap seemed to have no end. "No more soap," I moaned.

"More soap," NOLA repeated.

NOLA was E-vil.

I could barely breathe through all the flowery smelling soap. This was like a car wash but for people. I wondered if this was how they'd find me in the morning. Drowned while standing up in the shower and still fully clothed.

Having abandoned my attempt to free my hair, I just tried to remain standing, which was harder than it should have been for some reason. It didn't take long to figure out that certain parts of the floor were moving. Of course they were. What else could I expect from a bubble bath fun house?

NOLA's hands were now moving so fast that it felt like my head was going to vibrate off my shoulders. I reached up to steady it and something ripped. I thought it was my shirt. And what the heck was hitting my legs!

I couldn't see anything past the curtain of bubbles I wore, which explained why I didn't see whatever it was that slammed me against the glass.

"Oww! Bad NOLA, Bad NOLA! Stop. The. Shower!"

"Voice command not recognized."

Not recognized! "Cancel. Deactivate. Abort!" I shrieked desperately.

"Cycle ten aborted. NOLA deactivated."

The same glass panel that had sealed me in, the one I was also currently plastered against, abruptly disappeared. I fell out.

I never knew marble was so slippery when wet.

I skidded across the floor on my side and then crashed into the tub which spun me completely around. My three-sixty left me seated on my bottom with my legs stuck straight out in front of me. The first thing I noticed was my right shoe was missing. NOLA ate my shoe.

I sincerely hoped she choked on it.

I sat there in stunned silence. Had that really just happened? I was beat up by a shower? As the shock wore off, I tried to assess the extent of the damage. I didn't think I was hurt too bad, except for maybe my head and my eyes that were burning something fierce.

I swiped at the foamy lather attacking my eyes and slowly stood to my feet. Stepping over the Macy shaped outline of bubbles on the floor, I cautiously approached the sink. Eyeing it as best I could, I searched for any enemy controls. It looked like only the normal levers I would associate with a sink. I didn't see any gadgets or control panels, but I was not going to be fooled again.

Very gently, I pulled the nearest faucet lever toward me. "Just give Mama a little cold water," I pleaded.

Not coming any closer, I watched as the water flowed down the sink. When I was certain that it was just a normal sink with a normal faucet, I began getting the soap off my face and out of my eyes.

Grabbing a hand towel, I went to stand in front of the full length mirror next to the tub. I looked like I had been through a hurricane. My hair was sticking out every which way. There was also a big red spot on my forehead where a knot was rapidly forming. I moved the hair aside and leaned forward to inspect it a little closer. I wasn't sure my bangs would be sufficient cover.

Letting my hair drop back in place, I moved on to inspect my clothes. The shirt I had been wearing was barely recognizable. It had been a button up long sleeve. Now, one sleeve was ripped off entirely and pooled around my wrist. The other had a long gash in it. The top half of the buttons had been ripped off and it was split up the back. Amazingly though, it was still tucked into my jeans.

The right half of the belt loops on my jeans stuck straight out and they were stiff, like they'd been starched or something. Various rips and tears decorated the rest of my jeans until I reached the knees. Then, they were just shredded.

I took a deep breath, nearly gagging on the smell of roses coming from the soap. I seriously needed to rinse the rest of the soap off. Cutting my eyes in the direction of the monstrous tub, I regarded another potential foe. After a moment, I decided I just couldn't do it. I was not up to any more fights with plumbing tonight.

Instead, I opted for the known quantity, the nice normal sink. The sink was safe. The sink was my friend. Good thing the sink was deep. I had a lot of hair.

Having rinsed off the majority of the soap, I stood wrapped in a towel, staring at myself in the mirror again. Should I get ice for my head? Unless the goose egg shrank a lot, my bangs were not going to hide this.

Finding my eyes in the mirror again, I smiled at my reflection. "Well, Mace," I said to myself, "you survived the shower from hell. If that's the worst they throw at you, you'll be fine."

I briefly wondered how in the world I was going to frame this episode to Miranda. I was the one that went through it, and I hardly believed it.

My encounter with NOLA did have one positive side effect. I was now wide awake. I would have no trouble focusing on my question list.

I stepped away from the mirror and walked to the light switch. Suddenly, it occurred to me why Catman had that smirk on his face when he suggested that I enjoy my shower.

Someone was going to pay. Where was that notepad!

CHAPTER 6

COULD SLEEP JUST ABOUT ANYWHERE, so I was not surprised that I slept well in my new accommodations, especially given the comfiness of the bed. What was surprising was my unexpected wake up call.

I sat bolt upright in bed with arms and legs askew, gripping the covers like a lifeline. It took me more than a minute to be conscience of the fact that one, I was awake, and two, why.

Filling the room, playing ridiculously loud, was the familiar refrain of Reveille.

It sounded like it was coming from the bed itself. I had a moment of panic where I feared this could be another automated monstrosity. It had looked like a normal bed when I crawled in last night, but I was now regretting my decision to forego the inspection.

I glanced at the alarm clock beside the bed. It said it was five thirty in the morning. It was my normal wake up time, but it didn't feel like it. I just wanted to go back to sleep, but that wasn't going to happen with a bugler on the loose in my room.

I chuckled a little. Bugler on the loose. That was kind of funny.

Pushing my matted hair behind my ears, I slowly edged along the top of the bed in the direction of the music. When I didn't see anything, I slid from the bed and inched closer to the footboard. I used my knuckle to tap against what I thought had been wrought iron work on the leg. It was actually cloth. I was looking at a speaker.

Moving over to the other leg of the bed, I verified my conclusion. Yep, there was a speaker embedded there too.

This left me with one simple question. What the heck was wrong with these people? Couldn't a bed just be a bed and a shower a shower? What was next? Was I going to have to fight the toaster for breakfast?

I forced myself to a stand with a renewed sense of determination. I knew hands down who'd win that fight. No one and no altered device was going to come between me and my breakfast. With Reveille still blaring, I marched into the kitchen.

As I went, it occurred to me that the wake-up call was probably Olivia's doing, retribution for her embarrassment last night. That was okay. Let cheese face have her laugh. I'd plot my revenge later, after breakfast and any potential battles awaiting me there.

Saying a silent prayer for normalcy, I opened the fridge. Much to my relief, it offered no resistance. The contents were not too bad either. Fruit and bagels would do for starters. Then I spotted the half-n-half. Where there was cream, there had to be coffee. Hallelujah.

I begin opening cabinet doors and quickly found the coffee. And it was normal non-fufu flavored, yet another small victory. I got the coffee going and put the bagel in the toaster. The rest I put on the table and then went to see what they had placed in my closet.

I wasn't even the slightest bit hopeful in regards to finding anything comfortable. Neither did I think Olivia's definition of suit meant the throw blanket I was currently wearing. Though, it might be fun to see the expression on her face, if I let her believe this was what I intended to wear to the meeting with the Director.

Inside the closet, I stood in front of the rack, sliding the depressing garments past me one by one. "Let's see, there's black, off black, dark as night black. Ooh, pin striped black."

I slid the jacket off the hanger and laid it over my arm. On the opposing rack, I found the matching pin striped slacks. I paired them with a cream camisole that I found in a nearby drawer, and God bless them, the coolest pair of black boots I'd ever seen. They had silver studs, buckles and fur. They should have been gaudy and yet, they weren't.

I didn't think Olivia would approve of these. Someone else must have snuck them in. All the more reason to wear them.

I laid everything on the bed, which I noted had quit making noise. It wasn't my doing. It probably had a pressure trigger or a timer. Or video feed to one sadistic supposed assistant. I turned in a full circle, waving just in case.

I was returning to the kitchen, where breakfast awaited, when the importance of the day hit me. Today was the day that I'd meet this mysterious Director, find out why I was here, and hopefully, approve of what they wanted me to do. I didn't know what recourse I had if I didn't.

Sure, I could keep secrets. I'd been doing that for a while now. But these people didn't strike me as the kind that liked other people, who were not on their team, walking around with their secrets. Perhaps they'd perform a mind wipe, if that existed. I really hoped that didn't exist. I liked my brain just how it was. My livelihood depended on it.

I realized I was incessantly drumming my fingernails on the table and decided that getting myself all riled up was not going to help. Downing the last of my coffee, I set the cup aside and plopped the last piece of melon in my mouth. It was time to get ready for the meeting.

Everything fit perfectly. Thank goodness. I wasn't going to be wearing the clothes I arrived in. They were currently occupying the bathroom garbage can. All except for the one shoe. NOLA still had possession of that one, and I was not going back for it. It didn't take a genius to see where that might lead.

It was disturbing, however, to know that someone had put in enough effort to know my exact size, including my underclothing. Even more disturbing to think what that task might have entailed, but there was nothing I could do about that either.

Standing in front of the mirror, I inspected myself one last time. The knot had shrunk marginally, more like settled into place. But now it bore the distinction of being reamed in a purple-black color, like I'd highlighted it on purpose. I thought the bangs did a fair job of covering it as long as no one looked too closely. I just had to make sure I didn't brush them out of my eyes, like I sometimes did when I was frustrated.

I'd only applied a minimal amount of makeup. Trust me, no amount was going to conceal this knot.

I'd also managed to brush my hair out. Thanks to NOLA, that was no small task. It hadn't helped that I'd not bothered to brush it out last night or that I'd gone to bed with it still wet. At one point, I was so mad I thought it would be best to cut it all off and just wait till it grew out again. But I couldn't find anything sharper than a butter knife in the suite. So instead, it was pinned up in a bun. It wasn't my best look, but all in all, not too bad.

I frowned at my reflection. Aw, who was I kidding? The knot was like a blaring beacon on my forehead. I probably should have iced it.

Still shaking my head in dismay over my appearance, I retrieved the notepad from the office desk and headed for the receiving room to wait for Olivia. I'd managed to come up with three pages of questions and or comments in some instances. I now set to work prioritizing them in order of importance.

I really could have used a spreadsheet to organize them, but no computer was provided in the office. They seemed intent on cutting me off from technology. Well, technology that was normal and non combative. That left me with the old school method of sorting, which equaled flipping back and forth between pages and continual renumbering. It was tedious and irritating work.

A brief knock at the door interrupted my concentration, and I looked up with a frown. My new watch revealed it was seven a.m. on the dot. I made one last notation on the pad, finishing my thought, when there was another knock on the door.

"Dr. Greer?"

It was Olivia. Didn't she have a key? "It's open," I grumbled loudly. "As if you didn't already know that," I said just as loudly.

I waited for the door to open, but it remained closed. Perplexed, I got up and opened it myself.

Olivia stood there engrossed in the tablet she held in her hands. I thought she said that she didn't own a tablet. She must have upgraded this morning, which would explain the sounds of frustration she was making at the thing.

"Sleep well?" I asked her.

Totally oblivious to my question, she looked me up and down, pausing when she saw the tips of my silver studded boots poking out from underneath my pants. The right corner of her mouth pulled down, and she looked quickly up at me before nodding to herself.

That was very rude and dismissive. It made me wish I'd chosen the blanket route. I sniffed disdainfully and asked, "Do I pass?"

"You'll do," she said, looking up briefly from the device she carried.

I leaned against the door frame with arms and legs crossed, watching her in amusement. Today she was dressed in a navy blue suit. I'd yet to see her in black. I was beginning to wonder if apparel color was tied to seniority.

She looked up, finally realizing I was a witness to her frustration, and hurriedly turned the device off. Well, she tried to, but it seemed she couldn't remember how.

I let her struggle for a few moments before I held out my hand for the tablet. Reluctantly, she gave it to me, and I pushed the necessary button then held it out to her again. Without a word, she took it back, glaring at me with her lips pursed in either anger or embarrassment or maybe both.

That made the score two to one in my favor. I didn't try to hide the smile that suddenly appeared on my lips.

She regarded me silently, probably updating her appraisal of me. I could see the wheels turning in her head. She might not know how to work a tablet yet, but she was definitely smart. It wouldn't be wise to underestimate her. I knew from personal experience that great things came in little packages.

I withstood her scrutiny and waggled my eyebrows at her for no other reason than to irritate her. I didn't know why, but she brought out the competitive side of me. I normally didn't care about such petty things, but she irked me. The fact that she knew what was going on and I didn't was a big minus against her.

"We should get going, shouldn't we?" I said, tapping my watch.

The shake of her head was almost imperceptible. Without looking back to make sure I was following, she began walking down the hall.

I thought it strange how she and Catman both assumed I would follow them and therefore had no qualms about presenting me with their unprotected backs. One day, I might surprise them. But not today. Today, I wanted answers.

I shoved off the doorframe I'd been leaning against and followed her down the hall. I didn't bother to shut the door. What would have been the point in that? They could get in anytime they wanted.

Olivia led the way down one hallway after another, each looking exactly the same to me. But she was unfazed by the similarity and made every turn with confidence. We walked for about fifteen minutes generally in a downward direction. That explained the morphing size of the building when compared to the outside.

At one point, we cut across a cafeteria. My mood brightened immediately. I slowed down, but she was having none of it and quickly pulled me through and out the other side.

It was a disgraceful display of respect for nutrition.

I did however manage to scoop up one of those pancake and sausage combos posted on a stick like a corndog. Much to my delight and Olivia's dismay, it came equipped with the syrup built in. I offered her a bite, but she sneered at me. Who sneered at pancakes and sausage? It was one more indictment to add to the growing list against them.

We finally emerged into what appeared to be an office building. At the end of the hall was a large conference room ensconced in glass. Catman and several others I didn't recognize were milling around the room.

Catman looked different this morning. He was minus the black suit, dressed instead in slacks and a long sleeve button up shirt. The tie he'd paired it with had a green pattern that highlighted his eyes, causing them to almost glow. They were striking and nice in an unnerving sort of way.

The office we were passing had the door open, and I tossed my pancake stick into the trashcan that I spotted just inside the door. The occupant, who was on the phone, looked up at my intrusion, and I waved my thanks for the use of his trash can.

"What did you do?" Olivia demanded as I almost walked into her.

"I threw my stick away," I said defensively.

She tightly closed her eyes and sighed.

"What?" I asked, bewildered by her reaction. It was just a stick in the garbage.

"That was the Director's office," she hissed.

I smiled at her embarrassment. I'd thrown away some trash in the Director's office. Big whoop. She was acting like I'd peed in his plants.

"You need to loosen up," I chided.

Her blue eyes were like flint as she fumed at me.

"Shouldn't we be in the room before him?" I urged, anxious to put her lid back on.

"Please do not screw this up," she begged. "We need you on this project."

She had spoken with all earnestness. I looked away from the pleading in her eyes and found Catman staring at me. I wasn't trying to "screw up" anything for them. I didn't even know what there was to screw up. I was so tired of not knowing what was going on.

"I'm not trying to screw up anything," I told her.

"Just try to be on your best behavior?"

She'd stated it as a request, like she was dealing with an unruly child about to be presented to the public. She wasn't too far off with the unruly bit. I was definitely feeling the urge to act wild and rowdy, to mess up their agenda like they'd messed up mine. Maybe she wasn't too far off on the childish part either.

"Sure," I sighed. I could behave in a professional manner, swallow the part of me that wanted to rebel against their control—for a little longer. But I was making no guarantees beyond this meeting.

With Olivia in the lead, we walked into the conference room. She promptly left me and began talking with the men assembled in the room.

During my survey of the room, I happened to look down and spotted the tips of cowboy boots protruding from Catman's slacks. It made me smile a little. It could be that he wasn't as stiff as he appeared.

I looked up from his boots to find him staring at me again. His head was cocked sideways and his eyes were focused on my forehead. Uh oh, he had spotted the knot. I pretended ignorance at the question in his eyes.

Before he could verbally ask, there was a commotion at the door, and the Director walked in followed by two other men. It was actually more like a stride, like a man on a mission or a limited time frame. That probably meant that he wasn't going to want to spend a lot of time answering questions. I'd have to dispel him of that notion pretty quick.

I'd say he was mid-forties. His dark brown hair had just a hint of graying around the temples. He still looked muscular under the suit, which was black, but it was not standard issue. I didn't even think it was off the rack. It fit him like a glove, allowing me to know that he still had muscles.

Everyone took their seats except for the two guys who'd come in with him. They stood in either corner of the room opposite the door. They were also the ones in the standard issue black this time, and I assumed they were some type of bodyguards.

The Director took the seat at the head of the table and everyone else, including Olivia, who'd abandoned me, was on the other side of the table. As they were all looking at me, I pulled out the nearest chair and sat down.

"Let's get to it then," the Director said. "I'm sure you are anxious for answers."

"You got that right." Oops. Did I say that out loud?

One look in Olivia's direction confirmed it.

The Director only paused briefly, as if he'd chosen to overlook my indiscretion. That was good. I seemed to be getting less discrete by the minute.

"I'm Director Garrison," he started again. Indicating Catman, he said, "This is Agent Michaels. Agent Michaels is the team lead for this particular project."

I knew it and partial success on my mission to learn his name. I noted that he'd labeled Catman as an agent. I thought that implied some sort of government agency, which would confirm my suspicion and make me right again.

"Agent Needham, whom you've also met," he said, motioning toward Olivia. "She'll be your go to person for any requests that you have."

She'd already said as much. I could tell by the expression on her face that she was thrilled with her position. I smiled reassuringly at her, but that only deepened her scowl.

"Next to Olivia, we have Agent Juarez."

Agent Juarez had Native American Indian features. He was dressed casual in Khakis' and a long sleeve button up, which was unbuttoned with the sleeves rolled up. He'd placed it over a tightly fitted white t-shirt, once again, treating me to an impressive display of male musculature clothed in cotton. There must be some health plan included in the hiring package.

"Agent Juarez is our technology expert, meaning computers, gadgets, etc. He can make you seem larger than life or not exist at all. So we try real hard to keep him happy," the Director said with a smile.

Juarez inclined his head toward me, more in acknowledgment of his skill than in greeting I thought.

Don't get on the computer genius' bad side, check.

The Director's tone was more somber now as he introduced the last person at the table. "Agent Pike is our resident procurement specialist."

His pronouncement was greeted by soft chuckles around the room. Judging by their reaction, I took it that the term procurement was applied loosely.

Agent Pike smiled and waggled his eyebrows at me.

I scanned the t-shirt he wore. There was a squirrel standing on top of a pile of acorns, pointing out and saying, "Protect your nuts." Funny.

There didn't seem to be any rationale to the dress code. It seemed like the team members wore whatever they wanted. So why was I stuck in this suit when I preferred jeans and a t-shirt? My bet was on my look alike sitting across the table from me.

The score was once again even.

Introductions over with, Director Garrison looked at Agent Michaels and asked, "Assessment?"

Catman avoided my eyes as he began talking. "She maintains her composure well. Is not given to histrionics or belligerence, and she likes to eat. A lot."

Wait a minute. Was he talking about me? And he said the last part like it was a bad thing. I frowned at his assessment. First of all, it was absurd that they were discussing me while I was sitting right here. Second of all, why were they so against eating?

"Agent Needham?"

"Hold on a minute," I interrupted. "Are you seriously discussing me while I'm sitting right here? Shouldn't you have done this before now?"

"The reason I brought you here was not to hear your assessment of my job performance, Dr. Greer," the Director said somewhat coldly. "Do you have a problem with hearing what they have to say about you?"

"I couldn't care less what their opinion of me is," I said exasperated.

"But I do, which is the point." He stared angrily at me until I waved him on.

"Speaks her mind," Catman said, adding to his assessment.

I rolled my eyes to him in an obvious show of "bite me." The narrowing of his eyes led me to believe he heard me loud and clear.

"Undoubtedly," the Director said. "Agent Needham?"

"Mischievous. Scheming. You don't see the trap coming."

Well, someone was still upset.

Catman turned toward Olivia, confusion on his face, but she ignored him and finished her analysis. "Always thinking and figuring things out. Likable, in an annoying sort of way."

Likable in an annoying sort of way? What the heck did that mean? Seemed like an oxymoron to me. And besides, I hadn't even begun to be annoying yet.

The Director looked at me as if waiting for something. Did he want an apology? That wasn't happening. Maybe it was my turn. I liked that idea.

"Statues. One with not only the ability to anticipate my needs but a demonstrative willingness to do so." I nodded at Catman and then turned my gaze on Olivia. "And the other with a propensity for loud wake up calls and uncomfortable wardrobe choices. And, I would be remiss to omit her desperate need to chill out."

Olivia abruptly cleared her throat and averted her eyes. I knew it was her.

"What are you talking about?" the Director asked blank faced.

Tired of being talked about like I wasn't sitting right there, I said, "It was my turn. That's my assessment of your people. And for future reference, it is incredibly rude to discuss a person while they are with you. But putting that aside, why have you, assuming it was your call, brought me here?"

The Director stared at me, his gray eyes like chips of ice after my outburst. Maybe he was rethinking his decision. At this point, I was almost too mad to care.

Catman didn't seem too comfortable either. He was uncharacteristically squirming, if clasping his hands so tightly together that the white of his knuckles showed and rapid eye blinking counted as squirming.

"I've brought you here," the Director said with his voice reflecting the coldness in his eyes, "because we have a need that I think you can fill. I am familiar with your work with the hybrids in New Orleans. I'm sure you have noticed some irregularities with our Agents you have been dealing with."

I nodded. I'd only noticed any with Catman, but I'd suspected there were more.

"Your work with the HCF was mostly theoretical, academic. There was no experimentation or urgency with regard to your work. Now, there exists a need for you to step out of the book, so to speak, and actually perform."

Actually, perform? Like what I had done to date meant nothing? I hoped it got better than this. His comments were insulting and somewhat degrading.

"Our problem is of the utmost urgency." He paused, seeming to collect his thoughts. "We have made some astounding discoveries with our hybrids, had the birth of novel abilities." He paused again. He seemed to be wrestling with what or how much to tell me.

Why hadn't he figured out what he wanted to say before he came to the meeting? Annoyed with the delay his lack of preparation was causing, I offered, "That usually occurs with evolution. But I take it there is some problem."

He reacted as though my interjection confused him. I'd been waiting two days already to find out the reason for my abduction, and my patience was razor thin. I wanted to yell at him and tell him to just say it already.

He regarded me for a long moment, and, once more, I found myself the subject of scrutiny by a person I didn't know and therefore could not care less what he thought of me. Except, maybe I did. If he'd just tell me plainly what all this was about, I'd know if I cared about his impression of me. But then again, I was always just me, no matter who or what was involved.

The second he came to a decision concerning me, I saw it in his eyes. Maybe now I'd get some answers.

"The rate of evolution has increased dramatically," he said. "And, we are finding the abilities less predictable."

Predictability. There it was again. The HCF also had that as one of their goals.

"We are also experiencing difficulties related to proximity or exposure of humans to hybrids."

That was new. "What kinds of problems?" I asked before he could move on.

He sat back in his chair and pursed his lips.

It reminded me of Miranda when she didn't want to give an answer. If he was as stubborn as her, this could drag on forever. I couldn't let that happen. I was pretty certain Miranda was in close proximity and at some level of exposure with the hybrid she had left with.

"Look," I began, "as you know, I'm a molecular geneticist. I do not specialize in evolution per say. I work on the mechanics of the actual processes. Don't you have people that are able to work on this for you?"

He smiled briefly in a show of tolerance regarding how little I knew.

That grated against my already tenderized nerves. Irksome was a word that was quickly becoming universal for how I felt about all of them.

Too late, I realized that I had swept my bangs aside. A brief look around the room told me I wasn't the only one who had noticed. I also found that I was studiously drumming my fingernails against the table. Flattening my hand on the table, I cocked my head sideways as I swiveled my chair back to face the Director.

He glanced briefly at the knot, uncertainty written on his face. "I have been led to believe that you are tenacious, Dr. Greer. You get to the root of a problem, see the bigger picture, how everything fits together. Was I misinformed?"

Why the heck was he getting angry? As if I was wasting his time. He was the one who brought me here. For what I still didn't know.

I leaned into the table, put my "what did you say" face on and said, "Excuse me."

He leaned in too, mirroring my posture. "Was. I. Misinformed?" he said through clenched teeth.

"I don't know," I spat just slightly below a yell. "Did your source tell you that I would appreciate being kidnapped in the middle of the night and then made to wait until you deigned to show up and not answer my questions?"

The tension in the room increased dramatically at my response to his anger. As we leaned into the table, our gazes locked, I found myself in another staring contest. This was so juvenile.

"Just tell me plainly what is going on and why you have brought me here," I said calmly enough to pull us back from the brink of shouting, but forcefully enough to let him know that I still meant business.

He seemed to visibly collect himself at my demand. Taking a deep breath, he purposefully sat back in his chair. "I apologize, Dr. Greer. This matter is most serious, and I do not have time to waste. If I have the wrong person, I need to know."

I studied his face a moment, fighting the urge to yell and call him an idiot. The fact that I didn't see any malice in his expression aided my struggle. Pulling away from the table slightly, I clasped my hands in front of me and tried to keep my voice level when I spoke.

"How am I supposed to tell you if I'm who you need, when I don't even know what the problem is? Regarding the subject of hybrids, I am the best that I know of. That's not arrogance, just fact. And, I do have an uncanny ability to unravel the puzzle of it all. However, with the little bit of observation that I have been able to do, I can tell that your hybrids are superior or more advanced than what I have been working with. This means there's a whole field of research that I have not been privy too. A fact which greatly annoys me."

I didn't want to admit this next part because I wanted at the research that I had missed out on. But the sincerity of his plea and the potential seriousness of the situation convinced me that, as he said, he needed to know.

"I'm sure you have really smart people working for you already that are familiar with the genetics at work here. I would have to play catch up, and if time is a factor, then I'm not sure what I could offer that they haven't already provided or are on the brink of providing."

He nodded sharply once. "I appreciate your honesty, Dr. Greer, and I understand your hesitancy. You are not wrong in your assumption that I have plenty of smart people working for me. But they have tried to solve this problem and gotten nowhere. I don't need any more smart people. I need a brilliant person who's a problem solver. I believe that person is you."

How did I respond to that sort of statement? He'd just called me brilliant—aw shucks.

I let out a breath I didn't realize I'd been holding. I was definitely intrigued, but not enough to agree to anything without knowing the specifics.

He began absently tapping a knuckle on the edge of the table then quickly leaned forward. "Dr. Greer, the conclusions that you have reached singly in two years and with a meager budget, took my team of twenty four of the world's best scientists fifteen years to reach. And that was with an enormous budget."

Fifteen years? How long had they been at this? So, what, they needed my speed? And he had full access to my work?

When he didn't continue, I picked up my notepad. "What exactly are you Director of? What agency?"

After asking the question, I looked up at him. His expression clearly let me know that was not what he was looking for from me, but I wasn't agreeing to anything until I got some answers to my questions.

He folded his hands together on top of the table and once again engaged me in a staring contest. I maintained our locked status until I saw the resignation cross his face. That was a good boy.

"The HCF is an extension of the work we do here. At this time, any work you do for us will be under the auspicious of the HCF."

"But you are not HCF?"

"No, technically the HCF is part of us. But we operate at a more classified level than the HCF."

That was news to me. I didn't know there was a higher level, not when it came to hybrid technology. Considering I was the reigning expert, I really should have.

"So, you work for the United States Government?"

"Officially, no."

"Unofficially?"

"Yes."

His answer added to my anger with the government, who obviously had been holding out on me. Why was I not brought into this before now? Why had I been kept to the periphery when there was a whole lot more going on than what I had been working with?

Maybe that was the answer. I had played my part as defined by the government. I would be sure not to let them define me again.

"Do you work for any other government, officially or otherwise?"

"No."

"Are you funded by the US Government?"

"Partially. Though not officially."

I looked up at that. "Where does the rest of the funding come from?"

"Private sources and proprietary profits."

Profits? What part of hybrid technology could they possibly sell and to who? I jotted that down at the end of my list.

"If found out, could I be arrested for terrorist or terrorist related activities?"

"No," he said somewhat angrily.

Okay, not into terrorism. "Would I be betraying my country in any way?"

"By whose estimation?"

Touché. "The military's."

"Most definitely not."

Good. I loved the military. "Are you affiliated with the military? The US military."

He sighed. "The military is an interested party."

It seemed that I hadn't needed to worry about approaching

my contacts in the military. They already knew. Or, at least someone in their ranks did. It was not unexpected that they would want the technology for super soldier type stuff.

"Only the US military?" I asked.

"Yes," he drawled.

"Is the public at risk?"

We must have been reaching the very edge of what he was willing to tell me without any commitment from me. He stared at me for a full ten seconds before answering. "Possibly."

"Am I right to assume that you cannot answer any technical questions I have about the hybrids or their abilities?"

"That is correct. The boys down in the lab will be meeting with you for that."

"You do understand, Director Garrison, that I will not agree to anything until I know for certain exactly what I am agreeing to?"

He smiled at me. "I'm beginning to. However, I am so confident that you are going to agree to work for us, Dr. Greer, that I have cleared you for full disclosure with the boys in the lab."

He slapped his hands down on the table and pushed his chair back in an obvious sign of dismissal. Walking over to me, he extended his hand and said, "I'll let Agent Needham handle the rest of the particulars. She will give you access to whatever you need."

He placed his other hand over our handshake, "And Dr. Greer, I do mean whatever you need. We are not wholly government funded for a reason. Please make use of that fact. We need answers fast." With that, he left.

The bodyguards remained where they were. I guessed they were for me or against me, if necessary. Just what they thought I was capable of, I didn't know.

Belatedly, I realized he'd assumed that I'd say yes. I honestly didn't know what I was going to decide. I didn't have enough information to know. I'd only made it through half a page of questions.

Placing the pen on the pad in front of me, I began massaging my stiffened shoulders. This meeting had been more stressful than I had anticipated.

Agent Needham caught my eye across the table. "Need some stress relief?"

"That would be nice," I nodded.

"I thought we would start with a quick run. I can also give you a tour of the grounds at the same time. Then you have your appointment with Dr. Hollins, which will probably take the rest of the afternoon." She scooted her chair back and stood up. "We'll just stop by your room to let you change."

Oh, boy. I hadn't noticed any spare running shoes in the closet. "Does my closet have a pair of running shoes?"

"What happened to the shoes you came here with?" she asked.

I so did not want to say this, but she kept looking at me, waiting for me to answer. This was going to tilt the scale in her favor again.

"NOLA ate them. Well, one of them."

Catman, who had been in the process of standing up, stopped halfway with one hand on the table and one hand on the chair.

"NOLA?" Agent Needham's face said perplexed, but I could have sworn she had a smile in her voice.

"The shower," I sighed.

All eyes in the room turned to me.

"You got in the shower with your shoes on?" She asked with her head tilted to the side.

"I didn't mean to get in the shower with my clothes on. But NOLA is evil. She trapped me in, and then she started talking to me and engaged some cycle…" My voice trailed off as I stared at Olivia's open mouth.

Catman sat back down.

Agent Juarez put his hand up and said, "Wait, you got into the shower with all your clothes on and then started it?"

I sat back in my chair and crossed my arms over my chest. "I did not intentionally turn on the shower."

"What cycle?" This from Olivia, who was now clearly amused and no longer trying to hide it.

"Ten," I said reluctantly.

That was it for Catman. His head hit the table and his shoulders were shaking like a big ol'happy earthquake. The others in the room randomly dissolved into laughter.

I was never going to live this down.

"I don't see what's so funny," I protested. "She scalded me and tried to yank my hair out."

Those added details only led to more braying from everyone but Agent Pike. He was laughing so hard that he wasn't making any sound at all.

Through her tears, Olivia asked, "So how'd you get the goose egg on your forehead?"

Dang it.

"Well, there was a lot of soap because *NOLA* heard more soap when I actually said no more soap. Anyway, I couldn't really see what slammed me against the door thus producing this knot."

The tears were flowing freely now from all corners of the room, except where I sat. Though, I would have been justified in doing so.

"How'd you get out?" Juarez squealed.

"I managed to find a voice command she recognized and the door opened."

"The one," Juarez paused, momentarily overtaken by laughter, "you were leaning against?"

I sighed again. "That very one. I fell out."

Agent Needham was now sprawled in her chair, laughing really hard, loud laughs. Not very dignified if you asked me.

Everyone was so consumed with laughter that I thought maybe they wouldn't notice if I said the rest quickly enough.

"I then proceeded to skid against the floor, crash into the tub and spin around."

With every detail of my experience, more explosions of laughter erupted. Catman was silently pounding the table with his fist. Even the stoic bodyguards had lost it.

"It was then that I realized NOLA had eaten my shoe. What does NOLA stand for anyway? No One Leaves Alive."

It was a lost cause. I wasn't going to get anything from them until they got ahold of themselves. After several minutes, and a few more returns to Laughsville, they finally settled down.

In the fragile silence that ensued, Catman raised his hand.

I lifted my eyebrows in answer.

"What happened to the rest of your clothes?" he asked.

He was enjoying this way too much.

I narrowed my eyes at him before admitting the truth. "They didn't make it," I said flatly.

There they went again.

CHAPTER 7

"C OME ON, EINSTEIN," OLIVIA SAID once she'd regained her composure. "We'll skip the workout and head straight for Hollins. I'm sure he won't mind accommodating you. Anyway, I think my stomach's going to be sore enough as it is."

Ha, ha. Very funny.

As we went, Olivia informed me that NOLA stood for National Osmotic Lavatory Assistant. National being the company that produced them, and they were not standard issue. They were originally produced to aid the furrier of the hybrids who had difficulty maintaining the cleanliness standards required by the Agency. Cycle ten was the most aggressive program available and rarely used.

I, who was not the least bit furry, had been pranked. It was an initiation of sorts. They had all been through it, though none of them had a story quite like mine.

After Olivia checked her messages, she informed me that I was going down in NOLA history. Much to my chagrin, a video featuring my retelling of the NOLA experience had been broadcast to all the employees, and I was unanimously voted to the top of the plaque.

Apparently, at some time in the future, there was going to be an actual ceremony in which a shiny new plate with my name on it was going to be added to a plaque located somewhere in this facility. Nothing like delayed humiliation to look forward to.

I was very gratified to learn that Agent Michaels name currently occupied the number two slot. She wouldn't say exactly what happened, but I did learn that it had something to do with his manhood and not being able to wear underwear for a couple of weeks.

"So, where are we headed?" I asked, craning my head around, looking for some indication of where we were. Honestly, if these people ever expected me to find my way on my own, I may never be seen again. They could at least post maps at regular intervals like they did in amusement parks. I didn't even know where to go in case of emergency.

"I am taking you to meet Dr. Hollins. He is the head of our implementation team for the existing predicament we find ourselves in. He'll fill you in on everything."

That was what everyone kept promising, but here I was still with loads of unanswered questions.

"Yeah, you already said you were taking me to see Hollins, and I thought Agent Michaels was the head of the team?"

"Michaels is the head of the team handling this situation. Hollins is the head of the implementation aspect. Meaning, he is responsible for the actual doing of the solution or non solution in his case."

"What you're telling me is that he is going to be thrilled to see me."

"Overjoyed," she nodded knowingly.

I pulled up short at the end of another conjunction of hallways. I was completely baffled. One hallway looked exactly like the next. Even the name plates on the doors were all the same. There were no unique identifying marks anywhere.

"How do you find your way around?" I asked her. It was a mystery I needed answered because it was really bugging me.

"We are required to memorize the floor plan."

I glanced sidelong at her. Was she serious?

She held up her fingers in the familiar salute. "Scout's honor."

Well, that explained it. Though it was unlike any job requirement I'd ever heard of.

"About Hollins, did you mean current head of implementation as in soon to be replaced by me should I accept?" I was not going to accept reporting to some bureaucratic weasel, who objected to my horning in on his "project." I hoped they knew that.

"I suppose if that's the way you want it, you could negotiate that with the Director."

I'd negotiate it alright. She didn't seem to care one way or the other. In fact, since Director Garrison's exit, she seemed downright care free and way more forthcoming. Maybe the latter had to do with the total disclosure bit I'd been granted.

"You seem more relaxed now than when we first met," I told her.

"I suppose I am," she acknowledged with a smile. "You are here and assuming you can work your mojo, everything will be put to rights."

I had mojo? I thought it was moxie. "What do you mean exactly by work my mojo?"

"You are full of questions," she observed.

I waggled my notepad at her and said, "You ain't seen nothing yet."

She eyed me and the notepad briefly before explaining. "By mojo, I mean see what our guys are missing, solve the puzzle, and, over all, fix it. Whatever way you choose to phrase it is fine with me."

"Just get it done."

"Exactly," she said, doing a sort of voila thing with her arms.

"Now if only I had my magic wand with me."

"Don't be absurd, Dr. Greer. Magic isn't real."

"Big cat men and human bloodhounds, and any number of other hybrids, aren't supposed to be real either, yet they are."

She considered my recounting for a moment, but then shook her head. "I suppose so, but that's hardly magic, that's science."

She was right that it was science, but looking at some of the hybrids, it sure felt like I'd just crossed over into Fairy. If we could make magical looking creatures, then who was to say we couldn't someday make magic. Or what seemed like magic. It could be some sort of physics deal that we simply didn't understand yet or hadn't invented yet. That was about as far as my magic theory went.

Unwilling to argue from a point of weakness, I changed the subject. "Why were you so stressed over bringing me here?"

She cut her eyes at me, and I smiled baring my teeth.

"Besides the coercion and kidnapping," I said accusingly. "Don't you do this sort of thing all the time?"

"You noticed that, did you?" she said guiltily.

"The Clones are hard to miss."

"That they are," she said, smiling softly. "Kidnapping is not our normal mode of operation. And, it wasn't kidnapping, just detainment."

They weren't in the habit of kidnapping scientists extraordinaire. That would be encouraging if it didn't point to the extremeness of the situation.

Director Garrison had said it could affect the public. Originally, I thought he'd simply meant the exposure of continuing hybrid research. But I was beginning to think it was something more serious. I'd know for sure in a few minutes when I met this Hollins guy.

Glancing at Olivia and her still smiling face, I thought someone might have feelings for a particular Clone? Do tell.

"Which Clone is that smile for?" I asked.

She cleared her throat in obvious embarrassment. "No one in particular. They have just saved my life on several occasions. Kind of got a soft spot for them now." She lengthened her stride and pulled ahead of me. "That's the third time you've called them Clones," she tossed over her shoulder.

A subject change could only mean one thing. She was definitely into someone. Maybe not a Clone, but it was someone around here. Evidently, she did not want to talk about it.

"It was an upgrade from Goon."

"How generous of you," she quipped. "Are you patient as well?"

Was I patient? I didn't think anyone had ever attributed that virtue to me. "Does wanting what I want, the way I want it, exactly when I want it count as patient?"

"You mean like a two year old?" she said, turning to wait for me.

That was one way to put it. Not the way I'd define it, but accurate nonetheless.

"That's harsh, but exactly like," I confessed as I reached her. "But without the fits. There may, however, either independently or in any combination, be crying, yelling, snarky looks and or throwing things."

Even though we were the same height, it seemed like she was looking down her nose at me as she weighed my comment. "I fail to see how that is different than a two year old's tantrum."

"Oh, there's one huge difference," I said, brushing aside her skepticism.

"What's that?"

"I'm not two," I stated firmly.

She snorted in laughter while simultaneously rolling her eyes at me. She seemed to have ditched the elegance factor again in favor of down to earth. I liked this Olivia much better.

"Oh, that makes all the difference," she laughed.

Precisely.

We started walking again, and I thought I heard gun shots. "Is there a shooting range nearby?" I asked.

"Just down this hallway," she said, gesturing to another long expanse of identical hallway. "Want a peek?"

"Sure, why not," I sighed. Was I ever going to get to the bottom of this crisis?

She turned crisply, saying, "Follow me," as she strode confidently down the hall.

Like I had a choice. I didn't want to get lost in here forever. Become the ghost of the Agency, doomed to walk these halls. Get a nickname like Crazy Macy. My eyes found hers, and I realized she was staring at me.

With a funny look on her face, she asked, "You okay?"

I smiled at the picture I'd just painted. "Just my overactive imagination," I said without elaborating.

She stared at me a few more seconds, but didn't pursue any further explanation.

At the brink of the upcoming intersection, she looked back at me to indicate that we were turning. Before she could complete her next step, Juarez came barreling around the corner and ran smack into her. Their collision flattened Olivia while I was spun off to the side.

As they detangled themselves, I heard her ask, "Is there a problem?" The look in her eyes told me she was asking about something deeper than the reason for the collision.

"Might be," he said, pulling her to her feet.

He didn't let her go immediately, and I suddenly felt like an intruder. She cleared her throat and cut her eyes to me. He glanced behind him to find me leaning against the wall. He smiled, and I offered him a nod and a wave.

"Were you on your way somewhere?" she prompted.

"Yeah," he said distractedly. He rested his forehead against hers, and I just barely made out his whispered, "Stay close." Then he dropped her hands and sped off in the direction we had come.

I watched her as she watched him speed away. She hadn't technically lied. He wasn't the typical Clone, but he was obviously into her. By the blush coloring her cheeks, I knew the feelings were mutual.

"Should we forego the shooting range?" I asked, rousing her from her dazed state.

"Probably best," she nodded.

I pushed off the wall, trailing slightly behind her. "So, Juarez?" I said carefully.

"Don't start," she warned under her breath.

I smiled, throwing my hands up in the air in surrender. "Far be it from me to pry into personal affairs." I mean, you've only been prying into mine for how long? Even knew my underwear size and my taste in coffee. But far be it from me to ask a personal question and expect an answer.

Miranda was right. I did carry on lengthy conversations with myself.

We walked past a few more intersections before I attempted to question her further. "You mentioned that the Clones saved your life. Do I get the details about the life saving part, and more importantly, will my life need saving if I agree to work here?"

"No details this go round, and I seriously hope not."

She had resumed the professional demeanor she'd had when we first met. I was beginning to think it was some sort of defense mechanism. The collision with Juarez must have her worried about something. Maybe she'd tell me about it if I could keep her talking.

"What about an explanation for my life being observed? Nobody could have guessed my size this well, which to me means there was some definite personal prying going on."

She looked at me with that far off expression again. She was starting to worry me with her worrying. Finally, she looked away, as if she'd just comprehended my question.

"We observe everyone we consider for a position here," she said. "Consider it like a personality evaluation, but you didn't have to say what the pictures looked like."

"Yeah. That's probably good," I nodded. "They all look like one bacteria or another. Or burger parts."

She looked at me with disbelief in her eyes. "Burger parts?"

"Have you seen the ink blots? It's totally true," I argued.

She gave a dry chuckle at my assertion.

"Just a little?" I said, measuring the distance between my thumb and forefinger.

"Thanks," she said smiling.

"No problem. Just get me through this maze, and we'll call it even."

We turned one more corner and stopped in front of a huge set of stainless steel doors.

"Consider this the finish line," she said with relief in her voice as she motioned me to stand to the side.

Was I that hard to handle? I didn't think so. I just had what I called a strong personality. I was honest. I was frank. I was completely on guard as a panel rose and a small nozzle emerged.

I took two giant steps away from the emerging nozzle while Olivia stepped closer. As soon as it was eye level with her, it emitted a small puff of air directly at her face. She inhaled and then said, "Fear." The nozzle then retracted back into the ceiling, and one of the big steel doors opened

What the heck just happened?

"You can come back now," she teased. "The big scary nozzle is gone."

She could mock me all she liked. I was not going to be caught unaware again. Besides, I was more than justified in my new nozzle phobia.

I closed the gap between us. Flicking my hand in the direction of the ascended nozzle, I asked, "Care to explain that?"

"Finger prints, retinal scans, even DNA are too easy to replicate or obtain by nefarious means. Our security system is keyed to everyone's own personal skill set."

"Yours being?"

"One of my skills allows me to discern emotions through the chemicals or hormones that a person releases."

"You can scent hormones and the emotions they are connected to? In essence, you can read emotions?"

"Correct," she affirmed.

That could come in handy. I'd never come across that in any of my research. "That is very interesting," I told her. "So, you are the perfect liaison because you can address any worries or fears that I might have before they become an issue."

"That was the thinking. Why are you frowning?"

I raised my eyebrow at her, "Shouldn't you know?"

"Humor me," she said sarcastically.

"I was thinking this must be a really bad situation. Ya'll seem to be actually working at getting me to stay."

"It has the potential to be world changing. Bad? I don't know. Probably for some if not most. Maybe for everyone. It's not a predictable scenario. Let's go meet Dr. Hollins and see if you can make it all go away."

I was not encouraged by her uncertain answer, but we walked through the door anyway.

Ah, science décor. It looked like a nod to contemporary

design. It wasn't. At least, I didn't think so, and really, I didn't care. Just so long as it could be cleaned easily, I was good.

Most labs looked pretty much the same, lots of stainless and glass. This one was no different, except for the currently unoccupied really large line of cells I'd just passed.

"Are those for humans?" I asked, shocked at the possibility.

She nodded. "Willing and ready. Don't worry, you get used to it."

I didn't know if I wanted to. Human experimentation was taboo. Up till now, I'd only been analyzing the results of such experimentation. I wondered if that would change and how I'd feel about it. Swell. One more thing to possibly feel guilty about.

I wasn't the only one feeling guilty. That was the tenth time she'd adjusted her jacket since we'd entered through those stainless doors.

"Something on your mind?" I asked her.

She stopped walking and let her hands fall to her sides. "I feel I should warn you about Dr. Hollins."

Uh oh. Whenever someone warned you about someone else, it was never good.

"He's a little brusque."

"You mean rude," I interpreted.

She focused her eyes intently on me. "He's very engaged at the moment, as he should be, and he's easily upset."

"A pain in the butt who's easily irritated, got it," I translated.

Once again, I was met with her steely stare. "Not a diplomatic bone in your body, is there?" she stated dryly.

I raised my eyebrows innocently. Facts were facts, and these were hers, not mine.

She pulled a card out of her pocket and held it out to me. "If you run into trouble, just contact me."

I took the card from her and looked it over. It had only her first name and a number, short and sweet.

"Come on," she sighed.

She was too easy to upset right now. I wished I knew the source of her true concern, but obviously, if she trusted me to know, she would have already told me. We weren't even on a first name basis much less friends. I could work on that.

"Do you have a preference for what I call you? Olivia, Needham, Agent Needham?"

She looked at me ruefully. "I might regret this, but did I have a nick name before?"

I didn't hesitate with my answer. "Originally Non Flight Attendant Lady soon replaced by Food Lady."

"Figures," she mumbled. "You can call me Olivia or Agent Needham, if you prefer. Whatever you feel comfortable with."

I nodded. "Olivia it is, and please, call me Macy."

After rounding yet another corner, we stopped in front of another set of double doors, only they were wooden this time. The name plate said Dr. Heathrow Hollins. Catchy.

Her knock on Dr. Hollins door was immediately followed by, "Come in."

Once again, I noticed that she didn't open the door until given permission to. Awfully polite she was.

"Dr. Hollins, this is Dr. Greer," Olivia said, introducing me. "We've had a bit of a schedule change, but I'm sure you'll have no problem accommodating Dr. Greer."

Well, well. She'd whipped out her steel again. Wrapped in a seemingly innocent statement, she managed to hide both a command and a threat. Man, she was good.

I lacked the finesse or subtlety to pull off such a thing. By the look on his face as he regarded her, he'd picked up on it too and didn't care for it.

He made no move to greet either of us and, rather stupidly I thought, sat there looking me over. I didn't think he seemed appropriately impressed with my superheroness.

He was cute in a boyish kind of way. His hair was unkempt, and he had stubble that looked to be a few days old. In general, he looked tired. Great, now I was starting to feel sorry for him. Until he stood up with a sneer on his face and extended his hand.

"Greer," he said through clenched teeth.

I was surprised any sound could escape. I couldn't resist. I took his hand and mimicking him, I gritted out, "Hollins."

It was harder than I thought to say that without moving my jaws, and it certainly wasn't what I was saying in my head. But I refrained from using foul language whenever possible.

His eyes narrowed at my obvious mockery, and his hand tightened around mine.

I smiled at his display, and he let go of my hand. I wiped it on my pants while I continued to stare at him. I intensely disliked this man.

Olivia cleared her throat, signaling her disapproval and putting an end to our show. She needed to get some throat lozenges.

"Well, I'll just leave you to it then," she said, not trying to hide the hastiness of her retreat.

Before the door had fully closed, Hollins had retaken his seat and was viewing something on his computer. I took the seat in front of his desk, which he did not offer or acknowledge. He seriously wasn't going to sit here and try to ignore me? I'd had enough of that with the Clones.

I was about to enlighten him regarding his rudeness when his phone rang. He took the call, looking me straight in the eyes the whole time. If he was going for intimidation, he failed. I returned his glare but added a smile just to annoy him.

I wasn't normally so antagonistic. I didn't know if all the waiting had finally gotten to me or if it was him, but I felt like fighting. Being confronted with his attitude only increased that feeling.

Whoever he was talking to was loud, and the sour look on his face indicated he didn't like what he was hearing. He said a lot of "Yes, Sirs" and "No, Sirs", and then he puffed up like he was going to say more and just held it. One "Understood, Sir" later, and he hung up the phone and glared at it as if it had betrayed him.

He lifted his eyes to mine. "I understand you have an all access pass."

I flashed him a grin. "That's what they tell me."

He yanked open a drawer and pulled out a flash drive. "Follow me," he barked as he stood and left the office.

He walked really fast, and I quickened my pace to match his. He stopped at the end of the hallway and opened a door that led to another nondescript office.

"This will be your office," he said, waving me in.

I stepped inside, but turned to face him when he remained in the doorway.

Indicating the flash drive, he said, "This has everything that we know about the current situation." He held it out to me. "I have a meeting to get to. I should be back in an hour or so. We'll talk then." With no further explanation, he executed quite a nice pivot and left, slamming the door behind him.

I stared at the door still rattling from the collision with the frame. My phrasing of Hollins' personality was way more accurate than Olivia's.

Cataloging the room didn't take long. There was a desk with a computer and a phone. The usual shelves and file cabinets were present, and a coat rack with a lone lab coat stood in the corner.

My thoughts turned to the phone. I wondered if this one would let me dial out. I sat down at the desk and picked up the phone. Crossing my fingers, I dialed Miranda's cell.

As was her custom, she picked up on the third ring. "Macy Greer, about time you called!" she exclaimed. "Where are you?"

She was way too chipper for this early in the morning. Something was up. "Where's the sour Miranda I know and love?" I falsely demanded. "And how did you know it was me?"

"Who else would call me this early in the morning?" she accused.

Right. She was referring to my propensity to not respect the dourness of the rising sun which, as she frequently informed me, led to her propensity for despising mornings in general.

"Only madmen," I suggested. "Where and how are you?"

"Home and I'm fine. Just twiddling my thumbs till you get back."

I heard what sounded like a muffled man's voice in the background. Surely not. "Twiddling your thumbs, huh? So you weren't just putting your hand over your company's mouth in an effort to prevent me from hearing him?" I was met with silence. "Miranda?"

"You are too dang smart for your own good, you know that?" she scolded.

"And noisy too. I'm the complete package. So, do I get the whole story?"

"Only cliff notes for you."

I chuckled. She was fine. "Let me guess," I offered, "the couch has a starring role in this episode."

"Naturally. I couldn't let him sleep on my couch. You know how uncomfortable it is."

Unfortunately, I did. It was one of those modern numbers that wasn't even comfy for watching television. I think the afore mentioned situation was exactly why she kept the awful thing.

"The horrendousness of your couch is complete justification for your actions," I mockingly agreed.

"Exactly. It was the only hospitable thing I could have done, seeing as he drove me all the way home."

I wasn't sure hospitality ought to be the first thing on your mind when dealing with a kidnapper, no matter how southern you were. Considering she wasn't from the South at all, hospitality was a weak argument at best.

"You do know you're not from the South?" I asked.

"Be that as it may," she reasoned, "there was no call to be rude."

"Sure, it's not like you were kidnapped."

"You were kidnapped," she corrected, "I was chauffeured."

I grumbled my disagreement. That was quite a distinction she was making.

"So, how are you? Where are you?" she asked more earnestly.

I glanced around the office. For the umpteenth time since this whole thing started, I had no clue where I was.

"I don't know where I am. Apparently, I've been hijacked to head off a still unknown dire situation. The lead scientist, a Dr. Heathrow Hollins, seems like a real piece of work. He just handed me a flash drive, claiming it had everything I needed and left me in this office. I don't even know what's going on yet or why they want me."

Which brought to mind something Director Garrison had said about proximity to their hybrids. "Miranda, just how hospitable were you with your...*chauffeur?*"

"I know he looks good in blue satin."

What? When I didn't respond, she explained.

"My new sheets are blue satin."

Against my better judgment, I asked for clarification. "As in blue satin and only blue satin?"

"And coffee colored skin."

Alrighty then. As hospitable as you could be and too much info.

"Why?" she asked.

"Maybe nothing, I hope." I let the telephone cord I'd been coiling around my finger bounce back. "Is your companion still in the room?"

"In the shower. Again, why?" she asked more firmly.

"Without him knowing, can you look for anything you can find on a Director Garrison and a quasi-government agency responsible for hybrid development?"

"You mean other than HCF?"

"I'm not sure. Could be an extension of or not related at all."

"Ok, will do. How do I get in touch with you?"

"I don't know." I checked the phone and desk for a number, but couldn't find anything. "I'll just contact you when I can."

"You sure you're okay?"

I could hear the worry creeping back into her voice. "I'm fine for the time being," I assured her. "I need to get started on my reading, so I'll call you soon."

"Okay. Go get'em or save'em. You know what I mean. Talk to you soon."

"Miranda, be careful."

"Back at ya."

I placed the phone back in its receiver. Hearing Miranda's voice and knowing she was okay, soothed away a little of the anxiety I'd been feeling. I hoped finding out what was going on would take away the rest.

I started up the computer and plugged in the flash drive, only to discover that the computer was password protected. I stared at the screen in disbelief. I bet that prick Hollins knew this would happen.

Growing angrier by the second, I determined that I was not going to sit here and do nothing until he came back. I removed the flash drive and put it in my pocket. Grabbing the lab coat, I slipped it on and headed for the door.

Right before my hand reached the door knob, I had a brief moment of panic when I considered that the door could be locked. I did not relish the idea of escaping through an air vent. To my relief, it wasn't locked, and I swung the door open wide.

Peering out, I didn't see or hear anyone in the hallway. I stepped out and pulled the door shut behind me. With my hands in the pockets of the borrowed lab coat, I headed out in search of a computer I could actually use, possibly to never be seen again. Crazy Macy had a certain ring to it, didn't it?

I thought I might be stopped once I left the office, but I just walked down the halls like I belonged there and no one bothered me.

My search led me past several highly occupied computer labs, but not seeking to draw attention to myself, I kept looking. I didn't even bother to try and remember the way back to the office. If I was as important to them as they were saying, they'd find me soon enough.

I finally found a suitable lab that had only two other occupants. It was quite large and would allow me to use the end opposite the two already there. Quietly, I entered and seated myself at a bench in the back of the room. The two scientists, who were furiously working on their own projects, never even lifted their heads at my arrival. Nor did they notice my two moves down the bench before I found a computer that didn't require a password.

As I waited for the file to load, I thought about Hollins

again. He had disliked me from the first moment we met. Was he upset because they brought someone else in or because I was a female? Or was it just me in particular?

He had to know I wouldn't be able to get on the computer and therefore not be able to read the file. Other than preventing me from gaining access to the situation, what would that accomplish? Was he intentionally trying to keep me off the case, and if so, why?

The file directory appeared on my screen, and simply the titles of the files sent chills through me. The first few read, Physical Aspects of Hybridization Achieved through Nanobot Infusion and Temporal Effects of Nanobot Morphism.

Nanobots and Temporal Effects? Ooh, this was going to be good, like juicy ribeye steak good. I pushed the sleeves of the lab coat up and eagerly began to read.

CHAPTER 8

AN HOUR AND A HALF later, I sat, staring off into space and drumming my fingers on the table. "I don't understand," I said to myself. Thankfully, the other scientists had already vacated the lab, and I was alone with my muttering.

Alone and stunned on many levels.

I shrugged the lab coat off and threw it over the chair next to me. Lacing my fingers together behind my head, I leaned back against my seat and began to sort through what I had read.

Part of the report contained information I already knew. I was already familiar with the new RNA discovered that was responsible for the cellular machinery allowing for the seamless insertion of animal DNA into the human DNA strand. That was how all the hybrids I had been studying were created.

What was new to me was the introduction of nanobots into the process. The inclusion of nanobots revolutionized the creation of hybrids. It allowed for rapid bodily transformations in both directions. Changes such as eye re-contouring and bone reconstruction happened in a matter of seconds or minutes, depending on what was being transformed. It was shape shifting in a purely mechanical definition but on an astronomical cellular scale.

There was also a brief mention of nanobots altering brain wavelengths which allowed for hybrids bearing the same nanobots to establish an as yet undefined mental connection. Hollins had not seen fit to include any in depth explanation beyond the results achieved, an oversight I would have to correct.

But in general, the sheer scope of the strides they had made in this area were truly staggering, and to me, as a scientist, breathtaking. I presumed this was not the part the Director had a problem with. That was probably the last file outlining the impending epidemic of hybrid change about to sweep the earth.

I also thought it odd that I had to wade through all of the other reports before getting to the one report I was supposedly brought here for. It appeared to be another delaying tactic imposed by Hollins. I had yet to conclude that Hollins wanted the crisis to develop to its full potential, but it sure was looking that way.

According to the report, the crisis owed its origin to bacteria's prolific skill at horizontal gene transfer having combined with the carelessness of the Agency's scientists. Every hybrid gene the Agency had created had been transplanted into bacteria for study and experimentation. That in and of itself was not unusual. What did not compute was that the scientists working with them had been so careless as to spread every single strain of the altered bacteria outside of the lab environment.

Now, the bacteria had taken on a life of their own and begun to acquire even more abilities. The hybrid combinations that could possibly be produced as a result were truly horrifying to consider.

This crisis was serious enough to warrant any and all attempts at stopping it. But by the Agency's own account, the bacteria had surpassed all attempts at containment. Since the attempts made were not described, I couldn't attest to the legitimacy of their efforts.

In any case, the failure of their efforts spoke for itself. Most of the scientists working here and some of their family members were testing positive for one or more bacteria containing the hybrid traits. It was only a matter of time before the traits started manifesting.

What I didn't understand was why they needed me. The scientists working on this would have been as familiar, if not more so than me, with this material.

"They should have known how to fix this," I grumbled. "It's not even that hard."

They only needed to construct a nanobot kill switch. The nanobots could be reprogrammed with a chemical sensitivity or vulnerability to a certain radio frequency so that when they came into contact with it, they would self-destruct. The nanobots were already Wi-Fi enabled, so reprogramming wouldn't be that hard.

Hollins ought to have been able to end this crisis before it even got started. A protocol for just such an occurrence should have already existed. It would have existed if I were running the show.

But, beyond that, the likelihood of scientists not following protocol and that every hybrid gene had somehow escaped the lab had to fall somewhere below zero. It simply did not add up.

Spotting a telephone, I pulled Olivia's card from my pocket. She needed to know about this ASAP.

I slid from my chair and started toward the phone. Before I had made it three steps, I was plunged into total darkness.

"What now," I moaned softly.

I waited for a backup generator to kick on, but no orange emergency lights appeared. I was alone, in absolute darkness, in a top secret lab for hybrid development, from which mutant bacteria had escaped containment. That wasn't scary at all.

"Get out of the dark and creepy lab, Macy," I hummed softly to myself.

Why was it that whenever the lights went out, when there was no apparent reason for the outage, horror films started scrolling through your brain? I didn't even watch horror movies, regardless of the inclusion of food, and even I knew what happened to the lone girl when the lights went out. I was not going to be that girl.

Forcing myself to act, I reached back, making contact with the lab table. I grasped it and began inching my way backwards. As soon as my back pressed against the table, I turned and crouched behind it. I didn't know why. It seemed like the thing to do, to make myself as small a target as possible.

Once the momentary panic subsided, my mind kicked into overdrive. It was only ten in the morning, so it couldn't be an automatic lights out situation. It couldn't be a motion sensor scenario because I had moved, and the lights were out in the hall too. The backup generator was offline, which to me said this was not a glitch in the system. It was a darkness initiated with purpose.

Whatever the purpose, I really hoped it didn't concern me. I wasn't conceited enough to think that everything revolved around me, but lately, it seemed like the off the wall, movie quality stuff kept happening to me.

I never knew my life as a scientist would lead me from one terrifying episode to the next. But since I'd joined the HCF, that was exactly how it had been.

Seriously rethinking that decision right now.

Crouching underneath the desk, I realized I had another decision to make. My choices were walking into the unknown or sitting duck. Seemed sort of familiar, except the last time would have been walking into a bullet.

Maybe the blackout had nothing to do with me at all, and I'd be perfectly safe where I was. The first rule about getting lost was to stay put and wait for rescue, right?

A loud crash sounded at the other end of the lab, echoing throughout the room. That was all the convincing I needed. I wasn't a coward, but I wasn't stupid either. Decision made, I moved.

I sort of bear crawled toward the nearest door. Again, I didn't know why, it just felt right.

I made it to the door and slid my hand up its face to find the door handle already turning. Pulling my hand back quickly, I scooted back as quietly as I could and took shelter underneath the lab table again.

I could still hear someone slowly coming closer from the far end of the lab. Or maybe something. I thought I could hear what sounded like claws clacking against the floor.

Knowing my eyes would not be adjusting to this darkness, I closed them and listened instead. Whatever it was coming toward me, it was methodically searching the room.

Focusing on the door, I strained to hear whoever was coming

in there. My plan was to sneak by them with me exiting as they entered. I heard the small click of the door handle and as stealthily as possible, I started edging in a wide circle back toward the door.

My eyes flew open as my mouth and nose were engulfed by a large hand and an arm wrapped around my waist, pulling me backwards. Before I could offer any resistance, the smell of campfire and fruit washed over me. The fear that had seized me gave way to relief, and I relaxed against Catman.

He slowly lowered his hand and brought his mouth to my ear. "We have to get you out of here," he breathed.

I silently nodded, and he began to lead me backwards. Since we weren't bumping into things, I was guessing one of his abilities included being able to see in the dark.

I jumped at the sudden scraping sound off to our left. It still sounded far off, but the fact that it was there at all was way too close for me.

"It doesn't have enhanced senses," Catman whispered to me, essentially confirming that it was a something and not a someone.

The more I tried not to think about what was making the noise, the more it kept popping into my head. My mind kept conjuring claws, attached to very nasty things, scraping against the tile floor. Thank goodness Catman was solid against my back. I didn't think I would have been so calm if he wasn't there.

We reached the back of the lab and Catman stopped and began working on something attached to the wall.

Even though I couldn't see anything, I couldn't look away from the direction of my stalker. Was that slobbering? I reached back, placing a hand on Catman's back. Just being in contact with him made me feel safer.

In an effort to change the direction of my thoughts, I focused on him. He must have changed his clothes. It felt like he had on a t-shirt. I could feel his muscles working under the fabric. Yes, these were much nicer thoughts.

He leaned in, putting his mouth next to my ear again. "Go straight until you come to the first branch to the right. Take it and keep going. No matter what, keep going. I'll be right behind you."

Before I could ask where I was going, he pulled me in front of him and placed my hands on the edge of an entrance. Sliding my hands around, I measured the dimensions at about two by three feet. The cool air rushing past me indicated it was an air shaft. It seemed I'd only delayed my daring escape via the ventilation system.

"Get moving, Greer," he commanded and lifted me into the shaft.

I noted the strain in his voice. I didn't think it was from lifting me. Not wanting to add to his distress, I swallowed my protest of his handling of me. Keeping my shoulder tightly pressed against the side, so that I wouldn't miss the branch he'd specified, I started forward. But I hesitated when I heard the vent cover being reattached to the wall. So much for right behind me.

Surely, he wouldn't have stayed behind unless he knew what he was doing. I guessed it would be pointless to argue with him. For one, it would only draw attention to us, and two, he was the man with the plan to get me out of here. I was just the scientist trying not to get killed.

"Get moving, Greer," I mimicked in my head as I started forward again. He could use a little more finesse. I swung my head side to side in disbelief of my own criticism. I couldn't believe I'd just thought something Olivia would have said. Who was I to fault anyone for being direct? As long as he got me out alive, I would not hold it against him.

My heart sank at the sudden sounds of fighting that reverberated through the shaft. The stark realization that I'd left Catman behind to engage whatever had been in the lab with us felt like a lead balloon in my stomach. I wasn't one to run from a fight, and I sure as heck didn't expect anyone to sacrifice themselves for me. I was torn between going back and going forward.

"Get moving, Greer!" Catman's snarl thundered through the shaft.

"Guess that answers that," I mumbled.

He must be equipped with super hearing, too. How else would he have known that I had stopped? I was pretty far into the shaft already. But obviously, not far enough for him.

This time I moved quickly, racing to outpace the sounds of fighting. I refused to stop, even though I wanted to. I leaned hard into the shaft, nearly bowling over when my shoulder came up against nothing. I'd arrived at the branch with still no sign of Catman and no more echoes for company.

I briefly toyed with the idea of waiting for him, but he seemed pretty adamant that I keep moving. I didn't know what I was worried about, anyway. He could probably take care of himself.

Moreover, nothing else had joined me in the shaft. So either Catman had defeated the nameless beast, or they were both grievously wounded or dead. Geesh, I needed to stop scaring myself with reality.

Racing against some unknown clock set by Catman, I took the right and went about five feet when the tunnel begin to descend. At first, the decline was gentle, allowing me to continue head first. But soon enough, I had to switch to a feet first position in order to accommodate the steepening shaft. This resulted in me partially sliding, partially crab walking.

I was getting my fill of animal impersonations today.

The high heeled boots were not an asset for controlling the rate of descent, either. I was sure I probably sounded like an elephant tromping across the ceiling, especially when my left heel caught, flipping me onto my stomach.

Without any resistance, my speed picked up tremendously. Gone was my controlled slide. In fact, it seemed the material my suit was made of acted like a lubricant aiding my downhill plunge. If I stuck my arms out now, I thought there was a good chance of breaking them, so I tucked my face into my forearms and let her rip.

I tried to keep myself relatively centered, but three feet didn't leave much room for error. Being that it was also still dark as night, I basically bounced from one side to the other.

I really hoped this didn't dump me into some cavern. I momentarily considered trying to slow myself down again and even got as far as to place only my fingertips against the sides. The burning feeling that erupted at the points of contact abruptly ended that attempt.

I needn't have worried. The shaft didn't end. It leveled out and changed directions. I was summarily deposited headfirst into the wall when the shaft suddenly bent left.

"Didn't see that coming," I groaned as I struggled to sit up. Then I giggled. Pressing my hands tightly to my mouth, I tried to smother the errant sounds. Somewhere in the back of my mind, it occurred to me that I might have a concussion, but it didn't seem all that important. It seemed funny, and I collapsed in a bout of giggling.

As I lay there stunned by my impact and still consumed by the giggles, I mimed the roar of a crowd. "Greer wins the gold in shaft surfing. The crowd goes wild."

I was relatively certain that I passed out after that.

When I came to my senses, I realized that I had my arms up like I had scored a touchdown. I frowned and lowered my arms. Touch downs had nothing to do with gold medals.

Sitting up, I became acutely aware of my pounding head. With my fingers, I gingerly probed the source of pain. Just as I suspected, I had a new knot to go with the existing one.

"Looks like I'll have a matching pair. Dumb and dumber." Then I giggled again. I wasn't typically a giggler. Recognizing this only made me giggle more. Maybe the oxygen was thinner in here.

I started taking slow deep breaths as I studied the new section of the shaft. It was a relatively well lit corridor. There was still only one way to go, so no confusion there. I noticed the light was coming from fairly evenly spaced intervals in the shaft floor. Crawling forward, I approached the first light source.

It was connected to an office. From this distance, I could barely discern voices below the vent. Lying down on my stomach, I inched forward and angled my face to get a better view of the room. I could make out the figures of Director Garrison, Hollins and Catman? What was he doing there?

Director Garrison and Hollins were arguing while Catman stood off to the side and watched. Hollins was yelling he didn't need me on the project. Garrison informed him he would do what he was told or he could be removed altogether. Hollins' reply was too quiet for me to make out.

By now, we were way past the time that we were supposed to "talk." He probably knew I was missing. Obviously the Director did not, and Catman wasn't updating him either. I didn't know the reason for that, but I was getting the impression that there was a lot going on that the Director didn't know about.

Catman's head rose sharply and my attention shifted to him. I saw his nostrils flare as he sampled the air. His eyes found mine and he gave a quick jerk of his head, no. I took that to mean not to reveal myself.

Following his direction, I remained silent and watched as Hollins left the office. He sure liked to slam doors when making an exit.

Director Garrison moved toward Catman and began speaking to him. He was speaking too softly for me to hear what he was saying. As Catman stepped closer to the Director, a pang of guilt raced through me. Behind his left ear was a trail of blood that disappeared into the collar of his shirt. I was certain that had come from his recent fight.

I watched Director Garrison walk back to his desk, and then Catman turned to leave. As he reached the door, he looked up and mouthed "keep moving" to me. Then he left the office.

Keep moving? Why couldn't I just reveal myself to the Director and get out of this vent? For some reason, Catman wanted me to remain hidden. So the question was, did I trust him?

He hadn't harmed me, NOLA aside, and he'd seen to it that I was fed. He'd also just fought to keep me safe. I knew I didn't trust Hollins. The Director...? I thought he was just as clueless as me as to what was truly going on. It all came down to whether I did or did not trust Catman.

I found the answer to be yes.

I sighed as I accepted my choice. Trusting Catman meant I was going to be in this vent for a little longer.

"But you had better watch out," I quietly warned myself, "or you'll find the words, keep moving, stamped on your backside."

Yeah, that was all kinds of funny right there.

Moving as quietly as possible, I started forward, yet again. The shaft remained level this time, and I didn't encounter anymore branch points. I passed more offices, but there was nothing of interest going on.

I realized the shaft was slowly growing darker. The little light that the offices had provided was fading. Looking into the distance, the shaft disappeared into the darkness. It might have ended two feet past it or gone on forever. I just couldn't tell.

Straining to see into the darkness was causing my head to pound even more, and my stomach was starting to rumble. After a while, the rumblings seemed to pick a rhythm, like a drumbeat. It would have been comical if I wasn't the one enduring it.

"Maybe I should start carrying an emergency pack everywhere I go. Just the necessities. A flashlight, no a headlamp, so I can be hands free. Some water, food, first aid."

I would sure have appreciated an aspirin right about now for both my head and my other aching parts. I sat down for a minute to give my knees and back a rest. Sitting felt good, so I stretched out on the floor of the shaft.

"That's better," I yawned. "At least it's not hot."

While I was rolling my ankles, I realized they were not sliding across a smooth surface. Pulling myself back into a crouch, I inspected the surface with my hands. It felt like a roughhewn tunnel made of moist dirt and rocks. Definitely not something that had been cut with power tools.

I rubbed the dirt between my fingers and brought it to my nose. It smelled like clay.

"That narrows down my location to the majority of the planet," I muttered sarcastically. "I guess you're not the never ending shaft."

I was aware of the fact that I kept talking to myself, but I figured, as long as I didn't hear someone other than me answering back, I was okay.

I didn't think the shaft terminating into a tunnel carved out of the earth was part of the original design. So, why would someone attach an unplanned tunnel to a ventilation shaft? The most obvious reason was an escape route. That implied that someone knew there was going to be a need for escape. Someone like Catman? Why would he prepare a way of escape from his own Agency?

"I wish somebody would tell me what the heck is going on," I demanded of the ceiling. Disgusted, I wiped my hands off on my pants. "No response, really, I'm shocked. You people have been so forthcoming up till now."

I let my knees rest on the floor and folded my hands in my lap. It was time for a situation assessment. In lieu of pen and paper, I used my voice.

"Let me get this straight," I stated to the darkness. "I'm about to enter a tunnel, somewhere in the earth, with a probable concussion, not knowing who to trust, or why someone is trying to kill me, or where the heck I'm going, while a hybrid epidemic is poised to sweep the earth."

I pressed my lips together, considering if I'd left something out. I would never in a million years have guessed this was how I'd spend my day.

"Focus, Greer," I ordered myself.

I shook my head to try and clear it, but stopped when that only resulted in the tunnel spinning. Placing my hands on either side of me on the floor, I waited for the spinning to stop before continuing my assessment.

I could turn around and reenter the office complex. An image of Catman's stern face immediately appeared in my mind. No, he wouldn't like that very much.

I knew there were things going on that I didn't understand. I didn't know why Catman didn't want me to reveal myself to the Director, but he must have a good reason. It seemed to all come back down again to whether I trusted him or not.

"Uugh, this is not fair," I groaned. Why did I have to keep trusting a man I hardly knew? But something in my gut told me that I had to, that it was the right choice. And I had learned the hard way a long time ago to obey those promptings.

Then my lightning fast mind informed me that, given the environment, there was a good chance that creepy crawlies also inhabited the tunnel.

"Oh, Dear God, please do not let there be bugs in this tunnel," I begged.

I hated bugs fervently. I knew it wasn't rational, but they were icky with their sticky little legs and flailing antennae. My stomach rolled in revulsion at just the thought of sharing space with them. Maybe God would have mercy on me and send an angel with a flashlight and bug spray.

Unfortunately, regardless of my waiting, none showed up.

"They probably don't know where I am either," I muttered dejectedly. "I'm so glad I accepted this position. Oh wait, I didn't," I said with a dry laugh.

A few more minutes of sighing and staring into the tunnel didn't reveal anything new. Not that I thought it would given the fact that I couldn't see anything.

"I guess you've stalled long enough, Macy," I said resolutely. "Time to get your big girl panties on and conquer that tunnel. And this time, don't think about the possible outcomes," I instructed myself.

But I did it anyway. My mind just worked that way, seeing all the possibilities, like tunnel collapses or falling through weak spots. Dang it.

I took one more deep breath and let it out slowly. Then, I deliberately moved forward into the tunnel.

CHAPTER 9

TWENTY FEET INTO THE TUNNEL firmly established the fact that it was worse than just moist and roughhewn. Far worse. Each placement of my hands and knees was met with rocky, uneven, and sharp. What was this stuff? My hands and knees were being cut to pieces. There had to be a better way to navigate this.

I carefully set my feet underneath me and felt along the bottom of the tunnel. The edges of the tunnel where it started curving upward had fewer sharp edges. Assuming a plank position, with my hands and feet wide apart, I started forward again. I hoped doing all those chest presses would pay off now.

After thirty minutes, give or take a few, my arms started shaking. When the pounding in my head matched the shaking of my extremities, I crouched again. Rubbing my biceps revealed to me how tender my hands were. I knew they were cut up pretty bad, but the darkness prevented me from seeing how badly.

I didn't know how far I had come or how much further I had to go. Somewhere along the way, I had stopped keeping track of distance and just concentrated on not falling.

I felt along the floor again. Still sharp. Why would you make an escape tunnel that would bleed you to death before you actually escaped? Maybe they intended to use the ceiling. I felt along the ceiling, but there were no handholds of any kind. The only idea I had was to resume my previous position.

Suddenly, the tunnel was filled with thunder and the floor jolted underneath me, sending me sprawling. I managed to protect my face, but my forearms and knees took the full brunt of the fall. Scrambling, I tried to maintain my balance but the swaying floor was too much for my blood soaked hands. I felt the bite of the floor again, as I slipped.

Not wanting to risk another fall, I thought it best to stay put until the movement stopped. Little bits of debris continued to rain down around me as the swaying gradually slowed to a stop.

"What the heck was that," I said around my coughing.

Steeling myself for the pain, I gingerly removed my arms and then knees from the floor. I tried to lift them back in the direction they'd been impaled so as to minimize tearing. I didn't know how successful that was because I could feel blood from all the various cuts soaking through my suit.

I shrugged out of my jacket and began to rip out the lining. Using my teeth, I tore it into smaller pieces and wrapped it around the largest cuts on my forearms. Then I wrapped the remainder around my palms, securing them with knots on top.

I didn't have anything left over for my knees, but since they were not in contact with the surface while I was moving, I just left them alone. Not to mention, I would have had to sit down on the flesh slicing stuff to remove first the boots and then the pants.

When I determined there was nothing else I could do, I slipped my jacket back on and buttoned it. I didn't know if I was in shock or if the tunnel was actually chilly, but I was cold and shaking.

"All the more reason to get out of here," I said with chattering teeth. "This tunnel has to end at some point."

I shut my eyes tight against the images of blocked tunnels pummeling me, along with the new fear of having to retreat back the way I'd come. But on the bright side, there were no bugs. If I'd only thought to ask for it not to be lined with glass shards.

I slowly shook my head at my current state. Between the dirt, mud, and blood, I probably looked like some kind of tunnel rat. Thankfully, I hadn't run into any of those either. But I wasn't afraid of rats, or snakes, or spiders for that matter. That only applied to bugs of the six legged variety. Although, I had to admit, six legs probably would have come in handy for crawling through this tunnel.

Tentatively, I placed my hands back in their designated positions. Shifting my full weight on them caused sharp burning pain to radiate up my arms. I waited for the pain to dull to a throb before pushing on.

The padding helped a little. But, after a while, the blood soaked through, and they seemed more like skates than padding. I considered taking it off, but my hands would slip either way. At least this way they had some protection from more damage.

I had no idea how long it took, but I finally made it to the end. The last few feet of the tunnel floor had become mercifully smooth, and I carefully maneuvered myself to sit with my legs hanging over the side.

Past the tunnel itself, my outstretched arms couldn't feel anything. Using my legs, I carefully swung to the left and then the right. I gasped as my right foot made contact with the wall, causing stabbing pains to shoot through my knee.

Closing my eyes against the pain, I was grateful that at this particular moment, I couldn't see my knees. I didn't particularly relish the thought of seeing my own insides. And really, who wanted to see their own insides?

Balancing myself with my left hand on the ceiling of the tunnel, I leaned forward and placed my right hand on the new wall. I was hoping to find some sort of door, but instead I found steps. Not metal secure steps. No, they like the tunnel, felt like they had been carved into the rock. They were skinny little excuses for steps really, but they didn't seem to be sharp. That was a welcome change.

Bringing my hands back, I made sure the knots felt secure. I was well aware of how dangerous the task before me was. My body was already shaking with exertion and or shock, and my hands and forearms were wet and sticky with blood. My feet were okay because of the boots. The knees were a different story.

Too bad they weren't thigh high boots. My knees would have had some measure of protection then. Note to self...the next time I go crawling through glass, I would have thigh high boots.

I closed my eyes and took a few deep breaths. A few more experiences like this, and I thought I would have this meditation thing down. This was the most deep breathing I'd done my whole life. Not much call for it looking through a microscope.

No matter which way I spun it, there was no way around it. I was going to have to climb those tinker bell size steps, using my toes and finger tips. Why? Because, though I didn't recall voting for it, difficult was my new mode of operandi. Dad gum it.

I wiped my fingertips on my pants in an effort to dry them off. This was going to be tricky. I would need to propel myself off the ledge and onto the ladder, but not hard enough that I bounced off and fell to the depths below. The floor might have been only three feet down, but I wasn't going to test that out.

I had measured the distance between the steps at roughly a foot and a half. A little steep for me, but again, no other option presented itself.

Perching on the ledge, I grabbed ahold of the step.

"On three," I sighed, hoping this wouldn't be the last ladder I ever climbed. I closed my eyes, my prayer sincere this time.

"One." Please God, let my feet find the step.

"Two." And don't let me fall.

"Three."

I propelled myself up and out onto the ladder where I slammed into the wall hip first. That was going to leave bruises. My feet scrabbled furiously against the rock, trying to find a step. It seemed like they'd all suddenly disappeared.

"This better not turn into one of those movies where the steps disappear, and the tunnel magically morphs into a water slide!" I yelled at the shaft. I hated big drops almost as much as I hated bugs.

Hanging by my fingertips was causing the cuts on my hands and forearms to scream with pain. I recognized that my fingers were slipping, and I forced myself to search with only one foot rather than madly with both.

The toe of my boot finally caught the edge of a step, and I slid it forward as far as it would go. I brought my other foot alongside it just as my fingers slipped free of the step. Quickly shifting my weight, I pressed forward until I was hugging the wall.

I remained cemented in place with my heart hammering in my chest and my body shaking violently. I was officially on adrenaline overload.

"Oh, my God," I moaned. "When I get my hands on Catman, I'm going to beat the crap out of him."

As the shaking subsided, I brought my hands, which were fully extended and flat against the wall, closer to me. The cuts that had never really stopped bleeding were flowing freely again. I knew this would affect my climb, but there wasn't really anything I could do about it. I couldn't maneuver myself to rewrap my hands, and even if I managed to somehow do that, I didn't have anything else to wrap them with. Going back was not an option.

"I'll tell you how this changes things. It adds difficulty. Say it with me rock buddies, Dif-fi-cult."

I turned my head sideways and rested it against the wall. Did I really just say rock buddies? And to think, I asked God to help me get out here. He must be having a good laugh right now. The angels were probably taking odds. "Let's see her get out of this one," I mouthed.

Great. I had deteriorated to impersonating angels.

I wondered what my odds really were for getting out of here alive. Unfortunately, there was only one way to find out.

I didn't have confidence that my grip alone would support me, so I had to compensate by allowing my legs to bear most of my weight. But I had to position them so that my knees were not directly touching the wall. This left me ascending in a twisted sideways position, not the most favorable position for climbing.

It didn't take long for my quads to start protesting their continued use. I agreed they needed rest, but I thought I was working against the clock. I had never pushed my body this hard, and I wasn't sure how much it could physically take. There was also the probable concussion and blood loss to figure in. If I stopped, I didn't know if I'd be able to start again. That meant I was climbing until I couldn't anymore.

I was negotiating another step when something grabbed my ankle, causing me to emit a very girly squeal. I was then pressed into the wall as someone came up from underneath me. The smell of fire and fruit flooded my senses. Catman.

I was overwhelmed with relief right until the anger surfaced.

"You scared the heck out of me," I whispered furiously. "Why didn't you let me know you were coming?"

"I might have startled you, and you might have fallen, possibly knocking us both down the shaft, which goes down another thousand feet," he said calmly.

That was the most he'd ever said to me and good point. He would have startled me big time. A thousand feet? Yikes. How deep underground was this facility?

Even with him on the step below me, his head was still level with mine. He pressed closer and began sniffing vigorously.

"I smell blood. Where are you injured?" he asked.

"Stop that, you're tickling," I sniggered while shouldering him away. "It's my hands and arms. And knees, and legs. By the way, the next time I go tunnel crawling, I require thigh high boots."

He shifted back some. "Thigh high boots. I see."

I couldn't see his face, but I knew by the uncertain tone in his voice that he clearly did not see.

"It felt like I was crawling over broken glass. Thigh high boots would have given my knees some measure of protection," I explained.

His chest rumbled against my back as he growled softly. "The floor is actually layered with broken glass, among other sharp things."

Of course it was.

"You sent me down the tunnel, knowing I'd be sliced and diced," I said exasperated. "Was razor wire too expensive for you? You could have added flayed to the menu."

"It was not my intention to bring you harm," he bit back angrily. "It was never intended for human use, but it was the only way to get you safely out of the complex."

"Your definition of safely and mine are not the same," I argued.

A tense silence settled between us. I could hear both of us breathing heavily, mine mostly from exertion and his from anger. I didn't think he was used to having to explain himself so much. Oh, well.

He sighed and leaned in a little closer, placing his forehead against the back of my head. "It was the only way to get you out alive. A few cuts were deemed acceptable when compared to your death."

His anger was reflected in every clipped word that he spoke. He was also making it hard to stay mad at him with all these good reasons he had. But he was wrong about the extent of my injuries.

"I wouldn't call it a few," I snapped, but then more softly added, "But I do prefer living to dead."

"As. Do. I," he growled.

I could feel his breath against my hair as his anger escaped through his words. He inhaled deeply causing his chest to swell against my back. His voice was minus the anger when he next spoke.

"We should get moving again. I didn't expect you to start climbing on your own. I almost thought you hadn't made it when I arrived at the tunnel mouth and you weren't there, but then I smelled you."

I wasn't sure how to take that. Of all the smells I would associate with myself right now, I couldn't think of one good one.

I let the comment go along with the anger I was still holding on to. The spurt of energy that had come with the anger, left with it as well, and, as a result, my arms and legs felt like lead weights.

"Well, I did," I said, sighing loudly. "I've never been much of one for waiting. But if there is an elevator, I'd like to transfer to that now."

He snorted softly. "I'd love to oblige, but there's no elevator, just this ladder."

"Figures," I muttered.

Why should things be easy, when difficult was so much more fun? Should I clue him in to the new buzzword linked to me? Nah, he'd work that out on his own sooner or later.

Fingering the ladder—because that was about all that would fit on it—I reiterated my opinion. "It's not much of a ladder." I was clearly pouting, but it made me feel a little better.

He laughed and gently slapped the side of my leg. "Get moving, Greer."

Ignoring the pain he'd just caused in my knee and on trembling fingers, I started up the ladder again. He stayed right behind me this time. I wasn't so worried about falling now. I knew he'd catch me. It was quite the nice feeling actually. His body heat was an added bonus.

"Ok, I'm moving," I said after we'd climbed for a while. "You want to fill me in on why somebody is trying to kill me, and don't give me that BS line about the Director answering my questions."

"I won't. Director Garrison is presumed dead."

I was stunned. "What do you mean he's dead? I just saw him with you a few hours ago. What happened?" I asked, trying to reconcile the difference in my head.

"There was an explosion."

That must have been what rocked the tunnel. "How big an explosion?"

"Big enough. From reports I've received, it appears as if Director Garrison was the target. The blast radius places his office at the center of the debris field. Additionally, all of the preventative security measures and countermeasures for after the fact were disrupted prior to the explosion."

"Like the lights going out in the lab and the lack of emergency lights?"

"Yes, except you were no longer the target."

I wondered why I was a target at all and had my escape precipitated Director Garrison's death?

"You think he replaced me as the target?" I asked.

"Replaced, no. He inserted himself between them and their goal, making himself an obstacle to their success."

"By bringing me in and giving me full access?"

He was silent a long moment before answering. "I don't want you to think that you are responsible for his death."

Well, duh. I didn't blow him up. "Was he the only one killed?"

"As far as casualties, everyone in our Organization is accounted for. No one that you would recognize is still missing or dead."

If everyone was accounted for, then how could some be missing or dead? Unless he was talking about two different entities—Organization as in separate from the Agency?

"You're part of a different Agency?"

"Not an Agency, an Organization," he said, nudging me to continue climbing. I hadn't realized I'd stopped.

"Does this organization have a name?" I asked, pulling myself to the next step.

"The official name is a mouthful," he warned. "The Organization for Free and Unhindered Pursuit of Genetic Advancement and Development, which is why we call it simply, the Organization."

That was a mouthful. Even the acronym OFUPGAD was too much. "Did Director Garrison belong to the Organization?"

"He had no knowledge of our existence. That was not my decision, but it was a miscalculation on our part. Within the Agency, only the ones on your team, who are themselves members of the Organization, are aware of its existence."

"You mean Olivia, and Agents Juarez and Pike?" I asked as I struggled to find the next step. I kept lifting my leg higher, but it wasn't there.

"Yes. Are we taking a rest break?" he asked casually.

It suddenly struck me that this wasn't hard for him at all. "No. We are not taking a break!" I spat, breathing heavily again. "I can't find the step."

He grasped the underside of my leg above the knee and lifted my entire body to the next step.

Well, if he could do that, why wasn't he just carrying me, I thought grumpily. Mr. Super, Hybrid, Strong Man.

"You through?" he asked without emotion.

I was about to ask with what, when I recalled his mental abilities. Dang it, again.

When I made no move to resume climbing, he leaned in and softly urged, "Get moving, Greer."

I had a feeling I'd be hearing that in my dreams at some point in the future.

"Okay," I said, heaving myself to the next step. Either they were becoming further apart, or I was getting weaker. I wasn't sure how much longer I could keep this up.

"So, who is trying to kill me and why?" I said breathily.

"A consortium of people dedicated to the worldwide proliferation of hybridization. At least, that's what their mission statement says. We just call it the Consortium."

I gasped involuntarily as my right foot slipped off the step. Catman quickly placed his hand on my waist to steady me against the wall. Maybe I should focus more on the climbing and not so much the talking.

That reminded me. I needed to talk to him about the situation at the Agency, both my suspicions and the answer.

"How much further?" I asked.

"Not much. You okay?" he asked worriedly.

Was I okay? No. I was feeling weaker with every step. It was all I could do to make it to the next one. But, again, I was still alive. "I don't even know how to answer that," I finally said. "Let's just make it out of here, and then I'll grill you some more. Deal?"

"Deal," he agreed, and then he wrapped his arm around my waist and lifted me with him to the next step. That made it considerably easier to climb.

Aside from my grunting and occasional outburst when I hit my knees or a particularly sore spot on my hands, we climbed the rest of the way in silence. He remained fixed at my back, assisting me when I needed help, and carrying me when I couldn't do it at all.

When we reached the end of the ladder, it widened out,

allowing us to stand shoulder to shoulder, sort of. I also discovered that if he hadn't been here, then I wouldn't be getting out this way. As it was, he had to lean over me, incidentally squishing me painfully into the tunnel wall, in order to undo the hatch. Agents Juarez and Pike were waiting by the exit and finished lifting the hatch for us.

"Hey, why couldn't they open the hatch?" I grumbled, rubbing my forehead.

"It only opens from the inside," he answered.

"The next time you decide to rope me into your secret agent stuff, could you please include an informational brochure, or fact list, or maybe even a needed supplies list."

He pulled back and stared at me with a blank look on his face.

"What?" I asked testily.

It seemed a number of responses danced in his eyes, but then he very evenly said, "Let's get you out."

"Please do," I said angrily. With Catman lifting from behind and Juarez and Pike pulling from above, I made it out of the tunnel.

After being in the dark for so long, I was momentarily blinded by the appearance of light. I held onto Agent Pike's arm as I rapidly blinked tears away. My vision wasn't the only thing affected by my exit from the tunnel. I wasn't very steady on my feet either.

When I could see again, I looked down at my knees and sighed. This looked familiar. As one might expect when crawling over glass, the pants were shredded from the knees down. That made it sharp objects two, pants zero.

Shredding aside, there was a startling amount of blood. It appeared that even I had underestimated the extent of my injuries.

Pike kept ahold of my elbow while Juarez gave Agent Michaels a hand up. Since he'd saved me in the lab and probably again in the tunnel shaft, I'd promoted him to Agent Michaels. He'd always be my Catman, but he certainly pulled off the agent thing. Besides, I couldn't call him Catman to his face, and it looked like there would be a lot more face time now.

After Michaels cleared the shaft, he trained his eyes on me. I held my breath, knowing he wasn't going to be happy with what he saw. I watched his eyes narrow as they traveled upwards. When they met mine, I offered him a weak smile. The tightness that had been there softened a little, and he deliberately turned his attention back to Agent Juarez.

I closed my eyes and breathed a sigh of relief. I didn't know if I passed inspection, but at least it was over.

"Transport waiting?" I heard Michaels ask Juarez.

Pike's grip tightened on my arm, and I opened my eyes in response.

"It will be when we get there," Juarez answered. When Michaels continued to stare at him, Juarez rapidly gave an explanation. "This is not exactly the scenario we planned for, but we are making the necessary adjustments to make it work."

After a moment, Michaels nodded his acknowledgement, and Juarez looked away first. Pike who'd been watching the exchange seemed to relax, and his grip loosened. Obviously, I was missing something, but I just added it to the growing list of things I didn't know. I wasn't happy with how long the list was becoming.

Looking around, I was startled to see the empty space where the mansion had stood. Actually, it wasn't entirely empty. The remains were freely burning and looked like they had sunk into the ground, which I supposed they had.

I also noted the conspicuous absence of emergency vehicles. When you were a top secret facility devoted to illegal activities, apparently, you were on your own.

"I didn't realize the explosion was that big," I commented, and all of their heads swiveled to view the burning remains.

"It was quite devastating to the facility," Juarez said in a subdued voice.

"It wasn't devastating to the personnel?" I asked hopefully. Michaels had said that no one I knew was dead, but a lot of other people I didn't know were in there, too.

"No. Except for a select few, Hollins made sure most everyone was out," Juarez said with contempt.

How could Hollins get everyone out before the explosion that he didn't know was going to take place? Unless, of course, he knew about the explosion which would make him responsible for Director Garrison's death. I knew Hollins was angry when he left Garrison's office, but mad enough to kill him? Over me? And did that make him part of this Consortium that Michaels had mentioned?

I didn't know what to think as I stood there. There were way too many gaps in the information I had to figure out the one thing I needed to know the most. Who were the good guys?

I was also acutely aware of the fact that I was injured and surrounded by three potentially dangerous men, two of which I hardly knew and didn't trust at all. Likewise, I had yet to determine if they were allies or enemies. Keeping me alive, although a plus in their favor, didn't label them as one or the other. There could be lots of reasons for keeping me alive.

Michaels' gaze fell on Pike and then travelled to where he gripped my arm. In response, Pike's hand dropped, and he moved away from me. He seemed to shrink somehow, not visibly, but something in his demeanor shifted. He didn't return Michaels' stare either, but looked down and away.

As I watched the encounter, I felt like I was party to some sort of alpha male thing with me as the prize. I would have taken offense, but it seemed real, not some macho BS. I was guessing it had something to do with the hybrid DNA. But whatever the case, I wasn't going to make any sudden movements.

Michaels rolled his shoulders and then decidedly marched over to me. He scooped me up, and I hooked my right arm around his shoulders and wondered why the heck I was being carried. Seemed a bit possessive to me. I opened my mouth to say so when I got a good look at the blood trail behind his left ear.

Instead of voicing my protest, I asked, "Why do you have blood behind your ear?"

"Close encounter with a Furry," he answered, heading straight for the woods.

I noted that Pike had passed us and taken point while Juarez remained at the rear, covering our flank. Look at me, I could talk military, too.

"What's a Furry?" I asked.

"One of the Consortium's assassins," he said in the clipped tones he seemed so fond of.

We were just about to enter the woods. Pike had already disappeared. I didn't see a path, but I did see the large stump directly in front of us. I ground my teeth together as Michaels none too gently hoisted me higher as he jumped over the stump. The landing wasn't much fun either.

When I was sure I could speak without my voice conveying any pain, I asked, "Is that what was in the lab with me?"

"One and the same," he gritted out.

The look on his face was so intense. I couldn't decide whether to bust out laughing or be afraid. But, since he'd stepped in and saved me from death or mangling, I was going to give him the benefit of the doubt. I listed him as a good guy. A good guy who was really tense at the moment. His grip was a tad painful.

I squirmed a little, forcing him to adjust his hold. It wasn't any less tight, but it didn't put as much pressure on my knees which afforded me some relief. Hopefully he'd let up soon, or I'd have to say something that was sure to be construed as whiney.

I knew he didn't want to talk, but I just had one more question. "I don't understand why the Consortium would take out a whole government facility for just one man. Couldn't they just have killed him and left the facility alone?"

He continued his determined trek but tossed me a disapproving look.

"I know you said that Director Garrison put himself at odds with them, but are you sure this wasn't part of a bigger plan?"

"The Consortium always has plans," he said angrily.

Before I could respond, he suddenly swung me to the left, and I couldn't contain the gasp that escaped when he banged my leg into a tree trunk. As a consequence, I was now on the receiving end of his glare.

I removed the hand I had instinctively brought up to cover

my mouth and said, "Sorry." Almost immediately, I regretted my reaction. Why the heck was I apologizing?

He sighed heavily and loosened his hold on me to a more comfortable level. "You have nothing to apologize for. I am the one who should apologize. I did not mean to hurt you physically or otherwise."

I knew the words were not easy for him. He was honestly contrite over his behavior. I didn't know how I knew, but I did.

"I know," I told him. I wasn't excusing his behavior, but I could understand why he was so tense. All his plans seemed to have gone up in smoke, no pun intended.

Additionally, maybe he was tired of having to rescue me. I knew I was tired of needing to be rescued. Why he was bothering to rescue me at all was another mystery.

In an attempt to lighten the mood, I changed the subject. "So, I'm officially on the Consortium's hit list. Good to know. Since you've brought me here, I'm just winning all kinds of awards."

His grip eased a little more, and a smile played on his lips, probably recalling my first award. Whatever the reason, I was glad to see his smile return.

Though the words seemed to stick in my throat, it was only right to offer my thanks for the help he'd provided me. Manners were optional at the dinner table, but when someone did you a solid, I was taught to say thank you.

"Thank you for rescuing me. Again. The second time, I mean. Well, and the first time in the lab, too." Oh, that was smooth.

His smile widened at my mangled offer of thanks. "You're welcome. It was the least I could do, considering I put you in danger to begin with."

You got that right, I thought. But when I recalled my recent brushes with danger, I concluded that may not be a totally accurate portrayal of events. The shooter in the woods could have also been one of the Consortium's people. And if that were true, it meant that the Consortium had me under surveillance prior to my involvement with the Organization.

He tucked my head in and shielded me as we made our way through a patch of low lying branches.

As we cleared them, I said, "I think I was in danger before I became involved with you. A few weeks ago, I was shot at while gathering some data. The shooter was more than a crazy protestor. This guy knew what he was doing."

His smile retreated as he considered what I'd just told him. "This would be the time you spent three consecutive nights in the woods?"

My eyes widened at his question. How'd he know that? He'd only know that if he'd been watching me, too.

"You had me under surveillance!" I said sharply.

He glanced briefly at my surprised face. "The Organization had you under surveillance," he corrected, "and we were about to intervene when Kenny did our job for us."

"You watched me the entire time!" I had gone to the bathroom for goodness sakes. Repeatedly.

"Not me," he said, shaking his head no. "Olivia and a couple other female operatives you haven't met. We are not barbarians, Dr. Greer. Besides," he continued with a smirk on his face, "I understand it was not as if you bathed during that time."

I was now subjected to feeling his chest heaving in silent laughter. This was even more embarrassing than the NOLA incident.

"In fact, I have it on good authority that you were rather rank."

I pressed my lips together and thought, Miranda, that traitor. He must have talked to her. She was the only one besides me that could have vouched for my rankness. Why hadn't she told me they'd talked?

Regarding his amused face, I could think of nothing else worth arguing. It was a fait accompli. Any further show of embarrassment now would just be silly. Expressing my anger wouldn't accomplish anything either except to maybe widen his smile some more.

"You have an unnatural interest in my bathing habits," I said flatly.

He was still smiling when he admitted it. "Perhaps," he said with a tilt of his head.

I looked off into the woods, working really hard to ignore the smug look on his face. It was a task made more difficult by the fact that his face was only inches from mine.

My superfluous examination of the woods found that we were about to join a well-trodden path. As a result, Michaels picked up the pace quite a bit. The increase in speed, thankfully, did not equate with a great deal of jostling for me. In fact, the rhythmic swaying in his arms was starting to lull me to sleep.

I lifted my head from his shoulder where I didn't realize it had gone. "Not that I'm complaining," I said sleepily, "but why are you carrying me?"

"The hike before we rendezvous with transport is approximately two miles. You're in no condition to make that trek. At least not as quickly as we need," he answered, his face once again wearing a stern expression as he focused on something off in the distance.

Well, if you had to hike through the woods, being wrapped in two strong arms attached to tall, dark and delicious was not a bad way to go.

Thinking of Miranda brought a sudden pang of worry to my heart. Was her Goon part of Michaels' Organization or the Consortium?

"The Goon that took Miranda home, is he with you?"

"Goon?" he questioned, sparing me a brief glance. "I believe you are referring to Cedars. And yes, he is part of the Organization."

That was good news. "Will they be safe when the Consortium realizes I'm gone?"

His frown deepened as he continued to focus on something up ahead. I looked too, but all I could see was the surrounding woods.

"Not sure," he said, slowing down. "Juarez, has Cedars checked in?"

I turned my head, searching for Juarez, as he answered from behind us.

"He did check in this morning, but we haven't updated him on the current situation."

I wondered if Cedars had updated them on his current situation with Miranda. Hey, I thought happily, I might finally know something that they didn't. Although, I couldn't really classify it as important.

Michaels stopped walking, and I twisted back to the front to find out why. Pike was a few feet ahead of us, kneeling on the ground and holding his hand up to indicate a halt. He sprinted a short distance ahead, and then stopped again. Scanning the woods up ahead, he held up a closed fist and then flashed two. Juarez passed us to join him, and Pike indicated once left and once right.

"Michaels?" Pike asked.

Michaels sniffed the air. "Furries," he said.

If Pike couldn't smell them, I wondered how he knew something was there.

Juarez's eyes were a glowing amber color as he turned and looked at Michaels. "They're trying to cut us off."

"Agreed," said Michaels. "We are still half a mile out. We will have to dispatch them."

Juarez looked down at some digital gadget he'd pulled from his pocket. "We have to do it quickly," he advised. "They've called for reinforcements."

Nodding, Agent Michaels stood me on my feet, but kept a hand on my shoulder. Staring straight into my eyes, he pointed off to the East. "Do you see where the trees veer apart?"

I looked in the direction that he indicated. There was only one spot he could be talking about, so I nodded once for yes.

"I need you to head in that direction."

Alone? He meant alone. My eyes widened involuntarily, and I swallowed. I was bait. Injured, weak, stinking bait.

Sensing that I grasped the situation, he said, "That's right, you will draw them out of cover, but they will never reach you."

The look of disbelief on my face must have prompted his next comment.

"You have my word, Dr. Greer. They will not touch you. You have to trust me."

Wasn't I doing that already?

I squeezed my eyes shut. Trust. Such an easy thing on paper. Not so easy in the woods, in the company of three men you hardly knew, and being stalked by Furries—whatever those were. How did my life come down to trusting the word of a man I hardly knew?

"Dr. Greer?"

"It's Macy," I said, opening my eyes. "Just Macy."

It was his turn to nod.

"Okay," I said. "I'm ready."

He squeezed my shoulder and aimed me in the right direction. "We'll be right behind you," he assured me.

Where had I heard that before?

CHAPTER 10

I ALLOWED MYSELF ONE BREATH TO gather my courage, and then I started for the split in the trees. I didn't realize it while I was being carried, but my knees had stiffened considerably. Each step I took sent spikes of pain radiating through my legs. Being the trooper that I was, I gritted my teeth and kept walking. At least it overshadowed the throbbing pain in my hands and forearms.

He said half a mile. I could do that. No problem. Except for the unmistakable growling off to my left.

It was a high pitched growling and didn't sound at all like what I'd heard from Michaels on several occasions. I was assuming that it belonged to one of the mysterious Furries. I wanted to look and not look at the same time. Surely it was covered with fur. Why else would they have dubbed it a Furry?

The growling was getting louder, which I interpreted to mean it was getting closer. The adrenaline kicked in, and my steps quickened accordingly, but the growling kept pace with me. Why didn't somebody just shoot it already?

My increased speed erased the benefits of the reprieve my knees had experienced while I was carried. Blood began flowing again from the many cuts I had previously sustained. I could feel the rivulets flowing down my shins inside my boots. It didn't take long for every step I made to emit a squelching sound, upping the gross factor considerably.

A snarl pierced the air in the opposite direction of the growling and startled me into missing my next step. I landed on one knee, generating a snarl of my own. A loud yelp quickly followed the initial snarl. Score one for the team?

Using the nearest branch for support, I hauled myself up and resumed my trek, albeit, not as fast as before. I risked a look off in the direction of the growling. Not surprisingly, I didn't see anything but woods.

I turned back around just in time to watch myself plant the heel of my boot in a jumble of tree roots. Un-freaking-believable.

Ignoring the pain, I began to pull furiously at my boot. I couldn't believe I had pulled such a stupid, amateur worthy stunt. I wrapped my arms around a low lying branch and used my free foot to push against the root entrapping my boot. I'd just about worked my ankle free when I realized something was different.

With both hands still painfully gripping the tree, I froze. The difference was the silence. Everything was quiet.

Sliding my foot the rest of the way free, I leaned against the tree. I had no illusions about who was the prey, and that served to settle one thing for me. When and if I made it through this, I was going to invest in some training. Combat, weapons, whatever I could find. I would do my level best to see to it that I never again was unequal to a situation like this.

The high pitched growling suddenly resumed, but I still couldn't spot the source. I was about to step away from the tree, when Michaels flew through the air in front of me. My head swiveled in time with his flight, witnessing his midair collision with something that was aiming for me.

Michaels hit the creature, and they tumbled to the ground. As soon as they rolled to a stop, the fighting ensued at a pace that was almost too fast for me to follow. They twisted and turned around each other, seemingly not touching. Only, I knew they were by the snapshots of blood appearing at random intervals.

The something was ugly. It looked like a cross between a rat and a hyena with big poofy fur covering its entire body. This was undoubtedly what they were calling a Furry. Its appearance was made even uglier by comparison with Michaels'.

Michaels had not shifted his entire body, only the periphery elements. His long fingers were tipped with claws, and a quick profile of his face let me see that he was sporting cat like ears and very sharp teeth. He was intense, and wild, and fierce all at the same time.

Adding to the surrealness of the scene playing before me were the big chunks of fur drifting slowly to the ground. They seemed out of place amidst the noise and the fighting.

Every time the Furry broke free of Michaels, it headed my direction, enforcing my belief that its only goal was to get to me. But Michaels never let the Furry come within five feet of me before dragging it back into the fight. I briefly wondered if he was playing with the Furry. It would not be unlike a cat to play with its prey.

At one point, I made eye contact with it. I immediately recognized that I'd seen them somewhere before, but I couldn't place them. It was a disconcerting feeling.

My eyes widened in surprise as the Furry suddenly released a high pitched howl and jumped straight up in the air. Before it had a chance to land, Michaels leapt and grasped the Furry's neck between his jaws. The howling ceased immediately.

Michaels landed, as only cats could, and the Furry's body thudded heavily against the ground. Great drops of blood began to spatter on the dirt directly beneath the Furry's neck. Playtime was over.

When the Furry gave a few weak twitches, Michaels gave a quick jerk of his head, and I heard the sound as the Furry's neck snapped. Now clearly dead, the Furry's head lolled to one side, and Michaels let it go.

Unstrapping a canteen from his waist, he poured water in and around his mouth as he cleaned his face. He poured more water over his hands, rinsing them as well.

I couldn't take my eyes off him the entire time. He was just... whoa. In a good way.

The Furry on the ground before him began to shift, and I succeeded in pulling my eyes away from Michaels. The figure of Hollins soon replaced the limp form of the Furry. Hollins was a Furry—used to be a Furry.

It was easy now to understand that he worked for the

Consortium, which definitely explained why he'd made no effort to contain the situation at the Agency. And, why he'd despised my arrival.

The "oh" faded from my lips as I examined the events I had just witnessed. Total body shifting—amazing. This was science fiction come to life. The file had mentioned this but didn't go into detail regarding the actual process or how significant the transformation was. After seeing it firsthand, I didn't think words could have captured the wow factor of the transformation.

My attention shifted back to Michaels as he came slowly to his feet. He was moving very carefully, like he was afraid he'd frighten me away. Watching his approach, I had to say, not likely.

He wasn't any less fierce close up, and now I could clearly see his very sharp teeth. He was still Michaels, but every feature of his face had shifted to varying degrees. I wasn't afraid of him, but it wasn't every day you met a real live Catman.

I'd never seen a hybrid this advanced. Usually they had only one or two features of some other species, and they didn't shift back and forth. He looked like a real live shape shifter. I wondered if he could take the shift further like Hollins and if it would be rude to ask?

"We need to keep moving," he said quietly. "I'll lead, stay on my tail."

I cut my eyes to his backside. No tail. I looked back up to find him glaring at me with the upraised eyebrow. It worked even in cat form.

"What?" I exclaimed. "You could have had a tail. You have the claws, and the teeth—" The one hand I'd managed to pry loose from the tree had taken on a life of its own, jabbing in the general direction of whatever feature I indicated. "—and the ears. Did I mention teeth already?"

The eyebrow slowly descended, and he held out his steady hand to my wildly gesticulating one. I shut my gaping mouth and, careful to avoid the claws, slid my hand into his. Tugging gently, he led me from behind the tree.

"What about Hollins?" I asked, looking back over my shoulder as we moved away.

"Hollins made his choice." His tone left no room for argument. Not like I was going to.

We were soon joined by Pike and Juarez. Pike looked unhurt, but Juarez was sporting a gash across his forehead. It didn't seem to slow him down though.

I was moving pretty well myself. I must have been in shock. I couldn't even feel my knees. As evidenced by the smile that stretched from ear to ear, I felt downright giddy.

Michaels looked back over his shoulder at me and shook his head. But not even he could wipe this smile from my face. I had my very own Catman.

As soon as we passed the part in the trees, we entered a large clearing. Parked at the far side was some sort of SUV slash cargo van vehicle. I closed one eye and cocked my head to the side, but it still looked the same.

I probably shouldn't have done that, because it resulted in me stumbling. Michaels didn't miss a beat. He just scooped me up and continued toward the vehicle.

Pike sprinted ahead of us and opened the door situated in the center of the vehicle. It opened vertically and revealed a set of seats facing each other.

Michaels gently sat me down in what was technically the third row of seats and climbed into the seat opposite me. He unbuckled a first aid kit from the ceiling and began pulling out supplies. His claws didn't seem to hamper him at all.

I watched as he located a pair of scissors and started cutting my pants off right above the knees. Now I was going to have on pin striped knickers with high heeled boots. I snickered at my new get up.

He briefly looked up at me and frowned before returning to his task.

I snickered again at his expression. Maybe the blood loss was making me giddy. Or it could be the concussion. Or possibly the low blood sugar. Breakfast was a long time ago.

Apparently, not long enough. The contents of my stomach rolled at the first glimpse of the damage to my knees. I automatically grasped the armrests and quickly looked up and away. The pain that seared through my hands reminded me of my additional injuries and only added to the waves of nausea now washing over me.

Releasing my hold on the armrests, I closed my eyes and pressed my head into the back of the chair. Small quick breaths were all I could manage.

"Take this," Michaels said, holding an alcohol wipe beneath my nose.

I took it from his hand and pressed it to my nose. It helped keep the nausea at bay, but not so much with the hundred little cuts on my fingers that were burning like fire at the contact with the alcohol.

As the nausea faded, I slowly opened my eyes. "Thanks," I uttered feebly and then closed them again.

He grunted and kept on working.

My boots were the next to go. I heard the clunk of them hitting what was hopefully the floor and not a trashcan.

"Can you save them, Doc?" I pleaded. I didn't know if they were worth saving anymore, but I really liked those boots. We'd been through so much together in such a short time. The tunnel, the shaft, my first ever confrontation with a total shape shifting hybrid. They didn't even hurt my feet. They were the best boots I'd ever owned.

"I don't think I'll have to amputate," he said seriously.

I popped my eyes open again. "I meant the boots," I said as forcibly as I could. He was not performing any kind of amputation on me.

He looked up at me, his wide grin letting me know he'd been teasing.

"Your bedside manner is lousy," I complained, relaxing against the seat.

He leaned slightly forward. With a mischievous gleam in his eyes, he countered, "Considering you are not in a bed and have therefore not been a party to my bedside manner, the veracity of your statement is highly questionable."

Whatever. I was not going to discuss his *prowess* bedside or otherwise. But I couldn't help smiling at his obvious implication. Realizing I was still staring into his eyes, I deliberately shifted my focus to my knees.

It wasn't so bad once most of the blood was gone. But some of the cuts looked deep. Was that my kneecap? My happy feeling suddenly fled, leaving me queasy once more. I looked away quickly, focusing anywhere but my knees.

The vehicle looked state of the art, equipped like something out of a spy movie. At the front of the vehicle, I spotted Olivia. She was in the driver's seat but turned around facing me with her attention on Juarez. She winked a hello at me when I caught her eye.

"Not yet," Juarez hollered.

I hadn't heard her ask a question, but I guessed she had. I looked at Juarez seated to my left. The desk surrounding him had multiple screens and keyboards. He must be command central.

"Are we clear yet?" Olivia called back to Juarez.

He tapped a few more keys and yelled, "Just like we planned it."

This was how they planned it? Someone needed a demotion.

"Will do," she said and spun to face the front. "Everyone strap in. We're in for a bumpy ride," she warned.

Great. What use did I have for a smooth, quiet ride that might actually allow me to recover a little? Honestly, why would I want to do that to myself? Recover, only to be thrust into some other untenable situation. My inner rant was terminated by the sudden vibration in my seat as she started the vehicle. This was not going to play well with my already perturbed stomach.

I closed my eyes, but then opened them again as a rhythmic whining started overhead. I watched as the seatbelt automatically descended to within reach. Clumsily, I fidgeted with the clasp until Michaels reached across and fastened it for me.

"Thanks," I whispered, closing my eyes again. My voice sounded weak, even to me.

The constant spinning of the vehicle was not helping either.

Focusing all my energy on my breathing, I tried to draw measured breaths in and out. After a moment, in which at no time did the vehicle stop spinning, I felt compelled to voice my protest.

"Olivia, I would greatly appreciate it, if you would stop driving in circles."

My solemn request was met with her less than sympathetic chuckling. She wouldn't think it was so funny when I hit her with my projectile vomiting.

"Don't worry," said Juarez dismissively. "Olivia's a great driver." He leaned in and lowered his voice. "I should know," he said suggestively, revealing the true nature of their relationship.

"Juarez," growled Olivia from the front.

Juarez lifted his eyebrows momentarily as if caught and then ducked his head, feigning remorse. But his wink indicated he had no such feeling.

I chuckled softly at Olivia's discomfort. Glancing at Michaels, I saw that he was smiling, too.

Feeling the vehicle lurch forward, I opened my eyes but kept them averted from Michaels' workings on my knees. We were in the woods now, and Pike was in the passenger seat next to Olivia. I hadn't seen him get in or noticed when the door was shut. I must have dozed off for a minute.

"Any sign of pursuit?" I asked Juarez.

"They are all around us," he said without concern. At the look of alarm on my face, he explained, "They won't find us in this vehicle."

"Super shielding impenetrable to even the most advanced sensors?" I jokingly asked.

"Something like that," he snorted.

I gasped and looked down again as Michaels set fire to my knees. I thought for sure I'd see him cauterizing my wounds, but he was only cleaning them for real now. That knowledge didn't make them burn any less. I gave him credit for moving quickly from one task to the next without hesitation, but I was deducting points for the burning.

"You've done this before," I said through clenched teeth.

"The medic bit, I mean." I could have been referring to all of the other things we'd just been through. He didn't look like a novice there, either.

"A time or two," he said without looking up. "Some of these will require sutures, but I prefer not to sew while moving."

"I prefer not to be in need of sewing," I retorted.

"You and me both," he agreed.

Hmmm, sweet relief. Whatever kind of gel he was putting on now must have had some numbing medication in it. I sighed audibly as the pain edged off. Looking down, I watched as he held one large gauze pad firmly against my knee and then began securing it with adhesive wrap. The circular motion his hands were making with the wrap were too much for my stomach, and I looked out the front window instead.

Olivia was cutting a path through what was little more than a game trail. Tree branches were roughly slapping the vehicle on all sides as we passed, but no one seemed worried, and I was too tired to worry for them.

"Where are we going?" I asked Michaels.

"Safe House," he answered as he wrapped the other knee. "It will take a while, especially the way we are going. When I finish, you should get some rest."

"Sure," I replied, though I didn't think I would be able to with all the jerking and noise.

"What is your name?" I asked suddenly, causing him to look at me with the frown on his face again. "It's my mission for today," I elaborated. "I know your last name is Michaels. Assuming that is your real name."

"It's Adam."

"Adam Michaels?"

He nodded.

"Mission accomplished." A quick smile played on his lips, and I slowly closed my eyes. "So tell me, Adam Michaels, what you could possibly do to top this first date."

"It's our second, actually," he corrected.

I opened one eye and squinted at him.

"Our first was your detainment roughly two days ago."

Had it been two days already? Seemed more like a month.

"Macy."

Someone was jiggling my chin. It was very annoying.

"Macy."

This time I identified the offender's voice. It was Michaels.

"Macy, open your eyes."

He was so bossy. I figured I had better do what he said before he moved on to something more drastic than jiggling my chin.

I opened my eyes and was greeted by his glowing green ones about an inch from my face. Startled, I jerked backwards, and my head ricocheted off the back of my chair right into his forehead.

"Ow-wa!" I said angrily, making it a two syllable word.

He leaned back slightly while eyeing me sternly, as if this was my fault.

I returned his glare, softly rubbing my forehead with my newly bandaged hands. When did that happen?

"That is not how you wake someone up," I said sharply. I did not need another knot to go with the pair I already had.

"Duly noted," he said in clipped tones.

I tried to continue returning his glare, but my eyes were so heavy, and I closed them again.

"Macy, I need to take your jacket off."

Couldn't he just let me sleep? "Kay," I slurred, leaning forward.

I felt him maneuver the jacket from my shoulders and begin to pull my arms out of the sleeves. That was all I knew until the fire wash was applied to my arms. My eyes flew open, and I felt a rush of nausea.

"I think I'm gonna hurl," I warned him.

He held the bag in front of my face just in time. He also managed to pull my hair out of the way. How I could have anything in my stomach to throw up was amazing to me. I hadn't eaten in a long time. My head hurt too much to do the math.

"All done?" he asked, amusement ringing in his voice.

I held out the barf bag as my response.

Slowly, I leaned back into my chair. The nausea seemed to have dissipated with the emptying of my stomach.

"Why are you always amused at my discomfort?" I asked crankily.

"I am not amused at your discomfort," he said, letting go of my hair, which had long ago abandoned the bun and was now flowing wild and free. "However, the way in which you enact your discomfort makes you a very entertaining creature. I don't think I have had a single dull moment with you." He disposed of the barf bag and sat back down.

"Look who's talking, *Catman*. You're the one who looks like a hero in some paranormal romance novel."

Laughter echoed around the cabin from everyone but him. He simply stared at me with the raised eyebrow and then proceeded with the form of torture he called bandaging my wounds.

A few minutes passed, in which I endured my torture like a good soldier, before he inquired about my status again.

"Are you still dizzy or nauseous?"

"No, just really tired, and there's some serious pounding going on in my head. Do I have a concussion?"

"Probable. More concerning, however, is the blood loss. We were discussing the pros and cons of a blood transfusion."

They were? I missed that discussion. And had I lost that much blood? Blood loss would certainly explain why I was so tired and foggy brained.

"What was the consensus?" I asked.

"Three to one in favor of the transfusion."

I wondered who was against it. "Am I in danger of dying?"

"Possibly. But I am not a medical doctor."

That was what you wanted to hear from the one patching you up.

"What kind of doctor are you then?"

I saw him look over at Juarez who shrugged. "What do you think, Olivia?"

My eyes found Olivia's in the rear view mirror. I was sure she was trying to read my emotions at that very moment.

"She's got to know at some point. I'm not sure there is any time that is more favorable than another. Now might be better, if you consider her lack of energy for arguing."

That was rude, though accurate. I didn't have the strength to argue right now.

"But there is also the possibility that she will not remember any of this, and you'll have to do it again."

That was also accurate, but just as rude. It was also rude that they were discussing me like I wasn't present. Again.

"Look at me," I demanded weakly.

He secured the wrap on the arm he was working on and then lifted his eyes to mine.

Leaning forward, I put as much intensity into my voice as I could muster. "Do not lie to me. If, for whatever reason, you don't want to tell me, then don't. But do not lie to me. I hate lies."

Message delivered, I slumped back in my seat. That little bit of effort exhausted me and elevated the alarm I was feeling at my condition. This kind of tired was not normal.

"For the record, I wasn't considering *lying* to you." His eyes flashed with anger, and his voice conveyed the resentment he felt at my implication. "I was considering the potential risk, given your current condition, of telling you now."

Why would my condition even be a factor, unless this was going to be some kind of shock to my system? I, for one, had digested my fill of shock for the day. That reminded me, I still needed to talk to him about what I'd learned from the file and my suspicions.

"Listen," I sighed, "is this going to be some kind of big revelation something?"

He fastened the wrap on what I hoped was the final bandage of the day. "You could say that."

"Then let me make this easy for you. Not that I am opposed to world altering revelations, but it is becoming more and more difficult to focus, and I need to talk to you about the Agency before I pass out again."

He surveyed his work, methodically looking me over, then met my eyes. "Alright," he sharply nodded. "We'll wait until you are more stabilized."

He started gathering the used medical supplies into a plastic bag and, somewhat distractedly, prompted me to continue. "What did you need to talk to me about regarding the Agency?"

"The impending world hybridization."

He remained silent, his attention focused on the trash bag he was securing.

"There's a very simple fix."

This time he did pause, looking up and piercing me with his green eyes. They were kind of mesmerizing, actually.

"Which is?" he asked with upraised eyebrows.

Oh, right. I hadn't answered yet.

I noticed the constant tapping coming from Juarez's side of the vehicle had ceased and that my knees were hurting again. Well, actually, only one of them. I opened my eyes to find he had ahold of my left ankle, jiggling my leg. Dang it, I must have drifted off again.

"Macy, what's the solution?" He asked, his voice insistent.

I had better get this out fast before I nodded off again. "Reprogram the nanobots with a kill switch. Such as when they come into contact with a certain chemical, or temperature, radio frequency, whatever. You get the picture?" I asked hopefully.

"Killing the nanobots will halt the progression," he rightly concluded.

"Correct," I mumbled groggily, then added, "If you really want to get fancy, you could reprogram the nanobots for complete reversal and then terminate them."

Michaels nodded at Juarez who began tapping furiously on the keys.

"Can I sleep now?"

"One more thing." He leaned forward and placed one hand on each of my thighs. "We need to talk about the possibility of a blood transfusion. If it becomes necessary for you to have one, I will see to it that it happens."

I didn't follow the concern in his expression. Blood transfusions happened all the time. It wasn't like it was open heart surgery.

"Why are you telling me this?"

"Because there could be side effects," he said stiffly.

Side effects? Because of blood? Then it clicked. No, because the nanobots were in the blood. "You mean hybrid side effects?"

"Yes, and there is no going back."

I looked into his face with his bright green eyes, pointed ears, and sharp canines. Would being a hybrid be so bad? Being a hybrid surely was better than dead, especially if I could change at will. But, then I noted that he hadn't changed back.

"Why haven't you changed back?" I asked.

"It takes a large amount of energy for the transformation, and I don't know when I'll get to refuel or if there will be a need for me to be in this form before we arrive at the safe house."

Refuel? Who talked like that? "By refuel, do you mean eat?"

I could see the consternation on his face as he put together where I was going with this.

"Yes," he replied cautiously.

"But you can change at will?"

"Yes," he said again even more slowly.

"So, you are telling me, that I would get to eat huge quantities of food, which I could burn off by shifting forms?" I was not seeing a downside to this. This sounded like the greatest thing in the world.

"That's one way to look at it," he said reproachfully. "But only you would look at it that way."

I started laughing, softly at first. "I'm in."

He removed his hands from my thighs and straightened in his chair. Crossing both arms over his chest, he frowned at me.

"I am so in," I snorted through my laughter.

CHAPTER 11

SUDDENLY BECAME ALERT, STARTLED AWAKE by loud pinging sounds on my right. It took me a few moments to recall where I was. Groggily, I realized that I had lost consciousness again.

"What's going on?" I croaked. My throat was dry and my voice sounded gravelly. I forcibly cleared my throat and asked again, but no one bothered to answer me. I didn't have the energy to ask again.

My eyes flew open again when another round tapped across the vehicle. I could hear the others having a rapid conversation, but I only caught bits and pieces—something about there was only two of them. I thought Juarez said they weren't supposed to be able to find us.

The next thing I knew, I was stretched out on the floor of the middle isle. Olivia was gazing down at me. "She's so pale," I heard her whisper. "If you are going to do it, now's the time."

I tried to force my eyes to stay open, but they wouldn't obey me. I was so tired. Pale meant blood loss, right? They must be talking about the transfusion again, and he must be hesitant. Otherwise, she wouldn't have to urge him to do it.

I realized someone was holding my hand, and I squeezed as hard as I could. "I prefer alive." It was barely a whisper. I wasn't sure if I'd actually said it out loud, until I felt the breath of his reply against my cheek.

"As do I," he gently uttered.

Somewhere in my brain, I registered the pinch on my arm, and then everything faded to black.

I opened my eyes to find myself still in my previous prone position. Directly in front of me, I could see Olivia back in the driver's seat and Michaels occupying the passenger seat next to her. They were deep in conversation about something.

"Hello, Beautiful."

I turned my head in the direction of the voice. It belonged to Pike who was smiling down at me from what was previously my seat.

"How long was I out?" I asked softly.

"Approximately six hours," Michaels answered as he came and knelt by my side. He brushed the hair off my forehead and gently probed the knots still there. "How are you feeling?"

My stomach picked that moment to growl loudly enough for everyone to hear. "Hungry?" I offered sheepishly.

Michaels smiled as he extended his hand to me. Placing his free hand against my back, he said, "Think you can sit up long enough to eat?"

Did he realize who he was talking to?

I placed my bandaged hand in his, and he helped me to sit up. I was pleasantly surprised by the decrease in pain. Overall, I felt a lot better. I wasn't at a hundred percent. My head still hurt and my body ached all over, but I didn't feel like I was in danger of passing out again. Until I stood up.

"Whoa," I said and grasped Michaels arm. He helped me to my seat without commenting, but the look on his face telegraphed his worry.

"I'm okay," I assured him and looked down at my hands. "Hey, did you change these?" I asked, studying my new wraps.

"While you were firmly out, I took the liberty of patching you up for real."

I looked up as Pike approached. He held out a tray of food to me, but Michaels was the one who took it from his hand. Michaels then speared Pike with a glare until he slowly retreated backwards down the aisle.

As soon as Pike sat down, Olivia cut her eyes angrily to him. She was upset with him, too. I wondered what he had done to upset both of them.

Michaels placed the tray in my lap, and I turned my attention back to him. He had retaken the seat opposite me. After he removed the plastic wrap from the tray, I reached for the sandwich, but he stopped me.

"This first," he said, holding out a newly opened nutrition bar of some kind.

My face contorted in revulsion. I was sure it tasted like cardboard. When I looked at the sternness of his expression and the set of his jaw, I knew that, sadly, there would be no negotiations. Reluctantly, I took the bar from him and sniffed it. It had no discernible smell. That couldn't be good.

"So, how many stitches?" I asked in an attempt to distract myself from the unpleasant task I was about to undertake. Wow, never thought I would define eating in those terms.

"I stopped counting after a hundred," he said casually.

I looked at him sharply. There was no hint of teasing. I shouldn't have been shocked. I already knew it was bad. Nearly dying from blood loss had told me that much. I was sure he hadn't given me the transfusion for the fun of it.

Bringing the bar to my lips, I forced myself to take a bite. I knew when I started chewing that I was right—cardboard. Correction, dry as a desert cardboard. I struggled to swallow the grainy mix.

"Could I have some water with my cardboard?" I asked sarcastically.

I took the bottle from his outstretched hand. He'd been kind enough to open it for me. All this help was sort of making me feel like an invalid. And, what was with the lights? I didn't remember the cabin being so dark.

Lowering the water bottle, I asked, "Why is it so dark in here?"

"If you'll look out the front window, you'll notice we are no longer travelling via terra firma."

I leaned to the side and almost dropped the water bottle. We were under water. "There's fish swimming by us," I exclaimed.

"Nothing gets by you, Greer."

He was clearly mocking my confusion. Granted, it wasn't the cleverest thing I'd ever said.

I swallowed the last bite of the bar and picked up the sandwich. As I ate, I considered this latest development. I was riding in a submersible. No, a SUV that turned into a submersible. Whatever this Organization was, it didn't include a lack of funds. That much was for sure.

"Where are we?" I asked.

"We're in a tributary in North Carolina." He looked down at his watch. "We still have a few hours to go before we reach the safe house."

"That's a long tributary, isn't it?" I questioned.

"It's made longer because we are proceeding at a pace that will not draw the notice of anyone who happens to be watching. The tributary's not all that deep at this time of year," he shrugged. "It's a much slower pace than I would prefer."

As far as I knew, the only ones watching us were the Consortium. "Are you implying there are other bad guys besides the Consortium?" I asked him.

"There is never a shortage of those intent on accomplishing their goals at the expense of others. But currently, I did mean mainly the Consortium."

Mainly? That was a no and a yes in one sentence.

"Is that what all the commotion was about before? When I heard the pinging sounds? They were shooting at us?"

He nodded in response.

"So how come they found us? I thought Juarez said they wouldn't be able to."

He glanced briefly at Juarez and then tilted his head to the side and looked down. The expression on his face indicated he was concentrating on something. No, not concentrating, listening. He was listening for something and not answering the question.

I leaned a little sideways and peered at the front of the cabin where Olivia and Pike were. They were both silent. I looked to Michaels for understanding. He gave a quick shake of his head. O-Kay, didn't know what that was about.

"Are we still being followed?" I ventured carefully.

"Not currently," he said, studying Juarez who was now facing us. "But they are always searching."

"Michaels can you come here a minute?" Olivia called.

He unbelted his seatbelt and made his way to the front where whispering ensued between the three of them.

Juarez leaned forward over his desk and spoke to me in a tight whisper. "We did have two Furries that managed to track us after we'd entered the SubV, but I took care of them."

"By yourself?"

"Just me, myself and I," he said humbly.

I couldn't help but smile. I liked Juarez. He had one of those personalities that made a person feel totally at ease, like I'd known him all my life instead of only a few days.

"That's quite impressive," I said. I knew that Michaels had been with me a lot, and I figured that Olivia hadn't participated in the fighting. "Where was Pike during the fight?" I asked.

"In the wrong place at the wrong time," he said sourly.

Inwardly, I sighed. I knew there was more to the story, but my life was filled with enough drama as it was. I didn't need or want anymore. Ignoring my natural instinct to get to the bottom of things, I asked about something else he'd said. "What does SubV stand for?"

He immediately flashed me a grin. "Short for a submersible that is also a SUV. SubV," he said proudly.

"Did you have something to do with its creation?"

His eyes seemed to glaze over as he lovingly stroked the desk carousel that surrounded him. "This area is all mine," he purred.

Men and their toys. I wasn't sure my eye roll could have been any bigger, but he was too busy loving his desk to catch it. I could understand his affection a little, given my love for my truck. But he was talking about a computer, not a motorized vehicle.

Computers were not high on my list of things to praise. They ranked somewhere below green peas and grout cleaner. Both were beneficial to humans and maybe even necessary, but definitely not worth a love fest.

I couldn't keep my lip from curling as I watched his prolonged display. I must be seriously missing something about computers, and I really had no interest in finding out what that was. Switching gears before I vomited again, I turned to the one last thing that bore commenting.

"North Carolina's awfully close to Tennessee." At Juarez's blank look, I explained why that was significant. "The location of Mr. Randall's report."

His hands stilled on the keyboard. "That it is," he agreed but provided no further explanation, which upped my curiosity even further.

Had Mr. Randall actually captured the real thing, and if so, what would that mean for all of us? Also, there was the curious fact that he did not answer the question of why they had been able to find us. Of everyone on the SubV, I thought he was in the best position to answer that. He was also in the best position to provide that information to the Consortium as well.

Michaels returned and resumed his seat before I could form any coherent conclusions, and then I was distracted by the emotions playing across his face. He was obviously conflicted about something. Did I really want to know?

I plopped the last piece of fruit in my mouth and chewed it slowly. "What is it?" I finally asked

"Olivia thinks she's found a shortcut."

That didn't sound too bad. But he didn't look happy about it. "You don't think so?" I asked.

He fidgeted a moment before answering. "It is a shortcut."

Then what was the problem, and why couldn't he meet my eyes? "But?" I supplied.

"There are variables to consider."

Were we back to the vague answers that really answered nothing? I raised my eyebrows at him, and he sighed.

"If we continue on the current path, there are known obstacles.

The shortcut has not been reviewed recently and, therefore, may hold unknown obstacles. It was only ever intended to be used as a last resort, and the path is a good deal more dangerous to traverse."

He sighed heavily and lifted his eyes to mine. "The last time I sent you down a path not meant for you, it didn't turn out so well."

Oh, he was feeling guilty over what had happened to me. I couldn't tell him it wasn't his fault. It kind of sort of was. But not entirely. The Consortium had played a part in it as well.

"This is not entirely your fault," I told him.

"That makes me feel so much better," he said dryly.

I could tell. So, moving on... "We are in a river, right? What's so dangerous about travelling the river?"

"You'd be surprised," he grumbled. "In any case, it will be decided for us when we reach the first obstacle."

I was surprised by the yawn that engulfed me. I quickly brought my hands up to cover it. Only babies looked cute when they yawned.

"Sorry, I guess I'm still tired."

He unfolded a blanket he retrieved from a pouch under his chair and laid it across my lap. I pulled it up over my shoulders, and he began tucking it in on the sides. His actions brought his head really close to my face. I could clearly see that his neck still bore traces of dried blood and black smudges. The smudges were probably from where I had held onto him.

Without thinking, I licked my thumb and rubbed at the smudges on his neck. When he froze at my touch, so did I. Ever so slowly, I moved my hand back under the safety of the blanket.

"Sorry," I whispered.

"Nothing to be sorry for," he answered just as quietly.

His gaze bore no resentment at my incredible breach of etiquette. We sat there, studying each other for a few moments, and then he pulled away.

"Get some rest," he said encouragingly.

That was a change from his usual "Get moving" mantra. He

truly was taking good care of me. Too good. Like he was trying to repay me for the blood transfusion. I'd have to really talk to him about it eventually, but not right now and not with an audience.

"I'll wake you when we get there," he said.

Roger that, I thought, closing my eyes. Macy over and out.

At some level, I should have been alarmed that I was dangling upside down, held in place only by my seat belt, and my field of view wreathed by my crazy hair. But such was the state of my life that I was not surprised.

"Aw, come on," I moaned loudly. "I have got to stop waking up like this. I prefer a gentle nudge…"

Michaels' face suddenly appeared beneath mine. "Change of plans. We're leaving now."

My hair prevented me from seeing anyone past Michaels, but I could hear a lot of movement. With the fog of sleep still presiding, I resumed my prior protest a bit more loudly.

"A tender brushing of hair from my face…"

His hands reached up toward me. "I'm undoing your seatbelt," he said gruffly. "Get ready."

The familiar sound of metal sliding against metal preceded my stomach's collision with his shoulder. I gasped at the impact. Contrary to his advice, I wasn't ready.

He set me on my feet, and I took in the scene around me as I hugged my stomach. The others were scrambling around gathering up supplies and pulling on scuba gear.

A bolt of fear lodged in my stomach. I didn't scuba.

I slowly straightened up, gradually taking deeper breaths as I recovered. "I'd even take a soft calling of my name or perhaps a little ear nibbling," I said hesitantly. I knew I was just delaying the inevitable, but I couldn't stop myself. I seemed to have developed an annoying habit for rambling when I was nervous.

Michaels, who had grabbed an oxygen tank and was unceremoniously strapping me in, paused at the nibbling bit long enough to meet my eyes. "Ear nibbling?" he questioned.

Despite the skepticism in his voice, I was thankful he was playing along. It was all the opening I needed.

"Do you know how I've been awakened the last half dozen times? I don't know what's worse. The latest free fall position or the fire wash. Reveille wasn't very nice either, but then maybe the field goal should take first place? Disorientation isn't a favorite of mine either."

He clicked the last buckle into place, pulled the strap tight and then looked at me in confusion. "Field Goal?"

"Never mind," I sighed heavily. "It's just one of the many joyful experiences I've had since I met you."

His expression darkened at my comment, and I stammered a little, trying to explain that I wasn't accusing him. "I didn't mean…It's not your fault that…" I stopped abruptly, snapping my jaw shut. That wasn't true, it pretty much was his fault. "What I mean is—"

He placed his fingers on my lips to silence me. He effectively shushed me. Seriously?

"Have you used one of these before?" He held up a scuba mask.

I had a hard time focusing on his question because I was fighting the urge to bite his fingers off. I didn't, but the frown imprinted on my face should have been warning enough for anyone. Anyone but him. His frown mirrored my own, but I refused to respond until he removed his hand.

It seemed like he was moving in slow motion as his fingers left my mouth. I knew he wasn't, but he was, and then everything sped up. Confusion supplanted my anger. What just happened?

I looked around the cabin and then looked back at him. He was still standing there holding the mask and waiting for my response, like nothing abnormal had happened.

"No." It came out weaker than I meant it to. "No," I said more firmly. "What happened? Why are we upside down?"

"We flipped it on purpose. From an aerial view, the bottom looks just like any normal rock formation."

"Why can't we just swim?"

"We are not swimming because I want to remain concealed. I won't risk exposing you again."

Won't risk exposing me? What the heck had he been doing over the last few days? I was exposed to all kinds of things.

He recaptured my attention when he snapped very loudly two inches from my nose. I let my anger show on my face, but it dissipated when I regarded the sincerity in his.

"Macy, listen to me. I'll walk you through it, and I'll be right beside you. We are not going very deep. You just have to do what I say."

I looked around. Everyone else was ready and waiting on me. Not trusting myself to not say something I would regret, I nodded.

Olivia came forward and helped me into some diving pants and water shoes. She followed with some type of gloves that stretched all the way to my shoulders. This tight fitting stuff didn't feel too good on the stitches.

"Sorry for the discomfort, but it will protect you from bacteria in the river," she explained. Stepping back, she reviewed her work then gave me a thumbs up.

I couldn't say that I concurred with her assessment. I felt like I had been stuffed into a straw that was too small.

As soon as she cleared out, Michaels began instructing me in the art of scuba diving. When he finished his instruction, he placed the mask on my face and briskly adjusted various things on my vest.

According to what he said, it didn't seem that hard. I essentially only had to remember two things, breathe through my mouth and stay with him. I could do that.

Michaels had just finished pulling on his own gear when the back of the SubV began opening. The others braced themselves as the water started rushing in, and I followed suit. It was an eerie feeling, standing there as the water flowed over my head.

I did have a moment of panic before I remembered to breathe through my mouth. Michaels tapped my mouthpiece as a reminder. Oops, almost forgot point number one.

The others made their way to the back of the vehicle, and Michaels took my hand as we got in line behind them. Pike left first followed by Olivia. Then Juarez took off, leaving only us staring out at the underside of the river.

We walked forward to the very edge of the SubV. I looked at Michaels, and he gently squeezed my hand in encouragement.

Well, here I went again, about to do one more thing I didn't want to do, adding yet another skill to my resume of extreme talents. River scuba had to be right up there with shower wrestling and shaft surfing. Boy, I was living the good life.

I nodded to signal my readiness, and we surged forward as he pulled us from the vehicle.

It wasn't half bad. Visibility at times was really poor, but I made sure to keep Michaels in sight or touch at all times. Besides us, there were a lot of fish and turtles in the river, but I didn't see any fearsome creatures. After Michaels' comment about "obstacles" and with the week I was having, I was concerned I'd have to fight river monsters or something else just as impossible.

Michaels hooked his elbow through mine and started pulling us straight down. As our destination began to come into focus, I groaned inwardly. Again with the tunnels?

Our underwater swim had led us to what looked like a flooded mine shaft. I could just barely make out the wooden frame outlining the entrance.

The others were nowhere in sight, so I assumed they had already entered. I held on to one side of the entryway until I felt Michaels' hand on my back, propelling me forward. Not like I could stay where I was anyway.

The daylight gradually faded as we made our way deeper into the mineshaft. I reclaimed Michaels' hand before it became totally dark. No way was I getting separated from him in here.

A short distance ahead of us, little lights started flickering. Hopefully, that was the rest of the crew. To my right, Michaels suddenly lit up, and I stopped swimming as he reached over and turned the light on for me. Didn't even know I had a light.

As usual, they had no need to worry that I would reveal the route to their secret location. I couldn't find it again if my life depended on it.

We surfaced inside a well-lit cavern that was dominated by a large wooden pier. There was a long ladder leading from the water to the pier. This seemed to be a new pattern emerging in my life. Shafts and ladders. Two of my new least favorite things.

Juarez and Olivia were already on the pier, pulling off their scuba gear. Pike was a few feet ahead of me and Michaels.

Pike pulled the regulator out of his mouth and asked, "Do you need me to help with getting her out?"

He meant me? Why would I need help getting out?

"Your help is not required," Michaels answered while looking at me.

Why were they always talking about me like I wasn't present? "Hey! I'm right here," I said angrily. "And, I know how to climb a ladder. Had quite a bit of experience with it just recently, actually," I said with a pointed look at Michaels.

Pike reached the ladder and smoothly scaled it to the pier. See, piece of cake. "Don't say I didn't warn you," he called over his shoulder.

I looked back at Michaels. "Ladies first," he challenged.

Fine. I didn't know what they thought was so hard about climbing a ladder. Olivia and Juarez didn't seem concerned about me climbing the ladder.

Michaels cleared his throat, and I made a face at him before I swam the last few feet to the ladder. Putting my feet on the closest rung, I gingerly gripped the sides with my hands. I started to haul myself out of the water, but I stopped when I realized I wasn't moving. This clearly wasn't my fault, since I reckoned I'd gained a million pounds during the swim. What the heck?

"Michaels. What was in that nutrition bar you fed me?" I asked, confused by my sudden weight gain. I stopped trying to move up the ladder and just hugged it, trying to keep from falling off. "Why do I feel so heavy?"

Pike leaned over the side of the pier and grinned at me. "Told you, Beautiful."

Michaels made his way over and stationed himself at my back. "Part of it is due to the equipment," he said as he slid my vest off and tossed it to Juarez, who'd come to watch the show. "Some of it is the fact that you just swam for two hours."

Two hours? I didn't think it was that long.

He pulled the mask from my face and smoothed my hair to hang down my back. "There's also the fact that you are recovering from your injuries and the blood loss," he said. "And lastly, there is a lot going on in that body of yours right now besides all of the above."

I assumed the last comment was referring to the transfusion that for some reason he couldn't mention by name. I didn't understand why he was feeling so guilty about it. The transfusion had saved my life. But again, this wasn't the time or place to have that discussion.

Having been freed from my vest and mask, I tried again to pull myself to the next rung of the ladder. I started to look back over my shoulder to see if Michaels was secretly hanging on to me, but stopped when I saw both his hands firmly gripping the ladder under mine. It was me. I really didn't have the strength to pull myself out. No sense in pretending I did.

"Pike," I yelled, "get over here and help a girl out."

"On it," he said eagerly.

I watched as he charged face first down the ladder and draped himself upside down with his arms extended toward me. It was incredible to watch. Would I be able to do stuff like that?

"That's really a beautiful pose you got there," I said, looking up into his still grinning face.

"Aw, we both know there's only one thing beautiful on this ladder," he teased.

Michaels growled loud enough behind me to cause my chest to vibrate.

"You guys can argue about my beauty later," I told them. "Right now, heave man, heave." The last heave was said with my arms reaching toward Pike.

Careful to grab me above the elbows, he pulled, and I managed to clear one rung of the ladder. But it wasn't easy. I couldn't get my legs, which felt like spaghetti, to work correctly.

After I had clumsily made several more steps, Michaels picked me up, set me on his left shoulder and started to climb. This forced Pike to make a swift retreat, for which, he waggled his eyebrows at me.

I wasn't sure what was going on with Pike and Michaels or what Michaels thought was going on between me and him, but right now, I didn't belong to anyone. I'd have to make Michaels aware of that, if he didn't stop with the possessive display.

We reached the top of the ladder, and Pike steadied me as I slid from Michaels' shoulder. At eye level with Pike's chest, I got a look at his shirt. In bold black letters it read, *I'm a lover and a fighter*. Pike lifted his eyebrows in invitation, and I shook my head and chuckled.

Behind us, Michaels' growl was unmistakable as he stepped onto the pier. Pike threw his hands up and backed off in an obvious show of surrender. I wanted to elbow Michaels and tell him to knock it off, but that would have been supposing he'd actually listen to me.

Olivia quickly appeared at my side and began helping to divest me of my various scuba clothing. As she pulled them off, she handed them to Juarez, and he stowed them in a large plastic bin. The last piece came off, and I was back in the heavily stained camisole, cut off pin striped pants and bare feet. I just needed a sash, an eye patch and a parrot, and I'd be a full-fledged pirate.

Olivia hooked her elbow through mine. "Think you can walk?" she asked. The urgency in her voice left no doubt she was trying to fend off a confrontation between Pike and Michaels.

Oh yeah, I thought. I'd been carried enough lately. Time to stand on my own two feet. "Certainly," I replied with more enthusiasm than I felt. "Is it far?"

"Not too far," she answered.

The smile quickly left my face. She'd said something similar to me once before, so I wasn't sure I could trust her with distances.

When I didn't move, she elaborated, "It's just a lot of stairs really."

Stairs. It was more climbing. But what was I thinking, of course it was.

"Who doesn't love stairs?" I replied dolefully.

"Exactly," she played along. "They lead you up," she started.

"They lead you down," I finished.

"Will you two shut up and start climbing," Michaels snapped from behind us. He didn't even have the good sense to look ashamed when he was on the receiving end of our double glares. He just stepped around us and took the stairs two at a time.

"What is he so upset about?" I asked as I watched him bound up the stairs.

Olivia and Juarez exchanged a meaningful look, and then he quietly followed Michaels up the stairs. Her only verbal response was her usual throat clearing.

"You should really invest in a large stash of throat lozenges," I told her.

"See you topside, Beautiful," Pike quipped as he too side stepped us and headed up.

"That boy is going to get himself eaten if he doesn't stop," she muttered.

I looked back at Olivia. She was regarding me with disapproval clearly written across her face.

"What?" I demanded. "I do not belong to Michaels."

She looked like she was about to say something, but instead, she just shook her head. "Let's go, Einstein," she said, pulling me toward the stairs.

With the state I knew my knees were in, I honestly didn't know if I was going to make it. We moved slowly, but with Olivia's help, I made it to the top of the stairs. They led us to sort of a mudroom. There was a bench against one wall, and I ambled over and sat down.

Olivia closed and latched the door we'd come through and then keyed in some code that made it look like it had never existed. To be able to produce items capable of such things was another testimony to the financial status of the Organization.

"You really shouldn't tease Michaels," she said quietly while still crouched where the hatch had been.

I knew she was referring to my interactions with Pike. But

that would imply that I was trying to make Michaels jealous, and I wasn't.

"I'm not teasing him," I said completely serious.

"Whether you mean to or not, the fact remains that you are," she sighed.

She stood up and brushed her hands off. Then she turned her icy glare on me. I felt like I was in the principal's office. For something I didn't do! I held her stare, and my confusion turned to understanding and then frustration.

I was not aiming to stir up trouble on the team. I couldn't control what Michaels did or did not feel. And I certainly didn't want to walk around on egg shells, monitoring my every interaction for something that might set him off. He would have to learn to deal with me for who I was. Just like I was learning to deal with him and his issues.

Uugh, busted by my own logic. Ignoring who he was did not equal learning to deal with him. It was the exact opposite.

"I'll try, Olivia." I meant it. I would try to understand what he was feeling toward me, but that didn't mean that I echoed his feelings.

"That's all I'm asking."

The relief in her voice was annoying. "That doesn't mean that I belong to Michaels," I added sternly.

"Understood," she said without sincerity. Clearly, she did not agree with me.

"And, that doesn't mean I won't say something if I think he's getting out of hand."

"Wouldn't expect anything less."

By the look on her face, one would have thought I'd promised to marry him. I'd only agreed to try and work with him better. That knowing look in her eyes made me suspicious. What did she know that I didn't?

"You ready?" she asked.

"For what?" I asked suspiciously. She was up to something.

"To rejoin the others," she said innocently. "What else could I possibly be referring to?"

That was exactly what I was wondering and what still had me glued to this bench. I had the feeling I'd just signed a contract that I hadn't read. Dad gum fine print.

From my seat on the bench, I could overhear strains of conversation. One overly loud one in particular caught my attention. "Miranda?" I said, looking quickly to Olivia for confirmation. "She's here?"

Olivia nodded and held out her hand, which I gratefully accepted. Seemingly without effort, she pulled me to my feet.

"I know I'm not your best friend," she said, nodding in Miranda's general direction, "but, I hope you do consider me a friend or at least, not an enemy."

I looked into her face, which was so similar to mine. "I think we could have been sisters separated at birth."

Her eyebrows almost touched her bangs. "We do look freakishly alike, don't we?"

We were the same height, too. We spent a few seconds studying each other's faces before the laughter took over.

"Well, you know what they say," I exhaled. "You can never have enough friends."

"Do they? I thought that was money."

I frowned in concentration. "You might be right. In that case, does two count as too many friends?"

She eyed me thoughtfully. "Little low in the friends department?"

"Most require too much time and work. The first, I have little to spare, and the second, I have too much of."

She nodded in understanding. "Fortunately," she sniffed, "I happen to be mostly self-sustaining."

"Is that right?"

"I also believe honesty is always the best policy, life is worth living, and pasta is God's gift to mankind."

It took a moment for me to process the unrelated list. I agreed with the first two, and it was true that I rarely met a pasta I didn't like.

"This might work," I told her.

"Friends it is?" she asked.

"Friends it is," I repeated.

That was two deals I'd struck with her in a matter of minutes. Dang, she was good.

CHAPTER 12

W E LEFT THE MUDROOM AND entered a short hallway that opened into a large great room. The first thing that hit me was the smell. I closed my eyes, inhaling deeply in appreciation. Someone had been cooking. God, I hoped there was some for me.

"Macy!"

I opened my eyes to see Miranda rapidly crossing the room. She engulfed me in a bear hug that made me wince in pain.

"Sorry, sorry. They said you were injured." She stepped back, locking me in place with her hands on my shoulders. She gave me a quick once over, then she screwed her face up and asked, "What the heck are you wearing? You look like a shipwrecked pirate."

I laughed. "And you smell like garlic." I sniffed again. "And oregano."

She sniffed me in return and drew back in disgust. "I have to tell you, sister, that's a whole lot better than what you smell like."

I imagined it was. You could have put my picture in the dictionary next to the definition of filthy, along with a warning not to inhale when in the presence of.

"Come on then, let's get you something to eat." She pulled me into a sideways hug as she ushered me into the room. "You can't be all that hurt if you are focused on food," she said happily, and then muttered, "Let's hope your funk doesn't ruin everyone's appetite."

I wasn't about to argue. I just let her lead me to dinner. She knew better than anyone I could eat while at death's very door. Tonight, even "my funk" would not deter me. And, if the other's couldn't eat, well, that would be more for me.

As she led me to the table, I caught Michaels' gaze following me. My stomach did a little flip when I saw the brief flare of pain in his eyes. He quickly turned his attention elsewhere, in what I thought was an effort to shield himself from me. That made me feel even worse.

It wasn't my intention to hurt him. I wasn't trying to provoke him or stir up his alpha male whatever. Nonetheless, I felt like I needed to apologize, but for the life of me, I couldn't think of what to say that didn't sound insulting.

Miranda led me to the table, and I noticed the others were spread throughout the room, involved in easy conversations. They were all talking and laughing like old friends. It was a nice feeling. Hadn't had too many of those lately.

The meal tonight was lasagna. I took a seat and offered her a grateful smile when she served me a very large piece. After she'd plated the lasagna for everyone, she sat beside me. Cedars took the seat next to her. The others filtered in and filled the opposite side of the table. An obviously reluctant Michaels took the vacant seat next to me.

Uugh, I hated all this drama and tension. In a fit of spontaneity, I reached for Michaels' hand under the table and laced my finger through his. I didn't know what I was saying in hybrid lingo, but I was trying to convey my sorrow at offending him. I kept a tight hold on his hand until his fingers wrapped around mine. I hoped that meant he accepted my apology.

"Well," Miranda said when no one picked up a fork, "do you need a formal invitation?"

Obeying her directive to dig in, I let go of Michaels' hand and replaced it with a fork. The next fifteen minutes were filled with silence as everyone ate.

After my third helping, I leaned back in my chair and rubbed my stomach. "You outdid yourself this time, Miranda."

"There's more," she said with a gleam in her eye.

There was only one thing we ever had after lasagna—cheesecake.

Using my last piece of garlic bread to mop up the sauce from the lasagna, I absently queried, "Would the more entail cream cheese and sugar?"

She rolled her eyes, but she was clearly enjoying this. "Among other things."

I was going to have to work for it then. "Nuts?"

"Possibly."

"Chocolate chips?"

Her smile widened.

"Caramel?"

She got up from the table and reappeared with a chocolate turtle cheesecake. Wow. It was my absolute favorite. It brought me to tears.

She sat the cheesecake on the table and wrapped one arm around my shoulder. "You okay?"

I pretended not to notice the quiver in her voice. We didn't like crying. Not alone and definitely not in front of a crowd. I took a deep breath, determined to hold back the tears. It had to be a release of tension. I wasn't seriously crying over a cheesecake.

I snuck a look at Michaels. He was frowning at me again, which, of course, made me laugh. "I'm fine. It's just been an interesting couple of days. I'll tell you about it sometime."

"You'd better. And, I'll tell you all about mine."

I glanced at Cedars. I'd swear he was blushing. "No thanks. I think I'll skip that debriefing. Update," I quickly corrected. "I meant update."

Everyone responded with laughter except for Michaels. He opted for a quiet smirk.

Miranda got up to clear away the dishes, and Cedars trailed her to the kitchen like a lovesick puppy. The others had already cleared out, so that left only me and Michaels still at the table. When I glanced at him again, he was back to his frowning. Okay, enough with the Mr. Grumpy Pants.

I leaned in, hitting his shoulder with my chin. "Would now be a good time for your world altering revelation?"

He seemed unprepared for the question. The room also quieted considerably. I guessed they were all invested in this conversation. He scooted his chair back and sort of angled it toward me, but he seemed unsure how to start.

"You inferred that you were some other kind of doctor besides medical. Why don't you start there."

He nodded. "I am a Doctor of Genetic Manipulation. But currently, I am the Operations Director for the Organization."

I really was not expecting that response. Was he joking? He must be joking.

"There is not a school in the world that offers a doctorate in that. Try again," I ordered.

His tone was matter of fact when he said, "There is actually. Olivia's the acting Director."

I looked at Olivia as she moved to stand behind him.

"He's telling the truth, Macy. There really is a school dedicated solely to research and development in the field of genetics. There's a whole other sphere of knowledge pertaining to genetics and hybrids that the rest of the world doesn't know about. We teach it at the school. That knowledge is what created us."

Her voice had been soft when she'd spoken, almost imploring me to believe. She'd said it with a straight face, too. Were they all in on the prank? I couldn't help staring at them. What were they expecting me to say?

Miranda, who had made a swift exit when the conversation began, returned to stand on the other side of the table from me. Guilt was etched in every feature of her face. I had a feeling she was about to confess.

"I've been to the school, Macy."

Well, I had been meaning to address her lapse in judgment when she failed to tell me about her prior association with Michaels, but this went well beyond that. Just when exactly had she found the time to go visit a make believe school without my notice. I was sure my eyes reflected the doubt I had.

"My whole absence wasn't spent between the sheets," she said defensively.

Uugh, not why I was upset.

"I've looked over their curriculum," she continued. "It looks like a pretty good program, if you ignore the illegality of it."

"You managed to travel to this school and review the

curriculum all the while entertaining Mr. Cedars?" I knew it was petty and not the best setting to have this discussion, but she had deceived me. And, she started it.

Knowing how I felt about lying, she exchanged the defensive tone for one of pleading. "I was in Houston when you called. I only visited the school a day and a half. That was plenty of time to tour the campus and look over the curriculum." She was fidgeting with her shirt, but grabbed the chair in front of her when she realized it.

I fixed my gaze on Michaels. "And you had no contact with Michaels prior to then?" If she lied to me now, we were through.

"Well," she said, her voice uncertain.

I thought so.

"He did contact me, only to introduce himself, when we were camped out in the woods."

I swung my head to face her.

"It was the second day, and I was bored out of my mind," she said hurriedly. "He at least provided someone to talk to. You were all serious with your radio silence." She put air quotes around radio silence. The fact that she was now mocking me didn't help the situation.

"And, the reason you didn't tell me any of this?"

She pulled the chair out and sat down. "Honestly?"

"I'd say it's about time."

She frowned at me and then looked apologetically at Michaels. "I didn't believe him."

Michaels looked up to the ceiling and shook his head.

"The whole idea was really out there. I thought he was just a whacko and there'd be no need to tell you anything. When you did finally rescue me from exile, I'd already forgotten about it, and I had the added distraction of your grossness."

"He didn't tell you not to speak with me?"

"No."

"Did you know they were going to kidnap—"

"Detain," Olivia interrupted.

"Kid-Nap us?" I finished, eyeballing her.

"No. I didn't know what Michaels looked like then. The only contact I'd had with him had been over the phone."

"You used your phone during the stake out!"

"I was weak. I admit it!" she yelled, standing up.

I stood up too. "You told Michaels that I smelled bad!"

"He called to follow up with me. And, what I actually told him was that you could melt the petals off a flower from twenty feet away!"

This was ridiculous. It must be true. Miranda wouldn't prank me. We hated practical jokes. There was nothing practical about them. They were just mean.

I felt like I had just fallen off the planet into another universe. One where I was the least smartest person in the room. Except for Miranda. She was currently nowhere near my list of smart people.

Scanning the room, I noticed all their faces were still set, like there was more yet to come. I yanked my chair back under me and focused on Michaels.

"What else?" I demanded.

"The school is also the source of talent for the Organization."

I crossed my arms and sat back. "What exactly does this Organization do?"

"Whatever is necessary to protect the country."

"Such as stop the Consortium and its plans?" I snorted my derision. "Doesn't seem to be working out in your favor, does it?"

One look at his face told me he was not happy with my comment or my attitude. I couldn't say that I particularly cared at the moment.

"And just who decides what is designated as a threat to the country?"

"That would be the board overseeing the Organization."

"And where does the board get their information?"

Clearing his throat, Juarez stepped closer to the table. "Courtesy of moi. The Organization has...*access*," he said with a tilt of his head, indicating his use of invasive gathering methods, "to every agency, bureau, and entity within the United States

Government and beyond. Basically, my team gathers information from wherever we need to. In addition, I have created various computer programs that filter the information for us."

How convenient and scary to think of the things he must know about. I guessed nothing could remain hidden from him. Nothing included in a database, anyway, which was just about everything these days.

"Does the government know of your existence?" I asked.

Michaels answered this time. "The President and select security advisors. A few in Congress know, and every branch of the military has a representative that works directly with us to provide aid in whatever form we deem necessary."

The United States Government was complicit in deceiving the American public at a much greater depth than I had suspected. It not only was fostering illegal research of hybrids, but it employed the use of that research to what...backhandedly control the world? In short, I had left reality and entered the land of freaking comics.

"So," I began, huffing loudly, "you and your little supped up friends go around saving the world from evil villains, who are about to enact their dastardly plans on the earth. Like some science fiction movie. Is that it?"

Michaels' glare was glacial, and I met it with one of my own. Belatedly, I realized I'd just insulted everyone in the room, but come on. What they were asking me to believe belonged in fairy tales and sci-fi novels.

Placing both my elbows on the table, I leaned forward and clasped my hands tightly together. "One more thing, what does any of this have to do with me?"

Michaels' anger was almost palpable as he continued to glare at me. When he didn't respond, I raised my eyebrows at him in challenge. I wanted so badly to say, cat got your tongue, but that would just be throwing more fuel on the fire. He already looked like he might explode at any moment.

Olivia, ever in her role as mediator, stepped in to fill the tense silence. "We have been observing you for some time."

I dismissed her with a wave of my hand. "Yeah, I got that already."

Not dissuaded, she continued. "We have never come across someone like you."

"I find that hard to believe," I snapped angrily, turning my glare on her. "Apparently, I'm not even an expert in my field. I bet any kid at your school could outperform me."

"It's not a matter of performance," Michaels said. Though still clearly angry, he had regained some measure of control and rejoined the conversation. "The way your brain works lets you see things the first time that others do not."

I'd heard some similar sort of nonsense from Director Garrison already. I was about to say as much when he cut me off.

"Let me finish before you open your mouth again," he snapped.

Goose bumps raced down my arms as anger flushed through me. "Do not speak to me that way." It came out as a very quiet snarl, but the menace behind it was scary, even to me.

He took in my posture and the look on my face, and something akin to resignation flashed in his eyes. He tilted his head in acknowledgment of his mistake. That simple gesture had the need to pummel him easing off.

More reservedly, he continued. "If I put a thousand different scenarios in front of you, you would pick the solution every time, the first time. For whatever reason, your brain is wired to find the right solution."

Really? Cause I was trying real hard to find a way out of this loony bin.

"You do have an annoying knack for always being right," Miranda said flatly. When I shot her a look, she threw her hands up and backed away. "Just saying," she murmured.

"What about the Consortium? I couldn't figure out who was shooting at me or why." There, that should put a whole in their theory.

But immediately, Olivia piped up with, "Because your frame of reference was incomplete."

"When supplied with the knowledge necessary to solve the problem, you always do," Michaels concluded.

I began furiously scrolling through my past. Was I always right? I didn't know. It wasn't like I kept a record. But even if what they were saying was true, they still hadn't answered the central question.

"Once again, what does this have to do with me?"

Michaels exchanged a look with Olivia and then answered. "We want you to attend the school and join the Organization."

"You're recruiting me!" I yelled in disbelief. I found myself gripping the table hard in an effort to control my rising anger.

"You would be an invaluable asset," Olivia said, affirming Michaels' offer.

The audacity of these people was unbelievable!

"Aw, hell no." The words were out of my mouth before I ever had a chance to consider what I was saying.

Michaels shoved himself back from the table, a deep growl rumbling in his chest. His march to the back door caused the whole house to shake with his fury. Punching the door open, he pounded down the stairs. Utter silence filled the house after his departure. The slamming of the door as it rebounded seemed like an exclamation point on the whole event.

"Macy!" yelled Miranda.

Everyone flinched at the unexpected interruption of the silence. I knew she was shocked by my use of profanity, but there was only so much crap a girl could take, and I was well over my limit.

"Miranda!" I yelled back mockingly. "Have you any idea what I have been through these last few days? It all started with them." I pointed in Olivia's direction. "And now they want me to be one of them? I have been kidnapped." I glared at Olivia, daring her to correct me. "Hunted, and shoved into tunnels, where I have been forced to crawl over broken glass—"

"Macy." Miranda was calm this time. It should have been a clue.

"I've survived stitches, explosions and concussions. Two

knots. Look at 'em!" I stood up and lifted the hair out of my face, displaying my knots.

"Macy." It was Olivia trying to calm me this time.

"No!" I yelled at her. "I survived severe blood loss by transfusion from a hybrid. A hybrid, Miranda. I was close enough to death to choose that option."

"Macy! Look at your hands!" Miranda shouted at me.

Perhaps it was her no nonsense tone that got through to me. I stopped my litany and looked down at my hands. They were splayed on the table. Each fingernail had been replaced by a claw, which due to the force of my grip, had embedded into the wood of the table. I pried them loose and stared at them in surprise.

"Your eyes, too," she commanded.

I looked at her, and she pointed toward a mirror on the wall. I walked over and saw the same eyes that Michaels had, but mine were blue. I also noticed the tips of pointed ears sticking up from the mess that was my hair.

"MK's in the house," trilled Juarez in the background.

I found his reflection in the mirror quick enough to see Olivia punch him in the arm. "Really," she hissed at him.

"What? It stands for Macy Kat, with a K," he innocently protested. "Because she's so Kooool. You know, with a K."

His attempt at levity did not sway her mood. I thought it was kind of funny. If you ignored the trauma I was currently enduring because I'd turned into a she cat or she kat.

Miranda's image joined mine in the mirror. "I got fangs, did you?" She smiled real big, revealing her very sharp incisors.

I ran my tongue across my teeth, then pulled my lips back, revealing my newly sharpened smile. I let the smile fade and met her eyes in the mirror.

"You lied to me," I said softly.

"I didn't lie," she said, holding my eyes. "I just didn't tell you right away. It's like deferred truth."

I narrowed my eyes, considering her argument. Okay, technically she hadn't lied, but deferred truth was a stretch. Creative, though.

I sighed and leaned my head toward her shoulder. "You've already agreed to go, haven't you?"

Her gaze searched out Cedars in the mirror's reflection. She didn't have to answer. I could tell by the look on her face she was in. Done in by a Goon. I huffed again and pulled myself upright.

"It's hard to explain," she began. "I just…it feels more right than anything I've ever done."

"It's only been three days, you know." Bearing in mind that I was currently navigating day one with Michaels, I was highly interested in her outcome. But the look of adoration on Cedar's face made my argument weak at best. And it wasn't like I was an expert on love.

Maybe interested wasn't the right word, I thought while regarding the two of them as they gazed at each other. If I was in for something as sappy as what I was witnessing between those two, words like uneasy, worried, and terrified came to mind as adequate replacements.

"I know," she replied tenderly, still gazing longingly at Cedars.

Yep, definitely worrisome.

I flexed my hands in front of me, examining my new claws. I wasn't going to ditch my best friend because she'd potentially found love. But if there had to be a Goon in the family, I wanted him to come with bonuses.

"Can he cook?" I asked hopefully.

"Like a five star chef," she beamed.

"Well, that's something at least."

My shoulders slumped in defeat. I didn't have many options. Not until I learned to control this shifting thing. Right now, I had no idea how to return to normal. And, I was super hungry again.

"Got any lasagna leftover?"

"I made enough to feed an army." She left off staring at Cedars and returned her attention to me. "That's one of the best things about being a hybrid shifter."

I nodded. "It's the reason I agreed."

She laughed out loud in response to that bit of information.

"Come on," she said, lacing her arm through mine. "Let's find out how much lasagna you can eat."

"And cheesecake," I added.

"And cheesecake," she agreed.

Holding a fork when your fingers were tipped with claws wasn't as hard as you might think. Eating with the new teeth? That was tougher.

The food didn't taste as good the second time around, either. It tasted like there were too many flavors competing with one another. Miranda assured me it was because I was still in hybrid form. I hoped so. What was the use of being able to eat as much as you wanted if you couldn't enjoy it?

I wasn't alone in my second dinner. Everyone else decided to join me. Everyone except Michaels, who was somewhere outside. A fact I was feeling guiltier about with every minute that passed.

It didn't help when Olivia sent her special brand of disapproving looks my way. I figured she thought I'd already broken our contract. I couldn't say she was wrong. Thoughts of working with Michaels never entered my mind during the previous after dinner conversation.

When Cedars got up to talk to Juarez, it left Miranda and me alone at the table.

"Are we okay?" she asked, playing with her fork.

I didn't like what she'd done. Even though I knew she hadn't set me up, it felt that way. As a general rule, I didn't like surprises.

"I really wasn't trying to lie to you or betray you," she said.

Hadn't I said something similar about not trying to hurt or betray Michaels earlier? And there were definitely things I had kept from her. I knew she had no intentions of betraying me. It was only hurt pride at having been the last to know standing in the way of reconciliation.

With concerted effort, I let the feeling of betrayal go.

"I know," I said. Then I brightened at the memory of our tradition. Maybe something good could come out of this. "Where's my I'm sorry gift?"

She reached into her pocket and pulled out a medallion. It was an old medal of honor that had somehow found its way into an antique shop in New Orleans. She'd scavenged it on one of the rare occasions we got to actually venture into the New Orleans antique shops. I'd loved it right away, but since she was the one who had found it, I'd kept that to myself.

She held the medal out to me. "These guys are only telling you what I found out over ten years ago. You're one of a kind, Macy Greer."

I took the medal from her, allowing my fingers to trace the word Valor inscribed across its face.

"You're whole life is the definition of valor," she said, her voice betraying the emotion she felt.

She was one of the few people I'd trusted enough to let know about my childhood. How I'd struggled to overcome poverty, my perilous journey through college, and my rise in the world of science. She also knew about the thousand ugly details associated with each triumph and failure.

I blinked away the tears that had filled my eyes. She must have been planning this for a while.

"I'll accept it for now," I said. "But we both know you deserve it as much as me. When you need it, I'll return it to you."

She nodded with tears freely flowing down her cheeks. She hadn't come from poverty, but she'd had to leave an abusive family and strike out on her own. From there, our stories were similar. Like me, she'd learned the value of crazy bread, a big gulp, and a mean right hook in the fight for survival.

We sat there, shoulder to shoulder, wiping away tears until we'd had enough. Almost simultaneously, we pulled apart.

"Still going to be here in the morning?" Miranda asked.

"Like I have somewhere else to go," I muttered.

She sat there looking at me, waiting for a definite response.

"Yes, I will still be here in the morning," I complied, rolling my eyes.

Satisfied, she hugged me and then sauntered off to bed, intentionally catching Cedars' eye before she made it to the stairs. It took no time at all for Cedars to wrap up his conversation with Juarez and follow her up. During the course of our second dinner, I'd learned that my bedroom was next to theirs. That made my decision to hang out downstairs for a while easy.

As it got later, the others gradually turned in, and Michaels still hadn't returned. I planted myself in front of the picture window next to the back door. These cat eyes were better at night than my normal ones, but my improved vision still couldn't find him anywhere.

"He'll be back."

I turned and acknowledged Olivia's sudden presence. It bothered me a little that I hadn't heard her come down the stairs.

"You should cut him some slack," she said to my back. "Right now, he's a bit…"

When she struggled to find a word, I supplied, "Overbearing? Possessive? Rude?"

"I was going to say protective where you are concerned. The male hybrids, as a whole, are a lot trickier to handle."

"Juarez doesn't seem hard to handle."

"Juarez was not created with alpha DNA, but even he has his moments."

I was in no mood for riddles. "If you have something to say, just say it," I told her.

"It's his blood that flows through your veins now. Try to remember that, Einstein." With that admonition and no explanation as to what she meant, she left me alone.

I was beginning to think her use of Einstein was not a compliment. I watched her climb the stairs to a waiting Juarez, who had come looking for her. There was no mistaking the love on his face as he waited. He claimed her outstretched hand, and they ascended the stairs together.

That was altogether not what I observed in Michaels.

No longer content to watch from the window, I opened the door and took up a post on the porch. Leaning against the column at the top of the stairs, I resigned myself to wait for his return. I didn't think this knot in my stomach would resolve any other way.

Olivia's words kept playing through my head. She had said his blood now flowed through my veins. Was she implying that he felt some sort of responsibility for me now? Or something more than responsibility, like what she and Juarez had? That a simple sharing of blood had irrevocably tied me to Michaels? That was way more than I had bargained for.

The moon rose higher, the wind picked up and the clock marched on without a sign of him. Abandoning my post, I sat on the top step of the stairs and wrapped my arms around my legs. What I was feeling was confusing to me. I couldn't rectify it in any sort of logical way.

It made no sense to me that I should feel abandoned by a man that I had no relationship with. Yet, I couldn't deny that was what I felt. I had a sinking feeling that this was just the beginning of emotions I didn't want to experience. Clearly, they would not fit all neat and tidy into my scientifically geared mind, which meant, somewhere along the way, I was going to have to change. Grow emotionally and all that garbage. That was something else I had not bargained for.

Long before I saw him, his usual fragrance of fire and fruit filled the breeze. Standing in anticipation of his arrival, I watched him gracefully lope across the yard. He came to stand at the bottom of the stairs. His demeanor changed from anger to one of regret as he observed all of my new features that were smaller copies of his own. That stung a little, and I found myself unwilling to meet his eyes.

I didn't understand why he was so against me becoming a hybrid. If he wanted me to join his team, didn't I have to be a hybrid anyway?

The silence stretched between us, becoming more awkward and pain filled. Sorry kept playing through my head, but I couldn't bring myself to say it out loud. *I'm sorry I over reacted and for making you mad. Again. Though, I have to say, it's not that hard to do. I'm sorry for not knowing how to handle you or be with you.* Why couldn't I just say it to him?

You just did.

My eyes snapped to his mouth, then back to his eyes. *I can hear you now?* I said hesitantly.

We're on the same wavelength. He tapped his temple with his claw and growled a chuckle that was devoid of mirth.

"Can I always speak to you like this or only in this form?"

"It's twenty four seven access now."

A shot of fear raced through me at that revelation. In response to my fear, I felt him tighten his guard against me. It was like running into a wall that had suddenly materialized or a door slamming shut between us that I hadn't realized was open.

"But, you heard me sometimes, before this."

"I mostly got emotions when you were really agitated."

"Wasn't I always agitated when I was with you?" I teased.

"In the beginning," he conceded.

The silence returned, and I wiggled my fingers in front of him. "So, I'm a hybrid now. Just like you."

"I noticed," he said flatly.

"Why are you so against me being a hybrid?" I said angrily.

"I'm not against you being a hybrid. That would be hypocritical, don't you think?" he snapped back.

"Well, you certainly don't like it," I argued.

He looked down, kicking the step with his foot. "It's not that I don't like it…I wanted you to be able to choose, not to have it forced upon you. To choose…" He angrily kicked the step one last time and turned away from me.

To choose what? To be a hybrid? "I don't consider saving my life as having forced me to become a hybrid," I told him.

"You might change your opinion a month from now," he said, turning to face me again.

His eyes were so hard. This was the side of him I didn't understand. He looked like he was mad at me for having put him in the position of having to change me. Or, like he didn't want to be the one who changed me, to have this link with me. It was a little late for that now.

I smiled a tight smile and was rewarded by cutting my own lips with my new shiny teeth. "I don't know how to change back."

"You'll learn," he said, watching me wipe away blood from my mouth.

"Not if you don't teach me," I snarled.

We stared at each other without blinking, my blue eyes to his green. He finally looked away and took a breath.

"For me, it's like water flowing in reverse," he said. "Like I'm pulling the change back inside." His arms illustrated his words as he spoke, and I watched him shift back to human.

I closed my eyes and pictured my talons and ears receding. Then I visualized my eyes returning to normal. Opening my eyes and being greeted by a darker landscape confirmed success of that shift. Looking at my hands, I verified that my talons were gone as well.

"I did it," I said softly, a broad smile spreading across my face.

"You forgot something," he said, stepping close enough to tap my teeth.

Oh. In my mind, I saw them retract. I didn't have to touch them to verify they were gone. I could feel them recede. I smiled real big, showing my teeth for his approval.

"The first time," he said flatly. That was all I got in response.

The smile slowly faded from my face, and I crossed my arms over my chest. "I'm not a superhero, you know. I'm not a super anything. I'm just a scientist." Annoyingly, a single tear traced a path down my cheek.

Michaels' eyes widened, and he climbed the remaining steps between us. With one hand cupping my face, he gently brushed it away with his thumb.

"You are so much more than a scientist," he said.

"Okay, a hybrid scientist." Another tear escaped to run down the opposite cheek.

"More than that," he said, brushing away the new tear.

"A hybrid scientist who likes to eat?" I was running out of descriptives.

"More than that," he said, pulling my face toward him. Gently, he pressed his lips against mine.

I was not prepared for the breathlessness that came with such a gentle gesture. Pulling away, I hid my face in his chest, and he rested his chin on the top of my head.

I could tell that he was smiling. I couldn't see it. I could feel it inside me. Oh, he was pleased with himself.

He chuckled at my silent assessment. It was good to hear him laugh, and I laughed softly at his joy before unexpectedly yawning.

"Come on, let's get you to bed," he said provocatively.

"Alone," I said a little too sharply, causing him to laugh harder.

"Absolutely," he replied with false innocence. Releasing me and stepping away, he ordered, "Move it, Greer."

"Absolutely, Mr. Michaels," I mock saluted him.

He put a hand on my arm to stop me. "Call me Adam."

Well, he's had many names over these last three days. We'll see if this one sticks.

CHAPTER 13

MORNING CAME TOO SOON IN my opinion. Laying there squinting at the sunlight that fell across my face, I spotted my suitcase against the wall. Miranda had probably brought that with her. Despite her recent lack of judgment concerning my need to know, she really was the best friend.

I sat up and flung the covers aside. I had showered last night before turning in, but I was so tired that I hadn't bothered to find clothing.

Crossing the room to the suitcase, I stopped mid stride when I became aware of the complete absence of pain in my body. Bringing my hands up, I examined them but couldn't find a single stitch. My knees were the same way. I couldn't even identify any scars. Apparently, I now had super recuperative powers, too.

"That is so cool," I whispered in awe. "Definitely worth waking up for."

I laid the suitcase down and opened it. Rummaging through it, I quickly found and pulled on some underclothes and jeans. My search for a top turned up one of my favorite shirts. It was a rust colored, tie dyed t-shirt that read, *you had me at deep fried*. For sure, it wasn't fashionable, but it did capture my sentiments regarding all things deep fried. Plus, it fit really well.

I shrugged it on and went to stand in front of the mirror for inspection. I honestly didn't know why I kept standing in front of mirrors, expecting some reflection of normalcy. How in the world was I going to get a brush through this rat's nest? A knock at the door interrupted my consternation at the state of my hair.

"Come in," I yelled sourly. There wasn't much use in hiding, and anyway, I might need whoever it was to help me tame this mess.

The door popped open, and to my relief, Miranda walked in. I watched her eyes widen as she appraised the state of my hair.

"What's up with the hair? Get a little too cozy with the rodent population?"

Ha, ha. I stuck my tongue out at her and began to search for a brush, though a blow torch might be more useful.

"Look in the bathroom. There's a bag on the counter by the sink," Miranda instructed.

I found the brush and returned to stand in front of the mirror again. Gingerly, I separated a section of my hair from the rest and started working from the bottom. I noticed Miranda had taken a seat on the end of the bed, and she was uncharacteristically silent.

"You're up early," I told her. "Feeling alright this morning?" I watched her response in the mirror's reflection, trying to gather some clue as to the source of her discomfort.

She shrugged noncommittally, another sign of her distress. Miranda always had an opinion one way or the other. Looking up from the bedspread she was picking at, she found my eyes in the mirror. "How about you?"

"Great. Hungry," I said as I finished the section I'd been working on.

She remained quiet while I worked at freeing another segment for detanglement. When I looked back up, she was eyeing me intently. So intently, that I started checking myself, looking for the source of her concern. When I could find nothing amiss, I paused my brushing.

"Why are you staring at me?"

"You're not overwhelmed?"

That was an odd question. I thought about it a minute. No, just felt like me. But looking at her fallen face, I could tell that she was. I gave up the struggle with my hair and went to sit next to her on the bed.

Wrapping my arms around her, I asked, "You are?"

Tears started tracking down her cheeks, and I sighed. For two people who hated to cry, we were sure doing more than our fair share.

"Yeah," she managed to croak out. "It's just so intense."

"The shifting or Cedars?"

She sat up, pulling out of my arms. "Both. We have this bond thing." She stopped abruptly and looked at me. "Do you and Michaels have a bond?"

Now I was the one uncomfortable. "We can speak to each other telepathically, if that's what you mean."

"You don't feel what he feels?"

I thought about last night, how I'd felt his happiness from inside me. "Only one time. So far, at least. I think he can do some kind of shielding thing which shuts me out. I felt that, too," I said with a frown. I wondered if he was shielding me out right now and why it bothered me if he was. We weren't together, together. One tiny kiss did not a relationship make, right?

"Well, he's going to have to teach Jamie," she said, wiping her nose with the back of her hand and pulling me back from my own thoughts.

"Who's Jamie?" I asked distractedly before I realized who she meant. "Oh, you mean Cedars?"

"Yeah. His name is really Jamison, but I call him Jamie."

"Do you want me to mention it to Adam?"

"Would you, please?" She got up and grabbed a tissue from the box on the dresser.

"Of course, consider it done." I paused as she blew her nose. Now, the hard part. "You feel what he feels?"

"Everything," she said. "Anger, fear, desire. And I can't hide what I feel either. I feel so exposed." She threw her hands out wide.

Everything? That was a terrifying reality, especially for her. "Does he know about everything in your past?" I asked softly.

"Yeah. I couldn't keep it from him if I wanted to. Apparently, I project like a digital cinema."

That would be so embarrassing and humiliating. But maybe freeing, somehow?

"Does it help to not have to hide anything?" I asked hopefully.

"Time will tell, I guess. For you, too," she said knowingly.

That was what I was afraid of and something I didn't want to think about right now.

"About the shifting. When did your…When did you first shift?"

She cleared her throat, and she was actually starting to blush.

Oh, Jesus. I wiped my hands across my face. "Did anyone get hurt?"

"No," she said coyly.

I did not need a rundown of her sex life. I wasn't a prude, but I preferred to keep what was private, well, private. I hurried to my next question before she could elaborate. "So, how long have you been able to shift?" That should be a safe enough question.

"Since two days after we were separated."

These nanobots acted almost as fast as she did. "And what abilities do you have?"

She began to tick them off on her fingers. "I can shift my teeth, eyes, ears, and nails. And, I heal really fast. Food tastes different, too, but I don't think that's a super power."

Same as me. "Are you a cat too?"

"No, a wolf."

Really? I pulled my feet underneath me on the bed as I pondered that. The whole idea of me being part cat and her part wolf was utterly absurd.

"After the last two years with the Colony, did you ever think this would happen to us?" I asked her.

"Not like this," she snorted.

She threw the tissue in the trash and flopped down on the bed next to me. I lay back beside her, and we both stared silently at the ceiling. Seemed like I could see paw prints everywhere in the textured pattern on the ceiling. I wondered if that was intentional or just my imagination.

"So, we're like Xmen reborn," I said into the silence.

"Superhero Mutants," she retorted.

"Do we have costumes?"

She held open the cardigan, revealing the t-shirt it concealed.

I rose up on my elbows and read aloud. "If I were an enzyme, I'd be a DNA helicase, so I could unzip your genes. Good enough," I snickered.

"Wait till you see what Cedars' shirt says."

I pushed off the bed, sticking the brush in my back pocket for use later. "When's breakfast around here?"

"I cooked last night. You're up next on the rotation."

I searched in the bag on the bathroom counter for a hair clip. Bingo.

Miranda came to stand in the doorway, watching my meager attempts at taming my hair.

"There's a rotation?" I asked while twisting my hair up and fastening the clip.

"No," she said, picking at the paint on the door jam. "I just know it's not my turn."

I started brushing my teeth. She was trying to be upbeat, but I could tell she was still a little down. I didn't know what she was worried about. I saw no signs of rejection from Cedars. If she wanted to get rid of him, she'd have to beat him off with a stick. A very big stick.

I finished brushing and rinsed the last of the toothpaste out of my mouth.

"That was disgusting," she said, making a grossed out face.

"But necessary," I replied. "If you lived inside my mouth, you'd be thanking me right now."

"Yeah, I'll just leave that up to Michaels," she said, rolling her eyes and walking back into the bedroom.

"Thanks for bringing my stuff," I called after her.

"You're welcome. Thanks for listening."

I joined her in the bedroom. "Anytime. Shall we?" I said, heading for the door. "Someone told me I'm only getting breakfast if I make it myself."

She rolled off the bed and stood up. "I believe the actual comment was, you only get to eat if you make enough for everyone, or at least enough for me."

"Is that right?" I threw over my shoulder as I reached for the door knob.

"You're the new supposed queen of right. You tell me."

I turned from the door with the eyebrow cocked and ready. We stared at each other a few seconds and then burst into laughter.

"I've missed you," she said between laughs.

I whole heartedly echoed her feeling.

"Come on," I said, opening the door.

Our exit was met by Adam. His black t-shirt read, *get out of my way*. I failed to see the humor in that.

"What are you two hens cackling at?" he asked.

Hens? Seriously? What decade was he from? "I thought I was a cat," I replied haughtily.

Miranda snuck past me, squeezing my arm as she went.

We watched her go, then he said, "It's leopard, actually." When I turned to face him, his eyes were on my chest, reading my shirt. "Why am I not surprised?" he said, shaking his head.

"Deep frying is an art," I said defensively. "Hey, if we are leopard, then why do we have elongated pupils? Leopards don't have elongated pupils."

He crossed his arms over his chest and leaned against the wall, like he was preparing for a long explanation. Hopefully, it wouldn't be too long. I was hungry.

"Several of the proteins we use are slightly different than the leopards. It gives us the elongated pupil," he said.

"We didn't get the map for the leopard protein?"

"We did, but the nanobots consistently substitute the human protein."

"I'm sure there is a good explanation for that. They are following logic that was programmed into them, right?" I didn't want to even think about the possibility of rogue nanobots.

He smiled down at me with that condescending way he had. "There is and they are."

He knew I wanted more information, but he wasn't offering. I'd have to pull it out of him one little scrap at a time. Before I could delve any deeper, my stomach grumbled loudly. I rolled my eyes at my stomach's display and timing.

"I heard a rumor you were making breakfast," he snorted.

"Possibly," I quipped.

"You any good?"

That could be taken in so many ways. I raised my eyebrows at him for clarification.

"I meant at cooking," he growled softly.

"I guess you'll just have to find out for yourself," I said. Starting down the stairs, I threw out a challenge. "Better yet, help me, and you'll get to watch a master at work."

He barked a laugh at me while following me down the stairs, muttering, "Lead on, master, lead on."

Oh, I would. One could not love food the way I did and not know how to cook.

Standing at the bottom of the stairs, I could have sworn I'd entered a texted t-shirt convention. Pike's t-shirt read, *the cat did it*. I was sure that was a dig at Adam.

Juarez's was just scary. Somehow the words, *I can find you any time, any place and make sure you don't come back*, scrawled in bold black letters across a t-shirt didn't inspire the warm and fuzzes. Olivia hadn't come down yet, so that left only Cedars. I was trying to wipe from my mind what was written on his shirt.

"Do you guys own a t-shirt screening shop?" I asked, perplexed at the display and a little frightened that I had unknowingly mimicked their clothing choices.

"It's just a thing," Adam said as he picked up a coffee cup. "Something we do after a mission."

They got t-shirts? That wasn't much of a bonus.

"Just so we're clear. I like jewelry. Silver jewelry to be exact. I figure after what I've been through, I'm good for at least earrings, a necklace and several bracelets."

"Is that right?" Adam asked, looking sideways at me.

"Oh, yes. Yes it is," I nodded vigorously.

Adam added a copious amount of sugar and cream to the cup and then handed it to me. I eyed him suspiciously while cautiously accepting the mug. Just how long had he been observing me? I took a sip. Not bad. Being observed had its benefits.

To my surprise, Adam followed directions really well. He didn't argue once, and the deftness with which he carried out my instructions led me to believe he knew his way around the kitchen.

At one point, I almost burned the bacon. I got lost in the sight of him licking bacon grease from his fingers. He didn't say a word. He didn't have to. That smug look on his face said it all. He just took my spatula and moved me over. I retreated a safe distance away to the other side of the island, where I started compiling a fruit salad. I had to ignore his soft laughter I could hear behind me.

When we were done, we beheld our finished product. It wasn't exactly masterful, and there wasn't anything deep fried on the menu, but it was still a decent spread. There were biscuits and gravy, bacon and eggs, the fruit salad and cheese grits.

Adam came up behind me and placed his hands on my shoulders. "Nicely done," he whispered.

I looked down to hide the unexpected blush that stained my cheeks. I wasn't used to compliments from him, and much to my embarrassment, it showed.

Adam suddenly tensed, and I looked up to find Pike's gaze locked with Adam's. This was ridiculous and irritating and had to stop. I was no one's possession and fighting over me would not win them any points.

The problem was, I had no idea how to make it stop. As a general rule, I didn't manipulate people, and my relationship experience was tenuous at best. I'd had a few boyfriends here and there in the past, but nothing ever serious and certainly nothing approximating this situation. I concluded I was just going to have to wing it. I was becoming less and less a fan of on the job training.

I turned to face Adam. The movement forced him to drop his arms to his sides. Putting both my hands squarely on his chest, I said softly, "Adam." When he didn't respond to my verbal query, I switched to the nonverbal. Along with his name, I tried to convey my need for him to look at me. *Adam.*

He shifted his eyes to mine, and I wasted no time making my point.

Leave Pike alone. When his eyebrows knitted together in a frown, I argued what to me seemed obvious. *I don't belong to you.* That only deepened his frown. *I don't belong to Pike either,* I added quickly. *And I'm certainly not going to belong to someone because they won me in a fight.*

That seemed to get his attention. His eyebrows went back to their respective homes, leaving me staring into his bright emerald eyes. My courage, that had been fully present just a moment ago, left me high and dry. I swallowed at the sudden dryness in my throat. All this testosterone filled closeness was seriously cutting into my juju.

I looked down, freeing myself from his gaze, and absently began to trace the letters on his shirt. Without the distraction of his eyes, I was better able to concentrate, and I could tell that not all of the tension had subsided.

Think, I growled to myself. I had told Olivia that I would try to work with this. I didn't want to fail her again and be subjected to her schoolmarm looks of disapproval. They were beyond annoying.

So, what did his alphaness need? The realization of what he needed suddenly became clear—to feel more important than Pike. That was completely childish, doable, but childish.

I recognized that it was also childish to be flattered by having two guys vying for my attention. But try as hard as I might to deny it, I couldn't. So, here was a side of myself I'd never known. I felt empowered somehow. I had some measure of control over this man...beast? Probably more beast than man present at the moment.

I decided, by right of winging it, to test my new found power over him. On completely new territory without the slightest hint of knowing what I was doing, I leaned in and whispered, *Adam, who did I choose to help me with breakfast, and who am I standing really close to right now?*

I felt the last of the tension drain from him and ventured a look up. I was immediately ensconced in his eyes again. If not careful, a girl could get lost in those eyes. Wouldn't really take much at all.

Gathering what courage I could, I said, "We should call everyone to eat before the food gets cold."

My prompting effectively ended the intimacy that had developed between us. He sighed and brushed a rebellious strand of hair behind my ear. Then he let his hand drop and backed away from me.

Whew, crisis averted. Did Olivia have to do this all the time?

I was startled by Adam's sudden whistle. He followed it with a shout of "Breakfast!"

"Warn a girl next time, will ya?" I said with my hands still covering my ears.

He smiled mischievously as he walked to the other side of the island. There he went again with the happiness at my discomfort. We were going to have to do something about that.

Everyone served themselves and gathered at the table between the kitchen and living areas. As the meal wound down, Miranda leaned back in her chair with a satisfied look on her face and exaggeratedly rubbed circles across her stomach with her hand.

"That was a deliciously fat laden meal. I should work out," she remarked with faked indifference.

"You most definitely should," I agreed, already knowing what she intended.

She flashed fangs and claws and just as quickly they disappeared. I chuckled and Cedars shook his head in amusement.

Adam, always the reasonable one, said, "You shouldn't waste your energy. You'll have to refuel again soon."

"I know," Miranda said excitedly. "Isn't it great!"

Her enthusiastic reply garnered laughs all around. Even Adam couldn't help but smile.

During the ensuing discussion that triggered, I turned to Adam. "Is it okay if I ask you some questions that have been bothering me?"

"Ask away," he said.

"What happened with the situation at the Agency?"

"You're referring to the impending hybridization event?"

"That and why, if you belong to a totally different organization, were you involved with them to begin with?"

He shifted in his seat and signaled Juarez for his attention.

Juarez answered with a "Yo."

"Get her up to speed on the current hybrid proliferation crisis," Adam told him.

Juarez set down the coffee cup he'd been holding and scooted his chair closer to the table. "As soon as you told us the solution, in the SubV," he paused, waiting for my acknowledgment.

I nodded slowly. I dimly recalled the conversation.

"I passed it down the chain right then. The latest report puts it at a week for total containment."

A week? I drummed my nails on the table as I reviewed my life over the last four days. It wasn't hard to form the conclusion that a lot could happen in a week. "That seems like longer than necessary. Why so long?"

"The re-program for the nanobots is already done. It's just a matter of gathering everyone that was exposed."

I thought about the bacterial growth rates mentioned in the report and did some silent calculations. "If it takes another week, I think you will have missed your window of opportunity to maintain concealment."

The table quieted as a result of my evaluation.

"You're sure?" Juarez countered.

Why did everyone always ask me that? A quick sigh exited my lips as my fingertips gave up their pounding of the table and tried to ease the building tension between my eyes.

"Macy works in the gray," Miranda quipped. "It's the land of possibly, probably and most likely."

Yes, thank you. I leaned forward putting my elbows on the table. "There are too many variables to control outside of the lab." They couldn't even control it in the lab, but I didn't say that out loud. Then it clicked. "The Consortium was behind the breach?"

"We've traced the initial breach to Hollins himself," Adam provided. "It seems he was wholly vested in the Consortium's dream of worldwide hybridization."

Apparently. Fortunately, we'd never have to worry about him being a source again.

"It's really not that hard a dream to accomplish, if you can get your hands on the necessary bacteria. Bacteria in general can reproduce in the millions in a matter of hours. You've got some sort of super nanobot bacteria on the loose. The longer it takes the greater the risk of exposure. It may already be too late. And the moment someone not affiliated with the Agency sprouts fangs or claws it will be in every conceivable news outlet before the day is through."

Juarez turned to Adam who didn't look surprised at all by my conclusion.

"Make the call," Adam said.

Juarez pushed back from the table and disappeared into a room off the living area.

"Where's he going?" I asked.

"I'd already come to the same conclusion you have and set up contingency plans to manage the fallout. There was one last ditch attempt I wanted to try. He left to initiate that." He began tapping his fingers on the table. "At this point, I think maintaining our concealment is just a wish. I think the best scenario places us in a position of managing the revelation."

So, I'd become a hybrid just in time to enjoy all hell breaking loose. My life just kept getting better and better.

"And the reason for your involvement with the Agency?" I asked.

"You," Adam answered unashamedly. "I'm the Operations Director for the Organization. I needed your skills for my operations."

The table went silent again at his statement. I didn't think that went over the way he'd intended.

Quickly realizing his mistake, he added. "For the team, people."

Embarrassed looks were exchanged all around. Except for Pike. He looked more disgusted than embarrassed.

"What I meant was," Adam said, pausing to spear each of them with a look, "that Director Garrison was already aware of you and intent on bringing you in. To have you suddenly disappear would have aroused suspicions. I spun it so that you would be under our supervision."

"So, you were already associated with the Agency?"

"We maintain a façade of working for them," Adam nodded.

"But why didn't you just bring me directly into the Organization? Why wait until Garrison was interested in me?"

"It was a consensus," Olivia supplied. "And, the Agency needed you to clean up their mess."

Adam leaned back in his chair, throwing one arm across the back of mine. He regarded Olivia with a smirk on his face. He was obviously content to let her field this round of questioning.

"And?" I pressed her.

She folded her hands neatly on the table and pegged me with a superior look. "And, there was some concern that you might not handle the existence of us so well. Considering your performance last night, I think our fears were well founded."

She meant her fear was well founded.

I picked up my fork and started drawing shapes in my leftover gravy. Just because I yelled at them didn't mean I couldn't handle the revelation of their existence.

"Am I wrong in thinking you wouldn't be here now if not for the blood transfusion?" she asked with confidence.

I felt Adam stiffen beside me, and I placed my free hand on his thigh and gently patted his leg. As Adam relaxed under my touch, I became tenser. She had me. If I hadn't been made one of them, I wasn't sure if I'd still be here. But that was a moot point now. For better or worse, I was now a hybrid.

I glanced back at Olivia. Her face was set in stone. She wanted assurance that I wasn't going to turn tail and abandon them. In her own way, she was testing me.

To tell the truth, until that very moment, I hadn't thought

about it. But as I looked around the room, I realized I didn't want to leave. I wouldn't say I had enjoyed the last few days, but as a scientist, my thirst for knowledge was hard to ignore. And their school was a tall glass of cold water sitting right in front of me. Not to mention, they'd already shanghaied my best friend.

"In my defense," I began, "I have been through an awful lot in the last few days. I believe I enlightened you to a few of them last night. And, I might add, it was without the benefits of the hybridization you already have or any prior experience with all the special ops stuff."

I placed the fork neatly on the plate and clasped my hands in front of me. Looking up, I waited for her response.

"We know your transition did not occur in the most desirable scenario," she allowed. "But, you are one of us now, and whether you will choose to honor that responsibility is still a source of concern."

"You think honoring that responsibility means joining the team?" I asked her.

"Yes," she said forcibly.

I debated that silently for a moment.

"Do you believe in destiny?" she asked.

"No." My answer was immediate. Was this all some grand design that we were left to play out? I had no idea. "I believe in choices and consequences," I explained. "Opportunities taken and those missed."

It was so quiet you could have heard a pin drop. Even Miranda was holding her tongue. No small feat, I assure you.

"I don't know if my hybridization was due to choice or chance or some grand design, but for better or worse, I am what I am now. I don't see any way to go but forward."

"And if forward involves going back to school?"

She wasn't letting up one little bit. I felt like I was in the principal's office again. She must be one heck of a director for the school. But I was determined not to squirm in front of her.

Meeting her gaze, I answered her the best I could. "I don't know what forward means as far as the school and superhero gig goes. I'm withdrawing my no vote and submitting a wait and see vote." Seeing the uncertainty in her eyes, I offered, "That's the best I can do right now."

She held my eyes a few moments more, then looked down in defeat. "Your best was good enough before. Let's hope it is again."

What kind of scale was she using? My best may result in worldwide hybridization.

I looked across the table at Miranda. She had a huge smile plastered on her face. I twisted my head sideways and asked, "What?"

"We're going to be college coeds together," she sang for the table, eliciting grins and a few chuckles.

I sat back in my chair and laid my head back to rest on Adam's arm. How many turns could my life take in the course of a week? It was only the first part of the day. I could be on a spaceship to Mars by lunchtime.

CHAPTER 14

THE SUDDEN POUNDING COMING FROM the direction of the living room captured everyone's attention. Juarez burst through the door, exclaiming loudly, "We've got company!"

The room sprang to life. Chairs scraped loudly against the floor as everyone rapidly stood. Pike, Olivia and Cedars raced toward the stairs.

"How long?" Adam demanded of Juarez.

"Twenty, thirty minutes at the most."

Adam rounded the table and stopped before an innocuous looking old hutch. "How many and point of entry?"

"East by land. More than we can fight and hope to win."

"Set the timer for fifteen," Adam instructed and Juarez disappeared again.

Opening the doors to the hutch, Adam moved aside a serving dish. He typed something on a keypad that had been hidden behind the dish, and the back panel slid open to reveal an array of screens. He pushed the remaining items in the hutch to the corners and began tapping on the screens. I wasn't sure exactly what he was doing, but I did see the word delete pop up a number of times.

While he was absorbed with that, Miranda came to stand by me. She clasped my hand and looked back and forth between Adam and the stairs. Fear was easily visible in her now amber eyes.

I carefully extracted my hand from her clawed one and wrapped my arm around her shoulder. "It'll be okay," I told her as I watched Adam. "He's pretty good at this sort of thing."

"You know this first hand?"

"Oh, yeah," I replied with a nod of my head.

The others emerged from the stairs outfitted for a small war. Cedars had changed entirely. He looked like some sort of commando. He was carrying several small camouflage packs, one of which he handed to me. He helped Miranda slip on another one.

"Olivia," Adam called.

She approached him, and he strapped a watch on her wrist. "You, Pike, and Juarez will retreat the way we came in. Pick up the SubV and head in the opposite direction. When you are sure you're clear, head to Deep River." He tapped the watch. "This contains all the necessary info."

She nodded and walked back around the table where she engulfed me in a hug. "Don't let me down," she whispered, and then she sprinted for the door.

"I think Macy should come with us," Pike said.

I turned to him in surprise.

"Macy stays with me," Adam warned.

Dang straight I do.

"She'll have a better chance—"

He didn't get to finish the comment. Adam had him gripped by the throat and slammed into a wall in less than a second.

"Macy stays with me," Adam growled.

Was Pike crazy? Adam looked ready to kill him.

I walked over and placed my hand on Adam's back. *Let him go, Adam.*

He flung Pike in the general direction of the door, following him only with his eyes.

After he regained his footing, Pike grinned and saluted me. "See you soon, *Beautiful.*"

The way he said it left cold chills running down my back. Maybe I should have let Adam kill him.

"It's not an option. Yet," Adam spoke quietly, answering my silent thought.

This was about something more than me. It had to be. I stepped away from Adam and slipped on the pack Cedars had given me.

"We go west?" Cedars asked Adam.

"We go west," Adam confirmed.

Juarez bounded into the room again and skidded to a stop in front of Adam. "T minus fifteen and counting." He was sort of quivering. Too much coffee perhaps?

"You're with Olivia and Pike," Adam said, pointing to the mudroom. Juarez turned to go when Adam stopped him. "Juarez."

"Yeah, Cap?"

Adam's face reflected the indecision he was feeling. "Keep your guard up," he warned.

"Will do," Juarez said thoughtfully, as if the two of them had just come to some unspoken understanding. "Will do," he said again. He made it to the door in two leaping steps. "Good luck," he called over his shoulder as he disappeared.

Adam stared at the door where Juarez had been. I couldn't help but feel his unease. I thought for a moment he might go after them, but he finally turned back to the hutch and finished whatever he was doing there.

"So, Greer," he said, backing away from the hutch. "How are your ATV skills?"

Four wheelers? I could do some four wheeling. Finally, I got to do something that didn't scare the bejesus out of me.

"Let's go," Adam said as he faced us. He caught the pack Cedars tossed him, and we filed out the backdoor and down the steps where we jogged to a shed about thirty yards from the house. He entered a code, and the door whooshed open to reveal anything but a shabby old shed.

I stepped inside onto a pristine concrete floor. "I am noticing the very conspicuous absence of dirt and hay," I said.

Adam, who had disappeared around a corner, huffed at my comment.

The inside of the pretend shed was stocked with all kinds of high tech gadgets. One whole wall was devoted to weapons of some kind or another. I heard Miranda arguing with Cedars and ventured in the direction the others had gone.

As soon as I turned the corner, I saw the glass kennels.

Inside of the glass kennels were motorcycle four wheeler looking somethings.

I closed my eyes and hung my head. I should have known better. I should have known simply by the mischievous smile on Adam's face when he asked me about ATVs.

"Where do you people come up with this stuff?" I moaned.

Adam turned his grinning face to me as he opened the kennel door. "After you," he said and did a little bow.

I looked to my right to find Cedars in the midst of coaxing Miranda into his stall. She didn't look happy about it either.

Adam cleared his throat, and I took the necessary steps into the kennel. Once inside, I stood there staring down at the thing. How was I supposed to get on it? It was too low to the floor. And it had about fifty little wheels instead of the normal size four wheels. This just wasn't right.

Adam stepped in front of me and straddled the machine. It immediately lifted off the floor and rose until it met his backside. Grabbing the handle bars he sat down and looked at me while a blue bubble enveloped him.

He was floating in the air, on this unnatural excuse for an ATV, encased in a giant blue bubble. That wasn't unnatural at all.

"No helmet?" I asked lamely.

"Not necessary," was his only reply. When I still made no move to climb on, he added, "We are in a bit of a hurry."

Cocky. Arrogant. Mr. Know It All. Some day he was going to be the one thrown into unfamiliar situations without any learning curve. Some day. But obviously, not today.

Sighing loudly, I grabbed his shoulder and swung my leg over the seat behind him. I scooted up as close as I could get to him, eyeing the blue bubble warily as it swallowed me as well. I pushed against it with my finger. It offered only brief resistance before my finger plunged through it.

"What is this stuff?"

"Shielding. Something our lab techs cooked up. Don't ask me to explain. Physics is not my specialty."

It wasn't mine either. I could work an equation like nobody's business. Memorize whole complex systems? Piece of cake. But something about the right hand rule and optics gave me fits. I could do it, but unlike so much for me, it was hard work.

"Hold on tight," he encouraged.

Oh, I planned on it. I wrapped my arms around him and held tight, pressing my face between his shoulder blades.

Ready, he checked.

As I'll ever be.

He pulled his legs in and leaned forward slightly. The machine responded by moving forward, and he maneuvered it out of kennel and toward the door of the shed.

Miranda and Cedars had just cleared the shed, and she looked back at me. I offered her a totally fake smile, and she turned back around and planted her head in Cedars back. Then they took off fast. Way too fast!

Don't scream, Adam said.

What? Those were never good words to hear at any time.

Adam leaned sharply forward, and we zoomed out of the shed and into the woods that surrounded the house. It was a good thing he had warned me not to scream. I had to forcefully keep my mouth shut as the sudden acceleration hit my stomach.

Readjusting to his more forward position, I leaned into his back and tightened my grip. If he'd been sitting up, I wouldn't have been able to see a thing. Like this, however, I had a clear view of the trees hurtling toward us. I squeezed my eyes shut tight. That only served to heighten my fear of hitting the onrushing trees, and I quickly snapped them back open.

We were going uphill now. A loud explosion occurred somewhere behind us, causing the trees to rain down leaves and other little bits on us. To my surprise, the debris bounced off our blue bubble. I could feel the wind, but the leaves couldn't get through. Physics?

The house? I asked.

The house, he confirmed.

Won't that let them know we were definitely there?

They already knew that. I couldn't leave anything for them to find.

Little bits of gray ash started floating down around us. I hoped we hadn't just started a forest fire.

Flashing red dots on the panel located between the handle bars drew my attention. I thought it signaled we were being followed. Adam weaved us in and out of the trees, which were almost a blur now. I had no idea how fast we were going or how he was managing not to smack us into something. But whatever move he made, the red dots kept up with us.

To my right, Cedars brought his ATV level with ours. "We're not losing them," he yelled.

"We need to split up," Adam answered.

I looked at Miranda. She was staring at me and holding on to Cedars for dear life. Maybe this would rid her of the superhero bug.

"Roger that," Cedars acknowledged and veered off to the right.

I watched them disappear quickly over another ridge and then turned my attention back to the screen. Two more red pinpoints broke off and joined four already following us. They must be after us or just me. At least Miranda would be okay.

Do you smell that? He asked.

I inhaled deeply. Smoke. *Did we set the woods on fire?*

No, it's coming from upwind.

Alarm bells went off in my head. *We're being herded.*

Adam slowed the bike to a crawl. He swiveled his head from side to side, searching for a way out. When he spun the bike around, we were able to see the smoke closing behind us. We weren't totally surrounded yet, but it wouldn't be long. We'd flown right into a trap.

I could sense the intensity of Adam's emotions, both fear and anger, as he sought for escape. But I knew it was me they wanted.

Adam—

No, he said before I could finish.

If it's me they want—

No, he said more forcibly. *I will not give you up.*

I could just jump off. Separate myself from him.

Macy! You will do no such thing!

I hadn't meant for him to hear that. His anger felt like claws raking against my brain. *Okay, okay!* I exclaimed, quickly abandoning the idea. What else then? The red pinpoints were getting closer, and smoke was starting to fill the air. *Can we drive through the fire?*

Not without risking blowing ourselves up. There's no jumping over either, he growled. He was already accelerating as he said, *But we might be able to make it across before the loop closes.*

We rocketed through the trees. We were going so fast that tears were being forced from my eyes. That didn't keep me from staring at the approaching twin walls of fire as we raced to the gap. It was going to be close. I watched as long as I dared, and at the last moment, I tucked in tight to Adam.

Hang on! Adam yelled.

He didn't have to tell me twice. I gripped him so hard he'd probably have bruises. I felt the heat sheath us like a glove, followed by a loud whoosh. I turned back to look just in time to see the flames shoot high as the gap closed behind us. We had made it.

Relief washed over me, and I pressed my face into Adam's back. He didn't slow our pace, and the heat faded rapidly, leaving us drenched and filthy. It seemed to be my normal state these days.

My arms ached from my grip on Adam, so I loosened them as he continued to blaze a path through the woods. Glancing at the screen, I noted there were no more pinpoints of red following us.

There's no one following us now, I informed Adam.

I'm aware, he shot back, not acting relieved at all.

Where are we going?

Deep River, he replied gruffly.

I guess that was supposed to mean something. *We'll be driving for a while?*

Yep.

First time I'd heard him use that word. Clearly, he was concerned about something. I thought I knew what it was. It might help if he got it off his chest.

How did the Consortium know where to find us? I ventured softly.
Good. Question.

I got a brief taste of the strain those words embodied before he began putting up the wall between us.

Undeterred by his reluctance, I pressed on. *You think one of the team is a traitor?*

I know one of the team is a traitor. There was no hiding the pain of betrayal in his voice.

I thought about the members of our team. There was only one person I thought capable of betrayal. *You're sure it's one of them?* Then I realized what I'd asked. This must be what people said when they didn't want to accept an unwelcome truth.

Yeah, I'm sure.

I wanted him to explain how he knew, but I didn't want to push him any farther. He'd already tightened the wall between us again.

You want to know why, he accused angrily.

It was just stress, I told myself. It was not me he was angry with. *I trust you, Adam. If you say it's one of them, then it is.* My money was on Pike.

I felt his chest rumble as he growled in frustration. After a few moments of tense silence, he launched into his explanation.

We've had a series of security breaches over the last year. I've narrowed it down to Pike, Olivia and Juarez as the only common denominators related to the breaches. I even went as far as to stage a mock operation with only the three involved. It's one of them.

I'm sorry, I said. It's all I could think to say. I and my supposed super brain couldn't fix this for him.

Leaning forward, I wrapped my arms around him and pressed my chin into his back. As I did, I reached through our bond, willing him to accept my comfort. When I reached the wall, I pushed harder, and gradually, I felt the wall give way.

You and me both, he replied, his voice thick with sorrow.

I didn't ask him any more questions about it, and we drove in silence. Until I became bored. After a while, one blurred tree looked just like the next.

I propped myself up on my elbows, which I had placed on Adam's back. *Doesn't your back hurt leaning over like that?*

You get used to it, came his terse response.

I began to trace circles on his back with my right hand. *Tell me about the school,* I said.

What do you want to know? Wait, let me guess. Everything?

Though he said it in jest, his voice was filled with disgust. As if my curiosity about the school was somehow disgusting. I stilled my doodling hand, bringing both of them together on his back. Why shouldn't I be curious about the school? Apparently, that was my future, and outside of the little they had already told me, I knew nothing about it. I didn't see anything wrong with my request.

There isn't, Adam said. *Sorry. It's just...everything.*

Everything. One medium size word to encompass a boat load of trouble.

That could be my new catchphrase, I teased. *What's wrong, Macy? Everything. What do you want on your burger? Everything. What options would you like on your truck? I'll take everything.*

Adam chuckled at my joking, like I'd hoped he would. *So, everything?* He asked.

Please, I exaggeratedly begged.

The School, he sighed. *Only the best and brightest are invited. But only when we are sure they will accept.*

How do you manage that?

Each candidate is observed thoroughly and, without their knowledge, put through simulated circumstances to observe their responses. We make sure they accept the reality or truth of hybrids and are interested in continuing research in that direction before we ever invite them.

I wondered what all that entailed, especially the thoroughly observed part, but then decided I'd be better off not knowing.

We also, of course, make sure they are not certifiable.

Even me?

Nothing with you has been according to protocol, came his quick retort.

Even though his tone was sharp, I felt him relaxing as I continued to question him. It felt like a tightness in me was loosening, and since I wasn't the one uptight right now, I assumed it was coming from him.

I wasn't put through any kind of simulation?

There was no need. You were already working with hybrids and the related genetics. I felt him smother a laugh. *And besides, I already knew you were crazy.*

Ha, ha. How long was I observed?

Five years.

Five years! I rifled through my past. I could think of five, no, six episodes that could probably be classified as crazy. But it wasn't like I had initiated any of them. They just sort of happened to me. Like the NOLA incident. Crazy? Yes. Embarrassing? Most definitely. But still, not my doing. Pointing this out probably wouldn't affect his opinion.

Ignoring the previous thread of conversation, I changed subjects. *So, what are the classes like?*

We do not bother with unnecessary course work. No English or history classes or other such subjects. The only classes you attend are the ones that are strictly necessary for your development.

I would have sure appreciated that my first go round at school. Whoever decided art history was a necessary requirement for graduating was an idiot.

There are no time tables for degrees?

None. Everyone finishes individually based on their abilities. Whether that's two years or five is totally subject to the individual. As is the degree.

When it is determined that you are finished, then what? Where do the graduates go?

Our question and answer session was interrupted by the deer that suddenly darted across our path. My heart skipped a beat as Adam swerved to avoid a collision. His maneuver set us spinning, and being true to form, I flew off the ATV.

Amazingly, I hit the ground in a crouch, but the force of the throw sent me skidding into a tree where I smacked the side of my face against the trunk.

"Oww!" I growled in pain.

Adam was at my side in an instant. "Woman!" he yelled. "You make the easiest of things difficult!"

I glared at him while I picked the pine needles from my hair and clothes. He was lucky I didn't have laser eyes.

He took one finger and placed it under my chin. Turning my head, he looked at my new injury. "It's just a scratch," he reported. "You'll be healed before we arrive."

I repressed the urge to slap his hand, but I did jerk my head away. Scratch or not, it hurt.

He sighed and stood up, extending his hand to me.

I ignored it and stood up all by myself. As I walked around him, I saw him place both hands on his hips and look skyward. As if I were being difficult on purpose. As if I wanted to fly off the stupid bike ATV thing and smack my face against a tree. Furious, I waited by the bike with arms crossed over my chest.

Without a word, like the apology he owed me, he remounted the bike.

I climbed on after him, but I didn't want to wrap my arms around him. I didn't want to fall off again either. I settled for loosely wrapping my arms around his waist.

He growled and grabbed my arms, pulling me tighter against him. I had no choice but to lean against him.

When I couldn't take his anger beating against me any longer, I asked, *Why are you so angry?*

Because you seem intent on harming yourself, he said tightly.

I am not! I didn't mean to fly off the bike!

Just like you didn't mean to be shot at in the woods, injured in the shower, or the tunnel. Or at death's door from blood loss. You almost died!

Whoa. Where was this coming from? I was totally unprepared for this line of attack.

All of those incidences were beyond my control. They happened to me. I didn't cause them. I just had to cope with them, I said quietly.

My soft response seemed to defuel his anger. *I need you to cope better,* he said haltingly, *without becoming injured. It…bothers me to see you in pain.*

Bothered him? It bothered me, too. I wasn't sure how to respond to him, so I didn't.

As the silence stretched between us, I began to replay my gymnastic escapade. I still hadn't worked out just how I had managed to end up on my feet. Must have been a cat thing. It was comforting to think I might be able to always land on my feet.

I was hesitant to disturb the fragile truce between us, but I didn't like the stony silence either. And, I still had questions about the school.

Before my tumbling act—

He grunted at my description.

As I was saying, before then, you were going to tell me about what happens after graduation.

The ball was in his court now. He could answer or not. The silence continued, and I had just about resigned myself to the fact that he wasn't going to answer when he did.

There are essentially two tracks. You can step right into research and development at the school and subsequently the Organization. Or, if you possess the right skills or as in your case, a particularly needed skill, you will be asked to join the Expeditionary Team of the Organization.

The school and the Organization are closely linked?

Very.

Where is the school located? I just couldn't picture how some school devoted to hybrid technology could exist without being noticed.

The school is located exclusively in a valley that is tucked in between the mountains in Montana. But the Organization itself has locations all over the world.

Hidden valley, huh? Now I was having visions of broccoli and ranch dressing. Unless Adam had a replicator in his pocket, I didn't see that happening.

We just had breakfast.

I'm a growing hybrid. I need lots of food.

You always need lots of food.

The man was a genius.

Are there a lot of people at the school?

No. There are a couple hundred attending at any given time. Another hundred or so work in R&D or teach at the school or both.

What about the Team?

There are currently thirty three members that can be dispatched as the need requires.

That's not a lot of people to save the world.

He laughed softly. *I suppose it's not. More are in training. But it takes a while.*

What kind of training?

The usual. Weapons, survival, medical, a mix of martial arts. The list is long, depending on the candidate.

Sounded like it. *Who decides the makeup of the team?*

That would be me.

So that was what Operations Director meant. I figured him for the boss of something. The other team members certainly treated him that way.

Are you the head of the Organization too?

No, the day to day operations are run by the original founders. They were the original crafters of hybridization.

At Biometrics? I interrupted. *They're still around?*

Yes. Dr.'s Renard and Julia Latke. They are still there today and still in charge. Pike is their grandson.

That explained a ton of stuff. If I suspected Pike, Adam had to also. The fact that Pike was the Grandson of the founders had to add a tough dynamic for Adam. It was probably why he hadn't gotten rid of him yet. Maybe he was waiting for the founders to die off before confronting Pike or collecting irrefutable evidence. I didn't envy his position.

They must be really old, I concluded.

Actually they look exactly the same, only better.

I was startled by that bit of information. *You can't look exactly the same and better. What do you mean, better?*

It seems that the nanobots take it upon themselves to regenerate or repair whatever and whenever they deem necessary.

I knew about the healing, but not the anti-aging. *You're telling me we don't age? Ever?*

Not as of yet. Maybe not until the nanobots themselves stop working.

Well that was something new to think about. The implications were astounding. Were we talking immortality or just a really long life. And were the nanobots operating outside of their programming? There must have been some command code they were following. If the nanobots could repair the human body, that opened up a whole new world of medical science. I was almost beside myself with possibilities.

Somewhere in all my processing, I was lulled to sleep by the hum of the ATV and Adam's breathing as my cheek rested on his back. When Adam finally pulled the ATV to a halt, I rubbed my eyes and looked up hopefully.

He sat up, placing his feet on the ground, but made no further move to disembark. *Something's wrong,* he whispered.

My view was now obstructed by him, so I leaned to the side to stare around him. All I saw was a cabin straight across a small valley from us.

I don't see anything, I told him.

Exactly. No lights, no movement. He inhaled deeply. *No familiar scents.* He eased the bike back into the cover of the trees.

They should have been here by now? I asked.

He didn't answer.

Maybe they haven't gotten clear yet, I said, recalling his instructions to Olivia.

Maybe, he said doubtfully. He turned the bike around and slowly went back the way we'd come.

Where are we going now? I tried, somewhat unsuccessfully, to keep the disappointment out of my voice.

I have to find a place to hide the ATV.

He searched until he was satisfied that he'd found the best place, and then I helped him camouflage it with branches. I followed closely behind him as he headed back in the direction of the cabin. Just before we exited the cover of the trees, he located a hollow that would give us shelter from both the elements and anyone looking for us.

We'd driven the better part of the day. The sun was just cresting on the horizon when we sat down in front of the hollow to enjoy a dinner of cardboard bars and water. Except for the necessary teeth grinding, we ate in total silence while the dark descended. He kept his gaze fixed on the cabin the entire time.

"We should turn in," he said, standing and crumpling his trash between his hands.

I watched him retreat to the hollow and wedge himself inside. Placing my trash under a rock, I approached the hollow. There wasn't much room to spare. We certainly wouldn't have to worry about accidentally rolling out during the night.

I settled in the space that was left over, and Adam pulled a tarp from his pack and secured it across the opening.

All tucked in for the night, I knew that sleep wouldn't come. All I could think about was the rest of the team. The more time that passed without their appearance, the more likely it was that the worst had happened.

"Adam," I said softly. "What happens if the Consortium gets them?"

He sighed heavily before answering. "They'll probably be tortured for information. Killed, maybe."

I squeezed my eyes shut. "Information about me?" I asked weakly.

"Macy, this is not your fault."

"It kind of is. You're all here because of me."

"Because we need you. The Organization needs you. They are not strangers to the Consortium's tactics, and they are well aware of the risks associated with their jobs."

"We have to save them." When he didn't respond, I laid my head against his shoulder. "We can't just abandon them, Adam."

"I didn't plan on abandoning them," he replied coldly. "But right now, they are not my first priority. And before you ask, yes, getting you out of here is my first priority."

"How could I possibly be more important than them? They're your team, not me. They're counting on you!"

"Dad gum it, Woman! I know!" he snapped.

Of course he knew. I was just making things worse. "Sorry," I mumbled. "I didn't mean to attack you. I just don't see what's so special about me."

"We've been over this," he moaned softly.

Yeah, we had. I just didn't happen to agree with him on the matter. Then it occurred to me that the reason he hadn't already tried to find them was me.

"If you're holding off looking for them because of me, then you could just leave me here." I could already feel him bristling to respond. "I'll be fine. I've stayed in the woods by myself before. Country girl, right here," I said, waving my hand. "I've been camping since—"

"Enough!" he ordered. "When are you going to get it through your head that I am not leaving you? That is not an option." His hand sliced through the air, adding emphasis to his words. "Don't!" he warned, halting my rebuttal.

Roughly, he wrapped his arm around me, pulling me tighter to his side. "Macy, you are just going to have to trust me," he said gruffly.

I was trying to, but he wasn't making it easy.

"Try to get some sleep. Morning is a long way off." His tone informed me that the conversation was over.

I sighed inwardly. What was this alpha male BS? Olivia had it right. Tricky to handle.

"I can hear everything you're not saying," he snarled in warning.

Really? Then here are a few more adjectives I'm not saying, I thought, angrily crossing my arms over my chest. *Arrogant, egotistical, control freak*—pressed up against him as I was, I could feel his chest rumbling with the growl he was generating. I rushed to add, *bad putty tat.* There, I was done.

We both sat there in the dark, not speaking and not sleeping. Then to my surprise, he started chuckling.

"Bad putty tat," he repeated. I was jostled to one side as the chuckling turned into full belly laughs. "That's pretty good," he said between breaths.

Even though he couldn't see it, I rolled my eyes at him. "Jerk," I said sourly.

He finally quieted and an uneasy peace settled between us once again. Uncrossing my arms, I leaned back into him, and he adjusted his position to accommodate me. After a while, I felt his breathing settle into a steady rhythm. I wondered how he could sleep. Maybe it was part of his training.

Training. There was a whole other line of thought to pursue. When would I get my head above water? Every new piece of information felt like it was pushing me further under. I didn't like playing catch up or being the last to know.

And, I hated thinking about what might be happening to Olivia.

A single tear rolled down my cheek as I squeezed my eyes shut tight. I had a feeling that this was going to be one of the longest nights of my life.

CHAPTER 15

WHEN I AWOKE IN THE morning, I was alone in the hollow. Rubbing sleep crustees from my eyes, I spotted Adam a few feet away. He was sitting and staring across the valley.

Man, I needed to go to the bathroom.

"Toilet paper is in the pack. Don't go far," Adam said.

I so wasn't trying to broadcast that tidbit of information. I was going to have to get better at this shielding thing.

I guess it didn't say much for my survival skills that I hadn't bothered to scope out my pack yet. I pulled the pack in front of me and unzipped it. Scrounging around, I found more water. Uugh, more cardboard. Needle and sutures? I hoped we didn't need that. Last was one very smushed roll of toilet paper. It looked like I felt. I hoped it wasn't the other way around, but I wasn't getting my hopes up with all the recent images the mirror had reflected.

I crawled out, stretching to alleviate the stiffness the night in the hollow had provided. Now able to move a little more freely, I headed in the opposite direction of Adam.

My return found him still at his post. I already knew the answer, but I asked anyway. "No sign of them?"

"None," he said quietly.

I joined him on the ground and stared at the cabin. It reminded me of the one that was now ashes.

"It is an exact replica," Adam said.

I stood, looking for whatever it was on the ground that kept poking my backside. "So, if I ever come across a house like this, I can assume it belongs to the Organization?"

"More than likely," Adam said, looking at me briefly as I turned in circles.

I didn't see the offending poker, so I sat back down. There it was again. While I wiggled around searching for a comfortable position, my hand bumped my back pocket. I slid my hand up my pocket and pulled out my brush. Well, that was convenient.

Unclasping my hair clip, I sat cross legged next to Adam and started working on my hair. He shot me the occasional annoyed look at my efforts, but mostly he was intensely focused on the cabin across the valley from us.

"What are you looking for?" I asked.

"Shadows, light, reflections of light." He inhaled deeply and said, "Scents." His ears, which he had shifted, kept up a constant swiveling motion.

"Sound, too?"

He nodded.

I fell forward as the knot I had been pulling at finally gave way.

"Let me have it," he demanded with an outstretched hand.

He wanted my brush?

"Give it to me," he demanded again, his hand motioning his words.

Fine. I handed him my brush and angled myself with my back to him. Having your hair brushed always felt good. As long as you were not tender headed, which I was not.

Now our positions were reversed. He worked on my hair, and I watched the house. When the brush began to glide through my hair freely, I figured he was done and was about to scoot away when he commanded me to, "Be still."

Okay. Little bossy this morning. My eyebrows rose in surprise as his fingers began to weave through my hair. He was braiding my hair?

"Where did you learn to braid hair?" I asked.

"Little sisters and a busy Mom," he grunted.

So he wasn't born entirely in a test tube. Good to know.

"Hair clip." He took it from my hand and did some kind of twist and tuck thing with my hair. The clip he used to secure it.

I shook my head side to side. Nothing moved or came loose. "Pretty good," was all I said by way of thanks.

He grunted again and resumed his previous position.

I wanted to ask what was for breakfast, but I feared I already knew. "What's next on the agenda this morning?"

"Breakfast," he replied without moving. "Then, we hunt."

I translated that to mean he was not surprising me with anything already prepared. "You mean the cardboard?" I asked sullenly.

He shot me a look then went to the tree and retrieved a bar for each of us. Reluctantly, I took the bar from his outstretched hand. Studying the package, I had a thought. Perhaps if I ate it as fast as I could, I wouldn't taste it so much. It was worth a shot.

I tore into my bar and began chewing furiously. Adam stopped eating his bar and watched me with that cocked eyebrow. After I stuffed a few more bites into my mouth while continuing to chew rapidly, I came to a conclusion. Faster did not equal better. I was only inciting myself to gag.

"Water," I croaked out.

He wordlessly handed me a bottle, and I chugged it down. Finished, I recapped the bottle and looked up at him.

"What is wrong with you?" he demanded angrily.

"I was trying to beat the taste," I explained.

"You're a nutcase, you know that?" he said, shaking his head in exasperation.

Once again, I reviewed my recent past. It was a little on the extreme side. Maybe I was a nutcase. Maybe this whole thing was some sort of induced delirium, and I'd wake up to find out none of this had ever happened.

"Well, maybe I am," I said with growing anger, "but you're along for the ride. So you best buckle up or hunker down as the situation demands, because I gotta tell you, the last week of my life has been one big freaking thrill ride after another!"

When I finished, I realized I'd yelled the last part at him. Very wisely, he ate the rest of his bar in silence while I tried to flush out my anger.

Nutcase. What did he know about being a nut anyway? I'd like to see him do all the things I've had to do, without training or warning most of the time, in as however many days as it has been. Now I was out here in the woods, stuck eating cardboard and waiting for the team to show up. Correction. Hoping the team showed up. And, there went my anger.

I looked over at Adam. I didn't think he had moved since I yelled at him. I knew he was stressed over the whole situation with the team. We both were. We both knew what their absence could mean.

In the short time that I'd known them, I had come to depend on them. My radically altered future was now tied to them in one fashion or another. I really liked Olivia, too, despite her judgmental ways. It was terrifying to me to think she could be undergoing torture at this very moment. It was so hard to just sit here and do nothing.

"Shouldn't we be doing something?" I asked in frustration.

"We are," he said as he stood up. "Let's go." Seeing my confused face, he clarified, "Hunting."

"I meant doing something about finding Olivia and the others," I said as I followed him.

"Nothing we can do currently. We had a measure of protection while on the ATV. Now, we're sitting ducks." He slowed, allowing me to catch up, then scrubbed his hand across his face as if that could erase the unpleasant thoughts. "Either they'll show up or the Consortium's people will."

"And if the Consortium shows up?"

"We run." As if punctuating his words, he broke into a jog, which I had no choice but to follow.

"Why don't we leave now before they get here?" I yelled at his back.

"Several reasons. One, we'd have to go on foot. You might have noticed our ATV is not standard issue, and we are not that far from civilization. Two, we'd be travelling blind, possibly into a trap. Everything I need to see them, beyond the short radius the bike offers, is in the house. They are not so limited. And three, I'm still hoping the rest of the team shows up."

Hope? My experiences with him had him pegged as a realist. I hadn't thought hope was generally part of his personality. It was a welcome surprise.

It would also be a surprise if we caught anything with how much noise we were making as we tromped through the woods. Then it dawned on me. We didn't have any weapons. Unless he had some hidden somewhere on him that I didn't know about.

"Adam, how are we going to get anything? We don't have any weapons," I said.

He slowed to a walk and then stopped with his hands on his hips. Turning to look squarely at me, he said, "We have teeth and claws."

He expected me to kill an animal with my bare hands? Or worse, my teeth? Oh, I don't think so. Shooting Bambi from a distance was hard enough.

"Consider this your first lesson in wilderness survival," he continued while ignoring my panicked look. "You are part leopard now, which comes with the ability to move soundlessly. Follow me."

He stalked off, his body as lithe as, well, a cat. He wasn't making a sound as he moved through the woods. How was he doing that?

I started forward and cringed when twigs and leaves snapped loudly beneath my feet. This obviously wasn't the way he was doing it. I stopped in frustration and watched his sinuous movements as he weaved in and out of the trees.

"You have to yield to the leopard DNA. Just let it lead you on the hunt," he called back.

Yield to the DNA, I repeated silently to myself. Yield to the DNA. How the heck was I supposed to yield to the DNA!

He stood back up, clearly irritated, and looked back at me. "You are thinking about it too much. It is not that difficult. Just be the leopard."

That was it. "I've never been a leopard before. I've never even pretended to be a leopard before. I don't even have a leopard costume, so it's a little more complicated for me than just be the leopard!" I yelled.

He eyed me a moment then walked to stand behind me.

"What are you doing?" I snarled at him.

"Just be quiet," he ordered. He reached both of his arms forward and placed them on top of mine, covering my hands with his own. Then he did something with our bond, and I felt what he felt. "Do you feel that?" he asked.

"Yes," I said quietly as the feeling engulfed me. It was a singleness of purpose—to hunt.

"That's the feeling you are looking for," he said, and then he backed off, taking the feeling with him. "Let's try again."

He started forward again, and so did I. If I reached for just the feeling, I couldn't touch it, but when I just concentrated on hunting, it covered me like a blanket. Everything became more vivid, alive somehow. I noticed smells and sounds I never had before.

Adam paused and sniffed at a particularly pungent smell. *Deer*, he supplied.

He dropped into a crouch, and I copied him. We approached a cluster of trees, and Adam pointed, indicating the location of the deer.

Stay here, he said. He waited until I nodded, then turned his back on me and slunk into the trees. His movements were like watching a real live cat on the hunt. As he moved, he kept up his lecture on hunting.

Don't approach a deer from behind, you risk being kicked. Don't approach a male from the front, you risk being hit by the antlers.

I watched as a six point ambled into a small clearing directly in front of the trees we were hidden behind. I knew Adam was somewhere in front of me, but I was startled by his sudden appearance. Seemingly out of nowhere and quicker than lightning, he attacked.

He used the deer's hindquarters to vault to its neck, and then tore out its throat before it ever had a chance to respond. Straddling the deer, he gripped the antlers from behind and followed it to the ground. Its struggling subsided quickly as its strength failed, and I watched the light fade from its eyes.

Adam gently laid the deer's head on the ground, and then used his claws to tear into the deer's belly. All the good feelings of the leopard on the hunt fled, and I was afraid as I watched Adam.

"Macy, come here," Adam said.

I shook my head no. In horror, I watched as he plopped a piece of the still warm flesh in his mouth.

"Macy, come," he said more sternly.

"I am not eating raw deer," I hissed from behind the safety of the tree I was gripping.

He sat back on his heels and searched for me in the trees, stopping when his eyes found mine. "It's not going to taste like raw meat," he tried to assure me. "You are part leopard. That includes your taste buds."

I was not convinced.

"Remember you told me that when you ate the rest of the lasagna it tasted different?"

That didn't mean this was going to taste good.

"Macy Greer," he said impatiently, abandoning any effort to persuade me. "If you do not get over here and try this deer, I will chase you down and force it down your throat."

I glared daggers at him. He would not do that. But I saw the resolve etched on his face. Oh God, yes he would.

"Macy," he growled in warning.

Using every ounce of courage I possessed, I let go of the tree and came to kneel by him. "Why do we have to eat anyway? We just had our fill of cardboard." It was a totally lame thing to say, especially coming from me. And, despite my claim, I grudgingly acknowledged that I was beyond hungry.

"I promise you, you're going to like it," he encouraged softly and reached to cut me a slice.

"Make it small, please."

He rolled his eyes but did as I asked. He held the piece up for my inspection. Blood was flowing down his fingers into his palm. I leaned forward and closed my eyes while opening my mouth. He gently placed the piece on my tongue, and I closed my mouth around it. My eyes flew open almost instantly.

"Good?" he said with that cocky grin of his.

I nodded as I started chewing. It was so good. It tasted better than anything I'd ever eaten before.

"More?"

I nodded again.

He cut a larger strip this time and held it up.

My hands clamped around his wrist, holding it solidly in place. I ate the strip of meat he held and then proceeded to lick the blood from his fingers and then his palm. When I'd licked the last bit, I froze. The realization of what I was doing struck me, and in one motion, I dropped his hand and scooted away from him.

"Oh my God! I'm so sorry!" I exclaimed. Overwhelmed by feelings of shame, I hurriedly wiped my mouth with the back of my hand.

He just sat there, looking at me with a knowing grin on his face. "You've wanted to do that since you saw me with the bacon grease," he accused.

"What! No!" I protested. But the more I protested, the more he laughed. I finally just gave up and wrapped my arms around myself, totally humiliated.

Ignoring my embarrassment, he went back to pulling strips of meat from the deer and eating them. "Macy, come here and do this for yourself," he urged.

I didn't really have any call to argue now. Not with my live performance just moments old. I slid back over and watched him demonstrate the easiest way to eat a deer when you had claws.

After we'd eaten our fill, which was a surprising amount, Adam led us to a small stream where we washed up. Still plagued by embarrassment, I avoided eye contact with him.

"Macy."

"What?" I asked dejectedly.

"Look at me." He took my chin in his hand, forcing me to meet his eyes. There was no humor in them now, only concern. "It's okay. Your first experiences with the leopard DNA can be overwhelming or frightening." He let go of my chin but still maintained eye contact. "It's normal and with practice you will be able to control it."

He looked down, his mouth pulling into a frown. "At least they didn't starve you and set you lose in a chicken coup." He met my eyes again with a look on his face that said "top that."

"Wait, what?" I asked in confusion.

"Oh, yeah," he said, walking backwards. "It was me and about a hundred chickens. I didn't even bother to de-feather them." He pivoted and continued walking. "Leopard DNA or not, that was a bathroom nightmare."

There was an image I wished I didn't have. I shook my head, trying to dislodge the visual. Starting forward to join him, I asked, "Why were you munching down on chickens?"

"It was part of my training to hunt and eat. I could kill anything, but I couldn't force myself to eat it. So, they left me no choice. They locked me in a room until I was half starved to death. Then they put me in the chicken coup."

"And you tore into the chickens?"

"No. I still resisted. Until they cut the head off of one of the chickens. As soon as I smelled the blood, I was a goner. Haven't much cared for chicken since."

That was harsh. Both the whole event and his aversion toward chicken. "Wait a minute," I said, stumbling to a halt. "You knew that was going to happen to me?"

He stopped and faced me. "I knew you would have a reaction. I didn't know you were going to claim my hand as your dinner plate," he said mockingly.

"You still could have warned me," I chided.

"What would you have done?" he asked pointedly. "It affects you however it affects you. You just happened to be a little more," he paused for dramatic effect, regarding me through his eyelashes, "risqué than most."

At my groan, he laughed and wrapped his arm around my shoulder. "So, was I finger licking good?" he asked smugly.

Oh brother, he was never going to let this go. Just once I'd like this stuff to happen to him instead of me.

Our trip back to the hollow was made in relative silence. Except for the numerous times he interrupted with his snickering. I finally decided to let the embarrassment go. I couldn't change it, and if it had happened to someone else, like Miranda, I would have been laughing my butt off.

That brought a smile to my face. Enjoying someone else's embarrassing moments? Nothing like it.

We were approaching the hollow, when Adam stopped abruptly and put an arm out to hold me back. Peering over his arm, I saw what had stopped him. The yard surrounding the cabin was swarming with people dressed in hazmat looking suits.

I'm guessing those aren't Organization people.

Consortium, Adam answered tightly.

What we suspected had just became a known fact. Someone on our team was a traitor.

Have they spotted us? I asked.

Not yet. But they are looking. See the two gathered at the water pump?

I searched for the spot he was specifying.

That's an infrared detector. As soon as they aim it this way, they'll know where we are.

What do we do?

Back away slowly. No sudden movements to draw their attention.

I begin to edge backwards. *To the ATV?*

Yes.

We'd covered about half the distance to the ATV when we heard voices raised in alarm. *Run!* Adam commanded and leapt into a sprint. I followed right behind him, and we reached the ATV in what seemed like an impossibly short amount of time.

Throwing the cover branches aside, Adam pulled the ATV out and hopped on. I piled on after and wrapped myself around him. Once we crested the ridge, we could see the solid wall of flames approaching. Our quick getaway was forced to a halt.

I could sense the tension in Adam as he once again sought escape from the Consortium's flames. They'd learned since last time. The wall of flames was a complete circle this time

We can't drive through, right?

No.

I studied the flames. They were primarily on the lower half of the trees. *What about up and over? Can this thing climb trees? Or can we?*

We might be able to, he admitted slowly, *but you have no experience at it.*

I leaned in, hugging him closer. *Right the first time, remember?* I could feel his hesitation. I suspected he'd already considered this and rejected it because of me. *It's our only option, Adam.*

He acknowledged the truth by becoming all business. "Get off," he said. "Remove your shoes."

I slid off and bent over coughing. Smoke was starting to filter in around us. "I've never shifted on purpose," I told him as I sat and started pulling off my shoes.

He joined me on the ground. "What about during the hunt?"

"That just happened involuntarily."

"Well, it's not hard. It's the reverse of pulling it back. Just see your claws pushing through rather than retracting."

I grimaced at his description. It sounded painful. But I did what he said and was rewarded by their none too painful appearance. Wiggling my toes, I had only one thought. Yuck. This was way beyond needing a pedicure.

"Tie your shoelaces together," he said.

I tied them together and slung my shoes over my shoulders.

Adam stood and walked a few feet away to a large tree. He looked back at me and said, "Use your claws to grip the tree." His hands mimicked his words. "Jam your toes in to hold you up and use your hands to pull." Adam's ears swiveled.

I could hear them too. I scrambled off the ground and joined him by the tree.

"We'll try to climb above the smoke and then start angling sideways." Positioning me in front of the tree trunk, he said, "Now."

I kicked my foot into the trunk and was surprised when it stuck. The next kick was higher. Reaching up, I forced the claws on my hands into the wood and pulled myself up. I moved right hand over left and opposite hand with the opposite leg. Except for the feeling that my toenails were going to be ripped off at any moment, it was pretty easy.

We ascended the tree, making it to the cover of the branches, before they made it to our left behind ATV. I could hear their vehicles and shouts below as they searched for us.

Adam led the way, moving us from tree to tree. If the rising temperature was any indication, we were getting close to the flames. The branches themselves were starting to be warm to the touch. I hadn't considered that factor when suggesting this idea.

A high pitched whistle split the air, and I pressed my hands to my ears. I strained to hear what was happening and heard enough bits of conversation to know that they had figured out we were in the trees.

I enfolded my face into my elbow as I coughed loudly. We needed to climb higher, but I didn't think the branches would hold our weight.

Keep going, Adam urged.

I wiped away sweat dripping from my forehead into my eyes and reached for the next branch. My hand slipped, and I nearly fell. It seemed the sweat was mixing with all the grime just enough to make my hands slippery. Hearing Adam's sharp intake of breath, I quickly righted myself.

I'm okay, I assured him while I wiped my hands off.

I froze as a dart whistled in the distance between me and Adam. They were shooting at us now?

With a new sense of urgency, I quickly caught up to Adam. He was perched at the end of the branch, staring at the six foot gap to the next tree.

Another dart planted in the tree above our heads, and we both ducked. How could they even see us with all this smoke? And weren't they concerned about being caught in the fire?

Adam buried a cough before saying, *You can make this.*

I wasn't so sure. But like so many other things in my recent history, I was going to do it anyway.

You first, I said. I wanted to see how he got across.

He crouched and shot forward. He grasped the intended branch with his hands and then swung his legs up and over. It was a very graceful maneuver that he made look easy.

I wasn't expecting to perform anything near as pretty.

Crouching as close to the end of the branch as I could, I was just about to leap when a sharp stinging erupted in my right bicep. I turned and saw the dart sticking out of my arm.

"NO!" Adam yelled, confirming our location.

A barrage of darts blanketed the air between us, forcing Adam to stay back. I could immediately sense his anger with himself for his slip.

"Macy, hold on," he pleaded.

I pulled the dart out, but I could already feel the effects of the drugs in my system. I turned the dart absently between my fingers. Completely irrelevant to my current situation, I wondered what drug they were using in the dart. I'd never been able to find one that worked on Kenny. I looked up in time to see Adam preparing to jump.

Adam, No!

I dropped the dart and gripped the branch to keep from falling. Everything was starting to sway, including Adam's angry face.

You can't rescue me if you're captured or dead. If you show yourself, that's what you'll be.

I didn't think he was going to listen to me, but then I saw him move away from the edge of the limb. I tried to brace myself on the branch, but my hand must have missed, and I face planted into the limb.

Macy! Adam cried as he witnessed my slip.

Tilting my head so that I could see his face, I tried to reassure him. *I'll be okay. They want me for something. That means alive.*

Adam pressed his back against the trunk in an effort to avoid another volley of darts. I felt another sting as one of the darts found a home in my thigh. My eyelids were so heavy. I couldn't resist closing them.

I will find you! Adam snarled.

The power of his determination filled me, and I forced my eyes open. The look on his face echoed the feeling inside of me, telling me clearly that he would.

As the drug's hold over me grew, my grip on the tree loosened. I listed to one side, the weight of my legs pulling them free of the branch. I was left grasping with only my fingertips. Staring into his eyes, I found courage that replaced my fear.

He nodded, *I will find you.*

It was almost a whisper, but it had the strength of iron. I held on to his strength. He would find me. I knew he would.

I'm counting on it, I said weakly.

The anguish on his face was the last thing I saw before my fingers lost their grip.

CHAPTER 16

THE SENSATION OF FALLING WRAPPED around me like a thick blanket. I was tangled in it, having to fight and claw my way free. I pushed layer after layer aside until I became aware of pain. It played like the rhythm of a drumbeat. One strong beat followed by one soft, repeated over and over again. It was to that rhythm that I opened my eyes.

It was dark. I was tempted to close my eyes again, but the pain wouldn't let me. I realized the drumbeat was centered along my face and neck. I thought that might have something to do with the contorted position I was laying in.

I pushed myself upright and blinked several times as I tried to clear my mind. I reached up to rub my neck, but withdrew my hand quickly when my touch caused a sharp stinging sensation. Reaching up again, I carefully traced a slightly raised diamond pattern in my skin. It covered my right cheek and extended down the same side of my neck.

Where did that come from? I hoped I wasn't developing spots like a leopard. It felt like it had been burned into my skin. What left a diamond patterned burn? Had I been branded?

I fought with the fog in my brain as I tried to recall how I had gotten here. Slowly, the memories came.

We had been trying to escape. There were trees and fire...I snapped my head up sharply, the memory of Adam's face as I fell filling in the blank.

Adam!

His response was immediate. *Macy! Are you alright?*

I checked myself over for any other injuries. Now recalling

my fall from the tree, I assumed the burn was from my collision with the mesh of a net. As I'd never gone head first into one from forty feet up before, I couldn't say for sure.

I think so. Just got a little too friendly with a net.

His relief slammed into to me, causing me to gasp a little with the weight of it.

Easy there tiger, I breathed and leaned back against my enclosure for support. I sensed his momentary confusion before he figured it out.

Sorry, he whispered. *Where are you?*

I looked around. *It's dark. I think I'm in a box. I'm gift wrapped.*

Concentrate, Macy. Adam's irritation came through our bond loud and clear.

Hey! You're not the one with cotton in your brain, I fired back.

Just tell me what you see, he urged more gently. He was still irritated, but he eased up some with the emotion.

I ran my hands against the sides of my container. It felt smooth against my hands. *I think it's metal.* I noticed a pool of light on the floor and traced it to a small window. *There's a little window.* Coming to my knees, I looked out the four by eight inch cutout. *We are still in the woods. There are lots of trees. That's all I see.*

Can you hear anything?

I closed my eyes and listened. *There's a repetitive sound. A sort of roaring. Like something slapping water, maybe?*

A paddlewheel?

I don't know. I can't see anything but trees. I sat back against the box as a wave of nausea rolled over me. *Are you okay?*

Yes. Cedars showed up. Miranda is beside herself. Cedars has his hands full trying to calm her down.

She's a bit of a drama queen, I agreed groggily. Footsteps signaled someone's approach. *Someone's coming.*

Be careful, Macy, Adam pleaded.

Aren't I always?

Wherever he was, his sigh travelled all the way across the distance.

Hey, it's not like I keep signing up for this stuff, I said defensively.

Maybe not, but you're like a lure for trouble. You just keep reeling it in.

That was kind of like my shovel and digging analogy. Sadly, I couldn't disagree with his assessment.

I heard the click of a lock, and I pressed against the opposite end of my prison. The side with the window opened and a voice called, "Please join us, Dr. Greer."

I took a moment to slip on my shoes still hanging around my neck before scooting forward and out of the cage. Standing up, I brought my hand up to shield my eyes from the light.

I was met by a tall, skinny man with slicked back hair the color of glossy black ink. He was dressed like he was on safari in Africa during the 1930s. He even had the tan kerchief tied around his neck. All he was missing was the hat. But that would have mussed his hair, and I had the distinct feeling he wouldn't have liked that.

"The famous Dr. Greer," he said mockingly.

"Famous?" I repeated while scanning the area directly in front of me. Adam had guessed correctly. There was a paddlewheel and possibly a mill. I passed that information on to Adam. To slick, I asked, "Have we met?"

"You haven't had the pleasure," he informed me with his face stretched wide to accommodate his smile.

Yeah, that was creepy, and pleasure was not the word I would use.

He frowned as though he understood what I was thinking. "I'm Arthur Millsap," he said, like I should recognize the name.

When he continued looking at me expectantly, I responded with, "Doesn't ring a bell."

"How remiss of your friends," he sneered softly, momentarily losing the false smile. "I'm the President of the Consortium."

Before I could respond to his pronouncement, the wind shifted, and I almost gagged. "What is that smell?" I asked from beneath my hands which I'd reflexively brought up to cover my nose and mouth.

He looked around the area, clearly scorning what he saw. "That would be the many paper mills that dot this river." He looked back at me, and his smile reappeared as he watched my struggle with my gag reflex. "You grow accustomed to it," he offered with a shrug of his shoulders.

Uugh. Why would you want to?

I'm somewhere that has a lot of paper mills, next to a river. The smell is terrible.

You're doing great, Macy. Keep looking.

I tried breathing through my mouth to keep from gagging. It helped a little.

"You said you were with the Consortium? The one in support of hybrid proliferation?" As I talked, I searched the river for mills, looking for a name or town. Anything to help Adam find me.

"So, you do know of us?" he said delightedly.

"That's all I know about you," I threw out quickly.

My retort served to throw some water on his fire, causing his hundred watt smile to dim a fraction. I knew I wasn't making all nice with him, but pretending had never really been my strong suit. Staying alive, however, seemed to be, and I knew I was going to have to do better than this to keep that going.

Surely, I could pretend long enough for Adam to find me. I could act like...what? A wimp? That wouldn't work. Coward? No way. Submissive. That was how I needed to appear to appease his ego.

I almost laughed out loud at my conclusion. When had I ever been submissive? I wasn't sure I could pull it off. Maybe I could just keep him talking. In the movies Miranda made me watch, the villains always loved to talk.

"Why are you in favor of everyone becoming a hybrid?" I asked.

He was pleased by my question and launched into quite an extensive monologue. He was so into it, I didn't think he cared if I was listening or not.

Tuning him out, I focused on my search and spotted something blue further up in the trees. It was a sign. I just barely made out the faded lettering, Blue Ridge.

We're next to what used to be Blue Ridge Paper Mill.

Elation zinged through our bond, making me a little woozy. I put my hand against the nearest tree in order to keep myself upright. Millsap was still fully engaged in his speech and didn't notice my wobble.

We got you. Just hold on, Mace.

Yeah, I was holding. I would like to hold on to a stick while I knocked slick upside the head. Or a gun. Then I would only have to pull the trigger. That would take less effort on my part.

Macy, you need to let up a little.

Well, which is it, Adam? Hold on or let up? They are mutually exclusive, I snapped at him. Almost immediately, I regretted my retort. *Sorry. It's kind of been a long week. I'm just cranky.*

So, everything's normal is what you're saying.

Very funny, Catman.

Glad you think so. But seriously, Macy, it won't be long.

I glanced around the campgrounds. There were guards posted along the perimeter approximately every twenty feet or so.

I'm not going anywhere just yet. There are guards posted around the perimeter.

As if that could hold you.

I smiled at Adam's confidence in me. The crazy thing was, even though I might not have had confidence in myself to accomplish such an escape, I knew that I would absolutely do it anyway if given the chance.

Millsap's rising volume drew my attention back to him.

"…because it's time for the human species to evolve, Dr. Greer." He thought my smile was for him. Encouraged at my presumed interest, he became more animated, making great sweeping gestures with his arms. "To leave behind all the petty squabbles associated with beliefs in false Gods."

It was hard not to stare in open disbelief. *Millsap is insane,* I informed Adam.

He is a few fries short.

More than a few. I'm betting he opted for fruit. Who chose fruit with a hamburger? Unless it was deep fried.

A maniacal grin lit his face as he continued gibbering on in his grand finale. "…to embrace progress and reform and establish a civilized world culture."

And he thought this would happen by turning everyone into animals? Cue the crazy person music. How did I segue from that?

"So," I said, clearing my throat. "Are you a hybrid?"

He spread his arms and lifted his chin as the shift overtook him. Pincers emerged from his mouth, and antennae grew from his forehead.

My eyes involuntarily widened in horror.

Macy, what's wrong?

I was speechless as the freak show continued. Another pair of arms, segmented like an insect's, grew from his sides.

He's a bug, Adam. A giant freaking bug!

I take it, you don't like bugs?

No, I don't like bugs! I screeched at him.

I wanted to run away as fast as I could or pound it until it was dead. I couldn't control the shift that raced through my body.

Okay, Mace. Keep it under control. I'm almost there.

He wasn't quite laughing, but he couldn't entirely hide his amusement. It made me mad to think he was laughing at me, and that made the fear subside a little. Enough, so that I wasn't going to react out of panic. I knew I had to maintain control. Showing weakness in the presence of an enemy never ended well.

I planted my feet like they were in cement. I would not give in to fear. I hadn't ruled out fighting yet, but I was not running.

Millsap regarded me through insectoid eyes and then slowly began to shift back. Observing my shifted form, he said, "It seems like we have something in common."

I had to play this to my advantage. Realizing my breaths were coming in short gasps, I deliberately slowed my breathing. My lips I forced into a smile, but careful, so as not to show so much teeth as to look threatening.

"It looks like we do," I said, being extra careful not to cut myself with my own teeth.

He must have bought it. Without the slightest concern, he turned and started walking toward a row of tents.

Did I appear totally incapable of attacking anyone? I was getting tired of people turning their backs on me, dismissing me as a threat. True, I didn't have any experience fighting in this form, but I was more than willing to practice on him.

"Do come along, Dr. Greer," Millsap called.

My whole body felt hot as anger flushed through me. He was addressing me like I was a child and not an equal. I hated it.

Be submissive. Who was I kidding? I didn't know how to be submissive. What was submissive anyway? It was weak and useless. Submissive my—

Why are you thinking submissive? Adam questioned.

I am not submissive! I growled at him.

You don't have to tell me, he laughed. *But you are currently outmanned and outgunned. Be smart.*

I took a deep breath and immediately regretted it. Why did making paper have to smell so bad? But Adam was right, and there was no point in staying put. I moved forward, following Millsap at what I considered a safe distance.

"You're a lot more accepting of this than I was led to believe," Millsap said when I caught up.

Who was leading him to believe anything about me? That was what I had to find out.

"I haven't observed an appreciable bad side to being a hybrid," I told him. That was true, if I ignored my newly discovered urge to kill.

He stopped walking when he reached the last tent. "Too bad your friends don't feel the same."

A feeling of dread enveloped me when I realized what was coming. "I wasn't aware that they felt any different," I said hesitantly. "They've never given me any indication that they thought otherwise." I mentally braced myself as he reached for the tent flap.

"Interesting," he drawled, pulling it aside. "I have found them to be most disagreeable." His eyes were firmly fixed on me, waiting for me to look through the portal he had created.

My breath caught in my throat at the sight of Olivia and

Juarez in the middle of the tent. Stretched high above their heads, metal manacles secured their arms to tent posts that travelled from floor to ceiling. They were bruised and bloodied and unconscious.

I involuntarily took a few steps into the tent. The urge to run to them was strong, but I stayed where I was. Placing my hands on my hips, I rifled through the damage done to them. I was sure my face registered my shock. I was not that good an actress.

Millsap entered and stood beside me. "Don't fret, Dr. Greer," he encouraged. "They are healing quite nicely."

From my peripheral vision, I could tell there was a large grin of approval stretched across his face. It was completely opposite the disgust I felt. Then the disgust turned into something else. I felt oddly separated from what was going on. I was still there. I knew that I was. But it felt different. Maybe it was some sort of survival instinct, allowing me to function in the face of horror.

"And then, we can start again," he sang softly.

The glee in his voice at that prospect was unmistakable. Though I doubted he would dirty his hands with the task, he clearly enjoyed watching. Sick, evil, sadistic—

"Hello, Beautiful."

My eyes flew across the room, zeroing in on the voice. Strutting across the tent was a free and unbloodied Pike. That was not quite correct. He was wiping blood from his hands with Juarez's shirt. Olivia and Juarez's blood.

I was thrust from the surreal distance into the very real present. Rage filled my entire being. I now understood the phrase, I saw red. It seemed like my vision had been shrouded in red. All I could think was, he's dead.

Adam's concern penetrated the haze, and I answered him before he could ask. *They've got Olivia and Juarez. Pike, however, is amazingly free and unharmed.*

Adam's anger joined mine, adding yet another layer. With his boost, I felt stronger and even more eager to fight.

Pike stopped in front of me, and everything faded from my vision except him. He was within easy reach. A swipe of my claws across his neck was all it would take. I would have to make sure I hit hard and deep enough so that he wouldn't be able to heal from it. But it would be so easy.

Adam must have picked up on what I was contemplating. I recognized the effort it took for him to rein in his anger.

Macy, he said with his voice tinted with fear. *Don't do anything that's going to get you killed.*

They hurt them! Pike hurt them! I screamed at him. *He betrayed them!*

I know, Macy. I know. We'll get them out, and Pike will pay for his betrayal. I'll see to it.

I could see to it right now. Focusing on Pike, I let all the anger, all the rage I felt fill my eyes. My head tilted to the side as I located the pulse in his neck and measured the force I would need.

Sensing his mistake, Pike scowled and stepped back out of my reach.

"Now, now, play nice, you two," chided Millsap as he observed the exchange.

I felt anything but nice. Did he not realize how close to death he was?

You can't give in to the leopard right now, I heard Adam say as if from a distance.

But I could. I could give in to the rage. I could end them both. I thought it would even feel good. Every muscle in my body burned with the need to attack.

Macy, please, Adam pleaded. *You have to pull it back.*

It was the please that did it. I didn't understand his reasoning, but I'd learned to trust him.

Swallowing my anger was physically painful, but I forced it away, allowing the shift to go with it. Letting go of the rage left me feeling empty and numb. It also left me clear headed for the first time since I had awakened.

"That's better, don't you think?" Millsap said, as he acknowledged my down shift. "More civilized, hmm?"

This from the man who wanted everyone to be more

animalistic. I turned my face to him and watched his amused grin fade. I knew if I held his stare much longer he would be forced to look away, thus blowing my submissive cover. It felt like I was moving through concrete as I looked down at the ground.

Does Pike know I can talk to you? I asked Adam.

Once again, I was awash in relief that wasn't my own. But it felt good this time. It strengthened me rather than making me feel drunk, and I soaked it in.

Not to my knowledge. Prior to recently, it's only happened one other time in our history. And that was at the very beginning. Adam paused. *Cedars didn't tell him anything either. At the most, he would merely suspect a connection.*

I looked at Olivia and Juarez again. Obviously Millsap wanted me to observe the scene in front of me. The question was, why? As an implied threat if I didn't cooperate? Or to expose Pike's role in the torture? Maybe both.

"Were you always working for them, or did you just recently switch teams," I sneered at Pike.

He seemed truly confused by my anger. But feeling he was no longer in danger, the playful demeanor that had been his returned.

"This is the best way. You'll see," he assured me, complete with a waggle of his eyebrows. Then he reached as if to brush my cheek with his fingers.

I growled a warning, and he abruptly dropped his hand.

Millsap chuckled at Pike's embarrassment. Something that Pike clearly didn't like. The two studied each other with malice in their eyes. I knew they were working together, but they appeared to hate each other.

Regardless of their relationship, Pike wasn't the greatest threat in the tent. I turned my attention from him and focused on Millsap.

"If you don't mind me asking, what is your interest in me?" I asked Millsap.

"You, my dear Dr. Greer, are going to make our dream a reality."

Not if I could help it.

He held the tent flap aside, indicating it was time to leave. I exited under his uplifted arm without looking back. He smelled like a garbage dump, which was fitting for a roach.

I didn't know where he intended to go, so I stopped and waited for him to catch up. Was he bouncing?

"The fact that you are now a hybrid only makes it sweeter." He did a single pirouette and leapt over a tree root, landing squarely in front of me. He raised his eyebrows at me, daring me to comment, and then walked calmly away as if he had done nothing strange.

Well, that just added a whole new level of crazy. I stared at his retreating form, struggling to find a diagnosis that fit him. He was both evil pyscho and completely nuts. And, apparently, also a ballerina. He was a pyschonuterina.

Why would anyone willingly choose to let him be their leader? They'd have to be crazy or under a threat of some kind. Or programmed against their will?

I scanned the camp again, looking for any weak links. The guards were all blank faced which gave me no clue as to how they felt about his leadership.

As far as the camp went, it was a simple configuration. Two rows of tents formed a right angle with a single row of jeeps completing the triangle. Not much of a headquarters for a president.

I could tell by his fidgeting that he was eager to say more about his plan. It would probably be best if I played along.

"If you're counting on me to come up with a plan to enact this worldwide hybridization, you are going to have to send me to school. I have a lot of catching up to do."

He laughed derisively. That wasn't a good sign.

"My dear, Dr. Greer," he said smugly.

I really wished he would stop calling me dear.

"I am not interested in your brain," he said, looking at me like I was the dumbest person in the world for not knowing what he was thinking.

He wasn't interested in my brain? If he didn't want me to craft a plan, then what did he want me for?

He giggled at the puzzled expression on my face. "Well, not in the way that you think. It's your DNA that I want."

That was unexpected enough for me to be intrigued. "You're going to clone me?"

"You are too cute, Dr. Greer. I am not going to clone you. Clones are poor replications of the original. We both know that on the inside they are fraught with DNA mutations which over the space of a few years lead to the failure of the specimen."

Was everyone in this new world a molecular biology expert?

If he noticed my consternation with his level of knowledge, he gave no outward sign. He was too consumed with whatever juicy secret was concealed behind his shining eyes.

I still didn't see the connection between my DNA and his interest in my brain. He didn't want me to form a plan, and he wasn't cloning me. Then what did he need my DNA for?

"No, no," he continued, snickering and tossing his head from side to side. "We aren't going to clone you, we are going to make offspring from you."

My steps faltered, and I stumbled over a protruding root. Offspring? As in babies?

"That's right, Dr. Greer," he said. "Beautiful bouncing baby boys and girls. I will make a whole army of Dr. Greers. Then no one will ever be able to stop me again."

It was too much. *Adam!* I cried. *Where are you?*

We've reached the edge of the camp. There are more guards than I had hoped. Too many for just me and Cedars to handle—

I cut across Adam's thoughts. *He wants to make babies using my DNA.*

Adam's shock reverberated through the bond. *He what?*

Babies. He wants to make me into a supply house for a baby factory. I barely registered Adam's emotions through the fear that threatened to overtake me.

I will never let that happen! Adam roared.

His fury was unmistakable, and I swayed a little under the

force of it. I quickly grabbed the nearest tent to steady myself and hoped Millsap didn't notice.

"Here we go, Dr. Greer," Millsap said, eyeing me intently. "Your home away from home while you are with us." He watched me with interest until I stood up unaided by the tent.

I surmised his intentions were not to let me merrily go on my way when he was finished with me. All of my instincts were telling me to fight or run, but I knew that would just lead to more darts and a return trip to La La Land. If I wanted to escape, then I had to enter the tent. Those few steps into the tent were some of the hardest I'd ever taken.

"You are, of course, free to roam about the complex when not in use," he said.

Complex? It barely ranked as a decent campsite. He was delusional on so many fronts.

"Aren't you afraid I'll try to escape?" I asked.

The smile that crept across his face hinted at all kinds of evil. "Where could you possibly go that I couldn't find you?"

Once again, I fought the need to shift. I knew it was best to let him think I was still the submissive female and not fighting the urge to tear his head off. It would keep me alive and unbound longer and give Adam the best chance to forge a rescue attempt. I owed that much to Olivia and Juarez.

Unaware of my struggle, he let the flap fall. It slapped loudly against the tent. "Enjoy your evening, Dr. Greer," he called as he walked away.

I turned my back to the opening and waited until my eyes adjusted to the darkened interior of the tent. The accommodations weren't much. A cot stood against one side. A table with a tray of food was opposite that. I walked slowly to the cot and sat down, dropping my head into my hands.

There were moments in life that let you know what kind of person you were—what exactly you were capable of. Without any doubt in my mind, I knew when the opportunity arose, I was going to do everything possible to kill Millsap. In fact, I was intent on not leaving here until Millsap was dead.

No one was taking my babies from me. No one.

Peace descended over me as I accepted, even anticipated my new role. Strange how a little leopard DNA made killing my enemies totally acceptable. Or maybe it wasn't just the added DNA. People like Millsap didn't deserve to live. I just never figured myself as the executioner. But there was no gray with me on this issue. He was a danger not only to me, but to every other being on the earth. He had to die.

This must have been what Olivia was trying to get me to understand. If I had the ability to stop people like Millsap, then I had a responsibility to. I hoped I got the chance to tell her that I now understood what she meant.

Adam.

I'm here.

I think I'd like to join the superhero mutant team now.

The joy he felt accompanied his words to me. *Welcome aboard,* he said quietly.

I stretched out on the cot and laid one arm across my eyes. *When does Operation Get My Butt out of Here commence?*

As soon as reinforcements arrive. Should be a couple hours still.

Won't they be able to spot you? I didn't think my captors would miss a small army gathering around their camp.

Shouldn't. They'll come bearing mobile optic shield generators large enough to cover us. Until dark.

What happens at dark?

We glow blue or rather, the shields do. Sort of give us away.

You'd look good in blue.

Our bond was becoming stronger. I both heard and felt him snort in response. I'd never sensed so many emotions coming from him. In fact, before the transfusion, I thought he was rather cold and unfeeling. I was wrong.

Rolling onto my side, I put one arm underneath my head and tucked the opposite hand between my knees. *Adam, this rage thing...* I felt him still, waiting for me to continue. *I wanted to kill him with my bare hands. I wanted so badly to give in to the rage and rip out his throat.* I sighed, recalling the rage that had almost overpowered me. *It would have been so easy.*

But you didn't, he replied carefully.

*Is it always like this? This—*what was the word—*consuming?* Again, I felt him pause as he searched for the right words. If I closed my eyes, I could almost see him.

It will consume you, if you let it. Then you may do things that you will regret later. Once you start down the path of giving in to the urge to kill, it's a hard road back. But you don't have to let it consume you. Just like earlier, you can master it and use it strategically.

I thought of the many times over these last few days that I'd seen him visibly force down his anger. It could be done.

You've mastered it, I told him.

His response was very solemn. *Not without a few regrets. But you're better than me, Macy. You've already mastered it several times just today.*

Didn't feel like it. I rolled onto my back, pillowing my head in my hands. *You've suspected Pike all along, haven't you?*

Yeah, he said, his anger seething just below the surface. *But I had no proof. Considering his position, eliminating him based on a judgment call from me was not acceptable.*

His words were logical, but I could sense the regret that he now had regarding his decision not to act.

I hate him, I said.

I know, Macy.

Given the bond that we now shared, I knew he did. *He has to die.*

I know.

The tent flap suddenly flew aside, and Pike sauntered in, looking entirely too relaxed and happy. Before I knew what was happening, I had rolled to a standing crouch in the center of the tent.

Pike's bravado faded a little, and his forward motion stopped as he observed me. "How's it going?" he asked casually.

Seriously?

He ran his hand through his hair while mumbling, "Dumb question."

What's happening, Adam asked.

I rudely shushed him while I focused all my attention on Pike. Everything in his demeanor, his movements, his voice, the expression on his face, projected non-threatening. Everything except his eyes. They were intense, cold and calculating. And they were intently watching me. I guessed he was planning his actions based on my responses. It seemed Pike was the consummate actor.

The shift pushed against me. It was almost as if I could feel the leopard pacing inside me. I was already weak from hunger. I couldn't risk the energy expenditure of another shift, and I was not going to refuel by eating any food they supplied.

Still trying to project harmlessness, Pike stuffed both hands in his pockets. "So, Millsap told me you knew we were going to be parents."

My breath caught in my throat. "We?" I barked. "You're the male DNA supplier?"

The revulsion in my voice caused him to drop the act. "You don't have to make it sound so clinical. We could have fun with it," he said vehemently.

A come on veiled in threat. I couldn't help myself. My laughter bubbled up from deep inside. "You think, that you," I paused, bending over and letting the laughter have full reign. "Will ever touch me!"

My laughter increased his agitation, and he began shifting from foot to foot, creating a sort of ridiculous looking shuffling movement.

When the laughter was spent, all that was left was fury. "I'm going to rip your throat out," I spat at him. "Then I'm going to hunt down Millsap and do the same. Then I'm going to destroy everyone and everything associated with the Consortium."

He involuntarily took a step back. Realizing he'd given ground to me, he regained control and regarded me with a sneer. "You won't be so brave after you've been here for a while or when your friends pay for your rejection."

"They were your friends, too," I said through gritted teeth. "How could you betray them like this? How could you betray your grandparents?"

He began to slowly walk backwards. "Who says I'm not acting with their full knowledge and consent?"

"You're lying," I said automatically. But I knew that he wasn't telling the whole truth. I could smell it.

"Am I?" he laughed, starting out of the tent. "Oh," he said, pausing and turning back around, "I wouldn't count on being rescued this time, Beautiful. No one's coming for you."

Again, something about his statement was off, besides the fact that I knew he was wrong. He was still standing there, waiting for a response. He was fishing. He wasn't sure if Adam and I were in contact.

"I don't need rescuing," I said with a smile. "Super brain, remember?" I tapped my temple with my fingertip. "I'll be free, and you'll be dead."

He tried to hide it, but I caught the doubt that briefly flared in his eyes. "Time will tell," he said, backing slowly out of the tent.

Yes, it would.

I stood there unable to move for fear I would take off after him. I wanted so much to wrap my hands around his throat. But instead, I willed myself to calm down, and the need to shift eased somewhat. I shook my hands that I hadn't realized I'd fisted.

You're one tough Kitty Cat, Adam's voice whispered across my mind.

You heard that? I asked, suddenly embarrassed. I'd forgotten I wasn't alone. I guess I never truly would be again.

I even somehow managed to hear Pike.

That was probably because I'd mentally repeated everything he'd said, just trying to wrap my brain around it. I felt bare, exposed. This was what Miranda had tried to explain to me.

With head bowed, I waited for the condemnation I was certain was coming from Adam. But his reply surprised me.

When it comes time for the tearing out of throats, I'll help.

Relief flooded through me, my own this time. I sank down onto the cot again. My whole body was shaking with unspent adrenaline and anger. My stomach rumbled loudly. I was so hungry. Somehow, I kept forgetting that fact in the midst of all this drama. Never thought that would ever happen.

I'll bring more cardboard, Adam offered.

I uttered a sound that was half laugh, half sob. *Don't forget the water,* I reminded him.

CHAPTER 17

AS I SAT THERE WITH my head in my shaking hands, I replayed the conversation with Pike. His statement alluding to the founder's involvement with the Consortium needed to be addressed right away.

Adam, did you catch the part about the grandparents being involved with the Consortium?

I was not surprised by the long delay that prefaced Adam's answer. I imagined it was pretty difficult to acknowledge the fact that someone you had known and worked with for years had suddenly flipped sides and consequently, become your enemy. If what Pike said was true, then there would be huge ramifications. All of which would probably fall squarely on Adam's shoulders.

I did.

I knew Adam well enough now to know that short, clipped answers meant anger and reluctance to talk. But that hadn't stopped me yet.

And? I asked.

And, I don't know. It is possible, I guess.

Since when did Adam guess? He must be reeling from this latest bit of information. Welcome to my recent life.

But, there's nothing I can do about it right now, he grumbled. *Other than make sure this operation receives as little attention as possible.*

Would they know you called for reinforcements?

Only if they were watching for it. They maintain more of an oversight role in operations. I handle the actual doing. It is worrisome, though. I'm going to do some checking. You okay for now?

Just peachy, I assured him.

Peaches. One of nature's greatest smelling and tasting fruits. I cut my eyes to the table with the food. The platter had a big silver dome over the top, concealing its contents.

"Not gonna do it," I ordered myself. Rolling over onto my side, I put my back to the food. "Probably laced with something anyway."

While lying there fighting the temptation to eat, my thoughts turned to Kenny. Was this how Kenny and the others had felt? Captive? To them was I Millsap? Looking back, I couldn't believe how I was able to be so clinical about it all.

It was true that I had acted in the pursuit of science. But I'd played with their lives just like the HCF bureaucrats. I thought I was different. I meant to be different.

Originally, I had thought the hybrids were better off in the Colony. That they were protected there. It wasn't until recently that I acknowledged the boogie man was the one running the compound.

I didn't know how much it was going to mean, but I was really going to have to apologize the next time I saw them. Or maybe more than that, considering my pledge to help with whatever Kenny was cooking up. But I'd do it. I owed them too.

Macy, we got trouble.

What a surprise. *Yeah? So my lure is still in place?*

No kidding. I know what t-shirt I'm giving you when this is over.

Now that was just plain unfair.

What does trouble look like this time? I sighed.

I asked Renard and Julia's assistant if either of them had requested any operational updates. Only one of them had. Julia.

So Julia was in on it or at least aware of it. *Does she know about what's going on here?*

Not from this end. I managed to catch Lydia before she handed over the update. Instead, she gave a carefully worded report that will not incriminate her or us. And, she's going to keep me in the loop. I don't know if Pike or anyone else from this end is updating her. I've confirmed reinforcements are still on their way. It's possible she doesn't know yet. In any case, I'll move quickly when they arrive.

Lydia? *Why would this Lydia trust you more than her superiors?*

Because we have a history, he stated very calmly. He couldn't quite cover his reluctance to answer the question. That piqued my curiosity.

A history?

I brought her into the Organization.

I knew he was telling the truth. But he wasn't telling all of it, and he wasn't volunteering any more information either. History. Aah, he meant they used to be together as in a couple.

I suddenly felt very awkward, which didn't make sense. We'd only shared one brief kiss. It shouldn't bother me that he had been with someone else. And anyway, he was the one that always got possessive, not me.

Macy.

I could feel Adam squirming as I continued to mull over his "history." I was fully cognoscente of the fact that I was being ridiculous. I wasn't normally such an emotional person. I mean, I wasn't a robot before, but the strength of my emotions since I'd hybridized was overwhelming. And jealously was completely new to me.

Macy, it was a very long time ago. There is nothing more than friendship now, camaraderie between colleagues.

I accepted what he said. I wasn't trying to defend my reaction that I fully acknowledged I didn't have a right to. But that didn't make it go away.

Is this really necessary? He said in frustration. *Do you not have more important things to concern yourself with currently?*

Probably, but my mind seized on the long time ago remark. *How long ago?*

It was more than twenty years ago, Macy! Adam shouted at me.

Twenty years! He didn't look to be older than thirty-five. *Adam, how old are you?*

Adam's sigh reverberated down the length of my spine. I shivered in response. How the heck did he do that?

Macy, you know age is just a number. Especially, when you consider our nanobot engineering.

Yeah, yeah, you're only as old as you feel. How old?

You're not going to let this go, are you?

Do you know me? I smiled in anticipation of his response. This ought to be fodder for a good long while.

I am currently seventy eight years old, he said defiantly.

I blew a long slow whistle. Wow. Reverence. That was what this moment demanded. I bowed my head in respect.

"Moment's over," I announced loudly. Leaping off the cot, I danced around the tent, singing, *Grandpa's in the house.*

Adam's uniquely sour disposition sang back to me across our bond. I was sure I'd pay for this later, but for now, I was taking the joy where I could find it. I wasn't sure how long it lasted, but it felt good to be moving. Adam had given up and checked out long ago.

Once I started moving, I found I couldn't sit still. The need to run, to escape, to just do something was writhing inside me. I felt like I was trapped in a cage.

That brought an abrupt halt to the pacing that had replaced my dancing. Visions of big cats in zoos, walking back and forth in front of glass cages paraded through my mind. Did they feel like this? Great. Another thing to feel guilty about.

I needed to calm down, and I needed to think. Dropping cross legged onto the floor of the tent, I began to evaluate my situation.

What did I know? I was a prisoner, but a soon to be rescued one, so I wasn't too concerned about that. I trusted Adam would let me know what I needed to do when it was time.

I also knew that the Consortium was planning on mining my DNA to make more somethings like me. That was curious. Millsap did not say he was harvesting my eggs, only my DNA. Why did he only want a part of my DNA? Why not the whole egg? And what particular part of my DNA was he after?

If Pike was telling the truth, his DNA was supplying the Y chromosome. With his "have fun with it" comment, he'd hinted at a union of egg and sperm the old fashioned way, but I suspected that was not part of Millsap's plan.

I stood and shuddered as I pushed thoughts of me and Pike out of my mind. I settled back on the cot again while I tried to make sense of the Consortium's plans.

Had they advanced the science enough to mix and match individual segments of DNA from any number of contributors and end up with a viable living being? If so, then this was another huge leap forward in genetic engineering. And the question of how an army of babies would bring any kind of success for the Consortium's mission still remained. I needed more information.

Adam, will it interfere with any of the rescue plans if I take a stroll through camp?

Can you stay out of trouble? He asked flatly.

I frowned at his impossible question. I formulated several responses but knew they wouldn't satisfy him. I was attempting to answer again when he said, *Just don't die, okay?*

Okay? I agreed weakly. Not like I was trying to. No matter what my recent history said.

I rolled off the cot and approached the tent flap. Reaching for the flap, I pulled it aside and surveyed the scene outside. There were a few guards moving here and there, but it was mainly quiet. I crossed the threshold and headed back in the direction I'd travelled to get to the tent.

I hadn't noticed when I'd first arrived, because the smell of the paper mills was so overpowering, but there was another strong smell covering the camp. Passing closer than needed to a pair of guards, I inhaled sharply. I thought the smell was coming from them.

Adam, the guards smell funny.

They are Furries.

Can they all completely shape shift?

Yes.

Incredible. Now for the million dollar question I hadn't been brave enough to ask before. *Can you?*

I find that the longer I am what I am, the more of my body I am able to shift.

You mean the ability to shift is a progression of ever increasing shifts?

In my experience and most everyone else's on the team, Adam confirmed.

That would suggest that the nanobots are learning as they go. You think the nanobots will one day enable a full shift?

It seems probable.

That is so wild! I could be a were leopard one day.

It's something to shoot for, Adam laughed.

This was so amazing. To become an animal, a different species? I longed to study the nanobots and find out how they made this possible. Several guards regarded me warily as I passed them. I had better calm down. I wouldn't be able to study anything if I got killed. Not to mention, I had told Adam that I wouldn't die.

Now might be a good time to practice my stealth capabilities. It might allow me to avoid any more suspicious looks by the guards. What did Adam say? Be the leopard. Right.

I paused and closed my eyes, trying to remember the feeling without having to shift. There. I reached for it and opened my eyes. My vision was a little sharper, but not as if I was in full she cat mode. I guess there were degrees of shift even in the beginning.

Edging forward, I could hear voices on my left, behind the row of tents. Stepping between the tents, I stopped as I heard Pike and some unknown person with a whiney voice discussing the impending operation. It was coming from the tent on my right.

Leaning closer, I sniffed at the strange smell attached to the fabric. It was a smoky, funky smell which instantly made me need to sneeze. I hurriedly pinched my nose to stifle the feeling.

"What is your hurry? You still have to wait a year before training of the new hybrids can begin. It would be better to continue to *study* her during that time. She may have yet many secrets to reveal."

Sneering laughs followed the speaker, clearly indicating the sleaziness of the last statement. I assumed they were talking about me. But what was with the year time frame?

"It's too risky," Pike argued. "We are already risking too much. The DNA should have been collected already, and the body disposed of. She could be in contact with Adam right now."

There was a brief silence followed by Pike again. "Yes, the great and powerful Adam. Alpha of the pack. And a disgrace to all of mankind."

I frowned at his mocking of Adam.

"Macy must be saved. Macy must not be harmed. Macy blah, blah. Have you ever seen a man so whipped?" Pike shouted.

I didn't call that whipped. I was all for not harming Macy.

A new voice, deep and masculine responded in a monotonous tone. "We are doing sweeps of the surrounding area. There is no one out there."

As soon as he finished speaking, another round of laughing ensued. How was that funny?

"Besides, you know how the old man is. You'll never get a shot at her. He wants everything prim and proper for the process," said the previous whiney male speaker. His voice took on a mocking tone when he said, "Protocols are established for a reason. They must be followed."

Laughter filled the next few seconds. Then Pike spoke again. This time his words were filled with anger. "And you're sure the new process matures the fetuses in only a year?"

Matures to what? He couldn't mean full grown? I leaned in closer, trying to catch every word.

"We've done two trials already with the newest batch of nanobots. Each one was successful in the production of fully functioning hybrid adults within the time frame set by Dr. Millsap. You know this already."

They had nanobots capable of taking an engineered zygote from conception to fully matured adult in one year? This was science fiction even to my ears. And why did they keep laughing?

A scraping noise drew my attention to the top of the tent. Something was moving, but I couldn't quite make it out. I backed away from the tent. Standing on my toes, I could see a canister at the very top of the tent. It had a small hose attached that disappeared into the canvas. They were being gassed?

Focusing on the canister, I could, with great effort, make out a hand holding it. Flowing from there, I made out the body attached to the hand. It was extended from the tree above the tent. Even though I'd seen the hybrid, I still jumped when the eyes blinked, momentarily flashing white.

Adam, do you currently have a hybrid with the ability to camouflage in the camp?

Yes. He's performing a task for us.

I can see that. But only if I look really hard. Okay, just checking. Please go back to planning my great escape.

He didn't answer. I took that to mean he was doing exactly that.

Not wanting to chance blowing our operative's cover or being discovered myself, I resumed my trek between the tents and spotted the original reason for my side trip. Two guards chowing down on chili dogs.

They were seated on empty crates and had a large paper bag situated on the ground between them. It had the word "Frank's" written across it in red. They were too involved in their eating to notice me creeping forward.

"This is so much better than the crap Millsap tries to feed us," said the guard on the right.

"Yeah, I've had so much whole grain organic junk that my system is clogged up," the other one answered.

"This ought to fix that right up," returned number one.

They both laughed at that. Gross. But, hopefully, it was edible, unlaced food.

Drawing even with the back of their crates, I waited for my chance. It came when yelling erupted from one tent over.

Both guards stood, quickly stuffing their mouths with the remains of the hot dogs they were holding. Their hasty departure left the contraband unattended. Just the way I liked it.

I reached in and grabbed the first thing on top. I barely tasted it as I wolfed it down. The second one I managed to chew a few times, but it too was quickly gone. Hearing the argument winding down, I grabbed another and darted between the tents again. I finished the last one off right as I reached the edge of the tent alley.

I hid the hot dog wrappers under the bottom of the nearest tent. I used the canvas side of the tent to wipe the extra chili from my hands. It was hard not to lick them clean, but I didn't think it was worth the risk. I didn't know if my nanobots came with germ fighting skills too.

Pausing long enough to make sure the way was clear, I stepped out from between the tents. I wanted to get a closer look at the nearby mill. Angling toward it confirmed my assumption that it wasn't operational. The paint was faded and parts of the main building were collapsed. The paddle wheel that I had seen belonged to an establishment on the other side of the river. Even as I watched a barge floated past.

It was amazing how close someone could be to danger without them having a clue about it. I used to be one of those clueless people. Before HCF and Adam.

I watched as someone exited a door on the side of the mill that was still standing. They climbed the wooden stairs leading to the camp and started in my direction. I recognized the man. It was my old boss at the HCF, Norris Cain.

Oh man, Adam was going to love this.

Adam, I have a bit more trouble for you.

You're the gift that keeps on giving.

Ha, ha.

I felt him open the bond wide as he searched me for any sign of injury. *What's wrong?*

I'm fine, I assured him, pushing back against his probing. *I just saw my old boss from the HCF, Norris Cain, exit the mill.*

Positive on the ID?

Yep. Did you know he was associated with the Consortium?

We suspected. But our Intel was lacking. That was probably due to Julia's interference.

What does that mean for Kenny and the rest of the kids?

I don't know Macy. We will figure everything out when we get you out of there. Reinforcements are fifteen minutes out. You'll be out of there soon.

Do you have my cell phone?

On me? His voice was loudly incredulous.

Cool it, Gramps. I already presumed it was not currently in your possession. I meant do you have it at all? It's the only way Kenny has to contact me.

I'll have Miranda check your things for it. Otherwise, we can have Juarez or one of the other computer techs hack your voicemail.

Okay. Hold on Kenny, I prayed silently. One thing that Adam had said bothered me, though. *Adam, you did mean when you get us out of here? Me, Olivia and Juarez. Right?* He had better not try to pull some "you're the priority" BS with me again.

We are going to do everything we can to get you all out, but—

No! I yelled. *You will get us all out!*

The force behind my words shoved Adam out of my mind and effectively slammed the door shut between us. I hadn't meant to do that.

Adam? I whispered. It bounced back against the wall between us. Crap. Several more attempts to reconnect with him failed as well.

I decided it was time to move from my current location. I didn't want to attract notice by staying in one place too long. I began to wander around without a goal in mind other than to reconnect with Adam. I stopped when I realized I was in front of the tent that held Olivia and Juarez.

The flaps were hanging loose, and I could hear soft moans coming from inside. Glancing around and finding myself still alone, I slipped inside. I was disturbed by the apparent lack of guarding me they were doing, but the sight of Olivia crying silently eclipsed any further thoughts in that direction.

It looked like Pike had taken another shot at her. I knelt by her side and gently brushed the hair from her face. At my touch, she lifted her eyes to mine.

"Einstein," she whimpered.

"That's me." I offered her a small smile. "I should probably inform you that I've decided to join your motley team."

"You've decided this now that we're losing?" Her voice sounded hoarse, and her lips were cracked and bleeding.

Looking around the tent, I located a bright orange cooler with cups beside it. I started to move in that direction.

"Well, everyone likes an underdog," I said teasingly.

The word, "Don't," spoken harshly, almost gutturally, stopped me where I was. "It's drugged."

Of course it was. I hung my head. I wanted to help, but there was nothing I could do. The manacles and associated chains were way too thick to cut or break without a tool of some kind. Even if I did manage to free them, then what? Juarez was still unconscious, and I didn't think Olivia could walk on her own. We wouldn't make it far. I had to wait for Adam.

I returned to her side. "How much do you know about what they're planning?"

"Enough to be terrified by the thought of being surrounded by baby Einsteins. Think of the state the world could be in if that happens."

Yeah. All those trouble magnets running around. The potential for fireworks was astounding. The earth could end in a blaze of Greer filled glory.

I wanted so much to tell her that Adam was here, but I knew better. I wasn't naïve enough to think we weren't being watched, even if it appeared that way.

Juarez stirred a little, and I turned my attention to him. Scooting over next to him, I put my hand at his neck to check his pulse.

His eyes flew open, and he reared back at my touch.

I pulled my hand quickly out of the way of his teeth and gently coaxed him, "Whoa, Juarez, it's me. You're favorite hybrid Kitty Kat."

Recognition slowly filtered in his eyes, and he sagged against his chains. "Sorry, MK. Thought you were someone else."

I softly rubbed my hand against the one part of his arm that didn't look injured. "I know," I said. I wanted to tell him it was okay, but that would have been a lie.

"Olivia," he croaked, trying to turn enough to catch a glimpse of her.

I looked at her. She had fallen unconscious again.

"She's here. She's sleeping now."

He choked out a laugh. "That's a nice way of putting it, MK. I'm going to kill Pike," he growled as he passed out again.

"Me too," I agreed softly.

Realizing I was still rubbing Juarez's arm, I pulled my hand to my side and backed away from them. They would never make it out on their own. I hoped Adam was prepared for that.

Adam. I had to reestablish contact with him.

I walked toward the exit, pausing in the doorway to look back at the two of them. I hated to leave, but I knew I couldn't stay. I stepped out of the tent and walked right into Mr. Cain.

"Mr. Cain," I said calmly. I noticed his white suit didn't seem wrinkled at all, and there wasn't a speck of dirt on it.

"Dr. Greer, whatever are you doing here?" His tone of voice implied that bumping into me was not a happy coincidence.

"Probably not the same thing you are," I said flatly.

"My role here is merely in an advisory capacity. One of observation mainly." He adjusted his cufflinks as if he were someone of importance.

"Oh, so you've observed the torture of innocent people?"

I watched the horror march across his face and then disappear behind his bureaucratic mask. Maybe he didn't know.

"I assure you, I had no part in that. I am here solely to consult on the genetic manipulation that Dr. Millsap is in the process of developing."

I laughed. "Is that what he told you?" The sniveling idiot. I liked him even less than before. "Then you are aware of the army that Millsap intends to create to pursue forced worldwide hybridization?"

Shock and anger now touched his features. "That is not what this is about."

Poor, sad Mr. Cain still had his head buried in the sand. I should help him with that.

"Mr. Cain, that is exactly what this is about, and you're looking at the head DNA donor."

The look of disgust that passed across his face was insulting. "Why would he want your DNA?"

I was not going to give him any more information about me, but I did offer him some advice before leaving him behind. "Mr. Cain, don't ever play poker. Your face is easier to read than most books." I could still hear his huffing and sniveling as I entered my tent.

Before the tent flap slapped shut, I started calling for Adam. I reached as hard as I could, pushing against the barrier between us. I envisioned it opening, disintegrating, and blowing up. I tried imaginary keys of all shapes and sizes. I tried everything I could think of to make it disappear, but nothing seemed to restore the bond.

Growling in frustration, I flung myself down on the cot. I felt weird without him. It seemed like something was missing. Or like I had lost something. I felt uneasy, and uncomfortable, and alone. I stilled at that admission. I had always been fine with alone before. Since when did I need anyone?

Since I met Adam was my quiet conclusion.

There was no denying it. As much as I hated it, I missed him. That was right. Me, Dr. Macy Greer just flat out missed Adam.

Adam, where are you? I whispered.

Macy? Oh, thank God.

I sat straight up in surprise. I hadn't even tried that time. I wasn't even expecting an answer.

I thought I'd lost you, Adam said.

I'm sorry. I wasn't trying to push you out. It just happened.

Don't worry about it. The cavalry is here. It's time to go.

Olivia and Juarez will never make it on their own. They are both in and out of consciousness. I don't think either of them can walk. And the chains they are secured with are heavy duty.

Noted. Macy, don't fight me on this. I know what I'm doing.

He meant shut up and do what I was told. I never was very good at that.

You are going to attempt to get them out?

Yes. But I need you out of the way.

Okay. If Adam said he was going to try, then he was. I'd just have to trust him to do his best. That had worked out pretty well so far. Except for the me being captured part. But considering he'd been tagged with betrayal on multiple levels, and fighting the Consortium while being outnumbered, I cut him a little slack. Besides, he was about to rectify that.

Okay, what do you need me to do?

On the back side of the tent, I need you to cut an exit flap. A single cut should do.

You know which tent I'm in?

Yes, he drawled. *I know where everyone inside and outside the camp is. Move your butt, Greer.*

Alrighty then. *Operation Get My Butt out of Here, under way, Sir!*

Adam's amusement travelled across our bond. It was good to have him back.

Kneeling on the floor by my cot, I pulled it out enough to allow me access to the back of the tent. As I concentrated on my right hand, one sharp claw slowly extended from my pointer finger. With that claw, I made a straight cut starting at about two feet from the ground all the way down to the floor. Then I sliced sideways. Scooting the cot back in place, I let Adam know I was done.

In about five minutes, when you hear a commotion, I want you to slip out through the cut you made and walk straight back. Camo, the man you identified earlier, will be there. You probably won't see him initially, but he will escort you to transport leaving the area.

Leaving? What about Pike and Millsap!

Adam's words came out as angry as I'd ever heard him. *Given the current limitations I am working under, my only goal is to get you, Olivia and Juarez out safely. If I kill Pike or Millsap in my effort to accomplish that goal, then great. But now is not the time for that mission!*

I could feel his disappointment, his anger, his dread at having to tell me this. In light of that, my own anger dissipated.

Macy, I know what I promised you. I haven't forgotten. I just can't...If I make going after them a priority, I risk losing you or Juarez and Olivia...or I put the rest of the contingent at risk as well...Macy—

I know, Adam, I said quietly as I sat on the cot again. I understood his reasons, even agreed with them. But that didn't make it any easier to swallow. I was so mad at the thought of Millsap and Pike escaping unscathed that I wanted to rip the tent to shreds.

But we will end them as soon as possible, right?

You have my word, Macy.

It was small comfort, but it would have to do for now. Before Adam could say anymore, the tent flap was flung wildly aside, and Pike fell through in a tangle of limbs. As I watched him gather himself, a slow smile spread across my face.

Guess who just fell into my tent?

Fell? he asked, confused.

I was already shifting as I enlightened him. *One very high as a kite Pike.*

"Hello, lady Beautiful," Pike drawled, leering in my direction. He was doing the same side to side shuffling he'd done at our last encounter.

"Hello, dead man...wavering."

My comment caused him to double over in laughter.

I felt like laughing too. An unexpected eagerness to pounce on him settled over me. That had to be the leopard DNA at work. I sank into the feeling, and I found myself intently watching his every move in anticipation of the pouncing that was to come.

Macy, Adam softly growled in warning. He knew full well what I intended to do. *You're not trained to fight. Pike is. Even allowing for his current condition, this could end badly.*

Without disengaging my attention from Pike, I answered Adam's warning with a warning of my own. *Then you had better get your butt here to help me because opportunity just knocked, and one of us is not leaving this tent alive.*

There was a brief moment of hesitation, and then Adam made his decision. *Stall. I'm on my way.*

The adrenaline that surged through Adam into me left me feeling even more edgy and ready to fight. I wondered how Adam possessed the ability to physically affect me without being present. It must have something to do with wavelengths or frequencies travelling nanobot to nanobot. Physics stuff.

Focus, Macy! Adam yelled in irritation.

I am focused! I rose from the cot and walked to the center of the tent opposite Pike. *If I were any more focused, my eyeballs would pop out of my head. I just happen to be able to focus on more than one thing at a time. Some of us can do that, you know.*

I accepted Adam's snarl as acknowledgment of my superior focusing skills. I knew the situation before me was serious, but I couldn't shake the happiness I felt at this turn of events. Between mine and Adam's adrenaline and whatever else the hybrid DNA added to the mix, I felt giddy. Much to Adam's displeasure.

"It's like that, is it?" Pike asked with upraised eyebrows. His eyes raked my body, taking in my shifted form and the fighting crouch I'd dropped into. "You can't possibly hope to fight me alone. I know this wasn't part of your super brain plan."

He had mimed air quotes as he said super brain. His joy with his assumed cleverness almost caused him to collapse again. Obviously, he thought he had beaten me already.

But I didn't plan to fight him alone. I planned to, as Adam said, strategically use my leopard DNA to rip his head off.

I reached for the feel of the hunt and found it ready for me this time. All of my senses immediately sharpened. I almost gagged on the lust rolling off his body. I was once again amazed when everything else fell aside. All of my being was focused on one single purpose. To kill Pike.

With the giddiness gone, I was able to clearly formulate a plan of attack. He was almost a foot taller than me. I'd have to make every shot count, go for major arteries and all while remaining out of his reach.

"Come on, Macy," he said, reaching for me. "It doesn't have to be like this."

Seizing the opening, I twisted under his unprotected arm,

slicing my claws across his flesh. I immediately knew that I had succeeded by both the blood dripping from my extended claws and the sickly sweet smell. Bouncing back far enough to be clear of any counterattack, I resumed my crouch and waited for another opening.

How's it going, Macy?

I drew first blood.

You did?

Adam's surprise was distracting and irritating. I watched as Pike's drug laden senses finally relayed the information to his brain. He looked in disbelief at the blood running down his arm. Did he honestly think I wouldn't kill him? He was so very wrong.

How about saying something useful this time, I barked at Adam.

Okay. Let the leopard DNA lead.

Already doing that.

"Well, well, the kitty has claws," Pike scoffed.

And teeth I silently added. But I was in no hurry to taste him.

Pike's eyes cut to the door of the tent in confusion as noise from Adam's generated commotion filtered through. Since my bit of maneuvering had placed me directly in front of the tent exit, he'd have to go through me to get out. He didn't seem disturbed by that fact.

I caught the slightest shift in pressure right before he spun with a roundhouse kick that would have connected with my head had I still been there. Instead, I deepened my crouch and used my claws on the underside of his extended leg this time.

Once again, he didn't initially recognize that he'd been hit. At this rate, I'd have to tell him when he was dead. The smell of his blood blossomed in the tent. I must have hit a major artery this time. Almost in slow motion, he realized the relationship between the smell and his blood.

He took a moment to close his eyes and sniff the air. "Smell's quite nice, actually."

He was one sick puppy.

Then his eyes, alight with understanding, locked with mine. "We shall dispense with the pleasantries then, huh Beautiful?"

He pulled his shirt over his head and revealed a nice set of abs. Too bad it was attached to such a snake. He was barefoot already so there was no resistance as he slid his pants off.

Really? Was that necessary?

Don't look, Adam growled.

Are you crazy? I can't look away. He might attack. Adam was so angry over Pike's striptease act. His leopard perceived it as a direct challenge to what was his. *This is not the time for you to be jealous, Adam,* I snapped at him.

As I continued to watch Pike's transformation, his hair and nose disappeared. They were replaced by smooth patterned skin flowing over his head and down his body. Then his lips grew wide and long, flattening out his nose until it almost disappeared.

I could hear Adam's continual growling in my head. It made it hard to concentrate. *Either help me or shut up!* I yelled at him. The growling faded, but his anger was still present. I could use that.

Thin fangs dripping with venom descended between Pike's too thin lips. The transformation then proceeded to his hands and feet where his nails were replaced by long thin claws.

So, maybe not a snake, but definitely some type of reptile. Yep, Pike the lizard man now stood in front of me. Why he had chosen to fight naked, I could not understand. Wasn't that exposing a critical area for him? If he was trying to intimidate me, it wasn't working. Maybe he was proud of his manhood, like it was some part of a lizard mating ritual. Or Adam could be right, a direct shot at him. Whatever the reason, it was just awkward.

He took a few shuffling steps toward me which I countered with my own cat like ones.

In the background, I could hear snarling and the sound of gunfire popping around the camp, but my attention remained primarily focused on Pike. I added two new goals to the battle plan. Fang avoidance and gaining access to his neck. I knew a few moves from kickboxing, but I suspected they would not be enough.

Suddenly, he lashed out with another kick.

I managed to move fast enough to duck the kick, but not the follow up claws. Searing pain lanced across my back as I rolled out of the way.

Still standing in the middle of the tent, Pike made sure he had my attention as he slowly licked my blood from his claws. Then he made the critical mistake of turning his back on me.

Rage spiked through me. In one fast leap, I covered the distance between us and latched onto the backside of his knees. The force of the impact sent Pike to the ground on his stomach. A loud hiss issued from his lips as I tore through the tender flesh on the back of his knees with both my teeth and claws. Then just as quickly, I bounded away, once more outside of his grasp.

He pulled himself off the floor and stood facing me with liquid fury in his eyes. I spit a piece of his flesh that had worked free from my teeth directly on the floor in front of him. That act galvanized him into motion. He leapt at me with his arms extended.

I didn't know where it was coming from, but I did what I saw in my head. I shot forward underneath him and spun at the last moment to rake my claws across his midsection. He folded over in midair, but still managed to slash one of my calves with his claws.

We were both bleeding heavily now. Him more than me. We stared at each other from across the tent, neither one of us willing to make the first move.

"What's wrong, cat got your tongue?" he taunted. Pausing his sideways dancing movements, he crumpled forward in laughter.

While he was laughing, I identified the one thing I needed. Access to his neck. I leapt forward, somehow spinning in the air, and landed on his back. Locking my hands around his throat, I pressed my claws deeply into the skin at his neck and let his own frantic motions rip and tear the flesh.

Adam picked that very moment to burst into the tent. He was covered in blood and gore, but by the smell of it, I didn't think any of it was his.

"Everything alright, sweetheart?" he asked nonchalantly while folding his arms across his chest.

I smiled at him over Pike's shoulder. The smile caused the blood from my previous go at Pike's legs to roll further down my chin and neck.

Pike, who had momentarily ceased his struggle when Adam so dramatically entered, began again with increased urgency. The smell of his fear permeated the air as he put as much distance as he could between him and Adam.

At the same moment I sensed Pike's body tense, Adam's warning scrolled through my head. *He's going to roll.*

I waited until the last moment and then used my feet on his back to spring to the side. Or, at least, I tried to. He managed to hook one ankle and flung me into the table, which folded on me like a deck of cards.

Spaghetti. That was what was under the tray covering.

Brushing aside soggy noodles, I watched as Adam tackled Pike. It wasn't really much of a fight from there. Adam finished him off in short order. He didn't literally tear the head off his shoulders, but it was close.

Adam gave one final kick to Pike and then turned to find me still seated in the midst of the table wreckage. Standing with his feet wide apart and his arms braced at his sides, he regarded me with the ever familiar upraised eyebrow.

I'd never been so glad to see it.

"Planning on getting up any time soon?" he asked.

I made a couple of attempts to stand but kept slipping in the spaghetti mess.

Rolling his eyes, he crossed the tent and knelt down in front of me. With one hand, he sloughed off the spaghetti from my hair and the other he placed on my elbow. "Not bad for your first fight."

A compliment? "You didn't even see it," I charged.

"I saw enough to know that he was essentially dead before I showed up. I know you didn't waste energy or try for moves that you could never pull off. I know you were smart about it."

Standing to my feet with Adam's aid, I said, "What about the dismount?"

"An error easily corrected. When disembarking from an enemy, always tuck your feet in. It prevents the legs from being used as a lever to reel you back in."

Oh, that made sense. Before I could say anything else, Adam wrapped his arms around me and pulled me tightly to him. I barely had time to comprehend what he was doing when his lips locked on mine. At that point, any objections I might have had were lost in his kiss.

A loud voice interrupted our reunion, and I quickly ducked my head into Adam's chest. "Sorry, Sir. We're all clear."

Adam hugged me tightly and then whispered, "Let's go."

Amen to that.

Adam lead the way out of the tent, and I stepped out into what was left of the camp. Wow. I had been so focused on Pike that I hadn't heard all of this. My tent happened to be the only one still standing. The jeeps that were left were all on fire. Small explosions were going off all over the place.

As I jogged behind Adam, I asked, "Are Olivia and Juarez out?"

"They left a few minutes ago."

"What about Millsap?"

"No sign of him. I think he bailed directly before we came in."

"That would mean he knew you were coming," I said, disappointed that we'd missed this opportunity to get him.

"Yes, it would," Adam said.

More questions. It was going to be such a relief when I started getting some answers.

I touched Adam's arm, "Wait just a minute. Do you hear that?"

As we paused, I heard a weak, "Dr. Greer." It was coming from behind us. I turned, trying to locate the origin of the voice. Adam paced to a downed tent and pulled the covering aside. I recognized the white suit. It was Mr. Cain.

I limped over to join Adam. Cain's voice was weak because he had a pincer protruding from his chest. I guess he had confronted Millsap. A twinge of guilt raced up my spine, and Adam grabbed my hand and squeezed it for reassurance. I glanced briefly at him, nodding my thanks, then knelt beside Cain.

Taking Cain's hand in mine, just like Adam had done for me, I offered what comfort I could. As I stared into his eyes, I realized we both knew he wasn't leaving here.

"I'm sorry," he whimpered.

What could I say? I had no way of knowing what he had to be sorry for, and I certainly didn't possess the kind of power needed to absolve him.

A sudden thought struck me, and I leaned into Cain. "Does Millsap know about the Colony?" He was fading now, his eyes taking on a glazed look. I shook him. "Cain! Does Millsap know about the Colony?"

He was struggling to answer. I barely made out his sputtered, "Yes," as he breathed his last breath. His hand grew limp in mine, and I laid it by his side. Reaching up, I closed his eyes and said a quick prayer. Not for him, but for Kenny and the rest of the hybrids at the Colony.

Adam's hands were urging me up, and I stood. We were full on sprinting now as we headed away from the camp. Even with the injury to my calf, I managed to run without falling or becoming entangled with the foliage once. But I didn't get to celebrate my new found skill because Adam wrapped himself around me and took us to the ground.

A large explosion rocked the area and debris rained down around us. Little pieces of tent and metal and other unidentifiable things coated everything around and including us.

Looking from the shelter of his arms, I saw that the old mill was no more. "Was that really necessary?" I asked him. I was starting to suspect he just liked to blow things up.

He followed my eyes to where the mill had been. "It was their control center. And, we needed everything in small enough pieces to be carted away unnoticed."

"Mm hmm."

"What?" he asked, grinning like a kid who'd been caught with his hand in the cookie jar.

I shook my head as he helped me up. He kissed the tip of my nose and left me to begin giving last minute directions to the rest of the crew. Looking around, I didn't recognize any faces. But I did recognize the stack of cardboard they disguised as nutrition bars.

I picked one up and used my teeth to tear off the wrapper. I tried not to focus on the taste as I chewed. I didn't know if cardboard was accurate. It was more like chewing whicker or what used to be called particle board before MDF became the common name for it.

A bottle of water suddenly entered my field of view. I took it gratefully and turned to find Adam at my back. I raised my eyebrows as his eyes travelled the length of my body and back.

"You're a mess," he said without the slightest hint of sugar.

I maintained eye contact as I maneuvered my tongue across the front of my teeth, seeking to dislodge wayward bits of grain. He was covered in blood and guts, and dirt, and some unidentifiable gore, and he had the nerve to call me a mess?

"I hear what you're not saying," he reminded me with a tap of his finger to the side of his head.

Do you now, Grandpa? I teased.

His eyes narrowed in response to my dig. This was going to be fun, needling the old timer. Hey, he was probably around when they invented particle board.

CHAPTER 18

"How's the leg?" Adam asked with mild concern.

"It hurts as does my back." Remembering what he said about me and pain, I quickly added, "But, I'm alive."

"That you are," he said, watching me through hooded eyes. The intensity of his gaze was starting to freak me out. "Think you can stand taking a ride in my truck."

I paused mid chew. He owned a truck? "There is hope for you yet, city boy." I put the cap back on the water bottle and looked around for a place to toss it.

He ducked under the branch he was draped over and held his hand out for the empty bottle. "What makes you think I'm a city boy?" he asked.

"Your more city than me, that's for sure."

"Everybody's more city than you, bumpkin, which makes you unqualified to judge. Let's just say I was country long before you were ever born."

He might have me there. "That's just because cities weren't invented yet when you were born."

His face fell when he realized he'd walked right into that one.

I smiled in celebration of my small victory. But he had such a puppy dog, or should I say kitty cat, look in his eyes that I couldn't stand it. Walking up to him, I laced my disgusting fingers through his equally disgusting ones. "You were going to show me your truck?" I said.

I felt his delight at my making the first move filter through our bond. It was matched by the goofy grin on his face.

"This way, Ma'am," he drawled.

Oh, brother. I rolled my eyes at his corniness but couldn't smother the laugh.

He led me to a decent representation of a truck. It was an old blue ford with jacked up tires and a roll bar across the back. It even had the lights on top.

He opened the door and tossed the water bottle in the back seat. He started to lift me to the seat when I stopped him.

"Wait, do you have a towel or something. Look at me. I'll get the seats filthy."

Ignoring my complaint, he lifted me onto the seat. "Don't worry about the seat, Macy. As long as you're in it, I'll be okay."

That was so sweet and stupid. I didn't think I would have been as generous with my truck. Probably would have made him ride in the bed.

A smile lifted a corner of his mouth as he read my mind. Reaching up, he tucked my hair behind my ears. When he did, bits of what can only be classified as gunk fell off both him and me.

With disgust clearly on my face, I said, "We seriously need showers."

His eyes filled with what I was coming to recognize as desire. The feeling reverberating through the bond confirmed my conclusion. He moved closer, pressing against my side. "Macy Greer, was that an invitation?" he whispered in my ear.

"No." My voice actually squeaked.

He laughed softly and pressed a kiss to my forehead before pulling away and closing the door.

Was it hot in here?

Adam was content to leave me alone in thought as we drove, which I greatly appreciated. I had a lot to process.

From the victory of obtaining Kenny's DNA, to the complete worthlessness of it. The *detainment,* as Olivia liked to label it, by Adam. The painful crawl and climb through the tunnel and shaft. The stitches and concussion. Twice being stalked by Furries. The very existence of Furries and other astounding hybrids. My transformation into a hybrid. Another kidnapping. My battle with Pike. The escape of Millsap and what that meant for me and the Colony.

What would happen with the Organization now that Julia was a suspected traitor? What would happen to the HCF now that Cain was gone? Where did I fit in to any of this? And then, there was Adam.

It was too much to process for less than a week.

"Hell of a week," Adam commented.

I was seriously going to have to learn not to project my thoughts or at least, remember that I wasn't alone anymore. He'd probably read my whole list.

"You forgot the scuba diving and the fall from the tree. And being near death. Seeing Juarez and Olivia in their tortured state couldn't have been easy either," he said.

No, it wasn't. "Hell of a week," I agreed.

"They're okay?" I asked after a brief silence.

He undid the Velcro on one of his pants pockets and pulled out a cell phone. "The cell service out here is spotty at best." He handed the phone to me. "See if there are any texts."

I took the phone and pushed the message icon. There was one from Cedars. I read it aloud for Adam.

"It's from Cedars. On location. Juarez and Olivia recovering. All operatives accounted for. Lock down in place. Miranda says hi." I chuckled at the last bit. "What's he mean by lockdown?"

"When I discovered Julia's treachery, I issued the command for a lockdown. The long and short of it means that nobody gets in or out without my say so."

I handed the phone back to him, and he slid it back into his pocket. "We'll reconnect with everyone tomorrow and get all the updates," he said.

So, everyone for right now was okay. That was a huge weight off my chest. Apparently off Adam's too, his contentment was like a blanket over me. I didn't mean to, but somewhere along the way, I fell asleep.

I woke as we rolled to a stop in the driveway of an abandoned house. "Where are we?" I asked while stifling a yawn. Yuck. My clothes had dried and stiffened while I slept. Something just wasn't right when your clothes crunched.

"We are at a place where we can clean up before we enter the general population," he said as he opened the door and slid out of the truck.

I looked the place over again. Not sure how clean we could get in a place that looked as dirty as us.

He opened my door and stood aside for me to climb down. As soon as my feet touched the ground, he grabbed my hand and led me to the porch where he actually knocked.

I looked sidelong at him. Did he really expect someone to answer?

A loud crash sounded from inside, and I jumped in alarm. He patted my hand and with a big grin on his face, shook his head no at me. I tried to peer inside the little windows at the top of the door as another crash sounded. It was followed by a long string of creative swearing. And still, we waited.

I looked back at Adam and found that the smile had been replaced by the most contrite face I'd ever seen him make. I was completely baffled by his behavior.

Suddenly, the door flung open, and a surly looking old woman with striking green eyes, wearing a wrinkled dress and apron and holding a large rolling pin, stood directly in front of us.

"Well, looke what the cat done drug in," she wheezed with laughter. Then she gave him a once over and cocked her eyebrow at him.

It was the same look Adam had. I thought I might be looking at Granny Adam.

"Ya look like ya done slept in a pig pen," she said disapprovingly. Then she leaned in and sniffed him. "Smell like it, too."

He managed to keep the smile off his face, but not out of his voice when he said, "Always a pleasure, Granny."

Looking my way, she seemed to notice me for the first time.

With a twinkle in her eye, she said, "Well, my, my. Ya done gone and got yourself a she cat."

Her smile of appreciation was quickly replaced with anger, and she whacked Adam with the rolling pin. "Ya finally get yourself a woman, and this is the way ya treat her?" She whacked him again. "You'll never keep the gal this way."

I stood there gaping as Adam took what she dished out without so much as flinching. He would never have let me treat him this way.

She roughly shoved the rolling pin into his chest and wrapped her arm tenderly around me. Muttering, "Boy ain't got a lick of sense," she led me into the house. I looked back at Adam for help, but he only waved and grinned at me while making little shooing motions with his hands.

"I do apologize, Granny," he said with fake contriteness as he followed us into the house. "But when I realized I was in over my head, I came straight to you for help in rectifying the situation."

"Ain't me ya need to apologize to, ya dimwit," she yelled back.

Ushering me through another door, we stood in what was evidently her bathing area. She produced a brown paper grocery bag, popped it open and set it on the floor. I didn't know anyone still carried their groceries in brown paper bags.

"You can put those clothes in this bag right here, honey," she told me. Then, she gripped my arm, and I looked away from the bag and into her kind eyes. "I'll be back in a minute with everything we need to get ya cleaned up."

I was at a loss for words, so I just nodded.

She left and I began to disrobe. I unlaced my shoes while standing because I didn't want to dirty her floor any more than I already had. Pulling them off, I tossed them in the bag and then added my socks. Next came the jeans, which I had to peel off. The results were almost as good as waxing. Last of all was my shirt.

I sighed sadly as I held my favorite t-shirt in my hands. Like my jeans, it was covered in dirt and blood, both from the deer and Pike, and some other colored stains that I couldn't identify.

I tossed the t-shirt into the bag and quickly followed with my undergarments.

That was the second set of clothes I'd ruined since the Organization entered my life. Much more of this and I was going to request a clothing budget. That or wear only damage proof clothing. Maybe something in leather.

Standing there naked, I looked like I had on some kind of freakish camouflage. I located a mirror leaning against the wall and went to stand in front of it. I didn't realize my face was still covered in dried blood. Parts of it were flaking off like some kind of sick mask.

The dried blood in my blonde hair looked almost black. There were thicker things attached to my hair also, but I didn't want to pry at those too much. My overall image was gruesome, and I turned away from the mirror.

It was kind of curious that Granny didn't bat an eye at our appearance. Speaking of Granny, I could hear her ordering Adam around. I put my ear against the door to better hear the conversation.

"Ain't ya got no better sense than to take her on your missions with ya?"

So, Granny was in the know.

"I was rescuing her, Granny," Adam said with exaggerated patience.

I swallowed a laugh when I heard the snap of a towel followed by a small yelp. Granny was tough.

"Don't ya take that tone with me." I heard the towel snap again. "Ya couldn't do no better job? I know'd you was taught better-n-that. Don't ya laugh at me, boy."

A rich laugh flowed through the air, slowly building in volume. I'd never heard him laugh like that before.

"Put me down, ya overgrown cat," Granny cackled.

"I love you, Granny," Adam said.

The words were spoken softly and with such heartfelt sincerity. I could feel the love he had for her. It was strong and unyielding and unlike anything I'd ever felt before. It was beautiful. I leaned my head against the door. I'd never heard or felt Adam so happy before.

Granny sniffed, and her reply was considerably gentler this time. "Go on and use the shower out back now, ya mangy cat."

"Yes, Ma'am," he said, and then I heard a screen door open and shut.

Backing away from the door, I realized tears were streaming down my cheeks. He'd brought me to meet his Granny and let me be a witness to the love he felt for her. I was overwhelmed.

Macy? You okay?

It took me a moment to collect myself enough to respond. *Yeah.* What else could I say? Apparently, I wasn't shielding any of what I was feeling from him. I wasn't even sure what I was feeling. I thought envy might be the word—longing to be loved so completely. Wasn't everyone?

I could feel Adam's mounting concern as I tried to sort it out. *I'm fine, Adam.*

Macy.

Really, I'm fine. I'm going to try shielding you, okay?

Okay, he said slowly.

I could since the disappointment in Adam, but I was not ready to have a discussion with him about what I was feeling. I visualized a slow film enveloping me, and then I imagined the film thickening until only words were getting through.

How's that? I asked.

Can't feel a thing.

I couldn't feel him either. I altered the shield to allow his emotions through. He was not happy with me. The tears, which had slowed, began to flow freely again. I was a mess, both physically and emotionally.

A few days ago, I knew who I was and where I was going. Now, I didn't know jack. Not the limits of my physical or mental capabilities. Not my employment status or what my future held. I didn't even know where my next meal was coming from, and that was really important to me. It seemed like my life was completely out of my control.

My mind kept flashing back to me holding Miranda as she cried about the intensity of her relationship with Cedars and her feelings of being overwhelmed. I wished she was here now.

Is there anything I can do? His need to fix this travelled through our bond, adding greater depth to his words.

I just need to find my footing. Everything keeps shifting on me. That would be funny, if it wasn't so true.

You're going to be fine, Macy. In fact you're going to be great. I'm so proud of you.

His confidence in me was touching. Crap. I was crying again. On the other side of the door, I could hear Granny approaching. *Got to go, Granny's coming,* I told him.

She bustled through the door, carrying towels, soap that looked like it was from the fifties, and a nightgown that looked like it was from the Victorian Age. She paused when she saw my tears. Setting everything down on the counter next to the sink, she directed me to stand over a drain in the floor.

"Now, now, child. Ain't no need to cry. Everything's gonna be alright. My Adam will make it so."

She drug a stool over the drain and had me to sit down. Turning on the water, which came out of a garden hose, she started with my hair. The water wasn't cold as I feared it might be. But, honestly, with the state I was in, I'd have taken whatever shower I could get.

I kept my head down and watched the dirt and little bits of gore wash down the drain. When she was satisfied I was thoroughly soaked, she turned the water off and began to work me over with the soap. Granny had strong hands. She also had a nice voice. She hummed softly to herself as she worked.

Was it strange that I was sitting buck naked on a stool, in front of a total stranger as she washed me clean? Logically, in my mind, I thought it was, but it didn't feel that way. It felt natural. She was Granny. Maybe it was a cat thing?

She brought the hose up once more and rinsed the soap away. It left my skin with a soft citrusy smell. I thought I had just discovered the secret to Adam's scent.

Bringing the back of my hand to my nose, I inhaled. "Does Adam use this soap?"

She seemed pleased that I'd finally spoken. "Something like it," she said, "but more manly." She picked up a towel and began drying my hair. "I'd brush it out for ya, but I reckon Adam for the job."

I stood while she finished drying me off.

"Ya sure is a quiet one," she said uncertainly.

"I'm just tired," I assured her as she slipped the night gown over my head and started tying things in the back. "It's been a long week."

"I ain't got no unmentionables for ya."

Did she mean underwear? I didn't see the need given the depth of coverage this thing provided.

"That's alright," I told her. "What you've done has been more than enough. Thank you." Tears filled my eyes once again, and I wrapped her in a hug.

She patted my back a minute before sniffing and shaking me loose.

"Ya gonna let Granny take good care of ya tonight. Clear out them blues. C'mon," she said, rolling her eyes. "Let's see if that grandchild of mine got himself cleaned up."

She started to lead me from the bathroom, but then she paused. Taking both my hands in hers and looking deeply into my eyes, she said, "Ya ain't gone and got yourself into some trouble, have ya?"

I looked into her earnest face and had no idea what she was talking about. Thanks to Adam, I had gotten myself into huge amounts of trouble.

"I'm not sure what you mean," I said in confusion.

"You and Adam ain't expecting no little one, are ya?"

My eyes widened at her question. "No, Ma'am. I'm a good girl."

I immediately felt stupid for my assertion. Good girl? When did I start thinking like that? My only defense was that she had me rattled. Granny was fierce in her own right. Her eyes were like twin spotlights, and I was squirming. I wasn't guilty of anything, but I had a strong desire to confess to something.

She continued to stare at me, deciding the truth of my claim before she gave my hands a final squeeze and let one of them go. The other she kept as she turned toward the door again.

I heaved one giant sigh of relief. Under her interrogation, I was about to spill every thought I'd had about Adam, and they were not all G rated.

"That's good then. I weren't sure with the tears ya been crying."

There was a scary thought. If me being emotional equaled kids, then I'd have had a whole houseful this week.

I followed her back into the room that served as the living area. The house was a lot cleaner on the inside than it looked from the outside. It reminded me of a hunter's cabin in the woods. Not a lot of amenities, but what was there was highly functional.

The centerpiece of the room was a huge fireplace that took up one entire wall. I could feel the warmth of the fire from halfway across the room. I wouldn't have thought a fire would be necessary in the summer, but I guessed it got cold at night in the mountains. Being from southeast Texas, my experience with mountains and fireplaces was essentially zilch.

Adam was there too, seated on a small stool in front of the fireplace. He glanced up when we entered the room and smiled at our joined hands.

"Ya'll eat yet?" Granny asked.

The look that passed across Adam's face was comical.

"No, Ma'am," he answered guiltily.

She looked at him in shock. "Ya ain't fed the girl neither!"

"I had a nutrition bar," I offered in his defense.

Don't help me, please. I'm in enough trouble as it is.

"That ain't eating," she said with exasperation.

I wholeheartedly agreed, and I gave Adam a pointed look that clearly conveyed, "I told you so." I was starting to really like Granny.

She patted my hand and regarded me sincerely. "I'm gonna get ya something to eat child. Don't you worry none." Dropping my hand, she headed for the kitchen. Without turning around, she called, "Adam, fix her hair."

I had no doubt she fully expected him to follow orders.

Her muttering continued well into the kitchen. I heard bits of, "Girl done been traumatized," and, "He ain't taken care of her," interspersed with swearing that would win first prize for its innovativeness. I had never heard Adam swear once. It was a strange juxtaposition.

I glanced back at Adam, and he crooked his finger at me. "Come here," he said.

All of a sudden, I was nervous.

He rolled his eyes at my hesitation. "I'm not going to bite— unless you want me to."

I ignored his insinuation and crossed the floor with my lacey white night gown swirling around my ankles. When I stopped in front of him, his eyes travelled the length of my body and stopped at my eyes.

"Nice gown," he said sarcastically.

"It's very…" I stopped and looked down at the gown. It was old? Lacey, straight jacketish?

"Constraining?" he offered.

No, I could move freely. I looked back at him. The disgust in his expression was obvious. He meant it was a barrier to him. That was true enough. It surely did prevent any accidental viewing or contact. One would have to be determined to get through this thing. I didn't even know how to get out of it.

Still eyeing the gown like it was a worthy foe, he slid another stool in front of him and patted the seat. I sat down with my back to him. Seemed like he always had my back.

"I do," he said seriously.

I sighed heavily. Obviously my shields were back down.

"You seem to pick up a lot of things I'm not aiming at you," I complained.

He grasped my hair and pulled it behind my shoulders. As he had before, he began to work through it a section at a time. "You project really well," he said in explanation.

I cringed, recalling Miranda's words. "Like a digital cinema?"

He snickered at my comparison. "Not quite that vivid. You're getting better at shielding. You did it quite effectively earlier. We know you can do it. The fact that you shoved me totally out of your mind earlier today is also proof of that."

That wasn't something I wanted to think about. The fact that I had done it unintentionally or the fact of how much I'd missed his presence.

"For the record, I don't like it when you shut yourself off from me," he said quietly.

I pulled my feet to the top rung on the stool and rested my elbows on my knees. "I know," I said softly. "But sometimes, I need a little space."

He finished the section he was working on and slid it over my shoulder. "I know," he acknowledged.

We endured an uneasy silence as he completed another section of my hair. Another round of swearing, something to do with a possum's behind this time, erupted from the kitchen. It was so outrageous that we both laughed.

"She's very creative," I observed. "Is she really your Granny?"

"The one and only," he said.

For someone so strong, his hands were amazingly gentle in my hair. I wondered if more of his family was still alive. Wait. How was his Granny still alive?

"Adam, how is it that you are seventy-eight years old, and Granny is still alive?"

His hands on my hair slowed as he answered. "She may have had a little help in that department?" The inflection in his voice revealed his embarrassment.

"May have? You gave your Granny nanobots? Can she shift?"

"Yes and yes."

"The Organization allowed this?"

"The *Organization* had nothing to do with this."

He had broken the rules. Straight laced Adam had broken the rules.

"I couldn't bear to lose her," he quickly explained. "I had

already lost the rest of my family. She is—was the only person of importance left in my life."

Ignoring the obvious question of who was the other person of importance in his life, I asked, "She knows about you and the Organization? And she's okay with it?"

"She knows everything. She's fine with me being a shifter and what I do for the Organization. As far as herself, I wouldn't say she's okay with it, but she told me she'd stay around as long as I needed her."

He finished the last individual section he'd been working on and began pulling the brush from top to bottom through my hair. Granny's strange symphony continued to keep us company while we waited.

After a lull in the action, I asked Adam, "Think she needs any help in there?"

"Don't you dare," he said forcibly. "She'd have my hide if you, a guest, got up to help."

I believed him. I'd seen her with the rolling pin.

"She likes you," he said.

I liked her, too. Remembering her comment about him finally getting a woman, I said, "Probably because I'm the only woman she's ever seen you with."

"She's seen me with other women." As soon as the words were out of his mouth, I felt his regret. "What I mean to say, is, that in the course of previous missions, she has seen me with other women. But not *with* other women. I mean there have been other women."

I smiled as he continued to flounder.

Abruptly, he shut his mouth. "The important thing is, she's never approved of any woman with me, in whatever capacity, but you."

Granny was growing on me all the time.

Adam continued brushing my hair until it was almost dry and completely devoid of tangles. I was so relaxed that I hadn't realized Granny was standing in the doorway.

"You two young'uns finished?"

I blushed as if she'd actually caught us doing something, which she hadn't. I nodded.

"Well, c'mon then." She turned and headed back into the kitchen, leaving me and Adam to trail in her wake.

A small table stood against the far wall. On it she had laid out two plates piled with ham, mashed potatoes, field peas, and an array of other fresh vegetables. A tall plate of biscuits was stacked between them.

"Oh, Granny," I groaned.

She wiped her hands on her apron. "Ain't much," she said dismissively before showing us to the table. "Well, what'ya waiting for?"

That was all the invitation I needed. I sat down and picked up my fork with glee. Adam joined me and watched in amusement as I began to eat. With the first bite of ham, my eyes closed in bliss. Whether Adam and I made it as a couple or not, I was keeping Granny.

I opened my eyes and watched Adam bring his hand to his heart in feigned shock. Then he took his first bite, and I could feel the taste hit him. I raised my eyebrows at him knowingly. Mm hmm. Keeping. Granny.

Satisfied that we were in fact eating, Granny left us to begin the cleanup.

"You'd really steal my Granny?" he asked through a mouthful of food. "Maybe I don't know you as well as I think I do."

"If you don't think I'm serious about keeping Granny, you really don't know me. Food like this is hard to come by in the city."

"Thought you were a country girl," he said slyly.

"Born and raised, which is how I know Granny's a keeper."

His smile was from ear to ear. He was really pleased that I liked Granny. I caught just a glimpse of the fear he'd been suppressing that I would be repulsed by Granny.

Putting down my fork, I grasped his hand. "Adam, it's fine." I looked around to make sure she wasn't listening. "I'm quite fond of her."

He squeezed my hand and then released it to grab a biscuit. Couldn't really fault him there. They were so buttery and fluffy.

"Besides," I continued, "how many people can give a good scrubbing like she can?"

He lowered his fork. "She bathed you?" He was truly surprised.

"And, how," I said with a gigantic nod for emphasis. "From head to toe. And everywhere in between," I added with a shake of my head. I looked up from my biscuit to find him staring at me in disbelief. "What?"

"She, a complete stranger, can not only see you naked, but touch you as well, apparently including intimate places, while I, who have repeatedly saved your life, cannot?"

I shrugged. "It's different with you."

His frown remained fixed on me.

"And, she's Granny," I said as if that answered everything.

"She's Granny," he repeated.

"Yep, she's Granny," I said, filling my mouth with more biscuit.

"Of course I am dear," Granny said from behind me.

I almost dropped my fork. Dang, she was sneaky. That's the second time I hadn't heard her come in.

"Don't ya let my boy hear go pushing ya into nothing ya ain't ready for," she said, and then she pierced Adam with a look. Appropriately, he hung his head in shame.

It didn't escape me that Granny had good ears, too.

"Ain't no call for giving out the milk for free. Ya understand me?" She patted my shoulder while giving Adam one more glare.

I hid my grin behind my biscuit until Granny walked away. The rest of the meal was eaten in relative silence. Occasionally, I caught Adam staring at me with that same look of disbelief on his face. But I knew inwardly that he was pleased that Granny liked me too.

"Granny, can I help with the dishes?" I asked as I stood up and began to gather my dishes.

"Ain't no need. Ya'll can go to the porch and finish up your courting for the night."

Courting? I wasn't entirely familiar with the term. What exactly did courting entail?

Without a word, Adam scooted back his chair and put his dishes in the sink. He placed a kiss on the top of Granny's head and then left the kitchen. But not before she got him with the dish towel.

I heard the screen door shut, and I guessed he was headed to the porch to prepare for courting. Placing my dishes in the sink, I started to follow Adam.

"Not too frisky, now," Granny warned, causing me to pause.

"No, Ma'am," I said, and then I too headed for the porch.

I found Adam sprawled in a large porch swing under a pile of blankets. I pushed the screen door open, and he held up the blankets for me to crawl in. I slid in next to him and laid my head on his shoulder.

"You aren't really upset about her bathing me, are you?" I asked. I could feel him squirming inside, and my heart gave a nervous flutter.

"I'm not upset that she bathed you."

There was a ton of stuff not said behind that comment. I felt his guard click into place. See, I wasn't the only one who needed space.

"What *are* you upset about?" I asked softly.

He sighed deeply. I was getting the impression that he didn't want to have this conversation. Fine by me.

The sound of crickets filled the air as Adam slowly rocked us. It was so peaceful here. I wished I could relax, but there was too much swirling around in my brain.

"So, this is courting," I said.

He snorted in laughter.

"It's nice," I protested. "We're clean, and no one is trying to kill us."

Without warning, he scooped me up on his lap and hugged me close. Cradled in his arms, I relaxed against Adam with my cheek resting on his chest.

"Did you know Miranda awarded me the Medal of Honor?"

"No. Where did she get one of those?"

"We found it in an antique shop in New Orleans."

He tightened his hands around my waist, pulling me closer. Gently he began to nuzzle my hair. The nuzzling was soon replaced by soft kisses against my temple.

"She gave it to me as part of a tradition we have."

"Tradition?" he said distractedly as his kisses trailed down my face. I didn't think he was listening to me at all.

"Adam?" I said softly.

"Yes?"

"Should I feel guilty for being a part of killing Pike?"

Adam let go of me, and his head dropped back and hit the porch swing. If it weren't for the cocoon of blankets, I'd have fallen to the floor.

"You really know how to kill a mood," he groaned.

"Sorry, it's been bothering me. That I don't feel guilty, I mean."

He readjusted me on his lap, but held me more loosely this time. "He attacked you. He intended to kill you. Your actions were in self-defense and completely justifiable."

That was what I thought too, but I just needed to hear someone else say it. I'd never killed anyone before. The ease with which I took to the task was unexpected, as was the total lack of guilt.

"What happens now with the Organization?" I asked.

"This was not what I had in mind for courting," he grumbled.

"Fine." I pulled myself upright. "Kiss me."

The single eyebrow raise greeted my command.

"You heard me. Kiss me. Right here, right now, full-fledged kissing."

He did not obey. He still remained motionless, regarding me with suspicion.

I sighed. "I know you are not going to answer my questions, which I have so many of, until—" I wasn't able to finish my reasoning.

He launched himself at me, sending the blankets flying. We ended up with him on top of me and my head hanging off the porch swing. He quickly put his hand under my head and brought my face close to him. And kiss me he did. My face, my lips, my jaw, and that was when I saw Granny.

Adam.

He did not respond. He was struggling with the lace encasing my neck.

I grabbed his shoulders and shook him. *Adam! Granny's watching.*

He froze instantly. Slowly, he raised his head to look at Granny. "Granny," he said calmly, as if he wasn't lying on top of me and hadn't just been trying to rid me of my neck lace.

She smacked her lips and pierced him with her bright green eyes. "You gonna make me use this?" she asked, waving a water hose at him.

This was so humiliating. Busted by Granny.

"No, Ma'am." He eased back off me with his gaze still trained on Granny.

Then she turned her disapproving glare on me. Without the support from Adam's hand, I was looking at Granny upside down. She wasn't any less scary from this angle.

Her voice was laced with steel as she said, "Courting's over, young lady."

"Yes, Ma'am," I whispered.

I complied by righting myself and sliding off the porch swing. I made sure to avoid eye contact with Adam. I suspected the water hose was on a hair trigger.

She motioned me ahead of her when I went to stand beside her. I couldn't help myself. I gave Adam just the briefest of glances as I started forward. Before I could even turn my head back around, I felt the sting of the hose.

"Get moving, girle," she ordered.

I rubbed my backside where the nozzle had caught me and reached for the screen door. I now believed that nozzles and hoses might just be my new lifelong nemesis. Then it dawned on me that she'd whacked me with something. I must be part of the family. Despite my stinging backside, I happily went inside the cabin.

She led me to a room off the main living area that I hadn't noticed before. It was simply furnished with only a twin bed piled with quilts.

"Ya gonna sleep here tonight," she said as she pulled the quilts back and smoothed the sheet underneath.

At her direction, I slid in, and she lowered the covers over me. Sitting on the edge of the bed, she turned her spotlights on me again, and I looked down rather than into their glare.

"Ya love'em?"

My eyes snapped to hers.

She asked again. "Ya love'em?"

I closed the bond between Adam and myself as tight as I could. Then I answered as truthfully as I was able. "I feel something for him," I admitted. "I don't know if it's love."

She nodded as if she'd figured as much. "I'm tired," she said.

Okay, I thought, confused. Did I have something to apologize for?

"I've lived a good long life," she said, looking directly into my eyes.

The light bulb suddenly turned on. She meant she was tired of living. I so did not want to be talking to her about this. But then my reluctance turned to anger.

"Are you asking my permission to die?"

Her expression turned to one of guilt.

"Look, I know Adam has had you all his life, but I just found you. You absolutely do not have my permission to die. Even if Adam and me get married and have a slew full of cubs, you are not allowed to die."

She sniffed. "Ya got gumption, I'll give ya that." She took my hand in hers and gently stroked the backside of my palm. "He loves ya, ya know?"

Back to that again. "Granny," I sighed. "I've only known him five days."

"Ain't no need to get all prissy. I know'd you love'em too."

Granny of steel was back, and I was not going to argue with her.

"Ya gonna figure it out," she said, giving my hand one last pat. She shoved off the bed and started to leave. At the door she paused. "I think I might ought a stick around for a while. Ya'll gonna need help when the cubs come."

The closing of the door signaled her exit. Once again, I breathed a sigh of relief as the interrogation ended. Being around Granny was almost as difficult as being around Adam.

Macy?

Yeah?

Where did you go?

Nowhere. Granny was talking to me.

And you had to shut me out?

Do you want to know what she was talking to me about?

He thought about it a minute. *Probably not.*

Good call. Given his prior reluctance to talk about his feelings, I didn't think he would appreciate Granny confessing his love for me. He'd be furious at her hinting at dying.

Where are you sleeping? I asked him.

In the loft.

There's a loft?

Look up.

I did and saw a section of the ceiling lift away. Adam's smiling face appeared in the opening.

Care if I join you? he asked.

My eyes flashed to the door.

Relax, once Granny's asleep, she'll be out till morning.

Will you be out before she comes in?

He flipped himself through the opening and stood on the bed. Quietly he eased the latch shut. I scooted over, and he slid under the covers beside me. Even with him wrapped around me, there was no wriggle room.

You're going to get it if she catches you, I warned.

Go to sleep, Macy. I'm a big boy. I'll live.

Yeah, a big boy who is not talking aloud for fear he'll be discovered by Granny.

He snorted softly and kissed the back of my head. I felt like a teenager with all this sneaking around.

Sleep, Woman.

Well, one of us definitely wasn't a teenager. I guess old people needed their sleep.

Adam's soft growl reverberated in mock warning against my back.

Don't strain yourself, Old Timer, I laughed softly.

CHAPTER 19

WITH ADAM NEXT TO ME, I slept so soundly that my first clue it was morning was Granny's knock at the door.

Adam and I sat up simultaneously. In one sinuous movement, the *Big Boy* that he was rolled out of bed and dove under it. I barely had time to straighten the covers thrown askew by his acrobatic maneuvers before Granny opened the door.

She stood in the doorway, her eyes sweeping the room. I was terrified I would give us up as I fought the ridiculous urge to giggle. I repeatedly cleared my throat, trying to get rid of it. Her green eyes were hard as emeralds as she watched my battle for composure.

Sighing deeply, another trait she shared with Adam, she walked to the bed and sat down beside me. She took my hand again. I was learning it was her signal for a serious conversation.

"Adam told me ya'll's meaning to head out early this morning."

He hadn't informed me, but okay.

"I want to talk to ya about something before ya go."

"Okay," I said and waited for her to continue.

"Adam told me that your mama died when you was a little girl."

My face pulled into a confused frown. "Adam told you that last night?"

"Nah, he's been talking to me about you for quite some time."

Adam's unease with the direction of the conversation flushed through my mind. Why had he been talking to Granny about me?

"Anyway, I wanted to make sure ya was informed about certain womanly things."

I forgot the previous comment as alarm raced through me. Please tell me she was not going to talk to me about sex.

"Now, don't ya fret. There ain't nothing to be ashamed of about God's gift to married folks."

Where could I run, how could I escape? Adam's unease had turned to amusement and was only adding to my embarrassment.

"Granny," I hissed. It sounded harsher than I meant it to be. I swallowed, trying to calm down. "I know about the birds and the bees."

She dismissed me with a pursing of her lips and a tilt of her head. "Ya might know the how to in ya mind, but ya ain't got no experience in the doing. That's what I'm here to tell ya."

Adam's amusement quickly faded. He did not want to hear about his Granny's sexcapades, and neither did I. And how did she know that I didn't have experience?

"Now, I been a hybrid almost as long as Adam, and I know'd a thing or two about the subject."

Uugh, it got worse. Now she was going to tell me about some kinky hybrid sex scene. She was worse than Miranda. Adam's urge to run was almost as strong as mine. And yet, she seemed totally unfazed by my obvious humiliation.

Then, she started cackling. The cackling turned into large guffaws of laughter. She was laughing so hard she had tears streaming down her face. Letting go of my hand, she used her apron to wipe away the tears. "Young'uns is so gullible," she wheezed.

The rush of panic froze. She'd pranked me. I'd been pranked by Granny.

"I just wanted to tell ya, that *after* ya made your vows," she paused and gave me a meaningful look, "that ya trust one another when it comes to it. That ya leave fear at the door and just enjoy the learning of it." Reaching up, she gently patted my cheek, and then she stood and walked to the door.

Just like she'd done previously, she paused at the door. "Adam, ya can come out now. But don't think for one second, that if you'd taken your liberty with this gal here last night, that

I wouldn't a whooped ya up one side and down the other. Ya understand me, boy?"

"Yes, Ma'am," Adam croaked from his hiding spot.

Nodding once to herself, she left, pulling the door closed behind her.

The room was filled with a strange silence until Adam pushed himself out from under the bed. He made no further attempt to get up, but lay on his back with his knees bent and feet flat on the floor. The look on his face was one of contrite shock.

"I might be slightly afraid of Granny," he admitted.

That admission seemed like the funniest thing I'd ever heard. I covered my face with my hands as I doubled over in laughter. Adam's laughter soon joined mine.

When I could speak again, I said, "Me too."

After the laughter settled for the second time, I asked him, "Didn't you know she would be able to smell you?"

"I panicked."

"I'll say."

He flipped over onto his feet and stood up. "Ready for breakfast?"

I could eat, but I didn't know if I could face Granny.

"Think it's safe?"

"Come on," he said, taking my hand and pulling me free of the quilts. "She wouldn't really hurt you."

I was glad he thought so, but I was going to keep an eye out for wayward rolling pins and garden hoses.

We ate a quick breakfast of leftover ham and biscuits with homemade jam, and then she pulled me into a bedroom to choose some clothing. I'd swear there wasn't anything there past the nineteen fifties.

I finally settled on some white knickers paired with a powder blue button up shirt. She had found a bra, though I wished she hadn't. This thing was the definition of uncomfortable. What designer thought a pointed cup was a good way to go? A pair of Mary Janes completed the look.

I pulled my hair into a pony tail. It was the first time in days my hair wasn't in my face. That felt good all by itself. This whole ensemble made me feel like I was seventeen, except even when I was seventeen, I didn't dress like this.

When I entered the living room, Adam was already there. He stopped what he was doing and watched me walk toward him.

"Sort of feel like I'm robbing the cradle," he whispered as he helped me slip on a camouflage jacket.

I patted his arm reassuringly. "I imagine all grandpas feel that way when they are pursuing much younger women."

His eyebrows descended into a frown as he glared at me. I chuckled and starting rolling up the sleeves of the jacket that was slightly too big for me. Adam harrumphed and then helped me adjust the sleeves while Granny stood by silently watching the show.

When Adam slid on his jacket, Granny came forward and took each of us by the arm. "Ya'll be good to one another," she said in a rush and then wrapped us in a fierce hug. As abruptly as she'd pulled us close, she let us go and marched to the front door.

We followed her, and she swatted Adam's backside with a dish towel as he passed her. "Treat her right, ya hear?"

I'd forgotten about the towel. She had game with rolling pins, hoses and towels. She could be called Granny Whacker.

Adam turned and while walking backwards saluted her. "Yes, Ma'am."

When it was my turn to walk past, she simply said, "Don't make'em wait too long."

I cringed at her directive. She was something else.

When I reached the truck, I found Adam brushing off the passenger seat. I'd warned him. He finished and stepped back, allowing me to climb in. He shut the door and I used the handle, yes handle, to roll the window down.

We backed out of the driveway, and I waved to Granny who'd walked to the edge of the porch. Tears sprang to my eyes as I realized I didn't want to leave Granny behind. When I could no longer see Granny or the cabin, I pulled my head back in and rolled the window back up. It was still a little too nippy this morning to ride with the windows down.

"Where are we headed now?" I asked.

"A small public airport about twenty miles from here. From there, home."

"In Montana?"

"Yes."

I'd never lived anywhere but Texas. New Orleans was only part time, so I didn't count that. Montana was a long way from Texas. And, it hadn't yet been decided that Montana was my home.

"Has anybody told Renard about Julia?" I asked.

"No. Both he and Julia are currently unaccounted for."

That probably spelled more trouble. I glanced sidelong at Adam as he shifted uncomfortably in his seat.

"Has there been any more word from Cedars?" I asked.

"None."

Though he was sitting right next to me, I could feel the distance between us growing. Sadness flared within me as I recognized that he was pulling away from me. Apparently, Granny wasn't the only thing we were leaving behind.

Adam shifted in his seat again and leaned heavily on his door. I didn't know what was going on other than he was putting distance between us. His mind felt thick, dark. Not dark as in evil, just heavy. Me peppering him with questions he didn't yet have the answers to probably wouldn't help.

In an effort to ease this new tension between us, I offered to give him some space. "You want to shut me out and think for a while?"

He seemed startled by the question. Almost as if he'd forgotten I was there at all.

"You wouldn't mind?" he asked cautiously.

Actually, I did. But it seemed he was intent on it. Whether on purpose or not, he'd already pulled most of the way back from our bond.

"Take the space that you need," I said, making sure to lock down on my emotions before answering.

Six little words were all that he needed. With one swift click, he slammed the doors completely shut between us, and I couldn't feel him at all. But I didn't miss the relief that he felt prior to doing so. I couldn't deny that hurt.

He brought my hand up to his lips and placed a kiss there. "Thanks," he whispered.

I pulled my hand free and turned to look out my window. Angry, I slammed my own shields in place while I white knuckled the arm rest on my door. I didn't know why I was angry. It was my idea, after all. And certainly, I could understand the need to think. Hadn't I just done this to him last night?

I blew out a breath, slowly releasing my grip on the handle. I had managed to live all of my pre-Adam life without him. I could certainly do it again. And it wasn't like I didn't have plenty to think about.

We spent the rest of the drive each concentrated in our own little worlds. That worked for me. At least everyone knew me there.

When we arrived at the airport, Adam was more detached than ever. He began to work the second after we got on the plane. Seated at a desk at the front of the cabin, he delved into the work of the Organization and more or less ignored me.

I sat in the seats opposite him, watching him work and absently munching on the fruit in a nearby basket. Like the flash of a camera, an image of Kenny exploded in my mind. Oh, my God. I couldn't believe I had forgotten.

I sprang across the aisle to the nearest phone, causing Adam to look up briefly. When he saw me pick up the phone, he went back to work. I dialed Miranda's cell, hating that she didn't pick up until the third ring.

"Hey, Mace." She sounded happy. "Jamie said it was probably you. It is you, isn't it?"

"Yeah, it's me. Do you have my cell phone?"

"Hey, Miranda. How are you?" she said. "The rescue went great. I've been—feel free to fill in the blank."

"Hey, Miranda. How are you?" I dutifully repeated. "I'll fill in the blank later. I think Kenny may be in trouble."

"Oh," she murmured her understanding. "It may be in the things that weren't carted to the original safe house. Give me five and call me back." She hung up without saying goodbye.

I placed the phone back in the cradle and trained my eyes on the clock hanging over Adam's head. He never even noticed me looking in his direction. At least he was highly focused on whatever he was doing for the Organization. I had to give him that. When the five minutes were up, I called her back.

"What's your passcode?"

"Three, six, six, three." I heard the click signaling she'd entered the correct numbers.

"Does that stand for food?"

"Of course."

"Mine too," she said.

One of the reasons I loved her. Not for her passcode, but her love of food.

"You've got twenty seven voicemails. I'll put it on speaker."

"Okay, but if it's not someone related to the current situation, move on to the next one."

"Will do."

The first one began to play. It was from Kenny on the night I first met Adam.

"Hey, Doc. I've thought about what you said, and I think we need to have that conversation. Some strange things have been happening around here." As if he just realized what he'd said, he snorted. "Stranger than normal, I mean. Call me."

The next five or six were related to the university. Then there were the frantic and rude messages from Miranda concerning my where abouts.

"Sorry," she yelled over the ranting. "I was just worried, and you weren't available. Your voicemail was the next best thing."

I rolled my eyes in amusement. "Please skip any more rant filled messages from a certain Miranda person."

"Consider it done," she replied sheepishly.

The next message that she played for me was from Kenny again.

"Hey, Doc."

I sat up at the sound of his voice. It was tired and haggard.

"Starting to get worried here. It's not like you to not return calls." There was a pause and a lot of static filled silence before he spoke again. "Things are not right. People are disappearing."

I heard Miranda's intake of breath.

"They're not coming back, Doc." There was a large inhale. "I need you to call me." Then the line went dead.

"When was that from?" I asked.

"Two days after the initial call. So, three days ago," she calculated.

She skipped several more calls about various unimportant things. Then Kenny's frantic voice came on the line again.

"Doc, wherever you are, I pray you're okay." His voice sounded so strained, more like the sixteen year old that he was. "It's bad, Doc. I found Crystal." At the mention of her name, his voice broke. "She...they butchered her."

I clasped my free hand over my mouth. Miranda's soft sobs joined Kenny's.

"She's dead, Doc." He took a deep, rattling breath. "I got as many as would listen to me out. We are in the place where we came to our understanding. Please remember, Doc. I think they're listening." One more sob. "I really need you to find me." Then the line went dead again.

I closed my eyes, my breath coming in shallow gasps behind my hand. On the other end, Miranda still wept. I could hear Cedars softly comforting her in the background, and then he spoke.

"That was from last night. If you contact him and they are listening, you could expose his location."

"I'll call you back," I choked out and then hung up the phone.

"Everything alright?"

I lifted my eyes to Adam. Pulling my hand from my mouth, I waited until I was sure I could speak without crying.

"I have to get to the Colony."

"We are going to Montana." He held my stare for a moment and then went back to work.

He'd dismissed me. My eyes widened at his presumed gall, and anger flushed through my system. Who did he think he was?

"I need to get to the Colony." It came out as a growl. One I'd heard him make on many occasions.

He paused his typing and looked up at me. "*You* need to calm down."

"Calm. Down." I paced toward him. "Calm. Down!" I found his lack of emotion to be utterly insulting. "You do not order me to calm down. Neither do you dictate to me where I will and will not go." I was beyond furious as I stood in front of his desk with my hands fisted at my sides.

"Macy," he began in that patronizing tone he possessed.

"Don't you dare speak to me as if I were a child!" Suddenly I found myself face to face with Adam, my nose just inches from his. I had leapt onto the desk and was now crouched in front of him.

In an instant, his eyes shifted. He shoved his keyboard aside and gripped the desk with both hands. "You are certainly acting like one!" He snarled.

I found myself drawing ragged breaths as I stared at Adam. Was I seriously about to attack him? I reined my anger in some, but I didn't move from my position on the desk.

"The hybrids at the Colony may not mean anything to you, but they mean something to me. I will NOT abandon them," I snarled.

He was unyielding in his response. "The hybrids at the Colony are not your responsibility."

"Then whose are they Adam! The government's? That's laughable. Yours? They mean nothing to you! They are mine!"

Before I could move, he flung his chair aside and pressed his nose to mine. "You mean something to me!" he yelled.

We maintained our pose, him standing and me crouched on the desk, nose to nose and both of us breathing heavily.

"If I mean anything to you, then you'll honor my commitment to the Colony." This I spoke softly, pleadingly even, putting all the feeling I could muster behind it—for all the good it did. His shields were still tightly in place.

He pulled away and paced rapidly back and forth behind the desk. Not once did the growling stop as he marched back and forth. It was too focused to be simply driven by anger.

"You know what's going on," I said suspiciously.

He stopped, putting both hands on his hips.

"What's going on?" I growled. His reluctance to answer only fueled my anger. "Adam!"

He sighed deeply and turned to face me. "The Consortium has managed to infiltrate the government. I believe they are the ones responsible for the disappearances at the Colony."

Kenny had said Crystal had been butchered and left for dead. What were they after? In the next second, I knew.

"For research and experimentation?"

"And nanobots."

What? My head snapped back to Adam.

He seemed truly sorry to tell me this. "The Colony was not entirely made up of the original hybrids."

Light bulbs started going off all over my brain. The inexplicable differences I'd observed between the hybrids. Why some, like Kenny, seemed so much more advanced than the others.

The full realization of my betrayal hit me and my legs collapsed beneath me. "Kenny," I breathed with heartfelt regret.

There was no question that I had unwittingly participated in both the Organization's and Consortium's plans for the Colony. Now they were disappearing, destined for who knows what or being murdered before I would ever have a chance to make it up to them.

I drew in a deep breath. I knew I couldn't change what had already happened, but I could change things from here on out. Not all of them were gone yet.

"I made a promise to Kenny," I said. "I won't go back on that."

Adam would either accept it or he wouldn't. But there was no way on God's green earth that I was not going to do everything in my power to save Kenny and whoever he'd managed to save.

He sat at the corner of the desk furthest from me, one hand

planted on the edge, the other rubbing his forehead. "I can't just swoop in there and take over. I have to work through the logistics of the operation. I have to factor in the government, the populace, that reporter." He pushed off the desk and strode away from me. "Not to mention, the Organization is in shambles. We are one decision away from scrapping it all!" he yelled.

"While you plan, Kenny and whoever he's got with him are waiting for me to show up," I said quietly.

There was a long pause in which Adam didn't say anything. I turned to look at him. He was all the way across the plane, standing with his back to me. Could he be any more obvious? Realizing my shields had slipped, I pulled them back in place.

He turned and stared at me for the longest time. "You have to let me keep you safe."

That was the most egotistical, male chauvinist comment. My anger that had cooled welled up in me again.

He was in front of me in an instant. His hands were planted on either side of my hips and his nose once again inches from mine. "I need to protect you. Can you not understand that?"

I understood the need to protect. It was what I currently felt toward the hybrids at the Colony. But I couldn't say I was receptive to the way he expressed that need—if that was what it was. I wasn't convinced that this wasn't some kind of play for alpha dominance.

"One day," I said. "Then I go with or without you." I knew it wasn't what he wanted to hear, but I was done with trying to "work" with him. He'd gone too far this time.

"Then get your butt off my desk so I can work."

Truce struck, I slid off the desk and started to brush past him, but he grabbed my arm, forcing me to stop. While neither of us looked at the other, he said, "Macy. Don't ever challenge me again."

I slowly turned my eyes to him. I knew beyond a shadow of a doubt that all the revulsion I felt at that command shone in my eyes. I waited until he met my gaze before I responded.

"I am not yours to command. I am not one of your soldiers. I am not even officially your employee. But whatever I am to you, I will never be ordered around like a submissive cub. You don't challenge that."

Adam bristled with rage, but his hand dropped from my arm, and I stalked away from the desk. Shaking with my own suppressed rage, I was concerned that I wouldn't be able to make it back to the phone without collapsing. But I couldn't display weakness now. Not after all that.

Determinedly, I walked back to the phone and called Miranda. She picked up on the first ring this time.

"You okay?" I asked.

"We're going to get them, right? Please tell me we're going to get them."

"Yes." I didn't even look at Adam as I confirmed it, but I did smell the spike of anger that wafted from his direction. I knew he could smell mine too. We'd both shifted during the confrontation. His desk bore score marks where I'd been. I might regret that later, but not right now.

"When do we leave?"

I sensed her switch from grief struck friend on the edge of panic to woman of action. She was always good at compartmentalizing. I'd never needed to before, but I'd had a crash course in it this week. I had stuffed so much stuff in so many places that I hoped it didn't explode all at once.

"Adam's making a plan right now."

"Oh, that's good. You said he was good at this stuff."

Guilt shot through my heart. I did say that. And he was. I stuffed that into some already overstuffed compartment and confirmed her assessment. "He's excellent."

"So, we wait?"

"We wait."

"Are you okay? You don't sound okay."

I glanced in Adam's direction. He was still in hybrid mode. I wasn't going to answer right now while he could hear me. "I'll see you when we get there." It was tightlipped, and she deserved better, but it was all I could give at the moment.

She hesitated before answering with a sigh. "I'll be here."

I hung up before the understanding in her voice caused me to break down. There was one more thing I needed to address with Adam. "Do you know where Kenny is?"

"In the woods," he answered without looking up. "My operative just informed me."

Of course he knew. He knew what he was doing. I trusted him, right?

I closed my eyes and leaned back into the seat. This truce between me and Adam felt like nails being dragged across a chalkboard. I couldn't relax. The confrontation with Adam had left me shaken. I found myself simultaneously doubting Adam and my own abilities.

I'd had another uncontrolled shift. I wasn't naïve enough to think that I would become a hybrid and do everything perfectly right away. But I expected it nonetheless. Did that make me a perfectionist? I didn't know, but it did leave me disappointed.

As did Adam's implication that some of the hybrids belonged to the Organization. That little omission of his was another sore spot. When did the secrets end with him? Granted, five or six days may have not given him enough time to tell me everything. But this was different. This was personal to me.

Despite all the drama associated with the teen hybrids, which had nothing on the adult ones I'd been with this week, I loved them. I didn't quite realize that until this week.

Over the last two years of my substitute parenting, I'd gotten to know them. They all had my phone number on speed dial. Many a time, after an early morning phone call from a broken hearted teen hybrid, did I regret that decision. But, as we got to know each other, they'd become like family to me. I couldn't let them down, any more than I already had.

Adam spent the rest of the plane flight working, and I spent the rest of it worrying. By the time we got to Montana, I was exhausted. Adam hadn't said another word to me the entire trip. That didn't change when we landed. He left the cabin and me without delay.

I felt a burst of cool air as the door to the plane was opened. Adam exchanged a greeting with someone, even laughed a little. It was a miracle. He did still have the power of speech.

I got up and collected the jacket I'd discarded on the plane. Making my way to the exit, I spotted Adam already seated in one of those hunter golf cart ATVs. With the way he'd been acting, it wouldn't have surprised me if he pulled away and left me there.

I shrugged on the jacket as I jogged down the stairs. It felt good to move again, even if it was only fifteen feet. When I reached the ground, he was still there, so I guessed that meant he was waiting for me. I climbed in and without so much as a sideways glance, he took off.

All I could see were the surrounding mountains. It looked like Adam was going to run us straight into them until I spotted a natural looking rock gateway. Adam slowed down and part of the rock slid away, revealing an opening just big enough for the ATV.

As soon as we cleared the entrance, the entire scene changed. Nestled in a large valley between the mountains, was the largest log cabin I'd ever seen. It reminded me of a wilderness lodge you would see on a postcard.

We sped across the grounds to the back of the lodge. A servant came forward and exchanged places with us in the cart. Another person, a slightly older and rotund woman, greeted us and then ushered us into a large kitchen. Her cell phone rang, and she walked a few feet away from us to answer it.

"I'm going to go shower, you okay?" Adam asked coldly.

I was startled that he'd spoken to me, but not that he was dumping me here. "Sure," I said without feeling, because that was how I felt—numb.

Seemingly oblivious to my emotional state, he left, leaving me alone in the kitchen with Rotundo.

"That is truly not flattering," she said stiffly as she walked up behind me.

Crap. Was this another mind reader I had to contend with? I turned to her, ready to apologize, but my apology died on my lips. She wasn't looking at me. She was looking at a dead pig being put on a spit. I had to agree. Not flattering at all.

"Are the other's here?" I asked.

"Are you speaking of Agents Juarez and Olivia or the two procreating like rabbits?"

I smiled despite myself. I totally appreciated her frankness. "Let's start with the unengaged agents, shall we?" I said.

"It would spare these innocent eyes. In any case, you'd be entirely on your own. I've sworn off their entire hallway after my first encounter with Cedar's bare backside."

Better her than me. Though it made me worry how I'd get in to see Miranda.

"Just follow me," she said merrily as she led the way.

I increased her intelligence rating due to the fact that she hadn't tried to give me directions. I didn't really pay attention to where we were going. Everything was just sort of a blur. I stopped when she did. We were standing at the end of a hallway. The semicircle that it formed had two doors.

"Juarez is in the room to your left, and Olivia is on the right," she said. "You need anything else?"

I shook my head no and watched her leave. Looking at Olivia's door, I wondered if I had the courage for this. This was what I signed up for, right? The good, the bad, and the just plain I don't want to.

I took a deep breath and walked the few steps to Olivia's room. I knocked softly and eased the door open. Poking my head in, I saw she was in the bed amidst a swaddling of blankets and pillows.

"Hey, Einstein," she said weakly from her cocoon as she tried to sit up.

"No need to get up on my account," I implored, hurrying to her side, but she continued to struggle determinedly. Putting one arm around her back, I helped her to sit and then adjusted her pillows.

"You just lifted me with one arm," she said.

Did I? "Yay super hybrid me." It lacked any enthusiasm, but

I didn't think she noticed. Sliding a nearby chair close to her bed, I sat down. "How are you doing?"

"I've been better," she snorted and then winced in pain. "My ribs were shattered," she gasped out. "One or more of them punctured my lung. I cannot even remember all my other injuries. All that to say, it's taken a little longer than normal to recover. But the nanobots are hard at work."

I sat there caught between the need to help her and the need to scream. "Olivia, I'm so sorry," I finally managed to choke out.

"It's not your fault," she assured me. It was the same thing Adam had said. "Pike and the Consortium are the ones responsible." A dark shadow passed over her face. "Mostly Pike."

I didn't know what all he had done to her, but I knew none of it was good. "You won't ever have to worry about Pike again," I told her.

She fixed her school teacher's glare on me. "Is that so?"

"Yeah. He attacked me, and I fought back. Adam finished him off."

She nodded. "That's good." Her eyes closed for so long that I thought she might have drifted off to sleep. I shifted to get up when she opened them again. "Have you seen Juarez?" Her voice was filled with uncertainty.

"Not yet. I just got here." The pain displayed on her face right now wrapped a weight around my heart. "Do you two share a bond?"

She nodded and tears coursed down her face. I reached out and captured her hand. She squeezed it once in thanks.

"I couldn't shield him from everything." She was crying and wincing in pain simultaneously. "In the end, I shielded him from nothing." Her breath was coming in ragged gasps.

The weight on my heart grew and seemed to envelop my whole being. That must have been the worst thing in the world for both of them to go through. There was nothing I could say or do to make it any better. I just held her hand as she fought to regain control.

"I'm sorry I didn't tell you about the rescue plan. I thought they would be listening," I said.

She painfully cleared her throat and swiped at the remaining tears. "We always knew there would be one. It was just a matter of time," she said shakily.

"Is there anything I can do for you?"

The grip she had on my hand became hard as steel. "You can use your super hybrid self to help us stop them and those like them."

"That, I can do," I nodded.

She was clearly exhausted by our exchange, and I helped her lay back down. "Get some rest, okay?"

"Sure," she mumbled, already on her way to sleep.

I watched her sleep for a few moments, thinking about the price she'd paid. I desperately hoped it was in service to the Organization and not for me. But I couldn't stop the words, my fault, from ringing in my ears.

I felt like I was walking through water as I made my way over to Juarez's room. I found him awake and in better shape than Olivia.

His eyes lit up at my entrance. "MacyKat," he said warmly, setting his laptop aside.

I shut the door and leaned against it.

"What's wrong?" he asked softly.

I shook my head, but was unable to speak.

He looked at me puzzled for a moment then understanding dawned. "You saw Olivia."

I nodded and then blew out a breath. "Sorry. I didn't expect to have this reaction when I came in here."

He patted the bed beside him, indicating for me to sit. "It's okay. How is she?"

"Weak." My voice cracked under the strain, and I swallowed trying to rid myself of the painful lump that had formed in my throat.

He nodded and looked away. Then he crossed his arms, tucking his hands in like he was hugging himself. "She's shut me out," he said. "Won't speak to me or acknowledge me." Tears filled his eyes and the knot reformed in my throat.

C. E. GLINES

"She's hurting," I said, approaching the bed. "Not just physically, but emotionally, too." I sat down with my back to him. "I don't know everything Pike did to her."

"I do," he cut in furiously.

Even though I didn't have a bond with him, I could sense the anger rolling off of him in waves. I turned to face him, and he skewered me with his glowing eyes. Clearly, he was a man on the edge, desperately in need of an outlet for his anger and an even greater need to help his mate. Not wanting to antagonize him further, I remained motionless until the glow faded from his eyes.

"I heard you killed him," he said gruffly. Though the glow had faded, his voice still carried the authority of a predator.

I nodded once in confirmation.

"How," he growled at me. It was not a question.

"He came into my tent and attacked me. I fought back. Partially ripped his throat out, and then Adam nearly ripped his head from his shoulders."

"Good girl," he said vehemently.

I couldn't hold it in any longer. My feelings of guilt for their suffering were smothering me. My words came out in one long rush. "I'm sorry, Juarez. I never meant for any of this to happen. Not with the Agency or the Organization and not with you and Olivia. None of it." I held my breath and waited for his condemnation to justify my own.

But his expression softened. "Oh MacyKat, nobody holds you responsible for this."

How could he say that? "I do," I whispered.

"Then you're wrong. Not a very good analysis by your super brain, if you ask me."

I closed my eyes against his intense gaze. Why would he think that? The whole reason they were captured was because everyone was trying to keep me safe. And it had cost him dearly.

"Hey." He clucked me under the chin, causing me to open my eyes. "You did not do this."

That was what they all kept saying, but it didn't lesson the guilt I felt.

320

"Where's Adam?" he asked.

I shifted on the bed, struggling against the pressure in my chest that came with the mention of his name. "I don't know." I tried to keep the disappointment out of my voice, but it didn't go unnoticed by Juarez.

"You two have a fight?"

I played with a loose thread on the comforter until he took my hand in his, forcing me to focus on the question.

I blew out a breath and rolled my eyes to the ceiling. "I think I challenged him," I said softly.

Juarez inhaled sharply. "Whoa." He absently patted my hand as if to say, everything's going to be okay. "So, how'd that go?"

I barked out a laugh. "About as well as you might expect."

"I think it went better than that. You're not dead. Not even roughed up a little. Anybody else very well would be."

"No, I'm not dead," I agreed.

He waited for me to continue, but I chose not to elaborate any further. What would be the point? He hadn't harmed me physically, but he had damaged something between us. I couldn't quite decipher it myself. I wasn't going to hash it out with Juarez.

We continued to sit in silence with him stroking my hand before he asked knowingly, "Did he start pulling away from you?"

Maybe Juarez did have a good feel for the situation. "Pretty much," I said, unwilling to meet his eyes.

"It's nothing against you, MK. That's just Adam's way. Before any large scale operation, he withdraws from us. And, he has one heck of a mess to clean up here."

I knew he had a big job in front of him. I did. But, *they* didn't share a bond with him. "He shut me out." Saying it out loud did not bring any relief whatsoever. It only made it seem more real. And I knew he was shutting me out for more than just work related reasons.

"Oh," Juarez answered, his mouth lingering in the "o" position.

It was utterly inexplicable to me that I should have these feelings of rejection, but they were here nonetheless. In fact, I thought with every minute that passed they were growing stronger. It made me wonder what the heck I was doing here at all.

"Well, he's new at this," Juarez defended Adam. "Both the bonding and the girl. But he's smart. He'll figure it out." He let go of my hand and crossed his arms in front of his chest again. "You know, I've known Adam for fifty years, and you're the first woman I've ever known him to go gaga over. Trust me," he said at my look of disbelief, "when it comes to you, he has been one crazy cat. You don't know the half," he said with a wave of his hand and a roll of his eyes.

This was pathetic. Now he was trying to comfort me, when it should be the other way around.

"It's actually kind of nice, seeing Adam all rattled for a change," Juarez chuckled. "Now he'll be forced to see things from my point of view."

I couldn't help but chuckle despite the building hurt I carried. "You're impossible you know that. And I can clearly see why Olivia loves you."

At the mention of Olivia, the sadness returned to his face.

I stood up and tucked the blanket around him. "You'll figure it out, too. Just give her some time to process her feelings before she shares them with you."

"You women do that a lot, process?"

I shrugged. I guess we did. If processing equaled thinking, I was an elite model on the verge of overheating.

I got up to leave but added one more observation. "She's afraid of hurting you any more than she feels she already has by not being able to shield you from her pain."

I saw the flash of understanding in his eyes. "Thanks, MacyKat," he said with tears welling up in his eyes again.

His tears were like a spark to my well fueled reservoir of pain. I turned and left quickly before he could see the tears in my eyes.

Outside their suite, I rapidly searched for the closest private place I could find. It happened to be a small stone balcony at the other end of the hallway. But instead of being open to the outside, it was enclosed with stained glass. It looked sort of like a small chapel.

I stepped in and moved to the side until I would be hidden from the view of anyone that happened to walk down the hallway. Putting my back against the wall, I clasped my hands over my mouth as the first sobs hit. But there was no holding them back this time.

All the emotions I'd been stuffing into those compartments this last week erupted as the hastily built structure crumbled. I slowly slid down the wall as the sobs overtook me. My shields were the next thing to fall. Then everything came down on top of me.

I cried for Kenny and the Colony and the guilt I associated with my failures there. I cried for Olivia and Juarez and the pain they were enduring. I cried for the Macy that was lost. And lastly, I cried for Adam.

I slowly became aware of Adam's presence. He had wrapped himself around me both inside and out. We were gently swaying to the rhythm he had adopted as he held me.

With my head buried in his chest, I took a shaky breath and rolled my head to the side. "Sorry," I whispered.

He stopped rocking me and pulled me tighter within the circle of his arms. "I'm sorry," he whispered gently. "I didn't realize..." he stopped and cleared his throat. "It was not my intention to hurt you. Nor was it my intention to make you doubt me."

He buried his face in my hair, as if to hide from the pain and regret of his actions. But I could feel them resonating through our restored bond.

"I know," I whispered again. I knew he wasn't intentionally hurting me. Just like I knew my feelings of rejection were stupid. How could you be rejected when you were not even officially with someone?

He stopped stroking my hair and turned my face to look at him. "Nothing you feel for me is stupid or ridiculous." He pressed kisses to both my tear swollen eyes, and then he swiped his thumb under my nose and wiped it off on his jeans.

That was sweet and gross and so unlike the Adam of earlier today.

He lowered his head and gently kissed my lips. Resting his forehead against mine, he said, "This is new to me. I am not used to being challenged, or argued with, or questioned." He paused while the truth of his statement hung in the air. Taking a deep breath, he continued. "You stir things in me I didn't know existed. I am not who I was when you are near, and I'm..."

I could feel his struggle to define what he felt. There were so many emotions swirling around in him, that I couldn't quantify it either.

"Lost," he growled. "I'm lost when you are gone. You have completely remade me," he finished with a snarl.

It was the most Adam had ever admitted about the way he felt about me. It wasn't a declaration of love, and clearly, he didn't sound happy about it. Sounded more like, you're a pain in the butt I don't know what to do with, but it was honest. I could have taken offense to his categorization of me, but like Juarez, I kind of enjoyed this discombobulated Adam.

"I'm not trying to cause trouble for you," I said seriously.

He snorted at my choice of words.

"I didn't even mean to challenge you. I was just being me. Or, the new me. Sometimes I'm not sure if I'm more leopard or human. The strength of what I feel, the..." I ran through the emotions involving Adam. Want, need, they were undeniably present, but it was more than that. I didn't know how to label what this was between Adam and me.

Adam kissed me again as I searched for the right words, then he pulled back to look into my eyes. "We'll figure it out together. But regardless of what you feel or how ridiculous you think it is, you have to let me know."

I couldn't stop the retort that sprang from my lips. "What, not a mind reader?"

We stayed frozen in place, each silently regarding the other until the laughter overtook us in one giant rush. I much preferred laughing to crying.

"As do I," he sighed heavily. Pulling me close to him, he proceeded to kiss me thoroughly this time.

You better stop before this leads to something Granny would not approve of.

My comment had the desired effect of putting on the brakes. Adam pulled back in a fit of laughter once again.

"You're not playing fair, Macy. How am I supposed to woo you with thoughts of Granny in my head?"

Woo me? "First of all, I'm not playing at anything. Secondly, food is an excellent source of wooage."

"Must be, if you've ditched me for Granny," he said a little too sarcastically.

Silently, hopefully without Adam knowing, I measured his emotions. He really was slightly envious of Granny. Unbelievable, but true.

"Granny," I said, stressing her name for emphasis, "cannot provide me with everything that I need. She merely provides certain trimmings that I find delightful. Since you are my avenue to Granny, I'd say that makes you more important to me than Granny."

"Still, that was a low blow, invoking Granny on me," he said as he pushed off the floor.

"But effective," I countered. I accepted his hand up and he pulled me to my feet. "Especially considering my virtue is still intact."

"It's just my luck to find a woman who has moral standards," he said, pulling me close once more.

Wrapping my arms around his waist and looking directly into those big green eyes of his, I flagrantly batted my eyelashes at him. "You must have the most amazing luck," I teased.

"I do," he said quietly and then ducked in for another kiss.

CHAPTER 20

ADAM GRABBED MY HAND AND laced his fingers through mine as we left the enclosure.

"So, how did you find me?" I asked him.

"I had this feeling that something was wrong. I finally dropped my shields," he said, grinning guiltily at me. "I still couldn't feel you at that point. So I tracked you by smell. But when your shields fell, I could see our bond. I followed it to you."

"You could physically see it?" I said, pulling him to a standstill.

"I don't think it was with my natural eyes or hybrid ones for that matter."

"What did it look like?"

"Streaks of light twisted or braided together." His free hand traced a spiral through the air. "They just floated in the air. The closer I got to you, the thicker it became."

"Can you see it now?"

He released my hand and stepped back. Looking down, seemingly at my chest, a slow smile spread across his lips as he nodded. "Your threads are golden."

He moved his fingers through the air like he was strumming a harp. I felt a fluttering in my core, keeping time with him as he played.

"I can feel it," I said in awe. Frea-ky. There really was an honest to goodness bond between us. I knew there must be a scientific explanation for it, but I felt like I was in the presence of magic.

"They start right here." He touched a spot just below my breasts.

I tried really hard to see what he did, but I couldn't.

"I think the desperation that I had to get to you had something to do with enabling me to see the bond."

"Maybe," I nodded. "It seems to me, that we, as this new hybrid species, are still evolving."

"So it would seem."

We resumed walking down the hallway, turning right before we reached Olivia and Juarez's suite. Adam squeezed my hand when a twinge of guilt pulled at me.

"It really isn't your fault," he said as we started down the stairs.

I sighed, but didn't look at him.

"Macy," he growled softly. He swung around in front of me, stopping on the stair below me. "The Consortium has been one step ahead of us for a long time. We...I need you. Please trust, that for whatever reason, you have been gifted with a brain for strategy and problem solving unlike anything we've seen before."

Those were hard words to swallow. I wasn't one who sought praise. I much preferred to remain behind the scenes. Taking the credit for a job well done never really mattered to me. Getting the job done, that was what counted.

"Are you trying to say I am worth what happened to them?" I said, keeping my tone even. The last thing I wanted was to start another argument between us.

He dropped the hand he'd brought up to my face. "Do I wish with everything in me that it hadn't happened? Yes. If I could have prevented it, I would have. If I could change it, I would. But those were not options given to me. You are not the only one with guilt where they are concerned."

He turned and paced down the stairs, dropping a shield he'd had in place over his own culpability in the matter and making me realize how selfish and self-centered I'd been.

"I should have known," I said, jogging to catch up. "I'm sorry." I slipped my hand back into his.

"Me too," came his soft reply and he kissed the back of my hand.

"You just always seem so unaffected by it," I said.

He huffed in response.

"How do you get over the guilt?"

He slowed down as he considered his answer. "Time. As they get better, so do I. I've been in leadership long enough to know that I'll bear the weight of anyone hurt under my command. It's a responsibility I accept." He shrugged. "I do the best I can."

"I guess that's all anyone can do," I said.

I thought back over the last week. In every situation I'd faced, I had given it my all. It had almost cost me my life to do so. I paused. Slowly, I repeated the words to myself. It had almost cost me my life. Just like Olivia and Juarez. I didn't hold them responsible for everything I'd gone through. They had, excluding Pike, done everything they could to see me safely through it. I would have done the same if our roles were reversed.

I looked back up at Adam.

He nodded. "That's what being part of the team means."

The huge weight of guilt that had been lodged in my chest suddenly shrunk.

"That's my girl," he whispered.

"Do you hear everything I think?"

"Only when you think slowly enough," he said, picking up the pace again.

I frowned in confusion at him which caused him to laugh.

"When you get going, I only get bits and pieces," he explained. "You think at ninety miles an hour, Woman."

"It's a gift."

"You better believe it."

"Starting to."

"That's my girl."

A puzzled look came over my face as strange animal noises came from another suite just ahead of us in the hallway.

"What's that?" I asked worriedly. It sounded like someone was being tortured.

Adam cleared his throat. "*That* would be Cedars and Miranda's suite."

Completely flustered, I pulled Adam past their suite, adding more speed as the *noises* got louder. He let me pull him along, but didn't try to hide the smirk he wore.

"You know," he began in a drawn out voice, "there's no call to be ashamed of God's gift to married folk."

Really? He was bringing Granny into this?

"I'm not sure that's what God intended. And anyway, they are not married."

I didn't know where I was going, but I just kept pulling a smiling Adam along, and he seemed content to let me. I slowed our march when I was no longer an ear witness to Miranda and Cedars' antics.

When I ended up in another dead end enclosure, I let go of Adam's hand and stopped completely. Turning around, I saw Adam leaning against the entryway with arms crossed over his chest and that familiar smirk painted on his face. Someday, I tell you. Someday.

His half smile widened as he picked up on my thoughts.

"Are you ready to hear about the plan to collect the Colony hybrids?" he asked.

"Yes. Yes, I am," I said, looking away quickly.

"May I?" He said with his hand extended toward the hallway we'd just vacated.

"By all means," I said with a wave of my hand.

He resumed the lead and took us back the way we had come.

"You could have told me I was going the wrong way," I muttered.

"You were so determined to come this way that I thought I'd let you."

Whatever. Thankfully, we didn't have to pass Cedars and Miranda again. He brought me to a large suite of rooms that had windows for exterior walls on two sides. The view of the surrounding mountains was breathtaking.

"I've already cleaned up, did you want to before we get started?"

A shower would feel nice, but knowing the plan would feel better. "Nah, let's just get to it."

He nodded once and then walked to the far side of the room where a large open office area was centered around an equally large desk. He motioned for me to join him, and I walked around the desk to stand behind his chair. On his computer screen, was a map of the area surrounding the Colony.

"Our operative put Kenny and about fifty other hybrids at this location," he said, indicating a familiar swath of woods. "There's no way to mount a large scale operation without drawing the notice of the local authorities or the general public. I'm not trying to create a panic." He looked at me to gauge my reaction.

"Agreed," I nodded.

"I can get them out in small groups, here and here." He traced two paths leading from the woods and away from the Colony.

I felt him grow really still inside, and I braced myself for a big however as he swiveled his chair to face me.

"It is not strictly necessary for you to be there." He lifted a hand to forestall my objection. "I know you want to be there. I also recognize the responsibility you feel for these kids. I don't understand it, but I know it exists for you." He placed his hands in his lap and waited for my response.

I softened at the cooperation I felt coming from him. He really was trying not to run alpha over me.

"What is the danger in me being there?" I asked.

He visibly relaxed when he realized I wasn't fighting him on this. "There is movement at the Colony. Satellite Intel is not showing anything out of the ordinary, which is what I expected. Kenny says that the normal guards were swapped out with people he didn't recognize. Given the recent string of betrayals, I'm simply not sure who I can trust."

He picked up a pen and began to tap it against his leg. "I'll get a better idea of what is happening when I get some eyes I do trust inside the compound. I suspect our team will find something akin to what Kenny found with Crystal." He stilled the pen. "I don't want you to witness that, and I don't want to put you in harm's way should any of the Consortium's people still be there."

He wouldn't meet my eyes, but I knew what he wanted me to do. I sighed, knowing I couldn't oblige him. Sliding my hand along his shoulder, I climbed into his lap.

"I appreciate you trying to protect me."

He immediately tensed at my words.

"Adam, I do. Seeing them like that would be hard, and I certainly don't want to compromise any of your team because they are trying to protect me." I stopped and considered whether I really was ready to forgo a trip to the compound. "Are your teams going to sweep the compound for survivors?"

"Yes."

"Then, I'm okay with not actually entering the Colony grounds. But I really would like to be in the woods."

"Only the woods?"

"Yes."

"And whatever I say goes?"

My reply this time was a little more hesitant. "Yeess."

He dropped his head forward in frustration. "Macy, I have to be able to trust you to follow orders. You aren't trained in anything—"

I placed my hand over his mouth to silence him and received the single eyebrow raise as my reward. I gave a quick kiss to the offending brow.

"I understand that you are the boss in this operation. However, I do feel the need to remind you of the propensity for circumstances to crop up that I have no control over and can merely respond to as I see fit."

He gripped my hand covering his mouth, his eyes narrowing as he removed it. "That would be reason number one for you not being there."

"You can't keep me in a box or locked away somewhere. It'd be like trying to beat the buzzards off of road kill."

"You're telling me, that no matter what, trouble follows you?"

"Like Cedars follows Miranda."

He rubbed his hand across his eyes. "God, help me," he muttered.

I chuckled at his sincere plea while I patted his back. "There, there, Big Guy. It's all in a day's work."

"Feels more like a lifetime," he mumbled.

Having settled the fact that I was going, my mind turned to the Consortium. "How long before we leave?"

"Couple hours. Have you eaten yet?"

"No," I said absently. I slid off Adam's lap and walked over to a large dry erase board positioned perpendicular to the desk. I picked up the marker and turned to Adam. "May I?"

He had the phone to his ear, but paused to answer me. "Certainly. Got something on your mind?"

"Just thinking."

I wrote Consortium in black in the center of the board. Then I drew an arrow slanted downward and off to the left. I wrote the word Pike at the end of the arrow. From there, I drew another arrow and wrote Julia.

"We know the Consortium had access to the Organization via this route," I said.

At the top of the board, I wrote my name and connected it to the Consortium with another arrow. "We also know they were after me."

To the right of center, I wrote nanobots and tied it to the Consortium. "By their attack on the Colony, we know they wanted the nanobots the Organization created. Did Julia want me in the Organization?"

Adam left his seat and sat partially on the edge of his desk. "No. She was against it from the start."

"The Consortium wanted the Organization's nanobots. Julia had possession of the nanobots, but kept them from the Consortium. The Consortium also wanted me and she didn't."

I stared quietly at the board. Then I drew an arrow arching from Julia to me with a question mark in the middle. "Some piece of information is missing here. It would appear that the Consortium and Julia were working at cross purposes."

Adam didn't comment, only continued to watch me work. I focused my attention on the nanobots.

"Oh," I turned to Adam. "I forgot to tell you, that, according to overheard conversations of drug laden Consortium operatives, the Consortium has developed nanobots capable of maturing a fetus to adult in less than a year."

Adam's eyes widened in disbelief.

"You don't think it's true?" I asked him.

"I'd find it really hard to believe. Nanobot design is an extremely difficult and complicated task. It incorporates both bio and electrochemical elements. Not to mention, the programming itself is a beast. The best they've come up with is the Furries, and they're loaded with flaws. You'll learn about it at some point."

"Has the Organization developed maturation nanobots, and could the Consortium have gotten their hands on them?"

"To my knowledge, we've not ventured down that road. I haven't yet examined Renard's or Julia's office. I plan on doing that shortly. Juarez may find something there." He shrugged. "There is also the fact that every nanobot is keyed into the individual biochemistry of the recipient. It's not as simple as transferring from one host to another."

I shot him a look. "You did it with me."

"You were dying. I thought it worth the risk. The actual way you were dying, the blood loss, is what saved you. It allowed the nanobots to proliferate quickly enough to takeover and repair any damage clashing biochemistries would have created. You were like a clean slate they could write on."

Well, if I was dying...

Turning from Adam, I refocused on the nanobots. "Whether it will work or not, they believe they have these super growth nanobots." I drew an arrow upwards from nanobots and wrote super growth.

"They also may be in possession of Organization nanobots retrieved from Colony abductees." I added that to the board. "How long can the nanobots exist outside of their hosts?" I asked him.

"Indefinitely. Right now, they are programmed to hibernate outside of the host."

That needed to change immediately. "Whose bright idea was that?" I asked.

"Not mine, I assure you."

I studied the board and the connections I'd made. "They've developed quite a plan."

I drew a plus sign between super growth nanobots and Organization nanobots and added what I thought it might equal. Adam summed it up.

"Super growth nanobots plus Organization nanobots equals hybrid army." He stood and began to pace the room. "It doesn't make sense. Assuming they could form a hybrid with our nanobots, what would they use the super growth nanobot for?"

"They are not looking to integrate the nanobots into adults," I said, stopping Adam cold. "They are looking for embryos, fetuses as a last resort. Remember, Millsap only wanted a part of my DNA from which to create babies?"

"They've found a way to splice DNA strands from separate individuals together to form a whole being, along with incorporating animal DNA? Again, that seems way outside of their reach."

"Is it outside of Julia's?" I asked softly.

He swallowed whatever he was about to say and placed both hands on his hips. I walked over and placed my hand on his back.

"You've got to start considering the fact that Julia was obviously up to something outside of the Organization's operations."

I felt his back shudder as he drew a shaky breath. "I never would have suspected her of such treachery. She had, or at least I thought she had, integrity, loyalty. She was supposed to be working against this sort of thing," he snapped and walked a few paces away.

"I'm not saying she is working with the Consortium, but she's up to something she didn't want the Organization to know about."

He hung his head in acknowledgment of the facts. "I hear you, Macy. You're right." He chuckled softly at the irony. "Just one correction to your theory. If they cannot get their hands on enough embryos, I don't think they would view fetuses as a last resort."

It was definitely going to be difficult to get ahold of embryos. Ever since Congress passed the Medical Research Act, embryos were not allowed to be stored for longer than ninety days, and that was only if they met the criteria for being stored at all. Then the security measures required for storage were enormous. But, fetuses?

"Where would they get the fetuses?" I asked. "I can't see mothers lining up to volunteer for this."

"Did they strike you as the kind of people to care about collateral damage?"

I recalled Kenny's report about Crystal. Didn't they butcher her just to get her nanobots? "You're saying the mothers won't have a choice, that they'll just rip the babies from the mother's womb?" I asked in horror. "The baby couldn't exist without the mother."

Adam looked at my stricken face. "You said they had conducted trials already? The baby couldn't have grown to full size adult within the mother. They've found some way to sustain the fetus outside of the womb."

I absorbed his words, drawing the obvious conclusion. "Millsap wouldn't hesitate to take what he wanted. It wouldn't matter to him if he had to kill the mothers to do it. With what Kenny said about Crystal's death..." I let my words trail off.

"It would be a bloodbath," he nodded. "Over the last few years, the Consortium's actions have become more desperate. Each offensive more bold and daring than the one that preceded it. The reports that the extremist groups have been creating, who do you think has been the source of their material?"

The dawning realization of the possible future before us was staggering. I sat down in Adam's chair. Adam knelt in front of me, putting a hand on each of my knees.

"You need to accept that the people we are dealing with have no qualms about killing or worse to get what they want."

I looked up in shock at Adam. Even when they had held me

captive, and I knew they were torturing Olivia and Juarez, it had still seemed like a farfetched occurrence. Like I was living in some kind of altered reality.

"I know this is not what you are used to dealing with," he said gently. "It is, however, your new reality."

I swallowed and nodded my head once. This time, he was right. "They can't hope to continue without being discovered."

"I'm not sure remaining hidden is a top priority for them anymore," Adam said.

I squeezed both my eyes shut tight as I processed that. Right, not hiding.

"If they succeed in enacting this plan, they will reveal the existence of hybrids to the world in a way that presents them as the monsters the extremist groups claim them to be," Adam said.

"The GL's membership would swell overnight," I concluded.

We stared silently at each other as we considered the ramifications that would cause.

"We have to stop this from being the unmitigated disaster it seems to be turning into," I said.

He nodded helplessly at me with a look that said, what do you think I'm trying to do.

I was tired of the bad guys winning. "The bad guys don't get to win this one," I said definitively.

Adam smiled at me. "We've figured out their plan, and we've got you. We'll find a way to stop them."

"Somebody need me?"

We both looked up as Juarez walked into the room. Adam stood up, and I rounded the desk, heading for Juarez. He scooped me up in a bear hug.

"I just left you a few hours ago, and now you're up and walking around. How are you doing?"

"Ready to fight," he said, setting me back on my feet and releasing me.

"I guess that means you're doing great. And, Olivia?"

"She's better too. I can't thank you enough, MacyKat. What you said…it really helped."

I patted the side of Juarez's arm. "I'm glad," I said quietly.

Adam's face wore a puzzled expression. *Relationship advice?* he asked.

Something like that. I'm just glad it didn't backfire on me.

That would have been the more likely scenario, Adam sagely agreed.

I stuck my tongue out at him while I walked to stand next to Juarez who was studying the white board.

"What's all this?" he asked, indicating the board with a wave of his hand.

"That's mine," I said. "It's what I think the Consortium's up to."

"Super growth nanobot plus Organization nanobot?" Juarez read aloud.

Adam joined us at the white board. "Macy thinks the Consortium intends to merge the two inside of embryos or fetuses. She also thinks they may have found a way to splice DNA from two separate human individuals."

"Whew," Juarez blew out as he studied the board.

"Is that possible?" I asked him.

He scratched his chin as if deep in thought. "It would take some doing."

"But it's possible," I pressed.

He blew out another breath and then tucked both of his hands in his front pockets. "Assuming they could actually integrate DNA from two separate individuals, and assuming they could then add animal DNA, and then top it all off by maturing the embryo at an accelerated rate?" He shook his head in disbelief.

"The information I overheard while we were being held captive indicated they had achieved a maturation rate of one year from fetus to adult."

"The programming required for that, and the sheer quantity of details that would need to be addressed...that would take years to develop."

"Could Julia do it?" Adam asked.

As they regarded each other, I watched their changing

expressions. Disbelief, betrayal and hurt colored Juarez's face before it settled into a stern expression of acceptance.

"She might," he nodded slowly. "She could definitely think up the idea, but I think she would not have addressed a lot of details. Do you remember the Keeno Trials?" Juarez asked Adam. "That was Julia's doing."

A look of disgust passed across Adam's face, and he swiped his hand across it in an effort to clear the memory.

"What happened in the Keeno Trials?" I asked, looking back and forth between them.

"Julia wanted to create hybrids from the womb," Adam explained. "She wanted the abilities to develop as the child grew. To have what we have in Kenny, but created in the lab."

"I take it that didn't go so well?"

Juarez huffed. "You could say that. Like I said before, she left out a lot of details. Particularly in regards to the positional information within the embryo."

I grimaced as I understood what he meant.

He nodded. "It was bad. Limbs in wrong places, entire pieces missing. I warned her, but she wouldn't slow the project down to let me thoroughly review it."

"That is horrible. This whole thing is horrible," I moaned, covering my face with my hands. Those poor little babies. I was starting to have an intense dislike for this Julia. Genius or not, anyone that could subject an innocent life to such cruelty did not rate high in my book.

"What's horrible?"

We all turned to watch as Miranda and Cedars walked in.

"The revelation of mutant, disfigured hybrids in such a fashion as to explode the ranks of the GL," I answered her.

The smile left her face, and her pace momentarily slowed. "It's always something with you, isn't it? Can't we just have a normal get together? Go shopping or something. That's what normal people do, right?"

It was the first time I'd seen her since we'd separated the morning after I became a hybrid. She looked thinner.

"We're not normal," I quipped as I walked toward her.

She hugged me tightly and then pulled back quickly. "Yeah, we were never normal even before we were hybrids."

That was true and not the least bit comforting.

"Seems we have always been destined for uniqueness," I said.

"One of a kind," she agreed as she watched Cedars walk past her. "Designer originals."

As I stood there, watching her watch Cedars, I wasn't sure she was talking about us anymore.

"You've lost weight," I told her.

She lifted her shoulders in a shrug. "I've been busy."

"I heard," I said pointedly with a tilt of my head.

That was enough to briefly regain her attention. "You heard?" she asked, her eyes widening in understanding.

I leaned in and whispered conspiratorially, "Apparently, the walls around here are not soundproofed."

She frowned while biting her bottom lip, then with an ease that belonged only to Miranda, shrugged off the embarrassment. "They should really fix that. I wouldn't want our capabilities causing a disruption in the harmony of the team. Inspiring feelings of intimidation," her eyes were now trained on Cedars again, "or inadequacy and whatnot in the face of Cedars most profound capabilities."

Uugh, she had to go there. "Excuse me, but haven't you just recently eaten of that particular delicacy? And, we have things to do."

"Things," she said distractedly, gazing at Cedars.

Cedars was talking with Adam and Juarez, but I noticed the smile that played at his lips and the frequent glances he cast in her direction.

Macy, I need Cedars attention focused on me.

I'm trying, I said.

I glanced behind me at the sound of a cart being pushed into the room. Rotundo—I had to learn her name—entered, pushing a cart of food in front of her.

"Miranda, look. Lunch is here." I spun her around to face the cart.

"I am hungry," she said, eyeing the covers that protected the food.

"Of course you are."

I pulled the first cover off. The smell of smothered steak with gravy wafted through the air. Miranda and I looked at each other. The next moment found us rapidly ridding the trays of their covers. Did they have Granny stashed in the kitchen? It was a truly southern feast.

"What's your name?" I asked Rotundo without taking my eyes off of the food before me.

"Margaret," she said jovially.

"Margaret," I said with my hand extended. "We're going to need plates."

She whipped out one for me and one for Miranda. We wasted no time filling them. The men were smart enough to let us finish before venturing near the cart. With plates in hand, we sat on a large golden sectional couch that had a large coffee table in the center. By the time the boys sat down, we were going for seconds. Complete silence enveloped the room as we ate.

As soon as I'd eaten my last bite, Adam stood. "Everyone ready?"

It really wasn't stated as a question, and plates were set down all around. Except for Miranda. She picked up the plate Cedars had set down and began to work on it. A twinge of worry gripped me as I watched her. Something seemed off with her. The fact that she was currently licking the gravy off the plate might have had something to do with it.

Adam left our grouping and Juarez and Cedars followed. I stayed back and waited for Miranda while she finished off Cedars' plate.

"Are you okay?" I asked her after she set the plate back down.

"Yeah," she said, confused that I had asked.

"You licked the plate clean," I told her, pointing at the now shiny plate. Even though we didn't hold manners in high regard, licking the plate was a little extreme.

"It was good," she said defensively.

I couldn't argue that. So, I didn't. But I did watch her closely as she went to stand by Cedars.

Adam had walked behind his desk and slid aside a panel in the wall to reveal an elevator. When the door opened, we all got in. The elevator went down a few floors and then sideways. The glass sides allowed me to see the interior of the mountain, where the shaft had been carved out, race by as we moved. It was kind of nauseating.

When the doors opened, we stepped out into a large cavernous foyer. My attention was immediately drawn to the floor where the Organization's full name and emblem were etched. It formed a circle around a roving DNA double helix with images of various animals incorporated into the strand.

The most prominent animals displayed were wolf, leopard, and Komodo dragon, but there were various other predators veiled in smaller pockets of DNA. And, a human that looked surprisingly like Einstein. The last seemed oddly out of place, and I frowned down at it.

Crouching down for a closer inspection, I verified that it was definitely Einstein. Maybe he had somehow been involved in hybrid development. I couldn't think of another reason for him to be incorporated into such a prominent symbol of the Organization.

Rising from the floor, I noted that opposite the elevator was a gigantic archway that led out into the complex. I walked to the archway and placed my hand on the edge. It went on as far as I could see.

I turned around and saw that the men had gathered around one of two doors behind the receptionist's desk. Miranda had taken a seat at the desk. I read the nameplate on the door as I walked toward them. They were going into Julia's office first.

Juarez was intently focused on the door's security panel. It didn't take him long to turn the light from red to green. A loud clicking noise signaled the door unlocking. Adam opened the door and went in. Juarez and Cedars followed.

"You coming?" I asked Miranda.

She lifted her head, which she had rested on her crossed arms, and looked at me like she wanted to tell me something.

"What's wrong?" I asked, suddenly alarmed.

"You two coming?" Adam said from the doorway of Julia's office.

"Of course, we're coming," Miranda said as she stood up. "I didn't ride the nausea producing elevator from hell just to miss out on all the action." She made little shooing motions with her hands at Adam, and to my surprise, he obeyed.

"Hold on," I told her, grabbing her arm.

"It's nothing, Mace. Just sickened by the ride, that's all." She pulled loose from my hand and entered the office.

I didn't think it was just the funky elevator ride. She was hiding something. But, she obviously wasn't ready to tell me, or the time wasn't right. If I demanded to know, she may shut me out altogether.

Macy, you okay?

I smiled at his concern. I still wasn't used to somebody worrying about me. *I hope so,* I told him as I walked into the room.

His eyes met mine, and he gave a quick smile before returning to his examination.

Juarez had taken his familiar position at the computer. Miranda and Cedars were trolling through the file cabinets.

Scanning the entirety of the room, I said, "It's not going to be in here."

Adam and Cedars turned their heads to me, expecting an explanation.

"She wouldn't leave anything incriminating where Juarez or you could so easily find it. But, she would want it close if she needed to grab and go."

As I walked around the office, I began moving things and pushing random objects.

"What are you searching for?" Adam asked.

"A button or latch. Depression, maybe?"

"For a hidden panel?" Cedars piped up.

"Or compartment. Was there ever anywhere she used to stand frequently? Or anything she used to unconsciously touch?"

"The mirror," Adam said, abandoning his search of the files on her desk. "She used to look at herself constantly."

He strode to a very ornate wood carved mirror hanging on the back wall of the office. He ran his hands around the mirror's frame and then leaned in and sniffed it. Everyone, except Juarez, gathered around as he worked. Having settled on a location, he began prodding it in earnest. A small drawer popped open, and he pulled out an old fashioned skeleton key.

"Any idea where that goes?" I asked.

Adam and Cedars both shook their heads.

"I might," Juarez spoke. He was watching video footage of Julia on the computer monitor.

Uh, oh. I didn't think Adam was going to like this.

I walked over to stand behind Juarez's chair. Adam followed me and placed his hand on my shoulder. Miranda and Cedars joined us on our right.

"Six months ago, Olivia and I began to suspect that something was off with Julia." He looked away from the screen and up at me. "Olivia and her used to be close. Well, as close as she would let anyone get," he said.

Tapping another key, he zoomed in on Julia walking toward the mirror.

"Julia began pulling away. Making weird comments to Olivia. So unbeknownst to anyone, including Olivia," he looked apologetically to Adam, "I installed cameras in her office."

I felt Adam bristle at the action Juarez had taken without his knowledge or approval. Nope. Didn't like it at all. I leaned back into him and silently reminded him this was a good thing Juarez had done, even though he'd gone around Adam. He did not agree with my phrasing and replaced it with, *behind my back.*

Sensing Adam's anger, Juarez continued more cautiously. "I had the feed sent to a secure server that I maintain separately from the Organization. I've known she was doing something in that alcove, but I never knew what until now."

He slid the monitor over to give everyone a better view. "This is from two days ago."

We watched as a very disheveled Julia collected the key from the mirror and approached the alcove. The pictures that wrapped around the alcove vanished and an antique door appeared. She inserted the key and then disappeared behind the door.

Juarez fast forwarded the footage, and Julia emerged, carrying a metal briefcase. She did something in the alcove and the pictures reappeared. As if caught, she froze a moment, eyeing the velvet drapes that framed the alcove. She shook her head and hurried to return the key. Still carrying the briefcase, she left the office.

"I thought she was going in there to pray or something like that. Every other time she let the drapes loose, preventing me from seeing what she was really doing."

The tension in the room was so thick it was hard to breathe. Cedars had backed away and taken Miranda with him, which left me between Adam and a still seated Juarez.

He was trying to protect Olivia. Surely you can understand that. By extension he was also trying to protect the Organization, I argued.

Adam didn't acknowledge my assertion. *He should have told me.* The growl in his response caused me to grit my teeth.

Granted. But what it resulted in is good, I stressed.

I could feel Adam's rejection of my arguments. With the string of betrayals he'd endured so fresh, he could not overlook the indirect challenge to his authority.

Don't you think he feels guilty. Look at him. Can you not smell the sorrow rolling off of him?

I turned and wrapped my arms around Adam. I pressed into him as if that would convey the strength of my arguments. He refused to meet my eyes as he stared at the back of Juarez's head.

He might have avoided what happened to Olivia if he'd told you sooner. If he'd trusted you more. He's been through enough, Adam. Do not hurt him!

The last was said both in supplication and warning. It caused Adam to snap his eyes to mine. It didn't seem like he was going to agree with me, and I frantically tried to find another argument to placate Adam's anger.

Unexpectedly, he grabbed the sides of my face with both

hands. *Shut. Up. I'm not going to hurt him.* The command in his voice was unmistakable, and I didn't like that he'd used it on me or told me to shut up.

Realizing what he'd done, he pulled back and repeated more calmly, *I'm not going to hurt him.*

He flipped the key to Cedars, who caught it without flinching. "Try and find the way in," he told him.

Cedars and Miranda entered the alcove and Adam turned his attention back to me. "A moment, please."

I looked back at Juarez still seated and motionless.

"It's okay, MK. I deserve this."

The emotion in Juarez's voice served to erase the last of Adam's anger. It erased it toward Juarez, anyway. He growled at me for my display of concern when I squeezed Juarez's shoulder in sympathy. I failed to entirely hide the smile that generated.

When Adam saw my smile, he ceased the growling and put his hands on his hips. Closing his eyes in anger with himself for his reaction, he tilted his head up to the ceiling.

Through our bond, I could tell Adam was frustrated with the havoc the leopard DNA was wreaking on him because of me. For whatever reason, I was secretly pleased that I could cause him to lose a little of his control.

Not too secret, Adam said.

I released Juarez and pressed my hand to Adam's chest. Rising up on the tip of my toes, I gently kissed his cheek. *Do you want me to go shields up while you talk to him?*

He considered me a moment and then shook his head no.

Thank you, I said and kissed him again before joining Miranda and Cedars.

"So, that was intense," Miranda whispered as I stopped beside her.

I looked back at Adam who was now down on one knee with one arm wrapped around Juarez. I think Juarez may have been crying.

"What's up with the sweetness?" Miranda frowned.

"He can be sweet."

She lifted her eyebrows at me.

"He can," I insisted.

"Ladies, can we focus here?" Cedars said while dangling the key in our faces.

Miranda swiped it from him, and I began to examine the alcove. There were no obvious buttons to push. I began sniffing the panels.

"Good idea," Cedars said and joined me.

Soon, all three of us were sniffing. We agreed on one location as the most likely spot, but no matter what we tried, we couldn't get anything to move.

"Maybe it's geared to her personally," Miranda guessed.

If it was like the security in the lab, it probably was keyed to her.

I heard Adam's footsteps as he appeared in the entrance. "No luck?"

"Nope," I said.

He tapped the panels. "Glass?"

I shrugged.

He produced claws on his right hand. They left long gouges in the glass as he drew them down the panel. Pacing to the desk, he picked up a crystal paperweight. "Stand back," he warned. Then he slammed the paperweight against the center panel, causing it to shatter. Just as in the video, the antique door appeared.

He held his hand out for the key, and Cedars gave it to him. The lock turned over, and Adam opened the door. No one made a move to enter.

"That was dumb," Miranda chirped.

"Why go to all the trouble of a hidden key and door if you can just break through the glass?" I agreed.

"It does seem uninspired," Adam commented.

"Has this alcove always been here?" I asked.

"Ever since I can remember. Cedars?"

"It's always been here. I never paid it much attention. I just thought it was a sitting area."

"There are no seats," Miranda said.

Like a bunch of idiots, we all looked around for nonexistent seats. Apparently, we were all a little gun shy when it came to unexpected circumstances.

"Can we sweep it for booby traps or something?" I said, looking up at Adam.

"Done and done," Juarez called from the desk. "It's all clear. There are no trip wires or pressure switches. No electrical or bio components of any kind. Julia really wasn't much of one for subterfuge," he concluded, looking back at the computer screen. "Until recently," he muttered.

"Any indication of what awaits us?" Adam asked Juarez.

"It appears to be a small cavern."

Did I miss that on the video? I turned around to stare at Juarez.

"The geological scan just finished," he shrugged. "Whatever the room contains, it's been here since the beginning. It doesn't appear to be man-made. It's not that big either."

Juarez sure was a handy one to have around.

As no one else had taken the initiative, I decided to start the ball rolling. "I'll go first," I offered, taking a step forward.

Adam caught my elbow and pulled me back. "You will not," he stated firmly.

Like I didn't see that coming. I smiled mischievously at him as he slipped past me into the lead. Lights came on as he crossed the threshold, and one by one, we followed him in.

Quickly skimming the room, revealed it to be a small lab. Stacked against the far wall, like relics from the past, were beige metal filing cabinets. The majority of the room was furnished with stainless and glass, which made the inclusion of the filing cabinets even more suspect.

As the others spread out, I crossed the room to the filing cabinets. Running my finger across the top of one, it came back coated in thick black dust. Whatever she used them for, she didn't bother with the dusting.

Pulling out a drawer, I randomly selected a file. I was startled to recognize the name. It belonged to an individual from the

Colony that had died last spring. I returned it and continued scanning the names on the other files. They all belonged to the various hybrids at the Colony. On a whim, I looked for my name, but I didn't really expect it to be there. I was wrong.

With no small amount of trepidation, I pulled the file from the drawer. It had my name and a listing of numbers—1945MG001, 1956MG002, and so on. Under the bio, it listed my birthdate as March 28, 1945.

That was impossible.

"Macy, I think you should see this," Adam said.

I lifted my eyes from the file and walked to the lab table where Adam was seated. On the table in front of him was a file entitled Mindbenders. He flipped it to the page he wanted me to see. A brief paragraph gave the synopsis of the report.

> *The subjects listed herein were the Organization's attempt to create minds of great analytical skill. Embryos were hybridized with DNA from sources of known intelligence, including such great minds as Albert Einstein, Rosalind Franklin, Robert Oppenheimer, and other such distinguished scientists. This report chronicles the failures and successes of the endeavor.*

My heart rate increased with every sentence I read. Below the paragraph was a list of names under the title of subjects. Mine was the last on the list with the same date as the one in the file I held.

Suddenly, I felt weak. Adam pulled me in front of him and wrapped an arm around my waist. I placed the file I held on the table and picked up the report in front of me. Slowly, I turned the page.

The trials were broken into four separate attempts starting in 1915, well before the founding of Biometrics. This, I guessed, was the precursor.

There were ten subjects in all. The first five never made it to birth. Due to complications associated with the hybridization, the developing fetuses had been severely deformed. The details were too grizzly to read, and I flipped the page.

Having learned from their mistakes, the next round of implants starting the following year proceeded at a more restricted pace. The next two subjects made it to their early teens before expiring.

Encouraged by their success and their breakthroughs in nanotechnology, they followed with the next round of trials in 1930. By the time the subjects were teenagers, it was concluded that neither one of them would achieve the results the Organization was hoping for. Their conclusion proved to be true when one of the subjects died in a car wreck in the fifties, and the other in the Vietnam War.

The last section of the report was devoted to me.

I looked up and found the rest of the group staring at me with blank expressions. Adam nudged me, and I leaned into him, grateful for the support. Taking a deep breath as I turned the page, I resumed reading. Adam placed his head on my shoulder and continued to read with me.

Unwilling to let go of their aspirations, they embarked on their final attempt in 1945. In an effort to subvert the complications they'd encountered in previous subjects, they subsidized the initial embryo hybridization with additional injections of nanobots at critical developmental stages. Their aggressiveness led my body to hibernate for three separate time periods with the longest lasting approximately twelve years. It was an unexpected and unknown variable in their experimentation.

Each time, I had gradually emerged from stasis and resumed a normal human growth pattern into pre-adolescence. It seemed the hibernation periods were preceded by the injection of the nanobots. I had no memory of this. Maybe because I was so young at the time, but either way it was frightening.

I was placed with a family—my family in Texas, which I did remember. The family had no knowledge of the composition of their daughter. They were told only that she had some mysterious disease and required extensive medical examinations every few years, which the "adoption agency" was happy to supply free of charge.

The last annotation regarding myself was handwritten and stated that I had developed beyond all their expectations and was now ready to be drafted into the service of the Organization. I felt Adam cringe as he read the last statement. It was dated April 1st, 2011. It was quite the April Fool's joke.

I felt completely numb. Even Adam's arms around me were no longer a source of comfort. Maybe numb wasn't the right word. I was in shock, yes, but I was angry too. Angry that I'd been played with? Created for the Organization's purposes? But wasn't everybody created for a purpose one way or the other?

"Can I?" Miranda held her hand out for the file, interrupting my thoughts.

I gave it to her and leaned back into Adam, letting my head rest on his shoulder.

Even if I was created in a test tube in 1945, I was not going to freak out about this. I'd already had enough drama to last a lifetime. The only thing that had changed in the last five minutes was what I knew about where I came from. I was a hybrid before I was a hybrid.

So I'd been given DNA from some of the smartest men and women to walk the face of the earth. It was mine now. I was still me and whatever I made myself into.

"What are you thinking?" Adam whispered in my ear.

"Too fast?"

"Little bit," he snorted softly.

What was I thinking? That knowing this, didn't change who I was now. Also, Adam now had verifiable evidence and could feel justified in his assessment of me. I'd have to acknowledge his rightness in the matter. Eventually.

"I'm thinking this doesn't really change anything. How I came into being doesn't affect the direction my future will take." Then I barked a laugh at the irony in that. "Other than it already has. Hey," I said suddenly, "that must be why we could sort of communicate telepathically in the beginning, before I was your kind of hybrid. I mean re-hybrided? Whatever, you know what I mean."

"Because you already had nanobots."

"Yeah," I sighed.

Adam rested his cheek against my neck. His worry radiated through our bond.

"I'm okay, Adam. Really," I assured him.

I could feel him push against me, searching for anything I was shielding.

"I'm not hiding anything from you," I said sarcastically, mentally swatting him.

"You're really alright?"

"Mm huh."

He began to nuzzle my neck with his nose. "I couldn't offer you any comfort?" he asked, his lips replacing his nose.

I smiled at his playfulness. "You're pretty spry for an old timer."

"You're pretty hot for a seasoned citizen. You're what, sixty-seven?"

"You're still older than me."

"And, wiser," he agreed.

Walked right in to that one.

A loud slap of the report being closed interrupted Adam's progress down my neck. I felt him snarl in frustration as he eyed the offender.

"Hmm," Miranda said loudly. "So, you're like a geezer or geezette."

Adam laughed behind me. Leave it to Miranda to state the obvious most unimportant fact.

I rolled my head to face her. "You learn that I possess possibly the greatest mind of all time, and that is your comment?"

She tossed the report onto the lab table and walked toward me. "I already knew you were smart. Starting college at sixteen and earning your doctorate by twenty-one sort of clued me in. The why of it doesn't make you any less a force to be reckoned with."

Cedars picked up the report and looked at me with the question in his eyes. I nodded and he and Juarez started reading.

"I do pack a considerable wallop," I allowed with mock thoughtfulness.

"No sense denying it," she agreed.

"Couldn't if I wanted to. It's all there in black and white."

We both looked at the report held between Cedars and Juarez.

"One thing, though," she said thoughtfully.

"What's that?"

"They gave no explanation for your unquenchable desire for Tex-Mex."

I started giggling. She'd long bemoaned my penchant to use any excuse to have nachos, and flautas, and deep fried chimichangas for dinner. Neither did she agree with my assessment that chips and salsa went well with anything.

"Well, considering the incredible strength of mind behind my unquenchable desire, I'm going to let the ruling stand."

A disgusted look crossed her face. "Does that mean nacho night is reinstated?"

This was her one failing. How could anyone not like nachos? "How about we replace it with fajitas?" I knew she liked those.

Her face brightened with a smile. "Deal," she agreed, then added in a suggestive tone. "But we'll need to tone it down with the onions."

"Here, here," said Adam and Cedars together.

CHAPTER 21

"So, this really doesn't explain Julia's exit. And, it doesn't necessarily condemn her either," I said to their disbelieving faces.

"It does mean the Organization, or at least Julia, was willing to do fetal experimentation," Cedars said harshly.

The look of disgust on his face was unexpected. I mean, I didn't like it either, but his reaction seemed visceral. I was beginning to worry that he was ready to bolt from the Organization.

I slid from Adam's arms and started pacing around the room. I couldn't have Cedars running away with my best friend in tow.

"It also confirms that splicing together DNA from separate individuals is possible," Adam said, regarding me like he would a specimen.

Not helping, I growled.

But such a cute specimen.

I purposefully ignored Adam and focused on the other two men in the room. "Look, I know that it appears Julia made or was making the Organization into something it was created to fight against."

"We thought it was created to fight against," Juarez countered, waving the report at me.

I looked back and forth between Cedars and Juarez. I had to get a handle on this soon. "Okay, you were all deceived," I admitted. "But now, you have an opportunity."

"To clean up her mess?" Cedars asked angrily.

"To make the Organization what you thought it was, what you want it to be," I said softly.

Miranda walked up and draped herself against Cedars. Her presence had an immediate calming effect. I flashed her a look of thanks, and she smiled at me over Cedars' shoulder.

"The video footage alone may not incriminate Julia, but this does," I heard Adam say.

I turned to find that he had moved from the lab table and was now standing in front of an open fridge. I walked over and took the vial from his hand. The label read, Growth Nanobot Revision 3. The initials next to it were Julia's, and the date was relatively recent.

I handed the vial to the others to inspect and began to examine the rest of the vials in the fridge. There was all kind of stuff in here. Julia had been busy.

"That means she's guilty of working with the Consortium, right?" Miranda asked. She looked from individual to individual as no one seemed willing to speak into the heaviness that had settled over the room.

"It does," Adam finally answered. He closed the fridge and turned toward us. "Let's go examine Renard's office." His steps, fueled by his desire to leave, carried him quickly across the room.

Jogging to catch up with him, I asked, "What are you hoping to find?"

"It's more what I'm hoping not to find," he said stiffly.

When we reached the foyer, Juarez began working his magic on the lock again. Adam and Cedars flanked Juarez on either side. They all had their faces set like men ready for battle.

"I don't think Renard would be a party to this. Julia was always a little…distant, aloof," Adam said.

"She was flat out uncaring," Cedars argued.

Adam tilted his head in acknowledgment. "But Renard was the polar opposite. I often wondered how those two were together." Adam shook his head just as Juarez unlocked the door.

I saw Juarez look up and nod at both of them. "Ready?" he asked.

Adam pulled the door open and froze. I turned aside as the smell swept passed me, which made me a witness to Miranda's dash to the trash can under the receptionist's desk. She'd made me watch enough cop shows to know what was waiting for us.

"This is what you were afraid of?" I whispered, squeezing Adam's arm.

He gave a quick nod of his head and then entered the office. Juarez followed Adam, and Cedars did too after Miranda waved him away.

"Are you staying here?" I asked Miranda.

She had claimed the receptionist's chair and had her head cradled in her hands on the desk. "Yes," she moaned, unable to say anything further.

I patted her back a few times and then left her for the office. I found them grouped together over the body of Renard. He'd been shot point blank in the neck and heart. His nanobots never had a chance of saving him.

"That answers the question of his involvement," Juarez said as he reached over and closed Renard's eyes.

It didn't really. It just meant that he was murdered.

"You didn't happen to install a camera in here?" I asked Juarez.

"No," he replied softly.

Cedars stood up and looked steadily at Adam. "We have to institute a new board. You have to formally take the lead now. And, we have to inform everyone else of what's going on."

There was great force behind Cedars' words. I sort of got the feeling that this wasn't the first time he'd talked to Adam about this. He looked like he was trying to force Adam to take the job.

Looking at Adam, I wasn't sure how he would respond. The emotions churning through him were conflicting and loud, like a room full of people with everyone trying to talk at once. But as he regarded Cedars, I knew the future of the Organization was being decided. It all hinged on Adam's response.

"It's what Olivia and I want also," Juarez said as he too watched Adam.

I didn't want to unduly influence Adam's decision, but he was going to hear me anyway. Might as well make it count. I sent all the confidence and faith I had in him through our bond.

He slowly looked up at me.

You are the right man for the job.

Adam looked back down at the body of Renard. "Schedule an assembly for after our return," he said.

A very relieved looking Cedars nodded and left the office.

Straightening from his crouch, Adam picked up the desk phone. I was a little unsure of how to respond to the emotions he was telegraphing. There was sadness, of course, but also pain and anger, and an urge to get away from everyone.

"Margaret," he said, "I need you to come to Renard's office."

He hung up and held out his hand to me. When I reached him, he pulled me into a hug. "Not you, the situation," he whispered.

"Juarez," Adam called.

Juarez looked up at Adam.

"Margaret's on her way. Can you assist her with the disposal?"

Juarez grimaced at the description of the task presented to him but gave a quick jerk of his head in acceptance.

"She should be able to handle the cleanup on her own," Adam continued as he led us to the exit. Pausing in the doorway, he trained his eyes on Juarez. "And Juarez, after cleanup, the only people I want in Julia's office are you, Cedars, and Olivia, if she's up to it. Understood?" He waited for Juarez's affirmative before leading us out.

We returned to his suite of rooms where he insisted that I change. He informed me that he would not tolerate me standing out in any way and that I would wear what everyone else wore.

He prodded me into a nearby room where he began pulling clothes from a mobile hanging rack. "I had Margaret bring these in while we examined the offices. I don't know your exact size, so you'll have to find what fits best."

He held up a shirt and scrunched his face, looking back and forth between me and the piece.

"Thanks. I got it," I laughed as I snatched it from him. I knew his emotions were running in high gear right now, so I cut him a little slack with the bossiness.

He showed me what pieces I would need and then left me to

it. I had to choose a black long sleeve tee with a black projectile proof vest—Adam had corrected me on my assumption of only bullet proof. The pants were also black and lined with pockets. He returned long enough to stuff them with various gadgets I hoped I wouldn't need.

Left to finish on my own, I added the final piece to the ensemble, a pair of black military style lace-up boots. It took a few steps to adjust to their weight.

He walked out of his room at the same time I vacated mine. He was dressed identically to me.

"Has it come to this already?" I said, hanging my head. "We're twinkies."

He barely acknowledged my comment. He was already starting to adopt the all business attitude. From this point on, I knew there would be no joking, or teasing, or silliness of any kind. Which was why he was currently glaring at me with the raised eyebrow as I stood there with a big goofy grin stretched across my lips.

I did that thing where you pull your hand down in front of your face and the smile disappears. But it was back the moment he turned his back.

Macy, he growled.

Oh, alright. I was just strangely happy, maybe elated even. We were going to rescue the kids. Finally, I was getting to be the one doing the rescuing rather than being the one needing it.

Adam led the way and in seemingly no time, we were crossing the floor of a bay lined with aircraft I knew I'd never seen before, and yet, they looked familiar.

"Were these in a movie or something?" I asked Adam.

"Where do you think they got the idea?"

"You, the Organization, consulted on a movie?" There was a profitable income stream.

"Exactly," he answered my silent observation.

"Are you leaving Cedars in charge?"

"Yes."

I thought as much. "Is the founder's assistant accounted for?"

He shot me a quick look. I wasn't trying to start anything, though I wouldn't deny that I was curious about the woman that at one time he had called his.

"You've been keeping her away from me?" I asked amused.

"I thought it best. After our...altercation on the plane, I wasn't sure you had enough control over your new DNA to contain certain urges."

Now it was my turn to glare at him. What'd he think? I was going to attack her for her past involvement with him? More likely, I'd take a swat at him for even daring to be with someone else. Anger was beginning to breathe through me as I contemplated the idea.

"See," was Adam's only comment.

Oh. Guess I did have a few control issues. I forced myself to breathe normally and focused on the situation at hand.

At the end of the very long bay, I could see a group of people waiting by some sort of jet. The closer we got the more I could tell that they were all dressed exactly like us. We were the whole box of twinkies. They quieted as Adam walked into their midst.

I stopped at the outside edge of the crowd and listened to him begin his instructions concerning the operation. Watching the others as he dictated to them, it seemed they all accepted his leadership easily. I didn't know what I was looking for as I studied them, but I felt the need to gauge their reactions.

I zeroed in on their faces, looking for the slightest tightening around the eyes or downturn of lips, indicating displeasure. I suddenly realized I was looking for rebellion against Adam. Then the next question had to be, why?

I became very still as I searched inside myself for the reason. Something didn't feel right. It was an oily sort of slippery feeling. Much like what I had felt around Millsap.

Alarmed by the potential for danger, I began to search the crowd more earnestly. My head swiveled back and forth between the operatives. Without warning, my normal senses fell away. Everyone took on a strange watery appearance. I could see colors radiating from them. Most were tinged with blues or soft greens.

But one, a female, was encased in black with red streaks swirling through it.

I began to push my way through the crowd toward her. I noted Adam's position. He had his back to her and was talking with another guy about contingencies should anything go wrong. He turned his head in my direction as I approached, but I wasn't looking for him.

Macy?

I saw her reach inside her vest, but too many people were between us to see what she pulled out. I shoved aside a much larger cadet in order to clear my line of view. He started to protest, but shut his mouth when I quickly looked at him.

Out of the corner of my eye, I saw a quick flash of silver, but I still couldn't tell if it was a gun or a knife. It wasn't until I was about twenty feet away that I made that determination. Pressed tightly against her leg was a serrated blade about eight inches long.

Macy, what's wrong?

She raised her arm, and I started running. Time slowed down, and people scattered as I ran. I didn't understand how no one else was aware of her actions. It wasn't like she was trying to hide.

Do you not see the crazy woman with the knife?

No. I felt him pause, searching for what I was seeing. *I don't see anything wrong.*

She paused as Adam turned around. She went hazy for a moment, and I stopped running.

Turn back around! I shouted at Adam. *Act like nothing's wrong.*

He turned back around and started talking again, but I could feel his confusion.

It's okay, Adam. Everything's okay, I assured him.

She must have some kind of ability to alter what people around her were seeing. That was an extremely dangerous trait to have in the wrong person. Case in point, Exhibit Lady Stalking with Knife. I had no idea why it wasn't affecting me, but I was grateful for it.

I also realized that I was on my own. If I drew attention to her again, she might send out another wave that overpowered me before I could stop her.

Fortunately, she was so focused on Adam that she hadn't yet realized I was coming. She was probably confident that everyone was under her spell. What was the saying…Pride comes before a fall? Just call me Pride.

My heart skipped a beat as she quickened her pace. I wasn't sure I would get there in time to intercept her. That might mean I would take the knife instead of Adam. That was a sacrifice I was willing to make, for both Adam and my hybrids. Adam was well able to bring them home without me present.

With my final step, I launched myself at her. Her eyes widened when she saw me. By the time she switched the direction of her attack to me, she was too late. Her surprise had cost her time, and I was already there.

Planting my feet in her chest, I rode her to the ground. On impact, my feet slipped to either side of her, and my knees now penned her down. I had one fully clawed hand poised to strike, and the other was locked around her throat. The knife I had ripped from her hand was still skidding loudly across the concrete of the bay floor. Everything snapped back into real time, and I felt Adam spin toward us.

"Macy!" Adam said sharply.

I would not take my eyes off her. She had tried to kill Adam. She deserved death.

Macy, I need you to let her go.

She tried to kill you. My fingers began tightening and her struggle to breathe became more prominent.

She was close to Pike. She probably has information we could use.

No one thought it prudent to remove her from this operation! Even if she isn't part of the Consortium, she would have been an emotional wreck!

That was my oversight. With everything going on, I didn't think it through. Cedars questioned her placement on the team, but I didn't think they were close enough to warrant this.

You were wrong.

Clearly. Without physically touching me, he knelt beside me. *You assured me that I was boss on this mission.*

I cringed slightly, but said one word in response. *Circumstances.*

Agreed. But you've handled it as you saw fit. The danger is averted. Now, you have to step aside, and let me deal with it as I see fit. Argument presented, he waited for my response.

Me and my super brain couldn't come up with a rebuttal. Slowly, I loosened my fingers until I could let her go. Never once, the whole time I'd locked eyes with her, had she shown the slightest bit of remorse concerning her actions.

She's not sorry, and she fully intends to keep trying until the job is done, I told Adam. Implied was my intent to make sure she never completed her task.

Acknowledged.

In one move, I jumped off her chest and landed in a crouch a few feet away. The gathered crowd automatically moved back as I landed. Rising slowly, I kept my eyes trained on her and Adam.

"Rogers. Altman." Two men approached Adam. "Escort Ms. Langston to the brig."

Adam stood and backed away as the other two grabbed her under the arms and hauled her up. A look of pure hatred scarred her otherwise pretty face as she began to struggle. It seemed unnatural on her. The effort with which she was struggling seemed over the top, too.

She almost succeeded in dislodging her captors. Adam stepped forward, and with one swift punch, he rendered her unconscious. Rogers and Altman carried her out of the bay.

"Everyone else, on board," Adam commanded while striding a few paces away. He retrieved a communications device from one of his pockets and contacted Cedars.

I remained where I was while Adam updated Cedars. But I was cognizant of the wary looks I was receiving from the others as they filed past me onto the plane.

Adam completed his call and walked toward me. He stopped when the toe of his boots touched mine. "Alright?" he asked.

I nodded.

"Let's go then." He walked around me and stepped onto the ramp leading into the plane.

I heaved a silent sigh of relief at having averted a confrontation with him. Turning toward the ramp, my steps faltered as he called over his shoulder, "We'll have to have a conversation about your vigilante behavior later."

Dang it, I moaned inwardly.

Once on board, Adam was in the cockpit, and I was seated with the rest of the crew in the back. The only noise was from Adam and the copilot talking back and forth. Was it always this quiet before a mission?

The avoided eye contact from the rest of the crew and the two next to me sitting as far away as their seats would allow, led me to believe they were afraid of me. Which was ridiculous.

You didn't see your face when you tackled her.

But aren't they all hybrids? Couldn't any one of them whip my butt?

I don't think you fully grasp the situation. You carry the blood of an alpha. You attacked without permission, and you were fully intent on finishing the kill. They are just responding to that. Not to mention the fact that you saw what everyone else, including me, did not. It's a little intimidating, Mace.

Not the greatest of team building exercises?

Hardly, he agreed with laughter in his tone. *Try talking to them. Let them get to know you a little.*

That'll help? I asked skeptically.

Try showing them that you're not just a crotchety old woman, he snorted.

Great. Try to make everyone more comfortable with the unpredictable wild cat on board.

I looked around at their faces. They all appeared young, but so did I, and apparently, I was sixty-seven. I cleared my throat loudly. A few eyes darted my way before quickly retreating.

"Look, I think I should address what happened earlier." Even though they were already quiet, I felt them still at my words.

What had happened? I took a breath to explain and then said, "I have no idea what happened earlier?" Oh, that was going to inspire confidence.

My words were ringed with frustration as I attempted to explain again. "I sensed a threat. I followed that thread to..." I couldn't recall her name.

"Langston," someone supplied.

"Langston," I repeated, nodding my head. "I know that all of you are wondering what is going on. Adam's going to address that when we get back." I played with the Velcro on one of my pockets. "I can't thank you enough for agreeing to rescue my kids." I took a deep breath as I tried to think of something else to say.

"Are they really your kids?"

The bright eyed boy seated directly across from me had asked the question. "Biologically?"

He nodded.

"No, but I've been a substitute parent..." I stopped. I had failed them in so many ways. I hadn't been prepared for the responsibilities associated with the job. I wasn't even that much older than them, not including this new age that I supposedly was. "Actually, I guess I've behaved more like an older sister not prepared for the responsibility of parenting. They've had a hard go of it. I wish I'd done better by them."

Silence reigned again until a girl, on the end of the row I was sitting on, asked another question. "Did you really kill Pike?"

Just how much did they know already? I asked Adam how much was okay for me to say. I got the go ahead for complete disclosure regarding Pike.

"I defended myself against Pike. Adam's the one who finished him off."

"I never would have thought Pike was capable of betraying us," said another cadet at the far end of the plane.

Murmurs of assent filled the compartment. I understood their doubt. I hadn't wanted to believe it either. But that had quickly faded when I'd had to face it head on.

It didn't take long for others to start asking questions. Our time in the air was filled with me reliving the whole last week, up to and including Granny. Surprisingly, they all knew and were equally afraid of Granny.

They seemed especially concerned with Olivia's well-being. I gathered that she was some sort of mother figure to them. They'd also taken a liking to Juarez's designation for me, and I was now officially dubbed, MK. I was okay with that as long as they let me call them cadets.

We arrived at an air strip and switched our mode of transportation to military troop transport trucks. I'd seen plenty of them before in my lifetime, so we presented nothing unusual to the public.

Our drive ended at a spot I was also familiar with, the edge of the woods where I'd parked my truck for the stakeout. I could still see the tire marks in the gravel where I'd made the U-turn.

As soon as the truck stopped, everyone quickly hopped out and melted into the woods. I followed after them and stopped when they did. When I looked back, the trucks were already gone.

Adam joined us and began to assemble the teams. He was going to be on the team inspecting the Colony compound. Though this was not news to me, my heart filled with anxiety at the thought of separating from him. None of the previous times we'd been separated had been very pleasant.

As the teams divided up and began to move in their respective directions, Adam came to stand before me again. Spearing me with his emerald gaze, he said, "You are not to get yourself killed, or kidnapped, or hurt in any way."

The force behind his words was worthy of an alpha. It reached all the way inside me. I couldn't think of what to say in response.

"Not a scratch. You hear me, Macy Greer?"

He didn't move a muscle as I rose onto my tiptoes and pressed a kiss to his lips. "I'll do my best."

"You'd better," he said as I withdrew. Then he slapped me on the butt like he was a football coach sending me into the game. "Get moving, Greer."

I saluted him and jogged off in the direction my team had gone.

My arrival was met by the glares of a bunch of angry teen hybrids. Until they realized who I was. As soon as that happened, I was engulfed in hugs by the clearly distraught girls. The boys remained close but didn't give way to all the hysterics. Most of them just offered a quick hug or pat on the back and then backed away. Last of all, Kenny came forward. The others stepped aside to make room for him.

"Kenny," I said carefully, recognizing that his eyes held suspicion and accusation.

"Doc." He seemed reluctant to accept my new persona. "You smell different."

"I am different," I agreed.

"I thought you were dead or that you'd abandoned us."

There was the accusation. "Well, I'm not dead, and I didn't abandon you. Not by choice. The fact that I'm standing here now involves a couple of small miracles." I didn't look away from his eyes. I wanted him to witness the sincerity behind my words.

He walked a few steps toward me, sniffing the air as he came. "You were always strong before. Now, you're more." He stopped, still regarding me with uncertainty. "A predator."

"You are not my prey."

That was all the assurance he needed. He wrapped his arms around me in a tight hug. "Glad to have you back, even if you stink."

I laughed at his jab. I wished I could convey how sorry I was. "I'm so sorry about everything. About Crystal," I said softly.

He squeezed tighter for a second then pulled away from my grasp.

"I have a lot to make up for," I told him.

He simply nodded in acknowledgment of both my apology and my pledge.

"We ready to proceed, Ma'am?"

I looked at the cadet who had asked. I recognized him as the one that Adam had said was in charge on this side of the road.

"Reynolds, is it?" I asked him.

"Yes, Ma'am," he nodded.

"Let's get everyone out of here."

"Yes, Ma'am," Reynolds said.

With that, the work of the mission got underway.

The kids were divided into small groups of four or five and led off in different directions at various intervals. There were a lot more here than the original estimate of fifty. Kenny was truly amazing.

During the time it took to lead the groups out, Kenny filled me in on what he'd observed at the Colony. The tale he wove was gruesome and filled with danger. He also gave me a list of the dead and missing. Crystal wasn't the last name on the list. I tucked it away in one of my pockets.

When Kenny wasn't talking to me, I sat with one or more teenage girls wrapped around me. I listened to their stories while trying to pick up from Adam what I could. The images I was harvesting from him matched the descriptions in their stories.

The next to last group had just left, when I felt Adam disappear. *Adam?* There was no response. *Adam!*

I stood up from the fallen log I was using for a seat. Spotting Reynolds talking quietly with another cadet, I approached him. "Can I talk to you a sec?"

"Yes, Ma'am," he said, and then he dismissed the cadet in front of him.

"Can you establish contact with Adam?"

I waited impatiently as he tried to contact Adam or anyone from Adam's team. As his calls became more insistent, so did my fear. Something had happened to Adam to disrupt our bond, or he'd shoved me out intentionally. Either one was not an option I liked.

Reynolds turned to me with fear in his eyes. "I can't reach him or the team."

Looking at the uncertainty on Reynolds' face, I knew in that moment that I was the veteran on this team. Adam must have chosen all new recruits in an attempt to avoid having any trust issues. I couldn't panic now. The whole operation might fall apart.

"Reynolds," I said, placing my hand on his shoulder. "I'm going to need you to lead the other cadets and the last of the teens to transport."

He didn't answer me. Instead, he just kept staring at me. I thought he was trying to decide if he should listen to me or not. I looked over my shoulder as the rest of the cadets began to ready the last remaining teenagers for the trip to safety.

Kenny, who was one of those remaining, had been watching the interchange between me and Reynolds. He walked over and stood next to me. "Adam's gone?" he asked.

Not wanting to frighten him as well, I carefully guarded my expression. "We can't reach him."

"You are going after him?"

I met Kenny's gaze. That was exactly what I intended to do. Then I understood his reason for asking. "You have to stay with your group," I told him.

A look of defiance crept over his face.

"They need you. You're their leader," I implored. Whether officially recognized or not, he'd been acting in that capacity for as long as I'd known him. The Colony hybrids knew it, he knew it, and so did I.

"Which is why I have to go," he insisted. "I trusted Adam to do the job for me, but if he's gone…" He let his words trail off into silence.

I looked down at the ground. He meant he was going to assume the task of looking for any remaining survivors now that something had displaced Adam. I didn't want him going back into danger. I wanted him safe—away from the Colony.

I looked back up prepared to argue and saw the remaining five teenagers surrounding him in a show of support. They looked like seasoned warriors standing there with the light of determination shining in their eyes. Each of the ones he'd chosen to accompany him was more than capable, probably more so than me.

I breathed a sigh of resignation. Shy of incapacitating him, there would be no stopping him. That made the decision to include him relatively easy.

"You follow my lead," I said.

He sharply nodded once, and I turned back to Reynolds.

"I'm going to find Adam," I told him. "The remaining teens are coming with me. Take the rest of the cadets to the rendezvous point and lead everyone safely home."

I turned abruptly, my thoughts already on reaching the Colony.

"My orders were to shadow you in the event of unforeseen circumstances."

I froze, an arc of pain lancing through me at the memory of the origin of those words. I slowly turned, meeting Reynolds' eyes once more. The fear was gone. In its place was the same determination written on Kenny's face.

I took a breath and sighed deeply. It seemed all my efforts to free myself from being responsible for the lives of young people were for naught. I figured, at this point, I was pretty much waist deep in the whole. You'd think I'd put the shovel down.

"Welcome to unforeseen circumstances," I said quietly.

"Yes, Ma'am."

Without further discussion, I pivoted for the Colony. I heard Reynolds behind me quietly informing transport of our change of plans. Kenny, who knew the area better than I did, took point. His team flanked him, enclosing me in their center. Reynolds and two other cadets—I knew them as Smiley and Flash—joined our band as we sped to the Colony.

I leaned into the leopard part of me, letting it guide my body. The others were pulling on their hybrid DNA as well, and we ran faster than I thought possible.

The gravel road came into view, and I watched Kenny clear it in a single leap. He was quickly followed by several of the others doing the same. I'd never tried leaping before, but driven by my need to find Adam, I gave it a try. To my surprise, I overshot the road and landed in a crouch on the other side.

I looked back at the road. That had to be twenty, maybe thirty feet across, and yet, it felt like no more than three feet. I could get used to this, I thought before springing up and into a sprint again.

As I ran, I discovered that I could do all sorts of things that I never could before. It seemed that my body knew what to do without me having to think about it. Clearing obstacles with a single leap, weaving through the darkened woods, anticipating the movements of the others around me, it was as simple as breathing.

And, it was exhilarating. It was freedom in a way I'd never experienced before. I felt stretched, enlarged somehow. Like the moment just after you jump off the diving board, when you're sort of suspended in midair, weightless. Only, there was no falling to the water below.

The leopard part of me was thrilled to be hunting. My desire to protect Adam battled with my desire to destroy anyone responsible for harming him. I wasn't sure which one would win, but I transferred every bit of those needs into helping me find him.

We arrived at the fence that surrounded the compound. Kenny had led us to the one place where the woods met the fence. As a result, we remained hidden as we surveyed the sight before us.

Lights were out all over, and the guards were gone. There was no noise or movement of any kind. Not even the wind was blowing. The darkness and unnatural stillness only added to the feeling of dread building within me. I didn't need the leopard to tell me something wasn't right.

Kneeling next to me, Kenny leaned over and whispered, "The quickest way in is through here." He indicated the way before us with a wave of his hand.

It also provided no cover whatsoever. "We need cover," I said, shaking my head no. I didn't want to walk straight into an ambush.

"Follow me," he said.

He ran parallel to the fence, then turned away from the compound and headed back into the woods. I frowned at his decision, but didn't question him. I knew I could depend on Kenny.

He halted in front of a man whole cover attached to a slight raised piece of ground. I wondered who thought that wouldn't be suspicious in the middle of the woods.

With Reynolds's help, Kenny pried the cover loose and slipped inside. The members of his team quickly followed, leaving me and the Organization cadets standing there. I gave Reynolds an apologetic look then lowered myself into the hole.

It was a long drop to the floor, but my stomach didn't produce those little butterflies like it normally would have. I landed gracefully, yet another surprise, and looked up at Kenny. He smiled knowingly at me and then turned and ran down the tunnel.

Catching up to Kenny, I asked, "What is this?"

"It used to be an escape tunnel for people like you."

"You mean scientists?" I clarified.

"Yeah. A few years ago, me and some friends disguised it." He shrugged at the look I gave him. "I thought I should have an escape route of my own, should I need it."

I had to hand it to him. His instincts at self-preservation were impressive. "Where does it lead?"

"Everywhere. I figure the safest entry point is through the kitchen."

The kitchen was how they referred to the cafeteria. Normally, it was always crowded. What teenager didn't like to hang out around food? It would probably camouflage our smell for a while, too.

When we reached a vertical shaft, Kenny leapt straight up and grabbed ahold of a ladder attached to the wall. I didn't hesitate to follow Kenny this time.

The ladder terminated into a narrow crawl space. It was lit with some sort of weird blue lights. I watched the shadow that was Kenny pop open a panel and crawl through. I followed him and exited into the actual kitchen of the cafeteria.

The kitchen was empty of the normal hub bub that usually filled it, which made it seem extra creepy. I went to stand in the doorway that faced the dining hall. My heart sank as I observed the tables and chairs strewn haphazardly around.

One by one, I heard the rest of our group emerge from the cabinet. After verifying that everyone was accounted for, we crossed the expanse of the hall. I made sure my shields were wide open, but I still couldn't sense Adam. I also sought to see our bond as Adam had when he was looking for me, but I had no success there either.

Arriving at the exit doors, there was a brief discussion about where to go from here. That resulted in Kenny dispatching two of his group to case the upper floors. The rest of us moved on, crossing the grounds to the medical clinic.

Three quarters of the way there, the air became thick with the smell of blood.

"Doc," Kenny warned.

"I smell it," I growled. To my horror, I recognized one of the scents as Adam's.

My fear lent strength to my legs. Kenny beat me into the lobby by mere seconds. I skidded to a stop next to him where I remained, momentarily frozen in shock. I wasn't sure that I could have imagined anything worse.

At our feet were arms from two separate individuals. The bright pink nail polish on one of them looked out of place amidst the carnage. Various other body parts were randomly distributed around the lobby, leaving blood trails crossing each other like some kind of sick painting.

I took in the score marks left by claws on the furniture and walls and the medical supplies oddly scattered everywhere. But mostly, I saw the blood coating everything.

I closed my eyes against the scene, my mind almost refusing to accept what I saw. Fear threatened to overwhelm me, but as I heard the rest of the group filter in and around us, I forced the fear away.

Opening my eyes, I regarded the teenage hybrids' faces. They looked like something etched in stone. This wasn't the first time they'd been subjected to this.

Feelings of failure coursed through me as I left the lobby on the trail of the one scent I recognized. It led me down the hall where I identified pieces of one of the team members that had been with Adam. I only remembered him because I had thought his freckles looked like a mask around his eyes.

Pressing my hand against my mouth, as if that would keep the panic that was rising in me at bay, I stepped over the torso at my feet and moved on. Behind me, I heard the quick intake of breath as Smiley made the same identification that I had.

The end of the hallway was in sight when I recognized a second scent, Millsap. Anger replaced the fear, and I rounded the corner at a run. Kenny followed close behind me.

I refused to entertain thoughts of Adam torn asunder like what we'd previously encountered. He was not dead. He couldn't be dead. I would know if he was dead.

We slid to a stop at the set of double doors that framed the end of this hallway. I looked at Kenny, and he pressed the button. The doors whooshed open and the scent of Adam hit me head on as it escaped the room.

I stood perfectly still as I waited for the assault on my senses to pass. After the initial wave, I noted that Millsap's scent was stronger here, too.

In the flicker of the orange emergency lights, I could tell that it was some kind of operating room. I stepped cautiously into the room, stopping when I saw the large pool of blood on the floor. It seemed like way too much blood for any one person to lose and still be alive.

Kenny walked up and stood so close to me that our arms were touching. Neither one of us wanted to confirm our fears.

My heart was pounding so hard that I could hear it in my ears, but I forced myself forward. Kneeling, I ran my fingertips through the blood. I knew before I brought it to my nose that it was Adam's.

I closed my eyes and let my knees sink to the floor. There was so much blood. Was it too much? Could he still be alive? Tears rolled down my cheeks and dropped to the floor.

I knew the others had come in and that everyone was watching me. But I couldn't meet their eyes yet. Unwilling to look further than the pool in front of me, I remained crouched where I was, rubbing Adam's blood between my fingers. I just needed a moment to think, to recover.

I began to focus on the other scents in the room. I thought I recognized Julia's scent, but I called to Reynolds for confirmation.

"Reynolds, do you recognize anyone's scent?"

His voice quavered when he spoke. "Adam's."

I nodded. "Anyone else?"

"And Mrs. Latke, I think, though it's weaker."

Kenny approached and placed his hand on my shoulder. "We're going to continue the search."

I nodded my understanding, and he left with his team.

I couldn't stand not knowing any longer. I stood and searched the room for any other signs of Adam. There were none. The only thing left of Adam here was his blood. I couldn't even find a trail where he or Millsap had exited the room. Every smell associated with them ended at the pool of blood.

Frustrated, I began to circle the spot. "They couldn't have just disappeared," I snarled. Putting my hands on my hips, I looked angrily at the ceiling. Duh, I thought, feeling like an idiot. If they didn't go out, they had to go up.

I drug a chair over and stood in it. The scent did travel up. I jumped and pushed aside the ceiling tile. With the next jump, I gripped the edge and hauled myself up. Using my feet to straddle the opening, I grasped the flashlight that suddenly appeared.

"Thanks," I told Reynolds as I turned it on.

As expected, the blood trail went up. Stowing the flashlight in a pocket, I wedged myself in and began to ascend. I definitely smelled Adam and Millsap, but not Julia. I hoped someone was going to be able to tell me what that meant.

The duct opened into the night air, and I climbed out onto the roof of the building. I traced their scents to a spot about twenty feet away. Then they disappeared.

"They must have had transport off the roof," Reynolds said from behind me.

I concurred with his conclusion, but I didn't remember hearing anything. I looked up into the night sky. Surely they wouldn't have bothered to take Adam if he weren't still alive. The blood was probably a result of injuries sustained from Adam fighting them.

Then there was Julia. Though her scent was faint, she had been here. I couldn't tell how long before Adam or how her scent was only in the operating room.

I roared in frustration. Where were they taking him? Back to Tennessee? I didn't think so. Julia wouldn't be stupid enough to go back to headquarters, either.

I crossed my arms over my chest and began to pace the roof. I didn't know where to go from here. I didn't have any leads connecting me to Adam.

A slight breeze began to blow, and I caught a new scent. Reynolds' head popped up when mine did.

"Do you smell it?" I asked him.

"Yeah, but I don't recognize it."

"Smells like...old paper?" I walked forward, tracking the scent.

"It smells like the Capitol," Flash offered as he made it to the roof. "I used to work as an intern during the summers," he shrugged when we looked questioningly at him.

Millsap, Julia, and someone from the Capitol? What was going on?

Having politicians involved did increase my belief that Adam was alive. They never did anything fast. But I still had nothing concrete to go on. It would look really suspicious if I went around sniffing everyone in DC. My only hope was reestablishing contact with Adam.

I stopped pacing and closed my eyes. Focusing on Adam, I searched for our bond. At first, there was nothing. Then, I began to think about Adam. Those green eyes that could be so intense and hard. And the tenderness he'd shown when I'd essentially lost it. The way he was with Granny, and that relentless eyebrow.

It was just a glimmer. It would shimmer into view, but disappear quickly when I reached for it. In desperation, I flung myself at it the next time it appeared. Similar to what Adam had described, the image of various cords woven together began to solidify. Everyone on the roof faded away as I latched onto that image.

I flowed over and through the cords, searching for him. I moved faster and faster until an iron curtain materialized. It dissected our bond and extended in every direction as far as I could see.

Gingerly, I pushed against the curtain. Nothing happened. I pushed harder and still, nothing happened. I leaned against it using everything I had. I dropped to my knees, and tears streamed down my face as I strained toward Adam.

In my mind, I backed up and ran at the curtain. It seemed like I could feel the imprint of the mesh against my skin from thrusting myself against it. I tried again and again, searching for any way through.

The mesh suddenly gave way. One phrase flashed through my mind. *Find Granny,* Adam said. Then the curtain dissolved, and my connection with Adam was back to nothingness.

Adam! I cried. But he was already gone. I tried several more times, but they were all to no avail. I came back to myself, realizing that Kenny was shaking me by the shoulders.

"Someone's coming," he said. "We have to leave."

I heard what he said, but a strange sort of fog had descended over me. "I have to find Granny," I heard myself say.

"We have to leave, Doc," Kenny urged.

The urgency in his voice helped me to focus on the here and now. I looked into their faces. They were all waiting on me to make the call. The leopard part of me knew inaction would be equated with weakness. Adam's blood, the same blood staining my fingers, now ran through my veins, and Adam was not weak. Neither was I.

The fog melted away as I stood. In its place was the predatory certainty of what I was going to do. I would follow the lead

Adam had given me. I would find Granny. Then, I'd find Adam. And come hell or high water, I was going to hunt down Millsap, Julia and whoever else was involved and once and for all, put an end to this.

Looking back into their waiting faces, I nodded as my decision resolved into determination. I wasn't alone in that decision. Reflected in each of their faces was an equal desire for retribution.

"To find Granny," Kenny gritted through sharp teeth.

"Then Adam," Reynolds's affirmed.

Buoyed by their support, eagerness to begin raced through me. "Let's move," I growled.

With the rest of the team following behind me, I took a running leap off the roof.

RECOGNITION, ACKNOWLEDGMENTS AND OVERALL THANKS

Jeremy...Thanks for being the first one to encourage me after reading only one paragraph.

Jonathan...Thanks for believing that my book was going to become a movie even when I was only on chapter three.

Justin...Thank you for the many times you told me that you loved my book when you haven't even read it. I love your books too.

To my sister, who likes to be known to the world as Dee, but who I call Anna...For reading, for being my sounding board and offering suggestions, for contacts in the business, and for overall consulting on all things related to the book, Thanks. And mucho thanks for repeated affirmations, especially when directed to do so.

Mom...for reading the very rough, rough draft through in one long day and for concluding upon finishing that I was a great author. Thank you, Mom.

Jess...Thanks for reading and your positive support and words of encouragement. They were there when I needed them and greatly appreciated.

Kaley...You and Mom were the first ones I let read the book. Thanks for putting up with my nervous hovering, giving up your time and making the trip, and for catching one big error where the text was saying something I had not intended to say at all. You know what I'm talking about.

A special thanks to author Lacy Camey for answering all of my questions and offering valuable advice when I very first began on this journey.

Thanks to Kristi Clark at Under the Umbrella Photography for taking beautiful pictures that made me look like a princess.

Streetlight Graphics, especially Tabatha...for basically holding my hand and leading me through the process, for answering tedious questions, and always having a positive response, even when my emails were more like venting. And of course, the cover work. Thank you, thank you, thank you.

COMING WINTER 2013

REVELATION

AUTHOR BIO

C. E. Glines lives in southeast Texas with her husband, three sons and a dog named Scruffy. Besides the writing, her life is filled with chasing after her boys and one home improvement project after another. She loves to eat and hates to clean. She always enjoys good times with her friends and family and reading a good book, especially when the house is quiet enough to actually read it. She holds a degree in manufacturing engineering and was pursuing a degree in biology when she wrote a book, adding author to her resume. She won't force her opinion on you, but if you ask, be warned. She also longs for the day when she herself can become a hybrid and eat as much as she wants to and still look good.

www.ingramcontent.com/pod-product-compliance
Lightning Source LLC
Chambersburg PA
CBHW020818180626
46814CB00001B/17